P9-BYI-159

Hostage to Pleasure

"Singh is on the fast track to becoming a genre giant!"
—*Romantic Times* (top pick)

"Nalini Singh has penned another keeper . . . If you want a thrilling read with action, danger, passion, and drama, don't miss Nalini Singh's *Hostage to Pleasure*." —*Romance Junkies*

"An intriguing world that's sure to keep readers coming back for more." —*Darque Reviews*

"This series just continues to get better and more vibrant as it goes . . . *Hostage to Pleasure* is a must read for any paranormal reader." —*Night Owl Romance*

"I commend Nalini Singh for writing a completely unique and utterly mesmerizing series . . . *Hostage to Pleasure* is already a keeper on my bookshelf." —*Simply Romance Reviews*

Mine to Possess

"Singh has done it again. *Mine to Possess* grabs you and never lets you go. This may be the best book of an already outstanding series." —*Fresh Fiction*

"WOW! Brilliant is the best description for *Mine to Possess* . . . It just doesn't get better than the best!"
—*ParaNormal Romance Reviews*

"As plot points fall into place, it's evident that clever, mega-talented Singh has truly spectacular things in store."
—*Romantic Times* (4½ stars, top pick)

"Ms. Singh's world-building is as fascinating as the characters with whom she populates it." —*The Eternal Night*

"Nalini Singh has done it again . . . There is no doubt that *Mine to Possess* will be the must read for 2008!"
—*Fallen Angel Reviews* (recommended read)

continued . . .

Caressed by Ice

"Craving the passionate and electrifying world created by the mega-talented Singh? Your next fix is here! One of the most original and thrilling paranormal series on the market . . . Mind-blowing!" —*Romantic Times* (4½ stars, top pick)

"A sensual, dangerous adventure not to be missed."
—*New York Times* bestselling author Lora Leigh

"A compelling read with wonderfully developed characters and the strong world-building that has made Singh a star."
—*All About Romance*

"With a truly inspired mix of passion and danger, this story will keep you on the edge of your seat. [It] will surely earn itself a place among your favorites." —*Romance Reviews Today*

"A wonderful story . . . I cannot recommend it highly enough!"
—*ParaNormal Romance Reviews*

Visions of Heat

"Breathtaking blend of passion, adventure, and the paranormal. I wished I lived in the world Singh has created. This is a keeper!"
—*New York Times* bestselling author Gena Showalter

"This author just moved to the top of my auto-buy list."
—*All About Romance*

"Brace yourselves because the second installment of the Psy-Changeling series will set all your senses ablaze and leave your fingers singed with each turn of the page. *Visions of Heat* is that intense!" —*Romance Junkies*

"A page-turning, sexy read that fans of paranormal romance are sure to devour." —*The Romance Readers Connection*

"In a genre filled with talent, Singh really stands out . . . This is one of the best paranormal series out there!" —*Romantic Times*

Slave to Sensation

Branded by Fire

NALINI SINGH

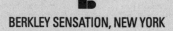

BERKLEY SENSATION, NEW YORK

THE BERKLEY PUBLISHING GROUP
Published by the Penguin Group
Penguin Group (USA) Inc.
375 Hudson Street, New York, New York 10014, USA
Penguin Group (Canada), 90 Eglinton Avenue East, Suite 700, Toronto, Ontario M4P 2Y3, Canada
(a division of Pearson Penguin Canada Inc.)
Penguin Books Ltd., 80 Strand, London WC2R 0RL, England
Penguin Group Ireland, 25 St. Stephen's Green, Dublin 2, Ireland (a division of Penguin Books Ltd.)
Penguin Group (Australia), 250 Camberwell Road, Camberwell, Victoria 3124, Australia
(a division of Pearson Australia Group Pty. Ltd.)
Penguin Books India Pvt. Ltd., 11 Community Centre, Panchsheel Park, New Delhi—110 017, India
Penguin Group (NZ), 67 Apollo Drive, Rosedale, North Shore 0632, New Zealand
(a division of Pearson New Zealand Ltd.)
Penguin Books (South Africa) (Pty.) Ltd., 24 Sturdee Avenue, Rosebank, Johannesburg 2196,
South Africa

Penguin Books Ltd., Registered Offices: 80 Strand, London WC2R 0RL, England

This is a work of fiction. Names, characters, places, and incidents either are the product of the author's imagination or are used fictitiously, and any resemblance to actual persons, living or dead, business establishments, events, or locales is entirely coincidental. The publisher does not have any control over and does not assume any responsibility for author or third-party websites or their content.

BRANDED BY FIRE

A Berkley Sensation Book / published by arrangement with the author

PRINTING HISTORY
Berkley Sensation mass-market edition / July 2009

Copyright © 2009 by Nalini Singh.
Excerpt from *Blaze of Memory* copyright © 2009 by Nalini Singh.
Cover art by Phil Heffernan.
Cover design by George Long.
Cover hand lettering by Ron Zinn.

ISBN: 978-0-425-22673-5

BERKLEY® SENSATION
Berkley Sensation Books are published by The Berkley Publishing Group,
a division of Penguin Group (USA) Inc.,
375 Hudson Street, New York, New York 10014.
BERKLEY® SENSATION and the "B" design are trademarks of Penguin Group (USA) Inc.

PRINTED IN THE UNITED STATES OF AMERICA

10 9 8 7 6 5 4 3 2 1

To my own personal brain trust—you know who you are. :)

CHANGE

Change can kill.
Devastate.
Destroy.

But it can also save. The Psy know this better than any other race on the planet. With the imposition of Silence, the protocol that wiped their emotions even as it saved their minds, this race of telepaths and telekinetics, foreseers and healers, a race both gifted and cursed, clawed its way back from the edge of the abyss.

As they stood looking down into the horror they had escaped, they shivered and turned away.

Years passed. And when the Psy Council declared that their once catastrophic rate of insanity had lowered to negligible levels, that there was no longer any violence in the PsyNet, they knew they'd made the right decision. The only decision.

Love. Happiness. Joy. What did any of that matter when the flip side was murderous rage, blood-soaked anarchy? The Psy preferred to leave such things to the "animal" races—and while the humans and changelings buried themselves in the

viciousness of emotion, the Psy evolved into the most powerful beings on the planet.

Cold. Pitiless. Silent.

But now, in the year 2080, more than a hundred years after
the "miracle" of Silence, the animal races are beginning to
rise. And change is pulling the Psy back into the abyss. Into
emotion and chaos . . . and nightmare.

CHAPTER 1

Mercy kicked a dry branch out of her way and glared. "Stupid stick." Of course, it wasn't the defenseless stick she was mad at—it just had the bad luck to be in her path as, shoulders hunched, she made her escape from the Pack Circle and the continuing revelry of Dorian's mating ceremony.

It was sickening how much her best friend was in love with his mate. In fact, all the other sentinels were starting to make her gag. "Clay making goo-goo eyes at Tally, and don't get me started on Luc and Sascha."

Then there were the worst offenders of all—Nate and Tamsyn. How dare they still be so crazy for each other after all these years! "Should be against the law," she snarled. She wasn't even going to think about Vaughn and Faith.

She decided to go for a run instead.

An hour later, and deep enough in the pack's heavily forested territory that she couldn't hear anything beyond the cautious whispers of nocturnal creatures moving about in the dark, she sat down on the smooth trunk of a fallen tree and blew out her breath. The truth was, she wasn't mad at any of the sentinels or their mates. Damn, she was so crazy-happy for them it hurt. But she was jealous, too. Everyone was paired up now. Except her.

"There," she muttered. "I admitted it. I'm a big ol' jealous baby."

Being a dominant female wasn't a bad thing in changeling society. Female alphas were as common as male ones. But being a dominant female in a leopard pack where none of the dominant males pushed her buttons, that was bad. And being a dominant female in a state controlled by leopards and wolves— where only the *wrong* one pushed her buttons—that was extra cherry-on-top bad.

Not that she was limited to their territory—Dorian had been nudging at her to go out of state, see if she couldn't find someone in one of the other packs, but she couldn't bring herself to leave DarkRiver, not when things were so dicey. Sure, life had calmed down a little since the failed kidnapping attempt on Dorian's mate, Ashaya, but it was an edgy sort of calm. Everyone was waiting for the next ripple in the pond—whether it would come from the suspiciously quiet Psy Council or the newly violent Human Alliance was anyone's guess.

That it would, was certain.

As a DarkRiver sentinel, she should've been considering their defense strategy, working out possible scenarios. Instead, she was going so insane with need she couldn't think of anything but the fever in her body, the hunger in her throat, the clawing *want* in every cell, every breath. Intimate touch was as necessary to her predator's soul as the forest she called home, but things might not have been so bad if she hadn't also been trying to cope with the impact of a conversation she'd had with the pack healer, Tamsyn, a few days earlier.

Mercy was the one who'd said it. "There's a strong possibility I'll remain unmated."

"You don't know that," Tammy had begun, frown lines on her brow. "You could mee—"

"It's not that. I might not be *able* to be with anyone. You know that happens."

Tammy had bent her head in a reluctant nod. "The chances

are higher with dominant females than males. It's an inability to give in . . . to surrender. Even to your mate."

And that was the hell of it, Mercy thought. She might want a mate with everything in her, but if he appeared, and he was the strong, take-no-shit partner she knew she needed, she might refuse to acknowledge him on the level necessary for a true mating bond. Oh, the mating urge would probably overpower her into taking him for a lover, perhaps more . . . but if the leopard in her didn't truly *accept* his right to her, then she might go roaming for months at a time, coming back to him only when she could no longer fight the need.

It was a special kind of torture reserved for those female leopards who got strangled up at the mere idea of giving a male any kind of control over them. And put it any way you would, unless her mate turned out to be a weak submissive— and she'd never be attracted to someone like that, so that was a no-brainer—he *was* going to try to dominate her.

"I don't need a mate," she muttered, staring up at the bright circle of the early autumn moon. "But can't you send me a nice, sexy, *strong* male to dance with? Pretty please?" She hadn't had a lover for close to eight months now, and it was starting to hurt on every level. "He doesn't even have to be smart, just good between the sheets." Good enough to un-snap the tension in her body, allow her to function again.

Because sex wasn't simply about pleasure for a cat like her—it was about affection, about trust, about everything good. "Though right this second, I'd take plain old hot sex."

That was when Riley walked out of the shadows. "Got an itch, kitty?"

Snapping to her feet, she narrowed her eyes, knowing he had to have deliberately stayed downwind in order to sneak up on her. "Spying?"

"When you're talking loud enough to wake the dead?"

She swore she could feel steam coming out her ears. Everyone thought Riley was quiet, practical, grounded. Only she knew he had a mean streak that delighted in annoying her as much as possible. "What do you want?" It was a growl from the heart of the leopard and woman both.

"I was invited to Dorian's mating ceremony." A slow smile that taunted her to retaliate. "Pretty hard to miss you burning up the place. And I'm not talking about your hair." His eyes lingered on the long red strands stroking over her breasts.

Mercy didn't get embarrassed easily, but her cheeks flamed now. Because if Riley knew she was in heat—like a freaking wild cat!—then so did the rest of her own pack. "So what, you followed me hoping I'd lower my standards and sleep with a *wolf*?" She intentionally made "wolf" sound about as appetizing as "reptile."

Riley's jaw tightened under a shadow of stubble a shade darker than the deep chestnut of his hair. "You want to claw at me, kitty-cat? Come on."

Her hands clenched. She really wasn't this much of a bitch. But goddamn Riley had a way of lighting her fuse. "Sorry, I don't beat defenseless puppies."

He laughed. He actually laughed. She hissed at him. "What's so funny?"

"We both know who's the dominant here . . . and you're not it."

That did it. She was a *sentinel*. So what if he'd been a lieutenant longer? That didn't change the fact that she occupied the same place in DarkRiver that he did in SnowDancer. The wolf had crossed a very defined line—and since she couldn't have sex, she'd settle for violence.

Feeling more than a little feral, she pounced.

Riley was ready for her. He took the kick on the thigh without flinching, but stopped her punch with a single hand. She was already shifting, sliding into the next position, ready to take advantage of any vulnerability. He blocked every one of her moves, but made none of his own. "Fight!" she yelled. She needed a good, sweaty workout—it would take some of the edge off the gut-wrenching fury of her need. Her booted foot connected with his ribs.

She heard a grunt and grinned. "Not so fast are we, wolfie?"

"I was trying," he said, blocking her next set of blows with his arms, "not to hurt you."

"I'm not a frickin' princess," she muttered, aiming for the most vulnerable part of a man's body—yeah, yeah, it wasn't fair. But Riley had asked for it. Oh, man, had he asked for it. " 'Kitty' this, Kincaid."

"Damn it, Mercy!" He grabbed the foot that had been about to connect with his crotch and flipped her. Effortlessly. Gasping as she realized exactly how much he'd been holding back, she twisted in midair and came to an easy landing on her feet.

"I'll give you one thing," he said, crouching opposite her as they circled each other. "You know how to move . . . kitty."

Adrenaline shot through her, a hot, liquid fire. "Better than a jumped-up sheepdog anyway." She kept her tone even, but she was sweating under the slinky black tee she'd changed into for the dancing, her heart beating at a rapid pace. "Claws out," she said and that was the only warning she gave as she went for him.

She didn't even see it coming. One moment she was about to slash his face—okay, so she would've just scratched him, it wasn't like this was a fight to the death—and the next, she was flat on her back with her wrists slammed to the earth, gripped in one strong fist. "Ooomph." All the air rushed out of her as Riley's lower body crushed hers to the ground. The bastard was heavy, pure muscle over solid bone.

"Yield." His nose was almost touching hers.

"You wish." She smirked into chocolate-dark eyes. "Come closer."

"So you can bite me?" A flash of teeth. "First you yield. Then I'll come closer."

"Not on your life." If she yielded, she'd be acknowledging his dominance, at least for tonight.

"Then I guess I've have to make you."

"Try it." Smiling, she went for his throat and almost had him, when—using a move that was all sorts of illegal—he flipped her again so her front pressed into the leaf-laden ground, her wrists still locked in his iron grip and pinned above her head. "Cheater."

"So says the woman who tried to kick my balls into my throat," he pointed out, even as he licked the salt off the skin of her neck in a lazy and highly provocative move.

"I'm going to kill you." It was more hiss than sound.

He bit her.

In the soft, sensitive place between neck and shoulder.

She felt her entire body shiver from the inside out at the blatant show of dominance. "Stop it." It came out husky, nothing like the rejection she wanted it to be.

He took his mouth from her. "I've pinned you."

"That's wolf shit. I'm a cat."

"You're still trapped under me." He nuzzled at her throat. "And you smell all hot and wet and ready." His voice was dropping, going wolf on her.

And the heat between her thighs was turning into a pulsing drumbeat. Her stomach twisted in a vicious wave of need. God she was hungry, so sensually hungry. And Riley had taken her, his hold unbreakable. At that moment, the leopard didn't care that he wasn't a cat. It just cared that he was strong, sexy, and aroused.

She found herself raising her body against him without realizing it, her bottom rubbing, enticing, inviting. "You tell anyone, I'll carve out your heart."

"Talking's not what I'm interested in right now." Releasing her hands, he let her twist onto her back . . . only to push apart her thighs and settle his erection snugly against her. It was all she could do not to moan out loud.

He raised himself up on his arms, looking down with eyes gone wolf—the black pupils circled by a ring of amber that echoed through the rich brown of the irises to turn his gaze night-glow. "How rough?" His sexuality was a primal force crashing against her skin.

"Hard." She wanted to be marked up, used until she was wrung out and comatose from pleasure. And she wanted to do the same to him. Fisting a hand in that thick, silky hair she itched to feel against her breasts, she pulled down his head and kissed him, snarling in the back of her throat. He gripped that throat with one hand, squeezing lightly. "Behave."

She bit him this time.

A full growl poured into her mouth as stick-in-the-mud Riley Kincaid gave in to his wolf and showed her exactly why he was SnowDancer's most senior lieutenant. Her tee was in shreds before she could blink, her bra gone the instant after that. His hand squeezed the rounded curves of her bared flesh, and when he tore his lips from hers to move down, she knew she was going to feel teeth.

What she didn't know was that Riley would suck on her nipple like it was his favorite treat before he sank those strong teeth into her delicate flesh. Her back arched up off the forest floor and she gripped the slick heat of his shoulders. Where had his own shirt gone? She didn't care. All she knew was that she had gorgeous male flesh under her hands and oh it felt good.

Ignoring his growl, she tugged up his head from her breast and bit at his lip again. For a wolf, Riley had a beautiful mouth. She'd been wanting to take a nip out of it for months. So she did. Then she slid her lips along his jaw and over the cords of his neck. Salt and man and wolf.

Wolf. Enemy.

Her cat snarled again.

But the snarl was buried in pure heat. He tasted good.

When he wound his hand in her waist-length hair and dragged her head back for another kiss, she didn't protest. It was as wild as the first, wet and deep and coated with the promise of raw sexual pleasure, no holds barred. "Now," she ordered as they broke apart, her body close to vibrating with ever-tightening need.

"No." He slid down her body and suddenly her dress pants and panties were gone. She felt the kiss of claws against the insides of her thighs and knew it had been on purpose. No pain, not even a real touch. Just a hint.

Just enough to remind her cat that he could take her.

More than enough to shove her arousal into the stratosphere.

"Goddamn wolf." A choked-out imprecation.

Spreading her thighs with strong, callused hands, he put

his mouth on her. She screamed. Riley was apparently in no mood to go slow and easy. He licked at her in hard, firm strokes, sucked then nipped. The orgasm tore through her so ferociously that she knew her muscles would protest tomorrow.

He continued using that mouth, those teeth on her until she could feel her body tightening again after a ridiculously short interval. But she wanted more than another burst of pleasure. Grabbing his shoulders, she pulled him up, knowing she wouldn't have been able to do it if he hadn't cooperated. It would've been annoying . . . in any other situation. "Do it, wolf."

A hand in her hair, wrenching back her head. "What's my name?"

She scratched trails down his back. He didn't even wince. "My name, kitty. Say my name."

"Mr. Mud Stick, Muddie for short," she said, even as she rubbed herself against the hard thrust of his denim-covered erection, the roughness of the fabric an exquisite sensation. She would've liked naked skin even more, but he wasn't budging.

"Say it, or no cock for you today."

Her mouth fell open. "Fuck you."

"You'll be doing that shortly." He kissed her again, a tangling of tongue and teeth and untamed male power. "Now"—he thrust against her, letting her feel the heavy, dark heat that she could have—"what's my fucking name?"

It was tempting to continue to snarl at him, but her skin was slick with sweat and he was big and wild and delicious over her. And she wanted him in her. *Now.* "Men and their egos," she muttered, just to piss him off a little. "Now do it, Riley. Or I'll find someone else."

He held her head where it was for another long second before lowering his face to hers, those amber eyes telling her exactly who was in charge inside him at that moment. "What did you say?" Quiet, quiet words.

She clawed his back again. This time, the wolf growled at her and the next few minutes passed in a fury of torn clothing and ravaging kisses, cries of pleasure intermingled with moans. And suddenly he was naked above her. Strong, hot, beautiful. She rose up against him, feeling her eyes go leopard as he put one hand on her thigh to hold her down and nudged at her with the aroused length of him.

She went to reach down, but he growled at her. Normally she'd have growled back, but he was making her feel so-damn-good. So she wrapped her other leg around him and thrust her hands into his hair, rocking her body upward. "I want you in me."

He began to push in. She sucked in a breath. The man was hard as rock and thick enough to make her muscles stretch to the edge of pain. She shuddered. "More."

He took her at her word, thrusting into her with a slow, intensely erotic focus that had her inner muscles starting to spasm in ecstasy even before he was fully inside. Then he was and she'd never felt so taken in her life. But he gave her only a few seconds to get used to him before his lips took hers once again, even as his body slammed in and out of her with a power her leopard gloried in. Wolf or not, this man was worth dancing with.

She moved with him, kissing him back, running her hands over his body and nipping at him just because. He kept her pinned to the earth as he took her, as if he knew just how damn much she needed a good, hard ride. When she orgasmed, it was with a sharp cry, a lush clenching around the thick heat of him, and a burst of starlight behind her eyes.

Lights that continued to flicker even after she came back down to earth. Riley was still hot and aroused in her, moving with unapologetically powerful thrusts that pushed her to another peak in moments. She bit his neck in the wolf way this time, and it finally pushed him over the edge with her.

CHAPTER 2

Early the next morning, a willowy Psy female walked into a breakfast and dinner—no lunch—restaurant just south of San Diego, and sat down, placing her briefcase beside her. She was dressed in a dark gray suit, with a jacket that cinched at the waist, and tailored pants in the same material. Her shirt collar was crisp and white, her nails manicured so they were short and clean.

The waitress smiled, but didn't expect a response. All Psy—well, except the ones who had defected recently—were emotionless robots. She'd heard rumors that they weren't born that way, that they trained the emotion out of themselves. Damn fool thing if you asked her. What was life without love, without laughter? Yeah, there were a few tears along the way, but hey, that was life. To be lived.

But she said none of what was on her mind—Psy were emotionless, but they tipped exactly on the correct percentage. Which was better than some cheapskates who ran her off her feet then left a quarter behind. She'd serve a Psy ahead of them any day. "What'll it be?" she asked, holding up the old-fashioned order pad. That was how this place stayed in business—folks came for the "ambience," as the boss called it.

She laughed at him—the old flirt was her husband, she had to keep him on his toes—but he was right. People liked the checkered tablecloths over wooden tables, the real-people service as opposed to order pads built into tables, even the crackling old jukebox they cranked up at night. That's why they got a lot of human and changeling traffic.

The few Psy who came in were mostly strays on their way to a meeting in the city. This one looked the type. Pretty, too, with those bright green eyes against skin that was a nice, pale bronze. Psy really were striking a lot of the time—probably messed with their genes in the womb, the waitress thought. "Honey?" she prompted when the woman didn't respond.

The Psy female blinked, staring at her.

And the waitress could've sworn she saw desperation in those eyes.

Then the briefcase exploded.

CHAPTER 3

Riley woke to find his brother, Andrew, sitting at the foot of his bed, mug of coffee in hand and a shit-eating grin on his face. "Nice trick, bro," he said. "Showering before you went to bed. Probably dunked yourself in a stream before you came home, too."

Riley just waited. Drew was really good at getting people to spill their guts with sly hints that he knew everything anyway. He blamed it on being the middle child. Riley blamed it on him being a smart-ass.

"But you forgot to empty the laundry hamper."

"Sniffing the laundry now?" He raised an eyebrow, knowing Drew had nothing. His clothes had been destroyed—he'd come home in wolf form. And he *had* dunked his ass in a freezing lake before he returned. "You really need to get laid."

"Oh, we're not talking about my sex life." Another smug smile. "Yours is much more interesting."

Riley remained on his back, feeling a soft ache in his shoulder. "Why are you here? You're supposed to be in Los Angeles this week." Drew had recently been promoted—to a role that necessitated him roving around all the different cities under SnowDancer control and reporting back directly to the SnowDancer alpha, Hawke.

It was a needed responsibility.

Because as SnowDancer had learned in the snow-white chill of the previous winter, not every wolf was good. Not every wolf protected. The lesson had struck the pack deep in the heart, and they were still bleeding from it. But that pain hadn't stopped them from fixing it so it couldn't happen again.

Hence, Andrew's new position as Hawke's eyes and ears among those who might otherwise be overlooked. He led a small team of men and women who were known to be absolutely loyal to SnowDancer, people who would cut out their hearts rather than harm the innocent. They were all also quick to smile, easily made friends.

Drew, in particular, could get anyone to talk to him about anything. Which was why Riley had learned to be very wary of his younger brother's apparently guileless questions.

"I swapped with Kieran," Drew now said. "He wanted to avoid somebody in the den."

Riley knew precisely who the other soldier wanted to avoid. "He broke up with his latest girlfriend." The fact that Kieran was technically human, having been adopted into SnowDancer as a child, didn't seem to stop him from acting the part of a wolf on the prowl. "Woman's out for blood, from what I hear."

"I figured." The glint returned to his eye. "So, who was she?"

"I thought you knew?"

Drew scowled. "I know you got laid. It's only a matter of time before I sniff out the truth."

"Knock yourself out." He began to get up, then realized why his shoulder ached. Mercy had scratched him hard. It might've given a human male pause. It made Riley's wolf smile. Wearing her claw marks was a badge of honor—because it meant he'd driven her to such pleasure that she'd forgotten herself. If she'd been his lover in truth, he'd be showing them off.

But he didn't know what she was to him. Except the woman who made him hotter and angrier faster than any other. So he remained on his back, brutally aware that once would never be enough. Not even close. His gut tightened. "Go away, Drew. I'll get up in a little while."

"Hmm, he wants me to leave. Why?" Drew sipped his coffee. "Could it be because the little she-cat marked our esteemed lieutenant?"

Riley barely kept himself from reacting to the "she-cat" comment. He had no intention of hiding his entanglement with Mercy—she might be frustrating as hell, a royal pain in his ass, but she was also an incredibly strong, sexy woman, someone any male would be proud to call his lover. But he needed time to figure out how he was going to deal with it. The instant that thought formed, he heard Mercy's voice in his head, a fragment of memory from their many scuffles.

"Jesus, Riley, do you ever just react?"

"When necessary."

"When necessary." She mimicked his voice perfectly. *"I'd call you Psy but I think that would be an insult to the Psy."*

"I feel."

"But your feelings go through about ten different filters before you let them out." She flipped her hair, tied in a high tail, over a shoulder. *"Doesn't bother me—except when you drive me insane with these plans."* The word "plan" was about seven syllables long. *"We'll deal with some situations as they arise. We don't need a color-coded flowchart."*

He hadn't had a flowchart, of course. Mercy simply liked to jerk his chain as far as possible. "I think you need to go see Brenna," he said to Andrew when his brother remained seated. "Word is, she and Judd had a fight." Riley liked Judd, but the man *was* mated to his baby sister—Riley reserved the right to hassle him periodically. And use him as fodder to distract Drew. "She won't talk to me—go make sure he didn't push her around."

Drew left so fast, he created a breeze in his wake. Riley wondered if Judd would punch Drew for his unwanted—and entirely unnecessary—interference. "Serves him right," he muttered, rising and stealing the coffee his brother had left behind. Judd would cut off his arm before hurting Brenna. That was why he was still alive. Because while Riley wasn't Mercy, with her breathtakingly vivid nature, he felt deeply.

And he loved his sister with a strength that made her call him an overprotective bear on a regular basis. He didn't care. The pack had helped—so much—but it was Riley Brenna had looked to after their parents' deaths, Riley who'd kissed her scrapes and soothed her nightmares. The fact that she was mated didn't change his right to look after her.

A knot of guilt and fury twisted around his heart on the heels of that thought. He hadn't dreamed last night, but the ache was there, as always. Because the truth was, he'd failed Brenna when she needed him most. That Psy bastard Santano Enrique had *hurt* his sister, hurt her so much that she'd almost broken.

"But she didn't break. She fucking survived, and the last thing she needs now is an idiot brother who feels sorry for himself." Mercy's voice again, words she'd thrown at him when he'd snarled at her one time too many after Brenna's rescue.

What would she say if she could hear his thoughts right now?

He reached back to touch his shoulder, a reluctant smile tugging at his lips as old rage retreated under a wave of the most primal desire. If he'd known it would be this good between them, he'd have said to hell with self-control and gone after her months ago. That, he thought as he walked into the bathroom, was one mistake he wouldn't be repeating.

By the time Drew dragged his sorry ass back through the door, Riley was dressed and eating scrambled eggs. "No visible bruises," he said, eyes going to Drew's chest. His brother had been shot through the heart last winter, his blood a scarlet flower across the snow—Riley's wolf couldn't help the near-automatic check. "Either Judd was in a good mood, or your ribs must hurt like hell."

"Laugh if you will," Drew said, an evil grin cracking his face. "But now Brenna knows something's up, too."

Great. If Drew was nosy, then Bren was relentless. "You have no life, Drew."

"Then you won't mind if I stick my nose into yours."

Mercy lay in bed way past her usual wake-up time, staring at the ceiling of her cabin. She was sore as heck, marked up with bites, scratches, and bruises, and she felt like purring. Not that she'd tell him—*ever*—but Riley knew what he was doing in bed. Or on the forest floor.

The wolf had not only ridden her into damn near unconsciousness, he'd given her the best orgasms of her life. And that was plain embarrassing. Her best sex had been with a wolf. Pa*the*tic. Except her body was telling her to shut up and wallow. 'Cause this felt gooooood. Good enough that she might even want to repeat it.

"No," she told herself the instant the thought reared its head. "Once—and most of the night definitely counts as once—you can write off as a mistake. But you do this again and he's going to start thinking he has rights over you." She knew predatory changeling men. They liked control. They particularly liked their women to submit. And Riley was one big giant hunk of testosterone-fueled Neanderthal wolf—he probably thought her submission was his right. She snorted. "Not in this lifetime."

Groaning as her muscles protested, she turned. She'd had a shower last night, but a hot bath was unquestionably in order. And a massage. One of her packmates would be happy to give her the latter out of simple friendship, but if they did, they'd see the marks on her body.

She could imagine their reaction when they found out she'd been getting down and dirty with a wolf. The SnowDancers were their allies, but leopard and wolf didn't easily mix. True friendship would take one heck of a long time. And, though she'd had great sex with Riley—okay, hot, monkey, freakin' wonderful sex—he wasn't her friend, either.

Most of the time, he irritated the hell out of her just by breathing.

She jumped as the comm panel beeped. It was an effort to stretch out a hand from the warm cocoon of her bed and pick up the portable handset. "Yeah?"

"Turn on the visual, Mercy."

All laziness fled. "Gran?"

"Of course it's me. Now, the visual. Hurry up, girl. Your grandfather's waiting so we can squeeze in some horizontal tango time before a meeting."

Mercy blushed. "I so didn't need that image in my head. And no visual—I'm naked." What she was, was worried that her eagle-eyed grandmother would spot the bite mark Riley had left on her neck.

"You haven't got anything I haven't," her grandmother said.

"Gran." She smiled despite herself. "I'm not one of your pack, so don't act the alpha with me." Her maternal grandmother led the AzureSun pack down in Brazil. Isabella's sentinels had stood by her as she aged, because it wasn't always about strength with changelings—age and experience counted just as much. Not that her grandmother wasn't also in phenomenally good shape.

"I don't act the alpha, Mercy girl. I am alpha." It was said with the calm confidence of a woman who knew exactly who she was and didn't give a damn what anyone else thought. "And this alpha has a present for you."

Every single cell in Mercy's body went on high alert. "Gran? What did you do?"

"Don't sound so worried, darling. I know you said you couldn't leave your pack to come see if one of my sentinels might work as a mate, but we're pretty calm down here so I'm sending Eduardo and Joaquin up to you."

Oh. Dear. God. "Gran, you don't need to play matchmaker. I already found someone." To have wild sex with, but she didn't think her grandmother needed to hear that part.

"Really?" A sharp sound. "Less dominant?"

Say my name, kitty.

Her claws sliced out, threatening to destroy the sheets. "No."

"Is he your mate?"

The leopard snarled at the idea. "We've only just—"

"Then there's no harm in having a wider field to choose from."

Mercy was all but strangling the handset. "Gran, I seriously don't need any help. Don't send your sentinels up here." Dodging two undoubtedly determined males was not her idea of a good time. Especially not when the only man her body seemed to crave was a wolf she'd threatened to kill more than once.

"Too late," Isabella said. "I cleared it with Lucas days ago—my men are probably already in your territory. And if they don't work out, I have several other unmated sentinels who all think you'd make an excellent mate."

Mercy thumped her forehead with a fist. "I'm sending them straight back. I don't need the complication."

"Of course you do, dear. And if the man you're seeing can't handle a little competition, he should get out of the game." Her voice changed, became pure alpha. "You need a tough man, Mercy. Otherwise, you'll stomp on his heart and eat it for breakfast."

"Thanks."

"Fact of life, kitten." A muffled whisper. "Speaking of tough men, your grandfather is out of patience. I'll talk to you after you meet Eduardo and Joaquin."

She was about to put the handset on the bed stand when it came back to life in her hand. This time, she checked the caller ID. "Lucas? What's up?"

"I need you to run a check out by the Grove. Something's there that shouldn't be."

Her mind shifted into sentinel mode. "Like last time?" Then, it had been a wounded Psy defector they'd found. The aftermath had almost gotten both Dorian and Ashaya killed.

"No"—Lucas's voice was grim—"tip was, there's a dead smell in the air."

CHAPTER 4

Ice water in her veins. "Psy, human, or changeling?"

"No confirmation—call me the second you know," he said. "One of the SnowDancers is already on the way to join you."

"Why?" Her leopard bristled. "The Grove's in our territory."

"It was one of their juveniles who sensed something off when he passed through—"

"Hah," Mercy said. "He probably came down to do mischief." As DarkRiver's official liaison to SnowDancer, there wasn't much she didn't know about the little turf war the cat and wolf juveniles—and young adults—were having. Anything that involved both packs and didn't need an alpha's attention went through her . . . and Riley. The bite mark on her neck tingled in sensory memory—she could all but feel his lips, his teeth against her sensitized flesh.

"Anything serious I need to worry about?"

Snapping back to the present, she shook her head. "No, they're just blowing off steam, trying to figure out the hierarchy between themselves." Both DarkRiver and SnowDancer ran disciplined packs—the younger members knew exactly how far they could go. "Maybe I can beat the SnowDancer to the Grove."

"We're allies." Lucas sounded very patient. "Be nice."

She knew he traded barbs with Hawke, the SnowDancer alpha, every time they met. "I will if you will."

"Shut up. I'm your alpha. Go look and see what's up."

Hanging up with a grin that quickly faded as she considered what she might find, she hurried to throw some water on her face—the bath would have to wait until she had a few hours to relax. Though her muscles were still a little sore, it was nothing that would hold her back. She was a sentinel for a reason—she was fit, lethal, and well able to take down most men twice her size.

Not including Riley.

Her teeth bared at the way he'd pinned her—maybe she'd enjoyed it last night, but if the wolf tried to use that to change the balance of power in the sentinel-lieutenant relationship between them, things would get seriously ugly.

Her mind filled with images of him blocking her punches, trying not to hurt her. She squelched the tiny tendril of warmth that threatened to rise to the surface. Because if there was one thing she knew about predatory changeling men, it was that they weren't good with boundaries—if she gave an inch, he'd take a whole country mile, start trying to protect her in the field.

Scowling at the thought, she wiped off her face, took a second to cover up a certain mark, then scraped her hair back into a high, tight ponytail before dressing in jeans, a plain white tee, and boots. Her cell phone was on the night table and she grabbed it on the way out, sticking it in her back pocket. The autumn air tasted crisp, sweet, almost too cold. She drew it into her lungs as she ran, ceding control to the leopard though she remained in human form. It knew instinctively where to put its feet, when to duck, when to switch direction because an easier path lay a little bit to the left or right.

It just felt like *being*.

Despite the bleak nature of what lay ahead, she was smiling when the first hint of scent hit her nose. Her stride faltered as she crossed into the large tract of land known as the Grove. "God would not be that cruel." But he was.

Because there was Riley, running to meet her from the opposite direction. His expression was the by-now-familiar impassive one—the one that made her want to needle him simply to get a reaction. If she hadn't seen that same face violent with passion, she'd have thought him an android. And for a predatory male changeling, especially one as dominant as Riley, that was some act to pull off.

"Coincidence?" she asked with saccharine sweetness.

His eyes—dark, intense, extraordinarily focused—went to her neck. "You can't heal a bite that fast." Cool words, but his jaw was a brutally hard line.

"Maybe I can." And maybe she had really good concealer. "Let's do this." She swept left as he went right. "Anything?" she asked as they met on the other side of the rough circle.

"No. Another sweep."

She growled at him. "I know what I'm doing. Don't give me orders."

Those oh-so-calm eyes didn't so much as narrow. "Fine." And he was gone.

That pissed her off. Which, she realized, was precisely the result he'd intended. Riley knew *exactly* how to push her buttons. Like he took a damn degree in antagonizing— She froze, sniffed the air, and picked up a scent that tied her stomach in knots. "Damn." Putting two fingers to her mouth, she whistled.

Riley arrived a minute later. "Some kind of cat," he said the instant he got close.

"Changeling lynx." Crouching to confirm the scent, she shook her head . . . and caught a vague whiff of the "dead" smell that had freaked out the juvenile. Her soul chilled, even as the leopard whispered that that scent had never belonged to a person. "She's here because there's a wild lynx population in the area."

Riley's shoulders locked, his hands fisting. "She's gone rogue."

"I hope it's not too late." Mercy swallowed and rose to her

feet. Rogues were changelings who'd surrendered absolutely to the beast, submerging their human half. If they'd turned into pure animals, it wouldn't have mattered so much—yes, it would've broken hearts, but the lost ones would've been allowed to live out their lives in peace. But rogues were smarter, faster, quicker. And they liked hunting those they had once called family. But this one . . . "It's a kid, Riley."

The wolf looked at her out of Riley's eyes. "You know her?"

"Willow's family had to get the okay to be in our territory." Predatory changelings had very strict rules. It kept the peace. And the most basic rule was—no going into another predator's territory without permission. "Her parents work for a company that relocated to Tahoe."

"How old is Willow?"

"Eight, I think." She drew in a deep breath, attempting to locate the source of the fading spray of blood and death. "Something has to have happened to her parents." She pulled out her cell and coded in a call to Lucas as they started following Willow's trail.

"Mercy, you found—"

"It's Willow," she told him. "You need to get someone to check out the Baker house."

Lucas swore under his breath. "Nathan drove out that way early this morning. I'll get him to go in."

She hung up as Riley motioned he was going left. Nodding, she went leopard-quiet as she circled right, sensing Willow was close. But it wasn't the girl she found. It was the body of what had been a small wild dog. Small, but muscled. "She's very close to the point of no return if she did this." Thank God it was a true animal, not a changeling. If the girl had killed a person . . . There was no coming back from that.

Riley crouched down beside her. "Girl didn't eat the flesh. This was pure rage."

"Poor baby." Her heart clenched—what could've driven a little girl to this? "She can't be far. The scent's too strong." Making a quick decision, Mercy began to pull off her boots. "I'll have an easier time with her if I shift."

Riley nodded. "I'll stay downwind."

"Good idea." A wolf would either terrify or antagonize the girl in her current state of mind. "Turn around." Changelings weren't prudes about nudity, but now that Riley had seen her naked in very intimate circumstances . . . well, things were different. And that irritated her. "I said, turn around."

He folded his arms and leaned against a tree, those chocolate-dark eyes watching her with unblinking focus.

Oh yeah, Riley knew just what buttons to push. But she wasn't a cat for nothing. "Fine." Shrugging, she ignored him to strip with changeling efficiency, balling up her clothes and shoes to cache in the tree.

"I'll do that." Riley's voice sounded from behind her. Then he put his hand on her shoulder.

Sizzle.

The electricity generated by that simple contact continued to rock through her, even as she whacked off his hand. "No touching." The cat swiped at her, wanting more, but she gritted her teeth and held on, knowing if she didn't set the ground rules now, Riley would push and push until something snapped. The man did obsession better than several of the leopards she knew.

"Give me the clothes." His anger was quiet, a gathering storm beneath the smooth surface he showed to the world.

Figuring he'd had an unwelcome surprise in her refusal to allow skin privileges, she thrust her things into his hands— "Fine, knock yourself out"—and shifted. Agony and ecstasy, pure pleasure and excruciating pain. All over in an instant.

Riley knelt down, clasping the fur at the back of her neck. "You're fucking bruised all down your back. Why the hell didn't you tell me it hurt?"

Because it didn't at the time, genius. Snapping her teeth at him, she pulled away and headed toward the lynx. She was aware of Riley falling slightly behind as he took care of caching her clothes, and then his scent faded altogether. Which reminded her. The girl would hardly appreciate sensing Riley in her fur. She paused to roll around in some fresh leaves, crushing them to overlay his scent with the mingled echoes of the forest.

That done, she made her way very, very carefully to the little grove that appeared to be the end of the scent trail.

The wild lynx saw her first. They greeted her with soft growls and went about their business when she made no "go away" sounds. Willow was sitting in the middle of a group of lynx cubs. Except she was bigger, her eyes different, unique. The way she held herself, the way she smelled, it all marked her as changeling. Walking over, Mercy batted away the other cubs, careful not to do harm.

They padded off, though an impish few tried to nip at her legs. One growl and they scattered. Willow didn't move. That alone set her apart. Instead of challenging the girl, Mercy sat down beside her, crowding her against a tree. Willow's little frame was cool against Mercy's side, her heartbeat not as ragged as it should've been.

The poor cub was in shock.

Mercy just sat there, let Willow know she was safe, protected by someone bigger and stronger who wouldn't hurt her. It took time but that shocky little body eventually relaxed a fraction. Then another. She felt the girl snuggle into her and breathed a sigh of relief—if Willow recognized and saw comfort in her, then she wasn't beyond saving.

Half an hour later, Mercy decided it was time for the next step. Getting up, she turned and nipped at Willow's ear. The lynx cub made a startled sound and scrambled up on all four feet, eyes wide. Holding that wary gaze, Mercy shifted.

Willow was still in lynx form when Mercy hunkered back down, her hair cascading over her shoulders. Damn, she'd forgotten to take out the hair tie. Not only that, the concealer was gone. Everything disintegrated during the shift. Even tattoos had to be done with special ink that bonded to their cells in some weird way she didn't particularly want to explore—it was enough that the two she bore didn't have to be redone after each shift.

"Hey, baby." She stroked her hand over Willow's head, flattening those adorable tufted ears.

The girl butted up against her but resisted shifting.

"I know you're scared," she said, kneeling so she could

pull Willow into her lap. "But I'm here now and I won't let anyone hurt you."

The girl lay motionless against her heartbeat.

Mercy's throat threatened to close at the vulnerability of the child in her arms. "Come on, Willow. I need to know who hurt you so I can help." Strokes through baby-soft fur, kisses on a cold little nose. "You're safe." She put all her dominance into her voice. It was considerable. She was one of the highest-ranking members of either DarkRiver or SnowDancer. For this lynx girl, that made her commands close to impossible to disobey. "Shift."

And Willow did.

Mercy didn't move a muscle as the cub disappeared into the magic of the shift, the sparkles of color bright and joyful. An instant later, a little girl scrambled off her lap, crouching down opposite her. Her eyes were huge with hurt. "They took Nash."

"Your brother?" Nash, she knew, was a student at MIT but he had visiting privileges to DarkRiver land.

A swift nod. "They came and they hurt Mommy and Daddy and they took him." Willow swallowed hard, and it was clear she was trying desperately not to cry. "My mommy and daddy wouldn't wake up."

Oh, hell.

"Willow, sweetheart." She stroked a hand over the girl's ash blonde hair, careful with touch now. Changelings were funny about some things. And while the cub may have had no problem with cuddling, a little girl wouldn't allow total familial skin privileges to someone who was almost a stranger. "I'm going to call a friend now. He's a wolf."

Willow stared at her, hurt and terror momentarily trumped by astonishment. "A wolf?"

"Yeah." She shrugged. "I know. But he doesn't bite"— *lie*—"so don't worry."

Willow didn't look particularly convinced, but she stayed in position as Mercy whistled. Riley appeared within a minute—with her clothes, boots, and phone. Grateful, she got dressed. When Riley shrugged off his T-shirt and offered it to Willow, the lynx hesitated.

"Don't worry," Mercy said, unable to stop staring at the claw marks on his back, "wolf germs wash off real easy." *Damn, she'd scratched him hard.* It made her cheeks burn to realize how far gone she'd been.

Willow took the T-shirt after a few more seconds and pulled it on. It covered pretty much everything. And they might be changeling, but sometimes, with strangers, they were human, too. The girl stood up and met Riley's gaze, showing a courage that made Mercy's cat growl in silent approval. "Thank you."

"You're welcome." He glanced at Mercy, a question in his eyes.

She gave a slight nod. "You tired, kitten?"

Willow shook her head. "I rested a lot."

But she'd run a hell of a long distance from home. Still, the girl was a predatory changeling. Smaller than a leopard, but a predator nonetheless. They had pride in spades. And this one had earned her right to that pride. "All right. Give me a sec and we'll be off." She coded in Lucas's number.

"Mercy," he answered. "We have Willow's parents. Alive."

"How?"

"Tranqs. Heavy-duty." A pause as if he was discussing something with another person. "Couple of pack medics living nearby are giving them the once-over, but they should be on the road soon. Bring the cub to Tammy's."

Hanging up, she smiled at Willow. "Your mom and dad are okay."

A flash of hope followed by distrust. "They wouldn't wake up, and they smelled really bad."

On occasions like this, a great sense of smell could screw things up. Especially for the little ones. "Someone drugged them—it made them very sleepy."

Willow bit her lip.

"This is a waste of time," Riley said. "She can see for herself when we get there."

Willow nodded like a little machine.

"Come on then," she said, wondering if the kid realized

she'd just sided with a wolf, "time to run." She went in front, Willow in between, Riley at the back.

When the kid began to flag, Riley simply picked her up, swung her onto his back, and kept running. Willow held on tight. The leopard in Mercy growled in approval—whatever his faults (and they were many and legend), Riley knew how to take care of the innocent.

CHAPTER 5

In the PsyNet, there was a ripple of reaction to the . . .
what had it been? A bombing? An accident? Whatever it was,
it made news uploads across the country. People asked for
more information, and those closest to the restaurant tuned in
to the local stations, hoping to supply it.

The public data was sparse as Enforcement and Rescue had
reacted within minutes. However, a human student had managed to grab some camera-phone footage. It was obvious the
Psy female had been at the epicenter.

There was a flurry of speculation—not unpredictable, especially after Ashaya Aleine's violent defection from the Net—
but the ripple eventually calmed. It was an isolated episode,
people said, most likely an accident caused by chemicals in
the woman's briefcase. She'd been a research scientist—from
the evidence, it appeared she'd made an error of judgment and
put two volatile substances together.

There was no cause to consider it anything else.

CHAPTER 6

Mercy led Riley and Willow to her vehicle, parked a little way from the cabin. "Buckle up," she said, starting the engine.

"Done." Bright eyes met hers in the rearview mirror. "See?"

Even as Mercy nodded, she glimpsed Riley twist around to look over his shoulder. "Good girl."

That light exchange set the tone for the drive to Tammy and Nate's place—but Willow got real quiet the instant they opened the doors and she stepped out. "I can't smell my mom and dad." Her hand clenched on Mercy's.

"They had a longer way to travel," Riley told the girl with a blunt honesty predatory changeling children appreciated. Most of them were very good at sniffing out lies. "Probably be here in the next half hour. Go on in and grab something to eat." It was well after the breakfast hour.

"I'm not hungry." Willow kicked at the grass.

Mercy tugged at her hand, making her look up. "Your mom let you skip meals?"

A shake of the head.

"So?"

A sigh. "I'll go eat." But she dragged her feet all the way to the house . . . at least until Tammy's twins came running out in human form, jumping up and down at the idea of a Big Girl to play with. Their new pet, a kitten named Ferocious, ran up on their heels, determined not to be left behind. Taking advantage of Willow's fascination with the gorgeous gray thing, the twins basically kidnapped their new friend with promises of letting her cuddle Ferocious.

"A kitten for a pair of leopard cubs?" Riley murmured.

Mercy grinned. "That kitten thinks it's the master of the universe—Jules and Rome growl at any other cat that dares swipe at her." Laughing at his expression, she nodded at the house. "Let me make sure Willow's okay." When she arrived in the kitchen, it was to find Ferocious purring loudly in the lynx girl's lap, while Julian and Roman stood on either side of her, their little hands on her bare arms as they told her all the "amazing" things their pet could do.

"Your boys are wonderful," Mercy said to Tammy. They'd understood instinctively that Willow needed caring, so they were doing the job.

The healer smiled in maternal pride. "Have you eaten?"

Mercy was shaking her head when Lucas's mate, Sascha, walked into the kitchen. "Morning, Mercy. Lucas said to let you know he's out front."

Satisfied Willow would be well looked after—and in all probability, petted and spoiled—Mercy headed out to find Lucas giving Riley's back a considering glance as the damn wolf turned to retrieve something from the car. *Fuck.*

Lucas, Mercy was well aware, would know for certain that those marks had been made with leopard claws. But he didn't say anything when Riley turned back, cell phone in hand. "Must've slipped out of my pocket. I'm going to let Hawke know what's going on."

Lucas nodded and moved a little distance toward the house to give Riley privacy. Changeling hearing was incredibly acute. But it was her alpha's eyes that worried Mercy as she followed him over. "Any idea what happened?"

"Nate said the house had obviously been invaded. The son is missing, signs of a struggle." Eyes narrowing, he looked her up and down. Then drew in a deep breath. "Good, you took care of it."

She categorically did not want to be having this conversation. "Yeah. Can we move on now?"

"No." A glint lit those intelligent green eyes from within. "Riley's got some interesting marks on his back, and you're not touch-hungry all of a sudden. And is that a bite I see on your neck?"

"What's one got to do with the other?" She tried to brazen it out, but couldn't stop herself from sweeping her hair around to hide the incriminating mark. Of course Riley had to bite her somewhere obvious—it was exactly the sort of thing dominant males loved to do, the first stage in claiming a female for their own.

Lucas's lips curved, the savage markings on his face—four jagged lines, like the claw marks of some great beast—standing out in stark relief. "Dorian's going to love this."

She glared. "I swear to God, you tell him, and I'll"—what the hell could you threaten an alpha with?—"I'll tell Hawke you want to go on daily bonding runs with him."

Lucas didn't stop grinning, but said, "That's just mean, Mercy." He glanced over her shoulder. "But if you don't want anyone else to know, get Riley a T-shirt."

"This is not an admission of anything," she said as she ran into the house and grabbed a spare tee from the stash the sentinels kept there. It made sense since Tammy was their healer and they often came to her bleeding or worse. The tee was a plain gray but when she threw it at Riley and he put it on, it abruptly became much more interesting—the man might make her hackles rise ninety-nine percent of the time, but he was built delicious, all hard muscle and contained masculine power.

Feeling heat bloom in the pit of her stomach in spite of her teeth-gritting control, she turned away just in time to catch Lucas's smirk. *"Luc."*

"I'm a sphinx," he promised. "By the way, you have visitors. Came in last night—staying in a cabin not far from your place."

Anger flared, eclipsing everything else. "Why didn't you tell me my grandmother was doing this?" She knew Lucas and Isabella had a strong alpha-to-alpha bond. Over fifteen years ago, when DarkRiver had been under attack by the ShadowWalkers, Isabella had offered her help, though she'd been dealing with serious territorial problems of her own at the time. In the end, the help hadn't been needed, but the offer had never been forgotten.

Now, Lucas folded his arms. "I thought you were drowning. Your grandmother was offering to throw you a life jacket." Blunt words. "And might be one of them turns out to be your mate." He switched his attention as Riley jogged over. "Hawke up-to-date?"

Riley nodded. "Since I'm down here, I'll stay on this. What did Nate find?"

Lucas gave him the same rundown he'd given Mercy. "Willow say anything?"

"Only that they took Nash," Mercy said, putting everything else out of her mind. "Why would anyone run this big an op to grab a college student?"

"Brenna was a college student when Enrique took her." The withheld rage in Riley was an almost physical thing.

Mercy understood—Santano Enrique, a cardinal teleki-netic, had killed Dorian's sister, Kylie, and viciously tortured Riley's sister, Brenna. Brenna had survived, but she'd been hurt in ways no woman should have to suffer. "Riley's right," she said, and the sky didn't fall in. "This could be another crazy, or it could be something specific to Nash."

Lucas nodded. "Parents should be able to tell us more, but don't count on scent—someone sprayed a heavy perfume throughout the house."

Riley's eyes grew flint hard. "Could be changeling."

Mercy hoped that wasn't true. Betrayal among the tight structure of the pack was rare, but when it happened it shoved an ice pick of the cruelest pain through them all. "We need to go back to the scene after we hear what Iain and Enid have to say." She met Lucas's eyes. "I want to stay on this."

"Works." Lucas nodded. "Nate's helping Emmett run some important training for Kit and the other novice soldiers. It'd be better if he could continue with that."

An instant later, they felt the vibration of a vehicle getting closer. Nate's SUV rolled in not long after. Two people who looked like they'd been dragged through hell itself got out the back as Nate stepped out from the driver's side.

Mercy heard the sound of running feet seconds before Willow screamed, "Mommy! Daddy!" and launched herself off the porch. Catching her in a bone-crushing embrace, her father wrapped one arm around his mate and pulled her into the hug as well. Mercy looked away from the private moment, her eyes locking with Riley's.

Pure, electric heat.

She held that wolf gaze, daring him to say something. He kept his silence, but those eyes . . . the intensity in them made her thighs clench in instinctive female reaction. She called him a stick-in-the-mud because he was so damn calm, so practical, and in no way hotheaded. But as she'd learned last night, when that intensity focused on a woman, it *focused.* Hunger tore through her, potent, rough, primal in its sensuality.

"Can you two keep from tearing each other's throats out during however long it takes to find Nash?" Lucas's dry tone did nothing to hide the feline amusement in his eyes as he broke into her line of sight. "Or maybe I should be worrying about clothes instead?"

Riley growled low in his throat. "Not your business." His voice was more wolf than human, heavy with the same need that had Mercy in its claws.

"What?" Lucas asked disingenuously as Nathan began to herd the sobbing family inside. "Come on. Playtime's over."

Mercy hung back a little as Lucas went in. "Keep your shirt on next time," she muttered to Riley, realizing the implication of her statement an instant too late.

"Keep your claws in . . . no, don't. I liked it." A pause. *"Kitty."*

She felt those same claws release. It took serious effort of will to put them back in. "What am I worried about?" she said instead, drawing blood in a much more effective way. If Riley wanted to mess with a cat, he'd better invest in armor. "I'm never again going to let myself get that desperate—I mean, a *wolf*? Do you know how many years it'll take me to live that down?" The words were almost subvocal, designed to carry to his ears alone. She felt him bristle, but all amusement died the instant she saw the way Willow's mom was clutching her.

"My baby," she was saying, kissing Willow's cheek, "my baby." Another kiss. Willow clung to her like a little monkey. Her father was sitting beside them, touching his child and his mate anywhere he could reach. The love, the connection between the three was a physical thing. Her chest grew tight with the force of it.

Then she felt Riley enter behind her, and the heat of him was a wash of wildfire on her back. "Iain," she said, feeling that fire snake into her very veins, "we need to talk to you." The sooner, the better. "And Enid, too."

Sascha came into the room from the kitchen right then. "Willow, why don't you come play with Rome and Jules for a while. They're starting to drive their mother crazy." A smile, but the eyes—the white stars on black velvet of a cardinal, the most powerful grade of Psy—were directed at the lynx girl's parents.

Mercy felt a sense of calm, of warmth, soften the stark edge of fear and desperation in Iain's and Enid's scent. It was no surprise—Sascha was an empath, a woman born with the ability to soothe emotional wounds. Now she'd taken a piece of the Bakers' pain, absorbing it into herself. Mercy wondered if doing that hurt Sascha, but knew her alpha's mate would never back off, no matter if it did.

Iain and Enid finally let Willow go with Sascha five minutes later. "She'll be fine," Mercy reassured them, taking a seat in front of the couple while Lucas and Nathan remained standing against the walls.

Riley, however, came to sit beside her, swinging around a chair to put his arms on the back. "She's a strong kid," he told them in his direct, no-nonsense way. "Escaped and hid out with a group of wild lynx."

Iain smiled, his pride open. "We thought they'd taken her, too."

"Did you see who came into your home?" Mercy asked, trying to ignore the fact that Riley's thigh was pressing against hers, the rough masculine heat burning through her jeans to incite her leopard to voracious sexual *want*. It was on purpose. Definitely on purpose. The wolf was getting back at her for implying he'd been nothing but a convenience. "Even a hint would help."

The Bakers shook their heads. "We were asleep," Enid said, voice husky from crying. "But usually, we'd wake up the instant an intruder even entered the yard. But this time . . . it was like we were drugged right from the start."

"Enid's right." Iain frowned. "I remember fighting to wake up, sure something was wrong, but I couldn't. I saw a black shadow bend over me, felt a push in my . . ." He shoved up his sleeve as if searching for something. "I felt it right here." He pressed a spot on his forearm. "Like a pressure injector. Next thing I know, I'm waking up and the house smells wrong, and I *know* the children are gone."

"Could've been some kind of gas," Nate suggested. "We'll have to check to see how they got it into the house."

Enid sat up, eyes distraught. "We had some work done under the house a few days ago—I was being paranoid, wanting to make sure everything was solid because Willow's always crawling under there. But they could've set something up then. If I hadn't—"

"Shh." Iain bussed the top of her head. "The only ones at fault are the bastards who did this."

Mercy wished she could give the Bakers more time to come to terms with everything that had happened, but finding Nash had to be the priority. "If it was a gas, how did Willow escape?"

Enid laughed, a choked-up sound. "She's been misbehaving lately. Sneaking out to go play in the woods at night. Drives me crazy. Probably saved her life." She clapped a hand over her mouth. "I didn't mean to say that. Nash's fine. He has to be fine."

"I'm sure he is." Iain's tone was so certain, everyone looked at him. "It's his work," he told them. "Somebody wanted him for his skills—my son's mind, it's brilliant."

Mercy's cat came to attention, seeing a parallel that might simply be an illusion. But if it wasn't . . . "I thought he was a student."

"Not an ordinary one—he started taking college classes at thirteen." Iain's pride was apparent even through his worry. "He's been working on his own projects for years now."

"All to do with nanotech," Enid said, and a bell rang loud and clear in Mercy's head. Beside her, Riley's thigh turned rock hard, and she knew their thoughts were running on identical tracks—three months back, Dorian's mate had been the subject of a kidnapping attempt by the Human Alliance. Though none of Ashaya's attackers had survived to confirm it, it had been clear they'd wanted her for her knowledge of a lethal virus. Depending on the nature of Nash's work, this seemed very much like the kind of operation the Alliance would run.

"Do you have details of your son's research?" Mercy asked, knowing the payoff had to be major for the kidnappers to chance reprisal by DarkRiver—because while in their territory, the Bakers were Pack. And DarkRiver never forgot its own.

Both Enid and Iain shook their heads. "It's all hush-hush," Iain said. "The university got a grant from some big company and that company has first rights to the results."

"But his professor would know," Enid added. "I'm sure he'd help you."

"Merce," Lucas said, "why don't you and Riley head out to the house. I'll organize the data collection on Nash. Enid and Iain can see if Willow remembers anything."

The shift of muscle against her own, a slight rasp of fabric against fabric that made every hair on her body stand up in attention. But this time, the wolf hadn't done it on purpose, his attention elsewhere.

"We have to guard against tunnel vision," he warned, his fury apparent in the vicious control with which he spoke. Riley,

Mercy knew, *despised* the monsters who preyed on those weaker and less able to defend themselves. It was one of the few things they agreed on. "Could be a professional relationship gone bad, a competitor, anything. We need to explore all angles until we have more intel."

The others made sounds of agreement, and Mercy and Riley drove off after grabbing a quick meal. Despite Riley's attempt at wresting control—even though it was her car—Mercy was in the driver's seat. It was obvious Riley hated that fact with a feral kind of passion.

"If you don't stop clenching your fists," she said sweetly, "your veins might explode."

"I'll take that under advisement, *Mélisande*."

She barely stopped herself from slamming on the brakes. "Who told you that?" She needed to know who to dismember.

He snorted. "I ran the background check on you."

"What?"

"Did you think SnowDancer was sitting on its ass while you cats set up your territory here?"

Given that she'd done some spying of her own, she couldn't exactly argue with that. But—"That name is off-limits. On pain of death."

"I'm quaking in my boots, pussycat."

She screamed. "Why do you live to aggravate me? Why?"

A smile that told her nothing. "One thing I've always wondered—why did you enter that bikini contest when you were a teenager?"

Her face flushed with a mixture of anger and embarrassment. "How far back did you trace me?"

"Far enough." A pause. "You didn't answer my question."

"And you didn't turn into a puff of smoke and disappear. The world is full of disappointments."

A low growl filled the vehicle.

CHAPTER 7

Councilor Kaleb Krychek sifted through the reports flowing in via his constant connection to the PsyNet, the vast mental network created by the minds of millions of Psy, and paused.

Living "jacked in" to the Net, without firewalls or shields, was not recommended, and such complete immersion, such obscene openness to others, was not something he'd ever practice. But as a Councilor, he had to be aware of everything the instant it happened. And, given that most Psy uploaded data almost without thought, the Net was the quickest and most efficient information highway in the world.

Hence his very, very well-guarded link.

"Silver," he said, as another report "pinged" in his mind, alerting him to news that had set off one of his keywords.

His most senior aide walked into the room, smart and coolly elegant despite the fact that beyond the windows, Moscow lay swathed in darkness. "Sir?"

"I've caught three reports of public violence by Psy in the past twelve hours," he said, and it was the word "public" that was important—because Silence had been meant to wipe out violence among their race. "Find out what's happening."

"Yes, sir." She paused, and waited until he'd raised his head from his desk before speaking. "There is a slight possibility that Pure Psy might be behind this."

Kaleb had considered that—the pro-Silence vigilante group had the potential to spin out of control. And Kaleb did not countenance anything outside his control. "Do you have any evidence to back that up?" Because Silver's family were spies, betraying Pure Psy without a blink because Kaleb was more powerful, and therefore had the potential to offer them a better gain—loyalty to anyone outside their own family was a cost-benefit calculation for the Mercants.

"No," Silver said. "However, I'll ask members of my family if they've heard anything. There's also a chance it's a cluster."

He didn't ask how she knew about clusters—he hadn't chosen Silver as his aide because she was stupid. "Make a list of all recent events that fit the parameters. Go back a month." Clusters of violence—when a ripple in Silence broke certain fragile minds—only took place over a limited period of time. Two weeks was the maximum. If this had been going on any longer, they had to start looking for another explanation.

Even as Kaleb spoke to Silver, another man, one known only as the Information Merchant, received a request through an e-mail address available to those who knew where to look.

The request was . . . unexpected.

It might even, he thought, be impossible to fulfill. But the Information Merchant was the best in the business. He did not accept failure.

Decision made, he tapped out a reply using the wireless keyboard beamed onto his desk.

Request received. Transfer one million dollars to the account specified below. Work will begin as soon as the transfer has been verified. Further payments will depend on hours of work, and, in this case, the level of threat.

CHAPTER 8

The echoes of Riley's growl reverberated inside the vehicle.

Satisfied she'd finally gotten to him, Mercy relaxed her hold on the steering wheel and literally shoved her mind into work mode. "So, the 'explore all options' stuff aside, what's your gut say on this? Alliance?"

"Has their trademark—or what we know of it." He stared out the windshield, his wolf very apparent in the tone of his voice. And this time, the edge was lethal. "Planned like clockwork," he continued. "Only mistake was Willow, and even that's not a biggie. She's a cub, was probably too scared to take much in."

"But if it is the Alliance, why would they be so stupid?" That, she didn't understand. "They have to know we'll come down hard—we took out their entire team last time."

Riley was silent for a few minutes. "What do we know about the Alliance?"

"We've had Keely doing some research," she said, referring to the Pack historian. "From what she found, it looks like it's a two-faced organization, but that second face—the paramilitary arm—is hidden so deep, most of their own members don't know about it, even though they're effectively funding it."

"That tracks with our intelligence."

"We don't know how long the militant arm's existed." She overtook a large truck with speed that made Riley's knuckles whiten . . . and the leopard smirk in unholy glee. "But obviously, they're beginning to get more open in their activities." Part of Mercy could understand why the humans were starting to act with such violence. Being considered the weakest race on the planet had to hurt. "What I don't get," she murmured, "is how the Alliance could sink so low as to attack women and children, families? Their business arm has always had a core of integrity."

"Been around a long time, too." Riley slammed a hand on the dash as she swung around a Porsche that was already going well over the speed limit. *"Mercy."* The dominance was back, dark and potent and thick in the confines of the car.

It was hard to breathe, but she kept her tone sweet, her leopard tightly held. "Yes, Riley?"

"I'm driving on the trip back."

"Nope."

"It wasn't a request."

"And I'm not a submissive." She bared her teeth at him, her own power flaring out in a scalding wave. "Suck it up."

The air filled with aggression. It skated over her body, along her spine, over her throat. And that quickly, she wanted him. He knew almost the instant she did, his indrawn breath harsh in a way that was utterly, erotically male. An instant later, his arousal mirrored hers.

"We are so not doing this," she said, having to force the words out past the constriction in her throat.

Amber eyes glinted at the periphery of her vision. "We already did."

She felt like she was drowning in the indelible *maleness* of him. "Once." Enough to take the edge off her need, to give her back control over her own body. "And it's going to remain that way." She pushed the button that lowered all the windows.

He took another deep breath, as if savoring the musk of

her damp heat, and her hands clenched on the manual steering wheel. If she hadn't been able to sense his own arousal, she'd have thought he was just messing with her. But he very definitely wanted her—the brutal hunger of him was a pulse against her body, powerful and boldly masculine.

"Stop the car."

She made an undignified squeaking sound in the back of her throat. "No way in hell." The instant she did that, she knew full well she'd end up on top of Riley, riding him to erotic oblivion.

Silence from the passenger seat.

The leopard clawed at her, more than ready to sate its hunger. "You know I'm right."

"Is it the fact that I'm a wolf, or the fact that I made you whimper?" Controlled words, so damn controlled. Except for the pulse of heat that kept slapping into her body over and over.

"It's the fact that you aggravate the shit out of me." She set her jaw. "I'm not a slave to my hormones." It was a reminder to herself.

A bark of laughter from the wolf next to her. Close, so close. His breath—hot, harsh, male—whispered over her ear as he said, "I don't know any woman more in command of herself than you."

She shot him a narrow-eyed glance. "And that gets your panties in a twist, doesn't it?"

"Yeah."

Okay, she hadn't expected that answer. Sweat beaded along her spine as her body fought the urge to give in to the sexual flames licking at every inch of her skin. God, but she wanted to crawl into his lap and just *taste*. "Let me guess," she said, thrusting aside the disturbing depth of her response, "you dream of a submissive little wolfie at home, barefoot and pregnant?"

"What's wrong with that? You saying your submissive members have no value?"

Oh, he was annoying her on purpose. "I didn't say that.

This is about you not being able to handle a woman who's your equal."

A very deliberate pause. "I don't see one nearby."

She was close to breaking the steering wheel. "I'm going to ignore you now."

To her surprise, he didn't say anything in return. When she glanced over, he had his head turned toward the open window. Strong jaw—stubborn jaw—a touch of dark stubble, lips that she knew full well could turn soft when they wanted, hair that lifted easily in the breeze, but was shorter than that of most changelings.

Since when did she find that sexy?

Blinking, she stared through the windshield. It was just a weird chemical attraction, she told herself. She'd been too long without sex and, judging from the ferocity with which he'd taken her, so had Riley. They'd scratched each other's itch and that was that. Done. Finito. Over.

Protesting way too much, baby girl.

It was her mother's voice. For some reason, whenever she got stupid, her mental voice turned into her mother's. Good thing her mom didn't know about Riley—she'd probably have a coronary.

Wolf and leopard?

Yeah, right.

Having somehow survived Mercy's driving, Riley nodded hellos at the DarkRiver soldiers Nate had pulled to watch the Baker home and asked one of them to check under the house. "See if you can spot anything that could've been used to pipe gas into the house. Don't touch it. Just check."

The man's eyes flicked to Mercy. She gave him a nod and he headed off. It irritated Riley that the male hadn't immediately followed his order, but the lieutenant in him was impressed. These men didn't yet know that Riley and Mercy were heading this together—if the soldier had obeyed him, it would've betrayed a lack of discipline.

"Owen," Mercy said to the remaining soldier now, "Riley's on this with me."

Owen gave a military-perfect nod, but as Mercy turned away, Riley glimpsed disappointment. Why? Then Owen's nostrils flared and he knew. Boy had been hoping to be the one Mercy would choose to break her sexual fast. Inside him, the wolf's lips curled up to display razor-sharp canines, and his next words came from a part of him Mercy alone seemed to awaken. "Ready, kitty?" He kept his tone low . . . private.

Her eyes dipped to his crotch. She licked her lips. And he came to raging, painful hardness in a second. "Why, yes, Riley. Let's go inside." She walked off ahead of him, her hips swaying in a way that was all sorts of provocation.

The wolf couldn't decide whether to snarl or open its mouth in a savage smile, the smile of a predator that knew it had been bested. Deciding to think on it, he followed her into the house, the noxious smell of the perfume the abductors had sprayed heavy in his nose.

It should've drowned out the sweet musk of Mercy's arousal.

Of course it didn't. Because Mercy was a she-devil who delighted in irritating him. Alright, he allowed reluctantly, perhaps the scent wasn't on purpose, but Christ Almighty, did she have to smell so damn good? He wanted to do what he'd done last night—bury his face in her neck from behind and take a long, deep taste.

His mind taunted him with the image of her panting and angry below him, wildfire barely contained. To deal with her, to *be* with her, he'd had to unleash the wolf. He didn't like being out of control. But neither did he plan on letting Mercy ignore the inferno between them.

The object of his thoughts met him in the middle of the house, having apparently gone straight through to the back and worked her way forward. "You pick up anything?" She was all business now.

He shook his head, telling himself to get a grip. Teasing was fine—she'd play with him, cat that she was. But if she got even a hint of just how badly he wanted her, she wouldn't let him within touching distance—just on principle. So he'd have to play this cat-and-wolf game until she gave in to the hunger between them.

Then he'd gorge on her. Until she was out of his fucking system.

Because no way in hell was Riley Kincaid about to be enslaved by a lust that seemed to know no boundaries—exactly like the woman who inspired that lust.

"Riley," she snapped. "Stop checking out my boobs and pay attention."

"I've seen them already," he said, reacting in a way he only ever did with this cat. "They're nothing to moon over." What they were, were ripe, succulent, perfect for biting. Her skin was the rich cream of a true redhead, dusted with a luscious hint of gold. It showed every kiss, every bite mark. He could still see the one he'd made last night—it took everything he had not to lean in, place his mouth over that mark, and suck.

"Yeah, same." Her eyes dropped meaningfully before lifting. "Now that we've both got that out of our systems, can we get to work?" Sarcastic words, but her scent was a stroke against his senses, cutting through the perfume as if it didn't exist.

His skin stretched tight over his body. But he was a lieutenant—and little Willow was relying on them to find her brother. "You take that side, I'll do this one."

With a nod, she walked away. He watched her move for a second before heading to do his own part of the job. He was used to working with a strong female—Indigo was his right hand in the pack. But where Indigo was calm and collected, a perfect complement to his practical personality, Mercy was red-hot passion.

He never argued with Indigo, not about anything personal. So the fact that Mercy was a powerful, dominant female had nothing to do with why he couldn't be around her for more than two minutes without losing the cool that was as much a part of him as his status as Hawke's most senior lieutenant.

Something scratched across his senses. Crouching down,

he tried to follow the scent hidden in the miasma of fading perfume. It was there, a shiny thread but worn through, thin, so very, very thin. There, he caught it.

Metal.

His first thought was of the Psy. A lot of the ones in the PsyNet had a metallic edge to their natural scent that repelled changelings. This was similar but . . . *too* metallic. There was no life to it. And the Psy, for all their coldness, were still sentient, living beings. Following it across the room, he saw something lying on the floor below an end table. "Mercy," he said softly, knowing she'd hear him.

"You got something." She was beside him moments later.

"There."

She crawled lower, her body brushing along his side. The wolf growled. And it wasn't in rejection. Then she whistled. "I've seen one of those before. It's the same as that chip thing the Alliance soldiers had in the backs of their necks when they tried to kidnap Ashaya."

"I figured as much—I haven't seen one but Bren described it to me." His sister was a highly qualified tech, part of the team working with Ashaya Aleine to figure out the chips. This one, he saw, was still attached to a bloody hunk of flesh. "Ripped out. Nash?"

"I'm guessing." She paused. "I know when my brothers used to sneak out when we were young, I always knew before my parents. Oldest sibling intuition. Maybe Nash was outside tracking Willow when they gassed the place?"

He had seen Mercy's brothers around but now wondered what they were like. Redheaded hellions probably. "Makes sense. He steps out, escapes the gassing, comes back in because he hears something, and that's when they attempt to grab him, not realizing there's another kid out in the woods."

Nodding, Mercy touched the floor and came away with a thin layer of dust. "He shifted. This is from his clothes disintegrating."

Riley sniffed at the finger she held up. "I can scent denim."

"You can?" She raised it to her own nose. "I can't."

He couldn't help it—she brought out the wolf's most wicked edge. "That's because I'm older and stronger."

She shot him an evil look. "As I was saying, Nash shifted. Most likely after he ripped that chip off."

"Could've done it in animal form, too. Lynx are small and agile, especially when they're pissed." He barely resisted the urge to stroke his hand down the sweep of her back and over her bottom. Mercy was beautifully built, all smooth curves and muscled grace. What would it be like, he wondered, to have the right to caress her as he pleased? The wolf was oddly intrigued by the idea.

"Hmm." She sat back up on her haunches. "But they still got him. Had to be more than one—the Alliance's modus operandi seems to be to overprepare rather than under."

"We've got enough flesh to get DNA if the attacker's in any database." There was no question of going to Enforcement. This was changeling territory, changeling victims, therefore changeling law applied.

Not only that, but Enforcement had so many Psy stooges, nothing ever stayed secret. Until they knew what was happening, they couldn't afford to tip off the Council. Having lost two highly trained scientific minds when Ashaya and her twin, Amara, defected, chances were the Councilors would try to commandeer the Alliance chip and Nash both.

As for the assailants . . . too fucking bad. "Don't move the chip. There might be trace around it."

"*Really?*" Doing an atrocious vocal impersonation of a Southern belle, Mercy fluttered her eyelashes. "Why, I'm so glad you're here to tell me, Mr. Kincaid—I might not have figured that out all by my lonesome."

He felt his lips twitch. "I think you have something in your eye."

He was certain he saw a flash of amusement but then she shook her head and her voice shifted to work mode, any hint of play buried deep. "The techs should do the whole house in case they left any other calling cards. Might as well call Ashaya, too, have her come out with her team."

As Mercy spoke to the M-Psy who'd mated with Dorian, Riley shifted closer—smiling inwardly at her slight responsive jerk—and bent to look at the chip. It wasn't tiny. Maybe one square centimeter. But even without a microscope, he could see that it was a complex piece of work. Some kind of neuroinhibitor, was the current theory.

But what exactly did it inhibit?

"She's on her way," Mercy said, folding up the phone and—surprisingly—not pulling away. Instead she pressed closer, their heads side by side. "It's a hell of a piece of work."

Her hair brushed his arm, and he remembered how the strands had felt sliding over his skin as she kissed her way down his body that last time. "Yeah." His voice was half growl, the wolf's frustration rising to the surface. "Let's leave this for Ashaya and do a sweep around the house—they might've left a trail at their entry point."

"Nate had the men take turns doing that already—nothing."

"None of them is a lieutenant or a sentinel."

A slanted glance. "Is that a compliment?"

"No, it's a fact." He watched her rise to her feet in a fluid move that was intrinsically feline. "I'm going to give Judd a call—he's got contacts in the Net, can get a feel for whether this was a Psy thing."

Mercy nodded. "I'll utilize our own contacts, too. But my gut says the Psy aren't involved, at least not directly." Her eyes met his, the leopard apparent in the sheen of gold that overlaid her gaze for a fleeting instant. "Time to move, wolf."

Adrenaline speared through his veins as he realized she was beginning to lose the battle to rein in her own hunger. "Lead the way, cat."

CHAPTER 9

Mercy finished the first pass around the Baker home and shook her head. Nothing. Nada. Zip. The scent trail had had hours to dissipate. Riley silently indicated the next pass and off they went, having decided to do this in animal form. As she left, Mercy wondered what anyone would think if they saw a leopard standing face-to-face with a heavily muscled wolf.

Changeling animals were usually bigger than wild animals, but the shift did strange things to body mass and size. It was never a zero-sum equation. Though she was on the tall side of average in human form, she was smack in the middle in leopard form. Riley, however, was big—and unlike most of his brethren, he wasn't built graceful. No, he was built for stubborn endurance—apparently, his nickname was the Wall.

No one, she thought, would ever mistake him for anything but a changeling.

Something crunched under her paw. Backing up, she brushed aside the leaves with gentle care. It was nothing. An old toy. Probably Willow's, from the proximity to the house. They didn't find anything in the third or fourth pass. The fifth had to be the final—they were going into more heavily populated areas.

It was on that last pass, as they were heading toward each other, that Mercy saw it. A glint of silver in the grass beside a curb on a dead-end street—one that backed onto the woods that separated the Baker home from this neat subdivision. Slowing her pace, she came to a standstill by it. With other houses so close, it could've been any of a thousand things. But she looked closer.

A chain. No, an identity bracelet, the silver bar marked with the name *Bowen*. She couldn't pick it up with her teeth. She tried a claw very, very carefully. It came. Riley bent his dark gray head and took it in his teeth, holding it as they walked around the area where they'd found it. Nothing else jumped out.

Nodding at each other, they ran back and shifted in the patch of woods where they'd left their clothes. Mercy took the bracelet the instant she was human, and turned it over. *Happy Birthday, Bo. From Lily.*

Disappointment sat like lead in her stomach. "Could belong to anyone."

"We might as well do a door-to-door—that street's the closest logical place for a vehicle to have waited."

"Yeah, the woods would've provided coverage." Gut clenching with a furious mix of worry and anger, she put the bracelet to the side and grabbed her clothing. "Wonder if we can get satellite images."

Riley pulled on his jeans and she almost moaned. *Focus, Mercy.*

"I'll check," he said, zipping up those damn jeans as she slid on her own. "But we might get lucky with an insomniac." When he turned, she saw the marks on his back were almost healed.

Fast, even for a changeling. Which meant Riley was more powerful than she'd guessed, more than he let on. There was nothing flashy about him. Just— "What the—" His hands were on her waist and his mouth on hers before she could do more than gasp.

Lightning. Bright. Sizzling. Perfect.

This time she did moan, wrapping her arms around him and luxuriating in his strength, in the sheer speed with which he'd come at her. With both of them only wearing jeans, her breasts were pressed against the exquisite roughness of the hairs on his chest. She rubbed against him, giving in to the leopard's innate sensuality.

He tore away his lips but they remained less than a millimeter apart. "This is your fault."

"Hell, no." She sucked on his neck, biting him a little too hard for emphasis. "You jumped my bones."

Tugging back her head with a hand fisted in her hair, he glared down at her. "You were all but licking me the way you were looking."

"Looking's not the same as touching." Her mouth watered at the idea of licking him. They'd been in too much of a rush last night. Even the second and third time. As if they'd both been hungry so long, they'd needed to gorge. But—"We don't have time for this."

He held her for another couple of seconds, pure male muscle and heated skin. "We need to make time."

It was an order.

The cat hissed. The woman narrowed her eyes. "What you need to do is let go of me before I give you some scars that won't heal over as quick."

One big hand skated down her back to tease the top edge of her jeans. "I bet if I touched you now, I'd find you silky and hot and damp."

Her stomach grew taut as his fingers slid in past the denim, a little rough, all determined. Pushing. He was pushing her. But she was no tabby cat. She was a leopard. Biting those sensuous wolf lips just hard enough to sting, she shoved away using a move that snaked her out of his hold. "I meant what I said, Riley. Once was enough." *Liar, liar.*

He didn't attempt to grab her again, watching her dress with eyes gone amber as he finished pulling on his own clothes. "That's not what your body says."

"Yeah, well, it's not the best judge of character." Ignoring the weight of his gaze, she scraped her hair into a tight pony-tail, having finally remembered stuffing a thick rubber band into her jeans as she left work a couple of days earlier. "I've got no room in my life for a male who's going to tell me what to do."

"This is just sex."

He was trying to make her mad. As if she'd fall for that. "Oh, puhleeze." Snorting, she went to grab her boots. "Nothing's just sex with men like you—the instant you take a lover, you become all 'I man, you woman. You do as I say.'" And no matter how much she wanted a mate, Mercy couldn't submit. Not that way. Not to a man who wanted her to be something different. It would break her. "Then you beat your chests and howl at the moon."

Riley wasn't amused. "You don't think you can handle me?"

Okay, so maybe he was *really* good at pushing her buttons. "I said I don't have the time." Hopping on one foot, she put on her boot.

Fighting the urge to trap her against the tree and bring this conversation down to the basics, Riley fisted his hands. Mercy sucked in a breath at almost the same instant. He froze. "What?"

"Nothing."

But her teeth were gritted in obvious pain. Looking down at the bare foot she was now holding off the ground, he quickly made the connection. "What did you step on?" His wolf rose to the surface, protective and more than a little possessive.

"Nothing."

Stubborn cat.

He headed over and knelt down in front of her, lifting her foot higher so he could look at the sole. "This nothing sure looks like a big, fat thorn." It angered him to see her flesh marred by the spike that had already drawn blood.

Her hand landed on his shoulder as she balanced herself. "I can take care of it."

Instead of dropping her foot, he held on tighter. "Have you had your shots?" he asked, knowing she'd hate any kind of sympathy. Mercy was as proud as they came. And for some reason, it was important to him that that pride never be crushed. "I don't want to catch rabies."

"Ha-ha," she muttered, but her voice was strained. "Since you won't let go, can you get it out?"

He checked the ground to make sure there were no other dangers. Mercy's opinions on the matter notwithstanding, he was a protector. Taking care of the woman he was rapidly coming to consider his own was as natural to him as breathing. "It'll be easier if you sit." He didn't offer to help her down, just watched to make sure she didn't hurt herself any more.

Once she had her back to the trunk, he put her foot on his lap and grimaced. "It won't be pretty—I think your skin's started to heal around it." That was the problem with changelings—they healed quickly, especially when it came to minor flesh wounds. But if this healed over, the thorn would remain embedded in her heel.

"Do it." She set her jaw.

Shifting so his back was to her, he pressed the flesh on either side of the thorn with enough force to send it through the surface. He heard Mercy suck in another breath, knew she was hurting. The damn thorn had barbs. His wolf swept over his skin, hackles raised. Every male instinct in him wanted to give comfort, but he knew Mercy would hate that with a capital *H*. "You know," he said, fighting to keep his tone even, "I think I see a family resemblance. Maybe that's why it was drawn to you."

"You think you're hilarious, don't you?" It was a little breathless.

Another hard press got the thorn most of the way out. "Say ahhhh." One final application of pressure and the ugly thing was out. He made sure to crush it using a claw before dropping it to the ground.

Mercy didn't say a word as he checked the already healing wound. He was fast about it, but thorough. "I don't think it left any traces. Get Tammy to have a look anyway."

"It'll be fully healed in another hour."

He shot her a narrow-eyed look, noting her strained expression. "Do you *want* me to report you to your healer?"

She glared daggers at him, color rapidly returning. "I want you to let go of my foot."

He kept hold, gently massaging the area around the wound, ensuring good blood flow. It would help her heal even faster. "Will you see Tammy?"

"Yes! Fine! Can we go now?"

"In a second." He checked the wound again. "It'll be a bit tender to walk on until it heals. Be careful."

It looked like she was going to snap something at him but she clamped her mouth shut and put on her remaining sock and boot. Standing, she tested the foot. "It's fine. The sucker just hurt like hell while it was in there."

Riley nodded, but kept his eye on her balance. It was good. His wolf retreated. "Let's head in." Grabbing the identity bracelet, he slid it into a pocket.

Mercy folded her arms. "Thanks." It was a grumpy acknowledgment.

"So gracious."

As she closed her eyes as if to count to ten, he felt the wolf rise again, this time with pure mischief as its aim. "You never answered my question."

"What?"

"Whether you're running from us because you don't think you can handle me."

"I did answer it. I said I didn't have time."

"Chicken." Said as they came within hearing distance of the men and women guarding the house.

Mercy's mouth fell open. Surely she'd heard wrong. Surely solid, staid, stick-in-the-mud Riley Aedan Kincaid had not dared her by calling her a *chicken*?! "What did you say?"

"You heard." He greeted the four others who'd joined Monroe and Owen. Two of them were wolves.

Monroe walked over. "I saw nothing under the house that could've been used to pipe gas into the home, but I'll make sure the techs recheck," he told them. "Thing is, Owen does some sharpshooting—he says if you were good enough, you might be able to get some sort of gas pellet through the little vent in the bathroom."

"That vent is tiny," Mercy muttered.

Riley made a sound of disagreement. "I know two men who could do it."

Dorian and Judd. Nodding, she glanced at Monroe. "Tell the techs to pay extra attention to that area when they arrive." Raising her voice, she held up a hand. "Owen and Monroe, stay on the house. Rest of you—with us."

Mercy hit pay dirt barely five minutes into the search. She knocked on the door of a small cottage with frilly curtains and a garden so neat that no weed would dare show its head, and found herself being scrutinized by a tiny woman with such strength of will in her that it fairly pulsed in the air. Bright brown eyes looked Mercy up and down. "So, you tumbled that wolf you were with?"

Mercy was too much a pack animal to take offense at the personal question. She grinned. "How did you know it was me?"

"Do I look senile to you?" Not waiting for a response, she continued. "I was coming out to you, but you took off too fast."

Every sentinel instinct came on alert. "You saw something?"

For an answer, the woman picked up a piece of paper from a table beside the door and shoved it at Mercy. "Registration number of the van that was parked here for much too long—I knew they were up to mischief."

"Did you call Enforcement?"

"'Course I did." A pause. "Got a nephew in there. Good kid. He says it was off a stolen vehicle. But I wrote down the description of the van, too."

Mercy was already pulling out her cell to get the Dark-River techs onto surveillance.

"So?" her informant prompted before she could code in the call.

"Yes," Mercy said. "And I'm not doing it again." If she kept telling herself that, maybe her traitorous body would actually notice and shut up with its demands.

The older woman gave her a sour look. "Damn shame. What, you like them prettier?" A snort. "In my day, we liked men who looked like men."

Mercy had no chance to reply, finding the door shut in her face. Everyone was a critic today. And coming on top of Riley's "chicken" taunt, it didn't put her in the best of moods. But the tech answered then and she gave him the info. He promised to get back to her the second they had anything.

Riley was waiting for her by the curb, explaining how the old lady knew what he looked like. "Get anything?"

The woman's words in her mind, she ran her eyes over him as she shared the intel. He definitely looked like a man, she thought, all hard and solid and rough. Strength, there was incredible strength in Riley. Which made the gentleness of his hold as he'd gotten that thorn out of her foot all the more extraordinary.

She knew what he'd been up to with those cracks of his. Damn wolf had been looking after her. And he'd done it *right*. Even now, the leopard didn't know quite what to make of it, so she concentrated on the hunt. "It's a good lead."

"There's something wrong with this," Riley muttered, rubbing at a jaw that already bore the faint shadow of afternoon stubble. "That chip tells us this was an elite Alliance force, but why would they leave the evidence behind if they're so organized? And being so careless with the van?"

"You thinking the chip could be a plant?"

He looked down the street, as if seeing what had happened the night before. "I had a call from Lucas while you were talking with your informant—Nash's professor says he's being courted by several Psy firms."

Mercy blinked. "Psy are very, very insular. Especially with R & D. Why would they want a changeling?"

"A gifted changeling. Nash's apparently a genius in nanotech. And we both know the Council is missing two of its top technical scientists."

Mercy blew out a breath between her teeth. "The Implant

Protocol crashed and burned with Ashaya's broadcasts." That protocol had been meant to turn the individuals of the PsyNet into a true hive mind, interconnected and seamless.

"Yeah, but what if someone's got the idea to keep it on the back burner for the future?" He shrugged. "It's a theory."

"But if you're right, either the Psy took Nash and pinned the blame on the Human Alliance, or—"

"The Alliance took him and did a sloppy job."

Mercy rubbed her forehead. "Or we could be screwing ourselves up by making this too complicated."

"I guess we'll find out when we find Nash."

She jerked up her head, hearing a very dangerous thread in his voice. "Hey, cut that out. We're in a human neighborhood."

The eyes that looked at her weren't brown anymore. "And this is wolf territory."

"Leopard and wolf." She refused to back down under that predatory gaze, though it chilled her to the soul. She'd never seen Riley lose it like that. And so rapidly. "What flipped your lid?"

"If Nash is hurt, Willow's going to blame herself for not being able to help her brother."

Oh. "He won't be—he's a predatory changeling. We're not easy to kill." She made her voice as arrogant as she could. "Now, pull yourself out of that slobbering mess of self-pity and get with the program. This isn't about you."

Riley stared at her with those cold wolf eyes, a rich amber that held pure menace. "One day," he said calmly, "your mouth is going to get you into more trouble than you can handle."

CHAPTER 10

Mercy felt a whisper of relief brush across her face. She was confident she could hold off Riley in a real fight long enough for help to arrive, but if he truly went wolf on her, there was a high chance he'd kill her. Unless she cheated. Which, in a fight to the death, she absolutely would. Sometimes, it wasn't about strength, it was about intelligence. "Oh?" she said, and very deliberately ran the tip of her tongue over her upper lip.

Riley sucked in a breath and the wolf was gone between one heartbeat and the next. "Using sex to distract me?"

"Whatever works." Oddly enough, much as she liked to piss him off, she didn't like to see Riley hurting. Not over this. He'd gone through hell when Brenna had been abducted. So now, she grinned and said, "Plus, I know you're going to be tormented by that image the rest of the day."

To her surprise, Riley's lips curved. Just a little. Just enough to make her stomach dive. "So, you want to play, kitty cat?"

"Men." A disdainful snort, but Riley saw the flash of something richer, hotter, far more enticing in those changeable leopard eyes. Good. Because this wasn't over. Not by a long shot.

"Can we get back to work now?" An arch question.

No one ever talked to him like Mercy. If he hadn't had her all but purring for him only a night ago, he'd have imagined she didn't know how. "There's not much more we can do at this stage." He thought over their options. "Lucas and Hawke have taken care of getting the word out to our informants, and looks like the Bakers weren't able to give us any other possibilities to investigate. Have the comm lines been tapped?"

She nodded. "Nate organized it. Techs know to check all other cell phones and computers in the house—data'll go through to Dorian automatically." The blond sentinel was a genius at computers. "He'll alert us if anything jumps out."

"I'll get Brenna to work on the satellite end of things."

Mercy knew SnowDancer had full control of at least one satellite so that made sense. "I also tagged some out-of-state packmates while we were back at Tammy's. They're going to go chat with Nash's friends at MIT."

"Then, until we get a tip about the van, or the scene processing team comes up with something, we wait. Could be the abductors contact us."

Mercy made a sound of frustration. "I hate waiting."

"Leopards are good stalkers."

"The human half of me prefers action." Kicking at the grass, she nodded. "Okay, you're right. Are you going to head back to the den or stay down here?"

He glanced at his watch. It was five after four. There was a chance something would break today. "We might as well go over the new training schedule."

"I'd rather eat needles." But she started walking back to their vehicle. "Why did we think it was a good idea for the cat and wolf juveniles to mix?"

"So the alliance would become stronger." Riley wasn't sure anyone had realized how volatile the combination would be. Leopards and wolves were both predators used to being at the top of the food chain. Add teenage hormones to the pot and you had a recipe for trouble. "It needs to be done."

Mercy's cell phone rang before she could respond. "Yeah?"

"Merce," came Rina's voice, "I'm tracking two *gorgeous* men heading to your place. Do I let them go?"

"They've got safe passage," Mercy muttered, rubbing at her temples. She loved her grandmother to pieces, but she was going to strangle her for this. "And I don't plan to be home anytime this century."

"You need to make time, because wow. Hot. Beautifully, lickably hot."

"You're welcome to them."

"Oh, no, I think they most definitely want *you*."

Mercy hung up to the sound of the younger woman's laughter . . . and realized Riley's wolf was in his eyes. "Don't go there." She immediately turned down the volume of her phone.

"Who are they?"

"No one you need to concern yourself about." Shoving the phone into a pocket, she raised an eyebrow. "You hungry?" Neither of them had eaten since before lunch.

It took him a long time to respond, but he finally nodded. "Yeah."

They ended up parking in front of a fast-food place along a small suburban shopping strip. "Meat and grease. Yum." She licked her lips, stomach rumbling. "I luuuuuuve burgers."

"It's crowded," was Riley's only comment.

"You can sit in the car. I'll bring you something after I finish eating." A smirk. "It'll be cold and congealed but hey, wolves have no taste buds anyway, right?"

He got out and followed her to the restaurant. When he paid for her order, she shrugged and decided that was one battle she didn't care to fight. With predatory changeling men, you had to make *some* allowances, or you'd give yourself a concussion. They were that bloody hardheaded. And since she still wasn't letting Riley drive, this was a good enough compromise.

Not that Riley thought so. His expression was so irritated when they took their seats that the teenagers sitting at the next table—a group of nonpredatory changeling kids—gave them wary looks.

"Relax," she told the kids. "He's just grumpy because they didn't have sweet-and-sour sauce."

One of the girls ventured a nervous smile, but the kids went back to their meal.

Riley thrust a burger at her. "Put that in your mouth."

"Are you telling me to shut my piehole?" She bit down on her burger and made a low purring sound in the back of her throat. "Nice." It came out "Niishe."

Riley ate half a burger with one bite, then started on the biscuits they'd both added to their orders. When she stole his fries, he didn't even growl. The cat decided to be nice to him during the meal, given that the food was clearly mellowing him out. She was on her third burger—hey, she was hungry—and he was on his fourth when the hairs on the back of her neck rose in warning, even as Riley went predator-still.

Both of them looked very carefully toward the door. A man had come in. A Psy, from the way he was dressed and the scent of him. He didn't have the ugly metallic smell of those who had become utterly lost in Silence, but the echo of it was there. *Tainted*, Mercy's leopard growled, the man was tainted.

She was moving before she stopped to think, aware of Riley beside her. The man at the door looked around as if confused, then reached into the paper bag in his hand. Mercy kept moving with silent, leopard grace, peripherally aware that everyone in the restaurant had gone very, very quiet. Changeling or not, all living beings had a primitive core in their brain that told them when danger neared.

The man's hand began to come out of the bag.

"Now!" She didn't know which one of them spoke, but by the time the man's gun cleared his bag, wolf and leopard both were moving at lethal speed. They slammed into him and took him straight through the glass doors and onto the pavement outside.

He cried out as he crashed onto the cement, pedestrians scattering in a rush of dropped bags and short screams. Glass glittered under the sunlight, but Mercy had eyes only for the gun.

"I've got him," Riley said.

Letting go of the Psy male, she grabbed the weapon and unloaded it with cautious but quick hands. "Jesus. It's a machine gun—he could've taken out the entire place." Her heart grew cold as she thought of those innocent kids, the mother she'd seen with a baby carriage, the elderly couple by the door.

"Call Enforcement," Riley said, ignoring the glass sticking to his skin. "And an ambulance. He's hurt."

The would-be shooter was moaning as he lay there, but his eyes were unexpectedly clear. "I don't remember," he whispered. "I don't remember."

"I called them already," a shaky voice said.

Mercy looked up to meet the gaze of the nonpredatory girl who'd smiled at her—a bird of some kind, her hair as soft and feathery as her wings would be in changeling form. "Good girl. Can I have your sweatshirt?"

Nodding, the girl pulled off the thin sweatshirt to reveal a pink baby-tee. "Here."

Mercy used the material to cushion the Psy male's head. The glass had been safety glass, so it hadn't cut, but they'd hit the pavement hard. The man was bleeding. "I think he's concussed."

"Good." A SnowDancer lieutenant's flat statement. "That means he's not alert enough to be a problem." He got up, likely to scan the area for any further threats. Mercy wanted to contact Faith, have her get word about this to her father, Councilor Anthony Kyriakus, but she couldn't chance making the call in such a public location. Anthony's rebel sympathies were a well-guarded secret.

Then her eye caught that of a woman dressed in goth black, her lips painted midnight blue, her hands half-gloved. But it was the tiny tat on the top of her left index finger that interested Mercy. A little rat. Relieved, she nodded at the woman. An instant later, the human Rat—a member of the spy network that had allied to DarkRiver—took off. She knew word of the near massacre would reach DarkRiver within seconds.

Riley crouched back down. "Rat?" he asked so low that no one else could've heard.

She nodded. "Another Psy crazy?" As things grew increasingly unstable in the Net, more and more cracks had begun to appear in the Psy populace itself.

"Seems that way." Frown lines marked his forehead. "We wouldn't have to guess if we could question him after he's coherent, but we won't get a shot—Enforcement will take him in, and ten minutes later, the Psy Council will quietly secure him for rehabilitation."

She gritted her teeth. "This is where I wish I had Psy powers." Because after the horrific psychic brainwashing of rehab, this man would be lucky to be able to tie his shoelaces.

Enforcement sirens sounded right on cue. Since the would-be shooter was Psy, neither DarkRiver nor SnowDancer had any jurisdiction. The cops assumed control of the Psy male and—after taking one look at the big-ass gun—gave Mercy and Riley no shit for what they'd done.

The Enforcement guys, Mercy thought, weren't actually all bad. But the fact was, the Psy Council had so many spies in the organization, it leaked like a sieve. "You know how to get in touch with us if you need anything else," she said to the grizzled old cop who'd recorded her statement.

"Shouldn't need to," he said, tone easy. "Just patched into the security cameras—pretty obvious he was about to go whackjob on you."

"Technical."

The officer grinned. "I call 'em like I see 'em. There's been a few whackjobs operating last few days. They had a bomb go off in a restaurant in San Diego, and another guy drove this monster truck through a diner wall out in L.A. All Psy."

"Casualties?"

A nod. "But not bad. The bomb only took out the Psy. Injured a waitress, though, but she's gonna be okay. The weird thing was with the truck. It jammed—almost as if the crazy had second thoughts and braked real hard—it gave folks enough time to leap out of the way. He put a bullet in his brain before anyone could get to him. But if things keep going like this, more people are gonna start dying."

Mercy nodded. The senior members of both DarkRiver

and SnowDancer knew that things were shaky in the PsyNet, but she'd had no idea it had gotten this bad. "So we're good to go?"

"Yep." He nodded at the kids huddled behind them. "We took their statements already. You driving them home?"

It was a reasonable assumption—predatory changelings ruled, but with it came responsibility. "Yeah." Watching as the crime scene techs began to vacuum up the glass, she realized they weren't going to be able to fit all the kids in the car.

Turning to them, she asked for names and locations. Three lived within walking distance, the other two a ten-minute drive away. "Right," she said, "we'll walk you three home, then drive you two."

The girl in the pink T-shirt—Jen—bit her lip. "We'll be okay. We were, you know, just freaked out."

"I know." She wrapped an arm around the girl. They were changeling. Touch was how they healed. "But I need to see you home safely." Or the leopard would go nuts.

A nod against her. The girl didn't move away until Mercy squeezed and released her. Riley came up beside Mercy right then, and she explained the plan. He began walking and the boys fell in with him, while the two girls chose to stick with Mercy. The girl Mercy hadn't hugged, the one dressed in a tiny miniskirt and belly-baring top, inched closer until Mercy took the hint and hugged her, too.

Ahead of them, Riley and the boys had paused, shooting the breeze. She saw him ruffle one kid's hair, pat another on the back, do that fake almost-hurting-but-not-quite punching thing guys do with the third. Taking care of them.

The girl tucked up against her—Lisha—relaxed and pulled away. "You were so fast," she said as they began walking again.

"Yeah," her friend said, almost jumping up and down in excitement. "It was like wow!"

"Totally." Lisha beamed at Mercy. "I heard that you were, you know, a sentinel but I never thought I'd see you in action. The boys sometimes say that, like—"

"You're probably not as tough as the men," Jen completed. "I'm so going to make them eat their words."

Mercy laughed. "You have to excuse them—boys suffer from an incurable disability."

"What?"

"Testosterone."

Both girls cracked up. And Riley turned to give her a look that reminded her of all the things she liked about testosterone. Especially when it was packed in the hard, muscled body of a wolf who seemed ready to devour her in small, sexy bites.

CHAPTER 11

Anthony Kyriakus dropped out of the telepathic conference and thought about the information he'd just received via his daughter. Today's violence was troubling, but given the time frame of events, it *could* be put down to an anomalous statistical cluster. The Net was normally a seamless river of data, without chaos, without emotion—but with the recent high-profile defections, as well as the activities of various rebel groups, it had begun to fluctuate with waves of uncertainty.

And since Psy were connected to the Net on the most visceral level, needing the biofeedback to survive, anything that happened there had real-life impact. It even made sense that the violence was occurring in this region—the PsyNet wasn't defined by geographical limits, but they'd had a number of disturbances in this area and the psychic effect would be strongest at the point of origin. A big enough surge could have short-circuited some aspect of the conditioning under Silence.

However, Anthony wasn't convinced. His fellow Councilors seemed to be ignoring the events, but—

The comm panel beeped. Glancing at the ID screen, he saw it was Kaleb Krychek, fellow Councilor and perhaps the most powerful telekinetic in the Net. From what Anthony had unearthed, he knew that Kaleb's control over the NetMind, the neosentient entity that was both the librarian and guardian of the Net, was close to complete. It was the very situation the Council hadn't wanted after Santano Enrique. The now-dead Councilor had used his power over the NetMind to hide his murderous crimes.

Kaleb was much more subtle. He let others believe they held power even as he played them for fools. A very dangerous man. And one whose history was close to opaque—though there were rumors he'd been Enrique's protégé.

"Kaleb," he said, answering the call. "It must be early in Moscow."

"Very," Kaleb said, but since the visual was blocked on both ends, Anthony knew the other man could be anywhere. It was difficult to tie a teleport-capable Tk to one location. "But it's your region I'm calling about—I saw the reports."

"There's been a new incident."

"The shooter," Kaleb said. "Data is already flowing in."

"The others appear to consider these occurrences a statistical anomaly."

"And you?"

Anthony leaned back in his seat. "I think we need to scan the shooter's mind." He paused as a message came through on his cell phone. *Interesting.* "Henry just sent me a note proposing the same thing—and he's offered to take care of the scan." But what exactly was Henry doing in California? His home was in London.

"I assume you'll be going with him."

"Of course." After all, none of the Councilors trusted each other. Anthony, as the leader of a rebellion determined to bring a new reigning order to the Net, trusted very, very few people at all.

In a room at the San Francisco branch of the Center, the shooter lay tied to a table, his entire body restrained. "Please," he said. "Let me go."

The M-Psy monitoring his room heard but didn't respond to his plea. Their job was to make sure he stayed alive, and, given his violent tendencies, the best way to keep him safe from himself was to make sure he couldn't move.

The fact that his mind had been locked in telepathic shields would have been termed inhumane by the other races, but those races had no experience with psychotic telepaths. This man could blow out other people's brains with a burst of pure power—it might liquefy his own brains, too, but if he was suicidal, that wouldn't matter.

So they sat silent and watchful as the man in the bed started to say, "I have to. I have to. I have to." But he never said what he had to do. And they didn't figure it out until it was too late.

CHAPTER 12

Mercy was about to bring her vehicle to a stop a little distance from her cabin when the news bulletin came on.

"The body of a twenty-nine-year-old Tahoe woman was found buried in a shallow grave near the western shore of the lake an hour ago. The grisly find was made by a local resident out for a walk with his dog.

"Enforcement hasn't yet released a formal statement, but sources close to the investigation tell us the condition of the body suggests she died recently, possibly within the past forty-eight hours. We'll keep you updated as the story develops."

Riley, having decided to ride this far with her, reached forward to turn off the feed. "We need to warn our people. Just in case." His tone was even. Too even.

Mercy didn't try to talk to him about the pain he held so fiercely to his heart, knowing she'd get a blank look at best— Brenna's abduction and its aftermath was the one thing Riley simply refused to discuss. It was instinct to want to touch him, to offer comfort, but she knew that right now, he'd accept nothing. So she stuck to the facts.

"Let's hope it was a one-off." She felt deep sorrow for the

murdered woman and her family, but a jealous boyfriend or husband would be quickly caught. A serial, on the other hand . . . "No use borrowing trouble. I'll get the word out and have some of our comm people follow the story."

Riley nodded as they exited. Leaning back against the hood, she returned to their earlier topic of conversation. "I'll call you the second we hear anything about Nash." The ground-work had been laid—the intel would come in, of that Mercy was certain. "Trying to hide an adult lynx in a city full of changelings isn't going to be easy." Especially with the Rats on alert for any sign of the missing male.

"We can't underestimate them," Riley cautioned. "They managed to grab a pissed-off male lynx and get him out pretty efficiently."

About to tease him for his caution, she glimpsed something in his hair. "Don't move." Reaching up, she removed a square of glass, putting it on the car's hood so it wouldn't lit-ter the forest floor. To double-check, she ran her fingers through the thick weight of his hair. "You're tense as a board." His body was so taut, it was a wonder he could breathe.

No answer.

Looking into his eyes, she felt her breath lock. The wolf glimmered amber bright, hungry and edgy and dangerous. "What is it this time?" She shouldn't have provoked him, but she couldn't help herself. It was like he was catnip. One sniff and she lost her mind.

Riley was barely holding back his wolf. The creature wanted him to throw Mercy to the ground, rip off her pants, bite down on her neck, and take her. Hard. Fast. Again. *And again.* Dear God but the man in him wanted to do exactly the same. Fighting the instinct, he squeezed his hands into fists so tight, his veins threatened to explode.

"Riley?" Mercy scowled, taking a step back.

The wolf bared its teeth inside him, but he held on to his humanity. She'd bled earlier today when her arms had hit the asphalt as they took down the would-be shooter. The wolf had gone insane at the scent. Riley had somehow managed to keep it together this far—he wasn't known for his control for nothing—but now the wolf was clawing at him, determined to get out. And do what?

Mercy didn't belong to him.

The wolf didn't care. Neither, Riley was surprised to realize, did the man. He wanted to take her, taste her, fucking bite her for daring to allow harm to come to herself. The possessive, protective thoughts hazed his brain, pushing him closer to the edge than he'd been for a long, long time.

Focus.

He closed his eyes.

And felt her breath against his neck. "So tense you're about to snap." Lips brushing his skin, hands on his shoulders.

"Mercy." It came out a growl.

"I'm being nice to you." Teeth closing over the pulse in his neck, a gentle reprimand. "Accept it gracefully."

He squeezed her hip with a hand that had somehow found its way to her body, but remained still. She *was* being nice to him, using touch to anchor him. It was the changeling way. But he didn't particularly want comforting from Mercy. He thrust his hand into her hair, pulling it out from the rough ponytail.

Her hand stroked the side of his neck. "Can't help it, can you?" A kiss pressed to the hollow of his throat. "You're going all wolf on me because I got a little bruised up."

He was too startled by her knowledge to answer.

"Didn't think I saw the way you looked at my hands, did you?" Sliding those hands under his T-shirt, she ran her nails gently down his back. "Poor guy—blinded by testosterone."

Now she was laughing at him. He should've snarled. Instead, he relaxed his hold on her hair so she could more easily claim a kiss. She was the uncontested aggressor this time. He let her taste his mouth, let her lick her tongue over his lip. Cat. She was such a cat. Stroking him with those cat claws, nipping at his lip with feline flirtatiousness.

When she broke the kiss to tug at his T-shirt, he cooperated and pulled it over his head. Her lashes dropped to shade the expression in her eyes as she shaped him with her hands, stroking down the planes of his chest. His hand was back in her hair, but he was no longer as wound up, no longer as close to going wolf.

Then she pressed an openmouthed kiss to his chest and he felt another kind of hunger overtake him. "More." It was a raw demand.

She laughed softly and leaned into him, tracing circles around one flat nipple. "I think you're fine, now."

"More." His hand tightened in her hair.

She stroked her own hand down his body . . . and stopped an inch from the erection threatening to poke a hole in his jeans. "Play nice." Fingers tap dancing a *quarter* of an inch from his straining cock.

"No." He pulled back her head, baring her neck . . . then let go.

She held the position, offering him her throat. A gift of trust, because in changeling combat, you could lose your life to jaws clamping over your throat. Relaxing completely, he slid a hand over her nape and kissed his way up the arch of her neck. She tasted of—

Air under his palms. A red-haired cat with her hands on her hips several feet away.

He narrowed his eyes. "Teasing?"

"You know that wasn't what I was doing."

He showed her his teeth. "Coward."

"See if I pet you next time you go all crazy."

Good going, Riley. "I didn't like seeing you hurt."

"We've been over this—I'm not your concern. The only reason I'm not spitting at you is because I know you literally can't help it." Then she was gone.

Riley shrugged into his T-shirt, his stomach taut with a knowledge he didn't want to consider. She was right—predatory changeling men were protective as a rule. But Riley was his alpha's second. His control over his reactions was legendary. He protected, but he didn't go feral. Not like this.

Today, he'd become a wolf in human form, a wolf fixated on Mercy alone.

Wanting to prowl after her but knowing that would be the absolute wrong move with this cat, he was about to leave when he caught two distinct and unfamiliar male scents on the air currents.

The wolf exploded to the forefront of his mind.

He was at the cabin before he knew it—to find Mercy standing at the foot of the steps that led up to her porch, facing off against two strangers he immediately categorized as threats. The growl that started at the back of his throat turned into cold focus between one instant and the next. His claws sliced out.

CHAPTER 13

At the same instant, Councilors Henry Scott and Anthony Kyriakus walked into the observation chamber opposite the would-be shooter's room.

"Has he said anything?" Henry asked.

"He's been mumbling that he has to do something," the head M-Psy said, "but we don't know what."

Henry stared through the glass. "The mind scan should give us the answer."

Anthony knew Henry was the Councilor most involved with Pure Psy, the group that had vowed to maintain Silence at all costs. He wondered what their reaction would be to these acts of violence, acts that showed the clear disintegration of the Protocol. "Let's go," he said quietly.

As they went to move into the room, they glimpsed an orderly undoing the straps on the patient's arm. Anthony blasted out with a telepathic order to stop . . . but it was too late. The patient wrenched out his hand, pulled a pen from the orderly's front pocket, and stabbed himself through the ear in the space of a single fractured second.

Anthony sensed the M-Psy running toward the bed, but he

focused on the man's dying mind, reading what he could before the shock of death petrified everything to stone. He caught the edge of compulsion, knew someone had been pulling this man's strings. He'd been nothing more than a puppet.

Easily used. Easily discarded.

It was clear the puppet master had implanted a suggestion that his pawn suicide after the completion of his mission, or if he was caught. Only the fact that the shooter had been stunned at the scene, and then under mental guard, had stopped him from using his telepathy to accomplish the task.

Even as the thought passed through Anthony's head, he saw the orderly crumple to the floor, and belatedly realized the man had been laboring under the same compulsion. Who had the access and ability to control this many people? The answer was—a significant number of people in the Council superstructure.

The real question was *why*.

CHAPTER 14

Mercy spun around to find Riley amber eyed and cold in a way that told her he wasn't thinking about anything but blood. "Riley."

He didn't look at her. "Who are they?"

The two men opposite her had gone hunting-quiet at his approach, and now she felt the promise of violence lick the air. "Why is this wolf near your home?" Eduardo asked, his leopard crawling in the menace of his voice.

"Quiet," she ordered, turning to the newcomers with furious eyes. "He has a right to be here. You're the interlopers so shut it."

Eduardo blinked as if he'd never had someone speak to him in that tone. Beside him, Joaquin retracted his claws, but she wasn't fooled. These men were sentinels. They could go attack-ready in a split second. But then, so could she. "Stay here." Stepping away from the porch, she headed toward Riley.

He still didn't take his eyes off the men. Snarling, she pushed him in the chest. His head snapped toward her. "Who are they?" he asked again in that cold wolf voice.

"Sentinels from my grandmother's pack," she said, livid at all three men, but mostly at Riley. She wasn't a bone to be fought over. He had no right to act territorial—she hadn't given him that right. "And I thought I told you to head back."

"I'm not leaving you alone with strangers." Quiet. Implacable.

Her temper rose. "We just had this conversation, Riley."

He didn't answer, his amber gaze shifting over her shoulder. "Why are they here?"

"Mercy's grandmother," Eduardo said from the porch, "thought she might have . . . chemistry with one of us."

Mercy decided she'd have to shoot Eduardo. That pause had been calculated, the innuendo unmistakable. Damn cat was enjoying this. And she could all but sense Riley's beast pounding against his skin, ready to savage and kill. "Out," she said, pointing her finger first at Eduardo, then at Joaquin. "You come near my home again without permission, I'll show you exactly why my grandmother calls me her favorite grand-daughter."

To their credit, neither man turned noticeably green. But they did come down off her porch. "I'm not leaving you alone with a wolf." Eduardo again. Acting as if he held authority over her.

Mercy had had it. She moved without warning, spinning her clawed hand out toward the other sentinel's throat. He shifted back . . . but not fast enough to escape the graze across his throat. As he swore, his friend grinned and said something in Portuguese that he probably thought Mercy couldn't understand. But she'd spent time roaming in their homeland.

Now she retracted her claws and said, "Joaquin is right. You asked for that one." She raised an eyebrow when they didn't move. "Why are you still here?"

Surprisingly, it was the quiet one who answered. "We like the night air." His eyes were on Riley . . . who'd stepped closer, until only Mercy separated the three men.

They weren't going to listen.

Fuck.

Tempted to leave them to it, she glanced at Riley, saw his

rage in the iron-hard line of his jaw, and felt her heart give a jagged beat. He was at the edge of his control after everything that had happened today—if she left him alone with these two, somebody would get seriously damaged. "You like the night air?" She smiled, sweet as pie. "In that case, let's go for a run."

Wolf and leopard both looked at her like she was insane.

"What? Don't think you can keep up with me? You're probably right." With that, she walked into the forest and took off, hoping the gamble would work. It did. All three followed her, the protectiveness built into their nature winning out over the possessiveness. Not that she needed protecting. Never had. Never would.

And the fact that Riley didn't understand that more than irritated her. But in a tiny, secret corner, she was surprised to find a hint of pleasure. The wolf saw her as a woman, something men were often too blinded by her status to notice. Too bad Kincaid couldn't compartmentalize—what she'd accept from a lover, she'd never accept from an ally who was supposed to be her partner.

Now she took them on one hell of a chase. All were fast. But Riley knew this land like the back of his hand. Quickly outstripping Eduardo and Joaquin, he tracked her to a spot leading away from her house and toward the Sierra. She kept up the run even when he came up beside her.

"Stop," he said, putting a hand on her arm.

She shook it off. "If I have to escort you home, then that's what I'll do. A SnowDancer lieutenant is not going to be injured on my watch on DarkRiver land."

"This isn't about the alliance." The wolf was riding him so hard, she could scarcely understand the words.

"Yeah, it's about you acting stupid."

"Mercy, damn it. Stop." Riley swung around to block her path. "You're tired and bruised from today. You need to be in a bath." It agitated the wolf that she was tiring herself even further when she should've been resting.

She halted, raised an eyebrow. "I know that. What do you think I planned to do before you three started pounding your chests?"

His vision glazed over at the mention of the other men. "They're here to make a claim on you."

"No one can make a claim on me that I don't allow. And if you don't know that by now, there's no point in this conversation."

He heard something in that statement, a cool finality that told him he could lose her right this moment. Pulling on every ounce of self-control he had, he reined in the wolf and said, "Let me escort you back home. I'll leave straight after."

"No." A flat refusal, but her eyes were full of fire. "I'll get myself home, and if necessary, I'll kick Eduardo and Joaquin's butts."

Riley felt the wolf buck at the reins at the mention of those names but he held on to his humanity. "They won't catch you. You move like lightning and this is your territory."

"Good answer." But she stayed out of reach. "Are you going to leave for the den?"

He wanted to stalk those two unknown leopards, make sure they knew he'd marked her, taken her. But that, he realized, would end any and all chance he had with the woman he wanted more than his next breath. Biting back a growl, he shifted into wolf form and stared at her.

She came down on her haunches and touched him at last, an intrinsically female stroke through his fur. "Go."

Fighting the violent natural urges of man and wolf both, he did as she asked.

Mercy knew exactly how much it had cost Riley to do what he'd done. Yet he had. For her. It shattered another barrier inside of her, made her wonder if perhaps they could do this, become lovers, without it destroying the working relationship between them—a relationship that was vital to the DarkRiver-SnowDancer alliance. They were sentinel and lieutenant, there was no getting away from that. Every one of their actions had the potential to rebound onto their packs.

She felt her phone vibrate as she walked in through her back door, having evaded both Eduardo and Joaquin. The caller ID told her it was her grandmother. Realizing she better not answer it in her current mood, she had a quick meal, then stripped and walked into the shower. The bath would have to wait. She wanted sleep.

But her rest was broken. She was worried about Nash . . . and, if she was honest, about her inability to stay away from Riley. She'd been truthful earlier when she'd told him she was touching him because he needed it. But that wasn't the whole story.

She'd needed it, too.

Those dark eyes that were too often solemn, that beautiful, thick hair, that stubborn male body, it all drew her. Solid, Riley was solid. His abdomen was hard enough to bounce quarters off, his thighs firmly muscled. Bitably muscled. But he was in no way slow—though he was very good at pretending to be. As Eduardo and Joaquin had discovered, Riley could move wicked fast when he wanted to.

He could also move with leisurely patience when inside a woman.

Her entire body sighed, wanting more, wanting him. And only him.

But powerful though the attraction was, she could deal. She was a woman at home with her needs—and it wasn't as if he didn't want her back. No, it wasn't the physical stuff that worried her. It was the other things that were beginning to be woven into the physical.

Like the tenderness she'd felt today.

She should've berated him for going all crazy because she'd gotten a little scratched up, but no, she'd stroked him instead. Because when she'd seen that glint of glass in his hair, her heart had skipped a beat. Irrational worry. But worry.

And later, when she should've left him to fight it out with Eduardo and Joaquin, what had she done? She made sure he left without any bloodshed. Part of it she could blame on a sentinel's duties—he *was* a SnowDancer lieutenant, and if he was attacked by guests of DarkRiver, it would shake the foundations of the alliance. But the rest . . . in spite of her anger at his unearned possessiveness, she hadn't wanted him hurt. Of course, she thought, kicking off the covers, in the mood he'd been in, he'd probably have made mincemeat of the other two.

She had to . . . Sleep finally crept over her in a stealthy wave, her dreams hot and dark.

Riley ran himself to exhaustion, but he dreamed, too. They weren't good dreams.

He was late. Always too late. Willow's broken body lay in a shallow grave, and he couldn't even pick her up, couldn't even hold her close.

Her eyes snapped open but they weren't her eyes. Only one person had such unique eyes—and that's when he saw it was Brenna in that grave, being buried alive. Her hands reached for him, but he was locked in place, unable to move as his sister screamed.

Until the dirt covered her face, filled in her mouth, stilled her hands.

Riley jerked upright with a scream of anguish stuck in his throat. His first instinct was to check that Brenna was okay, but it was two thirty in the morning. And there was no way he wanted her aware of the demons that continued to haunt him, night after endless night.

Shoving back the sweat-damp hair on his forehead, he got up, knowing he wouldn't be able to go back to sleep. Instead, he took a shower and dressed.

It didn't take long.

There were so many night hours left to go.

When he began to head down to the garage, he told himself to stop, but his feet kept moving forward. Grabbing the four-wheel drive closest to the exit, he drove through the pitch black of night in the Sierra and onto DarkRiver land. Normally he loved the night, the beauty and the peace of it. But tonight, the darkness haunted him, reverberating with a thousand echoes of nightmare.

Fighting those insidious whispers, he kept his focus strictly on his destination. And then he'd arrived. Mercy's vehicle was there in its spot. Something in him relaxed. Parking next to it, he exited into a world cloaked in the opaque hush of a moonless night. It was instinct to go to her cabin and sit on the steps. His wolf was still agitated, but here, he could think. Blowing out a breath, he decided to simply wait for dawn. For Mercy.

That was when the door opened. "Riley?"

Of course she'd known he was there—she was a sentinel. And in some part of his soul, he'd counted on that. "Don't ask me any questions tonight, Mercy." He didn't look at her, feeling vulnerable in a way that panicked his wolf.

"All right." Soft footsteps. "But would you like to come inside?"

Wary of her agreement, but *needing* . . . something, he walked in. She took his hand, her golden eyes luminous in the dark. "Come on, wolf."

He let her lead him to the bedroom.

"Boots off," she said, and crawled beneath the blanket.

Sitting on a chair near the vanity, he took off his footwear and just watched her, not sure he could do this. She'd given her word so she'd ask no questions, but she'd know, she'd see too deep, to things he kept hidden because they shamed him so utterly.

"No questions," she said again after an endless moment, and lifted up the edge of the blanket.

Man and wolf both hungered for the simple beauty of her touch. He had no power, no will, to resist. Standing, he crossed the carpet to slide into bed beside her, fully dressed. And when her arms came around him, when her fingers stroked into his hair, he buried his face in the curve of her neck and let the unexpected tenderness heal the wounds of the night.

Sometime before dawn, he slept.

Mercy woke to the knowledge that she was wrapped around Riley like ivy, her face against his chest, her legs tangled with his, her hands under the T-shirt he was wearing beneath a khaki shirt. The blanket had been kicked off but she was toasty warm, he generated such luscious heat. Her cat purred, wanting to stay like this all day.

So when the phone rang, she had a hard time extricating herself so she could grab it before he did. She succeeded only because the wolf was half-asleep.

"We had contact from the kidnapper," Lucas said. "He wants a meet."

She snapped upright. "It's mine."

"It's yours," Lucas agreed and gave her the details. "I'll call Hawke, have some wolves meet you there."

She decided not to mention she had one wolf right in front of her. Closing the phone, she ran her fingers over his stubbled jaw. "Time to move, Kincaid."

No words, but his muscles grew painfully rigid under her hands.

He only relaxed half an hour later, when she continued to keep her promise to ask no questions. She didn't have to. She knew what haunted this powerful, proud male, though he'd never spoken of it, never even acknowledged it. And yet when the demons had become too bad, *he'd come to her*.

It changed things, but that was something they didn't have the time to discuss. Not while Nash remained a hostage.

The kidnapper was waiting for them in the shadowy depths of a half-demolished building on the outskirts of San Francisco. Early morning light whispered over the site, but somehow failed to soften the harsh lines of plascrete and metal.

Everything about the place set Mercy's hackles to rising.

Her eyes scanned the black plastic that floated where the windows should've been, giving the building even more of a sinister cast. Neither side of her liked the place, but it mattered little. She went in first . . . after a furious argument with a Riley who was back to his usual infuriating self.

"Human males underestimate females," she said, "even more than stupid changeling men."

"He could have a gun."

"I'm wearing a bulletproof vest." She touched the light-weight fabric. "You go in, you're so mad you might tear off his face before he tells us anything,"

Riley's hand closed over her upper arm, dark eyes ringed with amber. "He deserves to have his face torn off."

"That won't tell us where Nash is, will it?" She gritted her teeth. "We haven't scented him anywhere near this building. If you kill this guy, we're back to square one."

"I don't like you going in there alone."

"There're ten of you out here! You'll only be a couple of seconds behind me. How is that going in alone?" She was nose to nose with him by now.

Someone cleared their throat.

Riley's growl scared them off. "Don't pull any shit because you want to show off."

"Wait a second." She looked down then back up. "Nope, I haven't grown a cock in the last few minutes. I have no need to prove whose is bigger."

He leaned forward and bit her lip. Hard enough to sting. She'd have kneed him, but she needed his mangy wolf ass covering hers. "Happy now?" she muttered, wondering if any-one *hadn't* seen that blatant display of ownership. She and Riley were going to have a long talk after this was over.

"No. I won't be happy until I have you over my lap."

She narrowed her eyes. "Try it and we'll see who still has his balls."

Two minutes later, she walked into the dim room in one corner of the building, the windows half covered by old curtains rather than the ubiquitous black plastic. Some light crept in, but it was dull, as if the room swallowed all energy—the kidnapper had clearly chosen the location for that very reason. His skin shimmered with darkness, and he used the shadows to turn himself into an uncertain silhouette. But she was a cat, her vision acute. She saw his height, the way he held himself, and knew this man could draw blood with a single sharp move.

"I'm armed but I have no intention of attacking," were his first words.

Mercy kept her hands in sight, too. "Excuse me if I don't take your word on it." His English was flawless, she thought, his accent too clean.

"Touché." That word fell far more naturally from his lips. "My name is Bowen." A flash of perfect white teeth. "Bo's what folks call me most of the time."

"Careless of you to lose your identity bracelet."

"The lynx was stronger than we thought." Another smile. "Can I have it back?"

Charming, she thought. And he used his charm like a weapon. "We're not here to be friends. Where's Nash and what do you want in exchange for him?"

CHAPTER 15

"He's safe." **Bowen** said, no hint of sweat or panic in him.

Mercy wasn't fooled. People could learn to regulate their breathing and bodily reactions if they practiced hard enough. "I'd like to see him."

"After we talk." No charm now.

"So talk. Explain why you traumatized a young girl and stole her brother."

Bowen blew out a breath, his hands fisting. "It was meant to be a straight grab, no harm, no foul. The little one . . . we didn't realize she was outside until it was too late."

"What do you want?" she asked again.

"To talk with the DarkRiver and SnowDancer alphas. There are things you need to know about the Human Alliance."

"And you want to tell us out of the goodness of your heart?"

"I have a price on my head as of the night of Nash's kidnapping," he said, tone blunt. "So do the rest of my men and women. We're a crack team, but there are only ten of us. We need to ally ourselves to someone stronger or we'll be dead in a matter of days."

Mercy raised an eyebrow. "I can tell you now, your chances aren't high." Maybe it wasn't what a human negotiator would've said, but if Bowen knew anything about changelings, he'd know a less hostile response for a lie. Even now, she could feel the tidal wave of enmity from the men and women at her back. Cat or wolf, it didn't matter—they all wanted to tear Bowen into a million small pieces.

"Yeah, well, it's better than no chance." Bowen shrugged, shoulders moving with a fighter's grace under a battered leather-synth jacket.

"Long as you continue to hold Nash, no one will talk to you." She made her tone as unyielding as his own. "Nonnegotiable."

High cheekbones cut sharply against skin the rich, exotic shade of the finest caramel. "He's sitting in room 10 at the Happy Inn down the street."

"Unconscious?"

"No." Bowen actually looked shamefaced. "We told him we'd gone back and grabbed his little sister so he'd cooperate."

That explained why the Rats and trackers had struck out. Hiding an angry lynx was a far different cry from holding a cooperative one. "Nice."

For the first time, the mask of civility slipped. "Hurt feelings can be mended. Dead men won't rise."

Mercy didn't say anything. "We'll wait while my people check out the inn."

So they did. In silence. Riley's energy was a violent heat against her skin, but he held his position outside.

Fifteen minutes later, there was a commotion at the front and then someone yelled out, "We have Nash!" A pause. "And he wants blood!"

Mercy met Bowen's eyes, not dropping her guard. "You going to make trouble?"

"I gave you back your boy, didn't I?"

"True. So I could kill you right now." She wasn't as hostile as Riley, but she didn't like those who preyed on the weak. Nash and Willow had been under DarkRiver's care—they were hers as much as Tammy's cubs were. "A claw slash to a few important spots and you're out of our hair for good."

Time stood still.

Many miles from the chill standoff in that abandoned building, a slender male drove his car into the San Gabriel Mountains. His face was covered with sweat, his hands white-knuckled around the steering wheel. There were no embedded roads this far up, no way to put his small, city-use car on automatic. Even if it had been possible, he wouldn't have chosen it.

He needed to focus, to concentrate.

His eyes saw only gravel and rock, an endless twisting pathway.

Take the gun hidden in the trunk of your car. Drive to the enclave of artists on the edge of the Mojave. Kill as many of them as you can before the ammunition runs out. Remember, save one bullet for yourself.

The car shuddered as it fell into a pothole, rattling his brain, throwing those whispering thoughts into chaos. He managed to get it out but the tire was flat. Hitting the hover-drive, he continued on his way. He couldn't stop. If he stopped, the gun would find its way into his hands. And men, women, and children would die.

The compulsion crushed his mind, creating pinpricks of darkness behind his eyelids—veins were starting to shatter, to bleed inside his skull. He couldn't go any farther. Twisting the wheel, he brought the car to a halt on the side of the rough mountain road. Then he got out—his gaze going immediately to the trunk. *No.* He willed himself to turn. That cliff, it was close enough. Holding his head in his hands, he forced himself to put one foot in front of the other.

All he had to do was get to the edge. He didn't trust himself with the gun. But a fall would shatter his brain just as well.

An hour after finding Nash, Mercy drove a still alive and uninjured Bowen out of the city, Indigo by her side. Bowen's hands were cuffed, his eyes blindfolded. Dorian had come out and used his toys to search for—and remove—two tracking devices.

Bowen wasn't worried. "I'd have been stupid if I hadn't had backup."

Assuming his team was following, Mercy took him out through a number of back roads, making any pursuit highly visible to the large SUV following her vehicle. By the time they circled around and pulled into a deserted section of the Golden Gate National Recreation Area on the other side of the bridge, Bowen was very much alone.

He held up his wrists when they removed the blindfold and let him get out. "I think you guys can take me on even if I'm free."

Mercy shifted in front of Riley as he exited the SUV and walked over. "Don't irritate us," she said to Bowen. The Alliance man might be a tough son of a bitch, but Riley was a very experienced wolf in a cold rage.

Jet-black eyes went from one to the other. "Something's going on that I clearly don't know about."

"The last time our people were abducted, one ended up dead and the other was tortured so badly most people thought she'd never recover," she said, letting him glimpse the leopard's need to hurt, to punish. "So your chances of convincing us of anything are about zero."

Bowen swore. "Our intel was wrong. We'd never have done it this way if we'd known."

"Excuse me if I don't sympathize." Mercy could all but feel Riley's wolf, a hot, angry breath against her nape. It was as well that Dorian had left after doing the technical search. She didn't know if she'd have been able to keep Bowen safe from *two* men who continued to bear the vicious wounds of their sisters' abductions.

It didn't matter that Willow was young, it didn't even matter that she was female and Nash male—the girl had been traumatized by being unable to help her brother, her fledgling confidence dented. Mercy knew that if she wasn't handled right, little Willow would stop sneaking out at night. And for a changeling to curl up like that . . .

She turned. "Indigo?"

"I've got him."

Letting the SnowDancer lieutenant escort Bowen into position, Mercy shifted to face Riley. "I need you to deal."

Amber glittered in his eyes but he didn't argue. "I'll hang back. Tougher to rip the bastard's head off from here." With that, he took a position close to the outer perimeter of the protective semi-circle around Lucas and Hawke.

Of the two alphas, Lucas was the more calm. Part of it was because he was built that way. But mostly it was because he had a mate who grounded him. Hawke, on the other hand . . . his ice blue eyes were those of a wolf, his hair the silver-gold of his pelt in his animal form. He looked exactly what he was—a predator uncontained by any loyalty save that to his pack. And by threatening SnowDancer's biggest ally, Bowen had threatened that pack.

The wolf alpha's eyes met Mercy's as she came up beside Bowen, and the hairs on the back of her neck rose. Hawke was fully capable of killing Bowen then and there. Glancing at Lucas, she saw him spear the Alliance man with a green-eyed look that spoke of the panther within. "You wanted to talk, so talk."

Yeah, Lucas could put on the civilized act much better than Hawke, but when you got down to it, he was as lethal as the wolf. "Why did you take one of us?"

"Because Nash was in danger of being captured by the paramilitary arm of the Alliance."

"Seems like that would be a stupid move on the Alliance's part," Mercy said. "After what happened to the last group that tried to come after one of us." Every single intruder had died, some falling prey to a sniper's rifle, the others to claws and teeth.

"You'd think so." Bowen's tone was bitter. "The men who died in your territory were my friends, my fellow soldiers."

"You're not going to get sympathy here," Indigo said from her position to his right, her voice icy.

"I didn't expect any." Bowen held Lucas's gaze. "They said Ashaya Aleine would help the Human Alliance take its rightful position in the world. We believed the rhetoric coming from the top. We thought they had only our future in mind."

Leaves rustled in the midmorning breeze, but even the gulls had gone quiet.

"Later . . . it was obvious we were inviting war." Bowen's voice grew rigid with withheld anger. "That wasn't what I signed on for. The leadership seemed to realize that at the same time and we were told to go quiet. But two days ago, we heard there'd been a decision to snatch Nash." He went to raise his cuffed hands but dropped them midway. "Look at the back of my neck."

Mercy nodded at Indigo to push down Bowen's collar, while she covered the SnowDancer lieutenant. "He's got a scar where the chip should be."

"We all got them, all the Alliance soldiers." Bowen lifted up his head. "They told us it would help protect us—we figured it had to do with shielding us against Psy interference."

Interest spiked in Mercy. Humans were the most vulnerable to Psy intrusions—changelings had rock-solid natural shields. "Did it?"

"Never tested." He shrugged. "One thing it *did* do was allow the leadership to track us. Like we were fucking GPS-chipped."

"We found one of those things in Nash's house."

"That lynx had sharp claws," Bowen said. "Three went in, but only one of us had the chip by that stage—so the Alliance would know who'd taken the boy, but not where. Nash saved us the trouble of removing the chip after the op."

"You telling us you flipped off the leadership?" Hawke asked point-blank.

"Yeah, pretty much."

"Why not just warn us so we could protect Nash?" Mercy asked.

"One—there wasn't enough time. Two—because we wanted you aware of what we can do," came the unflinching response. "We aren't easy prey, so don't mistake us for it."

"You're in our city," Lucas said softly. "We'll get each and every one of you sooner or later. Name Lily ring a bell? Sloppy of you to leave her alone on watch at your hideout."

Bowen froze. "Hurt her and we'll strike back. Your people will die for no reason."

Mercy guessed the intel about the hideout had come in while she was negotiating with Bowen. Likely, the Alliance people had given themselves away when they moved to protect Bowen's back—a fresh trail made all the difference.

"We don't kill innocents," Lucas said. "But you're not exactly innocents."

"What the Alliance is becoming"—Bowen's hands fisted—"it's not anything we want to be a part of. And we're not the only ones."

"So you want us to allow a pit of vipers to set up house in our territory?" Indigo's sarcastic voice.

Bowen looked at her. "Are you all the same? All the wolves? We believed in our leadership. We were betrayed. Now we're taking steps to move out of their shadow."

"And we're supposed to take your word for it, permitting you to ally yourself with two powerful groups?" Mercy shook her head. "Nice and opportunistic of you."

"Like vultures," Indigo added.

The two women's eyes met. Mercy smiled.

"If we don't," Bowen said, white lines of strain around his mouth, "they'll kill us through sheer strength in numbers. And I think both SnowDancer and DarkRiver would prefer that didn't happen. Because if it does, then the militants take complete control of the Alliance."

Mercy saw Lucas glance at Hawke and the wolf nod. Lucas clearly spoke for both of them when he said, "Go back to your hideout and stay there. Don't cause any problems. The second you do, you're dead." Flat, cold words.

"We can't sit still," Bowen argued, shoulders tight with frustration.

Hawke shrugged, and though he was in human form, it was as if the wolf had made the movement. "So move. And die."

"You want to play power games with your leadership—find another location." Lucas's face was pure alpha, no hint of give in him. "We'll take care of the Alliance our way."

Most humans would've backed down by now—hell, so would most changelings, but Bowen held firm. "We can help you," he said. "We're strong, well-trained, and we know how to be loyal." His mouth twisted. "At least until that loyalty is betrayed."

"Are you saying you're willing to swear allegiance to us?" Lucas asked.

Bowen nodded. "If that's what it takes."

"The instant you do," Lucas continued, "you fall out of Enforcement jurisdiction. I could tear out your heart for breaking Pack law, and they'd stand aside and let me."

"Forget about tearing out your heart," Hawke said casually, "I'd rip you limb from limb."

Riley spoke for the first time. "I don't want anyone in our pack who thinks kidnapping a teenager out of his home is a good tactical move."

Mercy knew the second Bowen realized that though two alphas stood in front of him, the real danger lay at his back. Riley was ready to gut him. The human male turned. "We saved Nash from a far worse fate. Check all flights from Europe over the past forty-eight hours. I bet you you'll find a hell of a lot of men and women coming in who walk like mercenaries. That new Alliance squad is still here."

"You're holding the information hostage?" Riley again, sounding oh-so-calm. It had taken her six months of working with him before she'd realized the calmer he got, the angrier he was.

"I don't have it," Bowen responded. "One thing humans

have gotten very good at over the years is blending in. The Alliance team is in the city, that's all I know. My contact at HQ tells me they also have a new target, but we don't know who or what."

"Mercy," Lucas said, "debrief and take him back to his people." To Bowen, he said, "As far as we're concerned, you're still the enemy. You prove us wrong, fine. But until then, you so much as lift a weapon in this city, we'll take you out."

In the San Gabriel Mountains, another struggle continued to take place under an unforgiving sun.

The slender Psy male was almost to the edge of the cliff when he fell. His knees bled as the gravel shredded his pants but he barely felt the pain. His head was about to explode. A trickle of liquid slid from his nose and when he touched it, his fingertip came away stained red.

The compulsion didn't like being denied.

Determined, he tried to get up. His body refused. It hurt. Everything hurt. But he had to get to the edge. So he pitched himself forward and started to crawl. A few more meters and he could end this without doing that which should never be done. He was Psy. He couldn't pick up a gun and mow down innocent men and women.

Inside his mind, the compulsion slammed up painfully against the solid wall of Silence. His nose bled faster. When he heard a wolf's howl on the breeze, he realized he might not have to make it to the edge. Perhaps nature would end this for him.

Mercy drove a still-angry Riley back to the cabin so he could head up to the den. "You're making my teeth ache."

The wolf in the passenger seat stared at her out of human eyes. "No questions even now?"

Surprised he'd brought it up, she shrugged. "Some promises you don't even think of breaking." He'd trusted her with his pain last night, and she knew just how difficult that kind of trust was for him. The leopard had been startled by it . . . but that startlement was growing into something stronger, something that threatened the distance she was trying to keep.

Riley opened his mouth as if to reply when something beeped into the silence. Taking out his cell phone, he checked the message and swore.

She tore her mind away from the implications of the previous night. Because she'd let him in. And that, too, was a rare kind of trust. "What?"

"Nothing. Just kids being stupid." He stuck the phone back into his pocket. "I have to go bust some heads up at the den."

"Why do you have to be the one to hand out punishment?"

"Because the kids got caught hatching a plan to toilet-paper Jon. Not Jon's home. Jon." He sounded like he had a spike being driven into his eyeballs. "And since I'm the Dark-River liaison, Judd finds it highly amusing to make me deal with it."

Mercy moaned. "Oh, God." Jon had been adopted into DarkRiver by Clay and Tally a few months back. He'd not only fit right in, he'd become the undisputed leader of his age group—and Jon wasn't changeling, which said something about his skills. "Jon probably did something first."

"And didn't get caught." Riley shook his head. "I wish this lot would've been better at hiding their tracks." His eyes glimmered amber when he glanced at her. "Where are the South Americans?"

Her leopard bared its teeth in a soundless growl at the unwelcome change in topic. "Don't know. Don't care." Though she had every intention of making her opinion of the pair clear to her grandmother. "And those two have nothing to do with whether or not we share skin privileges."

Riley snorted. "Please. Your grandmother threw them at you because there's a high chance your mate will be a dominant leopard."

"What's that to you?" It came out without thought, and she wasn't sure if it was a warning or a dare.

His phone beeped again before he could answer. Riley checked it with a grimace. "You'll have to come up with me."

"Hey, wolves are yours to deal with." She meant to have a hard chat with Eduardo and Joaquin during that time. No one was going to push her into a situation she didn't choose. "I have enough—"

"They had Jon duct-taped to a tree. Judd just sprung him—but he was found with a suspicious amount of itching powder in his pockets. And several of the wolf juveniles have been squirming for hours."

Mercy wanted to beat herself with a blunt object. "Please, God. Kill me now."

"I'd rather work out my frustration by stripping you naked and letting you use those claws on me."

And that quickly, all she wanted to do was to crawl all over him.

CHAPTER 16

At a quiet meeting room in the sunken city of Venice, four women and five men sat around a long, dark table. Outside the windows situated flush against the dome that kept this city and its inhabitants from drowning, water lapped in a gentle, blue-green wash. But inside, the quiet was sharp, spiked with the knife-edge of tension.

Two of the chairs around the table lay empty. Aurine and Douglas had both walked away during the discussion of the latest operation, unwilling and unable to see the long-range nature of the plans they'd helped develop. The chairman was frustrated by their lack of vision, but then, perhaps it was better they were gone—Aurine, in particular, had been vociferous in her opposition to the Nash Baker operation. She'd undoubtedly have used this opportunity to push for a less militant approach.

"Bowen's team has gone under," the chairman told the others. "But they're not our primary concern—I sent the information about the target with a brand-new team, yet Bowen and his people managed to acquire and act on that information before the others even arrived in the city."

"The leak—could it be Aurine?" another man asked. "She was vocal about her disagreement."

"No," a third man responded. "She's a woman of her word—I've had enough business dealings with her to appreciate that."

"Douglas?"

"Too weak," one of the women murmured. "He was on the board because he had money, not balls."

Some of the men grimaced, but the chairman nodded. "Which means it's either one of us, or there's a leak in our offices. I intend to plug that leak." A statement that carried the menacing darkness of a threat.

"Go ahead." This came from the same woman who'd spoken earlier. "But don't try to play the big man." A disdainful sniff. "You may have delusions of grandeur but this is a *group* effort. If you can't understand that, you shouldn't be here."

The chairman blinked, taken by surprise, though he hid it well. "Of course. I'd never presume otherwise. But you did ask me to be in charge of security matters—it's my job to close the breach."

And he would close it. No one was going to stand in the way of his vision—by the time this was over, humanity would rule . . . and see him as their god. Even if he had to paint the streets with Psy and changeling blood.

CHAPTER 17

The situation in the SnowDancer den turned out not to be as bad as Mercy had feared. Lucas had come up with Hawke so they could discuss the Alliance matter more in depth, and Sascha had accompanied him for reasons of her own. As a result, a suitably chastened Jon was sitting in the "brig" when they got back.

"Why does he look like he swallowed raw eggs?" Mercy asked Sascha, after she found her alpha's mate in front of said brig. One cell held wolf juveniles, the other, Jon. Now that she thought about it, every single miscreant looked prune faced. "What did you do to all of them?"

Sascha gave her a beatific smile as they walked out into the corridor and began to head south. "They had to say one nice thing about each other. Jon had to say a nice thing about every single wolf he dusted with that powder."

Mercy's leopard grinned. "I like this new evil side of you." The nature of Sascha's gift meant she couldn't hurt anyone without hurting along with that person. That didn't mean her spine wasn't forged out of unadulterated steel. "I had wild monkey sex with Riley." The speed with which it came out told her, her subconscious had simply been waiting for the chance.

Sascha almost tripped over her own feet. "Oh." A pause as she glanced around the corridor and lowered her voice. "Lucas mentioned it but . . . really? You and Riley?"

"Oh, yeah." Mercy rubbed her face. "I can't believe I just told you. It means I'm thinking of doing it again."

"Was it good?" Sascha slapped a hand over her mouth, cardinal eyes wide with mortification. "I've been living too long with cats. That was a horribly nosy question."

"It was fantastic," Mercy answered. "Fan-fucking-tastic. I want more. It's making me insane."

"What's stopping you from . . . ?"

"Aside from the fact that he's a wolf?" She raised an eyebrow. "And I'm a cat? There's all sorts of wrong there."

"Mercy, don't try and snow me. Changelings aren't animals. You're human, too. And there's nothing wrong with a strong woman like you finding Riley attractive."

Mercy reached up to redo her ponytail. "You know how predatory changeling men are." But now she knew he was more than that—she'd felt the depth of his hurt, seen a glimmer of a heart so strong, it made the leopard hunger to be invited in.

"You're hardly a cream puff." Sascha's expression filled with mischief. "I don't think Riley's going to know what hit him."

A shiver sizzled down her spine even as she grinned at Sascha's comment. Glancing instinctively to the right, she saw Riley heading out from the area where the boys were contained. "Finished?"

"This time." He looked at Sascha. "They're calling you the Devil Incarnate."

Smile wide, Sascha dusted off her hands. "My work here is done." She glanced at her watch. "I have to go see Toby," she said, mentioning Judd's nephew, "and then I'd better go rescue Hawke and Lucas from each other. You two going to sit in on this meeting?"

"I might swing by, see if they need us for anything," Mercy said. "After that, I'm gonna go for a long run, clear my head."

There was too much crap clogging her up—the Human Alliance going suddenly psychotic, juveniles acting up now of all times, and this damn, unquenchable thirst for Riley "the Wall" Kincaid. They'd been antagonists for so long, the increasing complexity of her feelings for him kept catching her unawares.

Riley didn't say anything as he accompanied her to Hawke's office, which didn't surprise her. The wolf could be very quiet when he was thinking—and strange as it was, she'd come to be comfortable with his silences. Because Riley never stopped *being* there, his focus as absolute as always.

Hawke was picking up a call as they walked in. Mercy leaned over the back of Lucas's chair, intending to ask if he needed her to do anything before she headed down, but Hawke swore, sailor-harsh, before she could get a word out. She looked up to find his face a mask of anger and, oddly, pity.

"Send it through," he said, and flicked on the comm panel to their left.

The screen filled with the image of a golden-blond Snow-Dancer soldier. "We found him collapsed on the edge of the cliff. Looks like he was trying to crawl over it. Hold on." The soldier turned his cell phone so they could see the rough tent that had been rigged a few feet away. Getting closer, he lifted the edge of the canvas to reveal the male who lay unconscious inside.

"He's covered in blood, and as far as we can tell he's continuing to bleed from the nose and ears." A pause. "Jem says it looks like the fine veins in his eyes are starting to go as well. We don't have the resources to treat him—I've called an Evac unit, but I don't think it'll get him to a hospital in time."

"Anything to tell us who he is?" Hawke asked.

"Full ID in the pocket—Samuel Rain, a robotics expert employed at Psion Research."

"That's a Psy company," Mercy muttered. "He Psy?"

"Doesn't have the smell," was the response. "But from the density of his bones, I'd say so. One more thing—he had a loaded semiautomatic in the trunk of his car."

Lucas tapped a finger on the arm of his chair. "We can get

word to someone who might be able to get him out of there in time, get him directly to Psy medics."

The SnowDancer alpha didn't hesitate. "Do it. Jesus, what a way to freaking die."

Mercy was already pulling out her cell phone, knowing exactly who Lucas was talking about. Anthony Kyriakus knew a very, very fast teleporter. "What are his precise coordinates?" Heading out of the office soon as she had that info, she made the call to Faith in private.

Riley met her eyes as she reentered. "Still keeping secrets?"

"Of course. Don't tell me you share everything?" She returned her attention to the comm panel. "What would drive a Psy to throw himself off a cliff?"

"He probably didn't want to use the gun," Riley said with quiet pragmatism.

Lucas shoved a hand through his hair. "If this kind of thing is the outer edge, what's going to happen when the Psy-Net really fractures?"

"Hell on earth," Hawke said, eyes on the screen.

"Whoa!" It came from the soldier on the cliff. "He's gone." He switched the camera to show the empty spot where the body had lain. "Fuck, that teleporter must be good to do it from a distance."

Mercy agreed. She'd rarely seen a teleporter in action, but Sascha had told her that most needed contact with their "passenger." "Well," she said after the comm screen cleared, "I guess that's that."

"Do you think," Hawke murmured, those pale wolf eyes contemplative, "they'd do the same for us if we were lying injured and bleeding in front of them?"

"Depends on the individual Psy," Mercy answered, having some idea of how much Hawke despised most of the psychic race. "Lucky for this guy we aren't the vicious animals the Council makes us out to be."

Riley stirred beside her. "You need us the rest of the day?"

It was Lucas who answered. "No. Go . . . play."

Hawke's grim look turned wolf-wicked as Mercy narrowed

her eyes at her alpha and left the room. She felt Riley exit beside her, though he didn't say a word until they were back in the main corridors. "I guess the secret's out."

"What're you talking about?" she said, the devil in her taking over. Seeing that bloody, broken body had been the final straw—she needed to decompress. And what better way than by teasing Riley?

"You," he said, his voice dropping as she stopped and turned to face him, "and me."

Her nipples hardened to aching points, but she made her expression dismissive. "Don't flatter yourself." She shoved her hands into the back pockets of her jeans and rocked back on her heels, decision made. Excitement was a taut bow inside her as she said, "I had an itch. You scratched it. End of story."

A low growl that made her thighs clench. But she smiled and wiggled her fingers. "See ya later, wolfie."

Riley was about to stalk after her when he belatedly realized he was no longer alone. Scenting the air, he found out how the intruder had snuck in under his defenses. His wolf didn't consider his younger sister any kind of a threat. "Bren, don't say a word."

Brenna took one look at Riley's face and bit back a laugh. Not fast enough. Her oldest brother turned to her with *that* look. The one that made everyone behave. But this time, she was laughing too hard to hold it in any longer.

Riley just waited until she'd gotten it out of her system before raising an eyebrow.

"You and Mercy. I love it!"

Silence.

She sniggered. "You wanted Little Miss Submissive and you got a DarkRiver sentinel." Her giggles started again, deep in her throat.

"Brenna, I'm still your eldest brother."

"And I'm mated to a big, bad Psy." She put on her best annoying little-sister voice. "Plus you know you love me."

"I know that right now, I wish I had some duct tape to put over your mouth."

Oooh, that was interesting. Nobody really ever *got* to Riley. She knew he loved her to pieces, but even she had to prod and poke at him for a really long time before she got a reaction. "Mercy and Riley sitting in a tree. K-i-s-s-i—" She shrieked as he picked her up, threw her over his shoulder, and strode toward her quarters.

Her laughter came unbidden. She was giddy with delight. Riley had always been mature, contained, but he'd also had a sense of quiet humor. He was the kind of man children loved because he was both patient and open. But he'd changed after her abduction, withdrawn all that warmth, become so hard that nothing seemed to reach him. She hated that. And she loved Mercy for refusing to allow Riley to be this stranger he'd turned into.

Her nostrils flared at the familiar scent of ice laced with something that was uniquely Judd.

"I assume you have a reason for manhandling my mate?" Cool words but his amusement was apparent.

"Riley likes Mercy," she stage-whispered, trying to twist around to look at her mate. "But she told him that h—oomph." Riley set her on her feet without warning.

She swayed, but Judd's hands on her hips kept her upright. Pushing her hair off her face, she leaned into her sexy Psy mate and smirked at Riley. "Sooo . . ."

"Judd." Riley ignored her. "You're obviously not interesting enough for my sister—she's got way too much time to poke her nose into other people's business."

Judd wrapped his arms around her from behind, his chin on her hair. "I'm more interested in you and Mercy."

Growling—Riley actually *growled*—her big brother turned on his heel and left. Brenna waited until he was out of hearing distance to say, "I hope Mercy puts him through the wringer and brings him out whole on the other side."

"He was changed by your abduction. He'll never be who he was before."

"I know." She rubbed her cheek against his arm. "But I want him to learn to be happy again."

A pause.

She waited, knowing her mate well enough to understand he was thinking things through. He was so logical that it delighted her each time he let go. And he had a habit of doing that in bed. Which reminded her, she needed to replace the iron headboard that had buckled under the force of his telekinesis last night. At least it had held up better than the wooden stuff. Hmm, maybe she should start thinking about futons.

"Your brother is used to being in charge," Judd said at last. "So is Mercy."

"Good."

"Why?"

God but she loved his honesty, his willingness to show her everything he was. "Riley," she said, turning to nuzzle at his throat, "has this image of a submissive female he'll be able to pamper and protect, but he'd never be able to truly *be* who he is with that woman." She shook her head. "He needs someone strong enough, tough enough, to refuse to put up with those walls he uses to keep everyone at a distance."

Even if he was too stubborn to see it.

After waving at Riley, Mercy took off at the speed of light. It didn't matter that Brenna had distracted him. She knew he'd come after her—she'd read the intent loud and clear on his face, in his scent.

It was why she'd pushed at him that way, picking at his possessive, territorial instincts—instincts she'd known would be running high after the events of the previous forty-eight hours. This time, he wouldn't be satisfied by anything other than a hard, sweaty bout of either raw sex or violence. And she knew very well which he'd choose. Her leopard smiled at the challenge, even as the feminine core of her tightened, readying itself in expectation.

Part of her wondered what the hell she was doing.

The rest of her didn't care.

Smile edged with excitement, she stayed in human form as she headed out of the White Zone, the safe area around the SnowDancer den, and into the huge tract of land beyond. This area wasn't patrolled, being pincered between the White Zone and the heavily guarded perimeter. It was the zone where the juvenile and adult wolves felt free to hunt, run . . . play.

Her legs jumped over a fallen log without her conscious command, her body moving with a rhythm that could come only from being changeling. She was fast, faster than any other female in DarkRiver. But she could feel him gaining on her. So she pushed and went impossibly faster.

If the wolf wanted her, he'd have to catch her.

Deep in her primal brain, she knew what she was doing. Dominant leopard women never came easily into a lover's arms. They tested their chosen male, made him prove he was capable of handling all the female had to give. More, that he was willing to fight to get it.

But Mercy wasn't ready to think about the implications of her challenge. All she knew was that this was the most exhilarating game of her life. She could scent Riley in the breeze as he ran behind her, feel the sheer weight of his intent. The wolf thought he had her. But she wasn't a leopard for nothing.

Not slowing down, she jumped onto a tree trunk, hooking herself with her claws. Climbing up with the feline grace built into her genes, she pulled herself up onto a branch, and quickly made her way to the end . . . to jump onto the next tree. And the next. There would be no trail below, nothing to tell him where she'd gone.

Well, except for her scent.

But he'd have to be fast to catch it . . . because her cat was cunning. She'd circled back on him, was going toward him as he ran her way. It would confuse the trail, make him head in one direction while she went in the other. And that was exactly what happened a few minutes later as he passed under her.

Disappointment cut through her, a hot, biting wound. She hadn't actually wanted him to fail. If she made it to the den before him, then she won, and though she might accept him back into her bed again, it would never be the same. Making a face, telling herself she wasn't *that* upset—liar, liar—she continued through the trees.

A hundred meters on, she realized she couldn't make a direct leap from tree to tree. Since Riley was way over in the wrong direction, she jumped off the branch and came to a crouching, catlike landing on the small clearing below.

A familiar hand closed around her throat from behind an instant later and she found herself hauled up against a firm, gorgeously male chest, his free arm clamping across her body to immobilize her own arms. Heat against her ear, the possessive brush of lips that she wanted to feel on every inch of her skin. "Gotcha."

She reacted on instinct, kicking backward with her legs as she attempted to wrench her body loose. All that got her was a grunt and some rough swearing before she was pressed front-first to a tree trunk, her hands manacled behind her back, her shoulders immobilized by his arm, and her legs held in place by heavy male thighs. He'd left her just enough leeway that she could turn her head.

Both of them were breathing hard, their animals at the forefront, but she was very aware of one thing. Through it all, Riley had taken every care not to hurt her. Even now, he was pressing into her with a fraction less strength than he should've done if he really wanted to keep her contained.

Test not only passed, but aced.

Because this was a game. Hurting your partner wasn't the aim. "Riley?"

"Yeah." He didn't break his hold, even as he pressed closer, his erection insistent against her lower back.

The tiny hairs on her body shivered in reaction. "I think you're sexy."

Riley narrowed his eyes at Mercy's teasing comment. "I'm not trusting a word that comes out of that pretty mouth until you acknowledge my dominance."

"If I do, will you use *your* pretty mouth to lick me between my legs?"

Christ Almighty! "Mercy, I'm this close to tearing off your pants and just mounting you."

The lush tang of feminine arousal had flirted with the air since the moment he put his hand on her, but now it blanketed everything around them. The wolf rose to the surface. Lifting his arm off her shoulders, but pressing his chest against her back, he ran his lips over the shell of her ear. "Or is that what you want?"

CHAPTER 18

Her hands were close to his crotch and now one of those hands closed over his erection. "Bite me."

"Okay." He sank his teeth into the sensitive zone between neck and shoulder.

She jerked. "Fuck!" Her hand tightened on him and it felt so good, he almost came.

Reaching between them, he pried her fingers off with his free hand as he licked his tongue over the bite marks on her skin. "No playing down there. You might use claws."

"I won't."

"Why not?" He kissed the spot he'd bitten, luxuriating in the clean, sexy, dangerous scent of her. Instead of growling, the wolf in him rolled around in it, demanding more.

Demanding she carry his scent pounded into her skin.

She angled her head slightly, giving him better access. His cock throbbed, his throat grew thick, but he held firm and avoided giving her what she wanted. Instead, he drew back. "Yes."

"What?"

"Yes, if you acknowledge my dominance, I'll lick you

between your thighs." And this time, he'd take his time. "I'll lick and suck and—"

"I yield."

Everything stilled. He couldn't believe he'd heard right. He'd expected a grudging acknowledgement of his dominance at most. But this . . . His wolf wanted to nip at her, pet her, make sure she knew he'd take every care of the gift she'd given him.

"*Only* for this, only now."

The time limit changed nothing about the value of the gift. And it *was* a gift. One dominant females very rarely gave. "Accepted." He released her hands and slammed them palms-down on the tree trunk. "Keep them there."

"If I don't?"

He slapped her lightly on the rump. "I don't think you know what yielding means."

A snarl lifted up into the air. "Hands off my butt."

"Yeah?" Spreading his hand, he squeezed in a deliberate tease.

When she shuddered, he moved away and put his hands on her hips. That got him a growl but she stayed in place. Sliding his hands up under her T-shirt, he stroked them over the silky warmth of her skin to close over her breasts. The warm, sexy weight of her filled his palms, her nipples beaded against the fine cotton of her bra.

"Skin," she ordered. "I want skin."

Since that was what he wanted, too, he withdrew his hands and used his claws to shred the T-shirt and bra off her. Then he returned his attention to her breasts. She cried out as his hands found her again skin to skin. And he just about came from the tiny, rolling movements of her body.

Trembling with the fury of his desire, he buried his face in her neck. But only for an instant. He had a promise to keep. And it was one he most definitely wanted to keep. Pulling back, he tore off her jeans and panties, leaving her dressed in nothing but a pair of boots and socks. It was so damn erotic, he decided he'd have to lure her into the woods more often. "Spread your legs."

"Make me."

His lips curved, even as the stranglehold of sexual hunger grew ever tighter. Putting a hand on the inside of her thigh, he reached up with the other to pinch one beautiful nipple. She cried out, her attention shifting . . . and he used the opportunity to push at her thigh. She spread for him instinctively. Realizing what she'd done, she blew out a breath. "My nipple hurts."

"Liar." He'd meant to drop down behind her, but it was so tempting to stroke the taut, muscled curve of her butt that he delayed, indulging himself. "Want me to suck it for you?" He tugged at the aroused nub of flesh. "So pretty and red. Like my favorite raspberry lollypop."

A choked-off sound. "Damn, Riley."

He grinned at the shocked words. "What?" He didn't wait for an answer, going to his knees behind her and angling his body so his shoulders kept her legs open for his mouth. But he didn't touch. Not yet.

Keeping one hand on her thigh, he spread her with the fingers of the other . . . and blew a soft, hot breath over her. She cried out, her body clenching to release another rush of exquisite need. His tongue was there to meet it as he licked at her with long, lazy movements. He was determined to learn every little sensitive spot, every scent, every feminine cry.

Mercy closed her eyes, the better to savor the most incredible pleasure she'd ever felt. She was never ever going to accuse Riley of being uncreative again. The man had plenty of imagination. *Plenty.* His tongue was doing things to her that she knew were illegal somewhere, and— "Riley!" Her body shook under the force of a wickedly powerful orgasm as he closed his mouth over her clit, sucking hard.

He petted her thigh, calming her down . . . then stroked those same fingers over the excruciatingly sensitive flesh of her opening. She tried to squeeze her thighs closed, but his strong, muscular body kept them open while his mouth ravaged her. Those teasing fingers rubbed a little harder, and then one began to slide inside.

She opened her eyes, but saw only a wash of color as her brain tried to process the amount of sensation going through her body. It failed. Color exploded in every direction, and the muscles in her body went taut, her claws slicing out to pierce the tree trunk as she gave in to the wildness and rode the pleasure.

When she surfaced, it was to the feel of a hot, hard, and lusciously naked male body behind her own, one strong hand cupping her between the thighs. Petting her. Easing her down. He might've been a wolf, but Riley knew how to deal with a cat.

Smiling, sated, she rolled her bottom against him. His growl was everything she could've hoped for. Cool, calm Riley Kincaid had lost control. His hand withdrew from between her legs to clamp over her hips, holding her in place . . . no, he was urging her to bend a little, to change her stance.

She cooperated, and a split second after she'd settled her hands on the trunk again, he slid into her. "Riley!" It was a short, startled scream.

He froze and his voice, when it came, was more wolf than man. "Hurt?"

She shook her head at once. "I—" Her throat was raw, her voice husky. "I'm so sensitive. And you're so damn thick."

He chuckled, and the wolf's arrogance was very much in evidence. "You like it." He rocked against her.

Moaning, she found that her body was tightening again, readying itself for another wild ride. "Do that again."

He did. And again. She was just getting into the rhythm of it when he withdrew almost completely and thrust back in slow, oh-so-slow. Sensitized nerve endings went crazy and she found herself making hungry sounds in the bottom of her throat. He growled in response and picked up the pace. Hard and thick, he was a perfect fit. He seemed to touch every single pleasure point as he went in, then again as he came out. Stomach tensing with the need to come, to take him with her, she cried out.

And the world exploded.

Mercy surfaced to the awareness that she was lying on something soft. Touching it, she realized it was what remained of her and Riley's T-shirts. He'd made her a nest. *Aw.* Turning, she propped herself on one elbow and looked down at the male lying beside her. He had his eyes closed, and for the first time, she noticed that he had the same rich chocolate brown lashes as his brother, Andrew. Long and lush and curling slightly at the ends. Pretty lashes.

Delighted by the discovery, she leaned over and rubbed her nose gently against his. His lips curved but his eyes remained closed. One hand ran in a slow glide up and down over her back. "How was your nap, kitty?"

She nipped him on the chin. "Don't push your luck, Kincaid."

His lashes lifted, to reveal warm brown eyes full of languor. "You're purring."

"Yeah, so?" She dared him to make something of it.

Of course, since it was Riley, he did. "So I made you purr." A smug smile.

She frowned. "This is now officially a two-night stand."

"It's not night." He kept stroking her back.

His big, deliciously callused hand felt so good on her that she almost sighed. "You know what I mean."

"Why?" The lazy lover was rapidly being replaced by the Riley she knew and . . . lived to irritate.

"Okay," she said, "maybe you're not the spawn of Satan as I originally thought—"

"Thanks."

"But"—she glared at him for the interruption—"you'd be hell to be in a relationship with. HELL. In capital letters." Part of her own mind vehemently disagreed—sleeping with him last night, it had been something special, an experience that wrapped around her heart and made her want to take the wildest of chances. But that Riley might never again make an appearance, not if the lieutenant decided to contain him using his formidable self-control.

"I do have an ego, Mercy."

Hearing the warning in his voice, she ran her fingers through his hair. Beautiful and thick, it slid over her hands like water. "Riley, you still try to order Brenna around, and she's mated, for chrissakes."

"She's my baby sister. I'll try to order her around when she's eighty and a great-grandmother."

"See!"

"No, I don't see. There's a crucial difference between you and Brenna. You're not my sister. Thank God."

Mercy made a sound of frustration and sat up on her haunches. "It's not about that. It's about the fact that you're anal about control. You'd try to handle me." And she was not a woman who'd take kindly to that. More . . . it would hurt her if she gave him her trust and he abused it by attempting to turn her into something she wasn't.

Sitting up, Riley looked at her for several long minutes. "How about if I promise not to treat you as anything but my lover?"

"You can't," she said, curling her fingers into fists to stop from reaching out to caress him. "You're a dominant wolf male." Possession was in his blood.

"Fine." He scowled. "But the fact is, we burn up together and we both have no one else that we see as a potential partner. What's wrong with helping each other release the tension until we find our mates?"

Mercy wanted to snap at him for that blithe assumption. But the truth was, he probably would find a mate. His chances were higher than hers—dominant males had no problem mating with less dominant, or submissive, females. And Riley, of course, was looking for exactly that type of woman. "What if I don't want to be your fuck buddy?"

He kissed her. Slow and wet and openly possessive. "You do." Another kiss, a quick nip at her lower lip. "Do the words 'nose,' 'spite,' 'face,' have any meaning to you?"

She was not cutting off her nose to spite her face. She wasn't. Okay, maybe she'd considered it. "If we do this, you have to know—the *instant* you go 'Me Tarzan, you Jane' on me, I'm kicking your wolf ass out of my bed." Her hands closed over his shoulders, claws kneading. "Understood?"

"I understand you'll try to kick me out." A smile that began as a bare curve of his lips, and ended up creasing his cheeks with lean male dimples. "Maybe you'll win."

Since when did the sight of his smile tug at things low and deep in her? "Maybe you're delusional—and I'm undeniably insane for even considering this, but let's try it."

Riley's wolf bared its teeth inside him. He wanted Mercy, craved her until it was a gnawing ache in his gut. It was far more than sex now, even if the stubborn cat wouldn't admit it. But since it was patently clear that a full-frontal assault wouldn't work, he'd adopt cat methods and stalk her. And if he had to swipe the competition away with his claws . . . well, they shouldn't have gotten in his way. Because Mercy was *his*.

CHAPTER 19

Midmorning the next day, Riley talked to Judd as they supervised several eight-year-olds in the White Zone while their teachers went on a break. "So, did your contact come through?"

"Says the Council's downplaying any link between the shooter and the other incidents of violence." His voice was cool, his eyes intent. "It *could* be the truth."

Having learned something of how the PsyNet functioned, Riley took a moment to think. "The rebel activities in the Net have anything to do with that?"

His fellow lieutenant nodded. "Silence didn't magically happen one day—Psy chose it because we were going insane on a phenomenal level. If that Silence is now starting to fragment . . ."

"Then we're going to see more of this. Like that murder-suicide Dorian found." An entire family butchered after the head of the family shattered in the most lethal way.

"Yeah." Judd's face was bleak.

Riley could understand why. The Laurens had left the Psy-Net, but they still cared about those trapped in emotionless

Silence . . . and yet that very Silence might be all that was keeping those others alive. "But say it's not because of the trouble in the Net," he said. "How high are the chances of that?"

"High," Judd said to his surprise. "Apparently, there's evidence the shooter was acting under a compulsion. It's possible the others were, too." He glanced at Riley. "If that guy from yesterday survives, we might find out more."

Riley thought of the images he'd seen. "His brain was all but leaking out his ears—even if he survives, he might not remember anything."

"But if he was coerced, the telepath who programmed him might've left a psychic fingerprint." A pause. "I won't be passing on the info about the survivor to my contact."

"I think that's a good call—DarkRiver's being very close-mouthed about their source." The SnowDancer lieutenant understood their care, but the man didn't like the evidence of the continued separation between the two packs, seeing in it a solid barrier to his pursuit of Mercy.

"Can't blame them—trust is an expensive commodity in the Net."

Riley kicked back a soccer ball that had rolled to his feet. "Your contact, would it be the Ghost?" he said, naming a rebel so notorious, he'd started to become known outside the Net.

"Yes."

"Do you know who he is?"

Judd watched the children play, but his mind was clearly elsewhere. "I have my suspicions, but he's been very, very careful. I'm not even going to speculate until he's ready to blow his cover."

"Fair enough." Riley folded his arms. "But you sure his word is gold?"

"He's dangerous," Judd said. "Brutal at times. He'd do anything to protect the Psy, lie, even kill. But then, if it concerned the pack, so would Hawke."

"Point taken." The SnowDancer alpha had honor, but it came second to defending those under his care. "You think the Council will keep playing meek? We haven't had any real problems with them for months."

"They're up to something. We'll find out about it sooner or later." Judd's eyes narrowed. "It's the Human Alliance that concerns me right now."

Riley nodded. The recent slew of violence spoke of an organization that cared little for its own people, much less those they attacked. "Did you find anything in the surveillance footage from the airport?"

"Bowen's intel was solid—a number of mercenaries got off three different planes from Europe. They're hiding in our city."

Riley didn't ask how Judd had recognized them—the man had been an assassin, after all. "Fuck. That means this isn't over."

Learning that mercenaries had entered the city worried Mercy as much as it did Riley, and she conferenced with Clay to make sure the Rats knew what to look for. The spy network run by Teijan, the Rat alpha, and his people, was extraordinary. But the Alliance people were somehow managing to stay under the radar.

Still, after a SnowDancer-DarkRiver discussion, they decided to increase their visible presence in the city. It would let the mercenaries know they were under surveillance, which might be enough to derail their plans.

Since she didn't have a shift in the surveillance rotation until the next day, Mercy intended to use her time to catch up on her work for CTX, the communications network run by DarkRiver and SnowDancer. She was in the process of upgrading the security protocols for all stations, a vital precaution since CTX was breaking more and more inflammatory stories.

However, first she had to deal with another problem. Tracking Eduardo down to the guest cabin he and Joaquin were using on DarkRiver land, she folded her arms and looked him full in the face. Dark eyes, dark hair, bronze skin, perfect bone structure, sinful smile. "So, you come to me," he said in deliciously accented English.

And, Mercy thought with inward amusement, the arrogant

cat knew precisely how he sounded. After having grown up with three gorgeous younger brothers, there was little she didn't know about the male ego. "I came to tell you we have no 'chemistry.' Zero. Zip. Zilch. So go away."

His smile changed into something dangerous, determined. "You haven't given me a chance. Spend some time with me—a mating isn't always obvious."

"Eduardo, you're not an idiot. You have to know I'm with Riley." She still couldn't quite believe she'd agreed to be his lover. Part of her was convinced it wouldn't work—they clashed far too often. But another part of her was exhilarated, ready to take on the wolf on every level and then some.

Eduardo shrugged, tone insouciant when he answered. "You don't wear his scent. You haven't accepted him as a leopard female needs to accept a male. Means the coast is clear."

The way he said that disturbed her enough to agitate the leopard. "I might never wear any man's scent." The leopard liked running wild. To be tied that intrinsically to another, until their scents melded, was something that made it restless, wary. "But even then, we'd have zero chemistry."

He stood from his half-sitting position against the railing and gave her a smile that she figured would've sent most women into orgasm on the spot. "How about a kiss to test that theory?"

"How about you stay right there." It was a command. "I need to get to work—and you should go home."

A very Latin sigh. "You break my heart, Mercy."

"I'm sure you'll find someone to patch it up for you." She'd already had a few inquiries from interested parties as to whether "the sexy one with gorgeous eyes" was off-limits. They continued to be a little wary of the "dangerous bite of beautiful." "I've told the women of the pack that you're free to a good home."

"Such cruelty." But he smiled and it was real this time, stripped of the charm he'd used as a mask till then. Eduardo was as lethal as any of the sentinels in her own pack, his protective nature honed to a fine edge—he'd make as possessive a mate as Riley.

She scowled. All this talk of mating was starting to affect her sanity. Riley would never be her mate. Heat aside, she wasn't what he was looking for, and he was exactly the kind of man who made her cat the most wary . . . in spite of the fact that it was his strength that drew her to him.

A painful paradox.

Maybe she'd been right in what she'd said to Tammy—perhaps she'd never be able to surrender that absolutely to a man, to trust him with that much of herself. It was a real possibility that one day soon, she'd have to watch Riley mate with someone else. Her hand fisted. "Call it what you like," she said to Eduardo, "but don't say I didn't warn you."

He shrugged. "I'll stay—after all, Joaquin's still in with a shot."

Not deigning to answer, she turned on her heel and left, arriving at her current CTX station just after lunch. She had every intention of working with single-minded focus, but couldn't forget the disturbing ferocity of her reaction to the thought of Riley mating with another woman, a woman who'd have the right to touch him, kiss him, hold him when his demons got too bad. Even now, as she made her way to the garage, the idea made her blood ignite.

"Security cameras, check, weapons detection system, needed," she muttered in an effort to drown out the cat's angry hissing. "Can't do much about Psy teleporters, though. How do you detect someone who poofs in?"

A familiar scent came to her on quiet air currents. "Talking to yourself, big sis?"

She pecked her middle brother, Sage, on the cheek. "I smelled you a mile off, Herb." It was an old joke, one that never failed to make him scowl.

It didn't today either. "Ha-ha. This is my I'm-not-amused face." That done, he put his camera equipment on the floor and rubbed the back of his neck. "Guess where I just was."

Based on the now genuinely pained expression on his face, she said, "Lifestyles of the rich and famous?" Sage normally covered the crime beat.

"Close. I had to sit through an interview with Bibi Pink."

He looked like he was about to throw up. "If she has three brain cells, I'm a frickin' wolf."

Mercy's stomach dipped at the way he said "wolf." What would her family say if they realized she was consorting with the enemy on a very intimate basis? "Who did you piss off to get on that?"

"Nobody—it was Eamon's turn to do the celebrity stuff, but he got called out to a shooting at the Berkeley campus. I was the closest to Bibi so I covered."

"Another shooting?" Frowning, she turned to look at her brother. Sage had inherited the family red hair, but on him, the red was tangled with so much brown, most people didn't realize he had any red at all until he walked out into the sun. "Details."

Deep hazel eyes frowned. "Would it hurt you to say please?"

"Would you prefer I broke your arm?" She'd grown up with three little hooligans who didn't seem to understand the meaning of a closed door. If she'd let them, they'd have swarmed her like a horde of locusts. "Give it up, hotshot."

"Abuse," he said, but then gave her a smacking kiss on the cheek, the scent of him a familiar and much loved touch of firs dusted with snow, and the sweet crushed nutmeg of home. He'd hate to be described that way, but that was how she saw him—if Bastien was the rock, and Grey the sea, then Sage was the tide. Fluid. Enduring.

Now he put an arm around her shoulders. "I'm getting this second hand," he said, "but apparently it was so much of a mess that there's no way the Council's going to be able to keep it quiet. Some senior Psy professor put a gun to his head and pulled the trigger."

"Suicide by a Psy is news, but you're talking breaking news bulletin if Eamon got pulled off schedule. Why?"

"'Cause the professor held his physics class captive for twenty minutes beforehand. He shot himself in front of them."

"Jesus." Mercy rocked back on her heels, datapad dropping to her side. "You hear of any other episodes like this?"

"I got a buddy up in North Dakota—he says they've had a

couple of incidents of Psy acting out violently. One guy almost beat another to death before they managed to pull him off. And Garrick, up in Chicago, he's had a couple of hits on his radar, too."

Which meant there were probably even more that hadn't yet filtered down through the grapevine.

"Oh, and this broke a few minutes ago—they found a human male stabbed to death in an alley in Tahoe. Looks like random violence, but it's the second murder in that area in less than a week. First one was that woman in the shallow grave."

Mercy nodded, wondering if there was any connection between the two killings. Might be time for Dorian to hack into an Enforcement database. "Thanks, Herb."

"Cut it out." Turning, he grabbed her in a full hug, squeezing tight, his forehead lined with a heavy scowl. "Take it back."

"Puh-leeze. I can flip you in one second flat."

"And how will you explain the bruises to Mom?"

"Tattletale." She fought not to smile.

His eyes narrowed, but she saw the cat's laughter. "Take it back."

"Or what?" When he bared his teeth in a mock growl and squeezed her even tighter, she blew out a breath. "Fine. I'm sorry. Happy?"

He let her go with a grin that had caught her heart from the moment her mom had first laid him in her arms. "I'm still telling. You know how mad Mom gets when anyone makes fun of our names, Mélisande."

About to respond, she caught another scent entering the garage. "I've got company. Talk to you later."

Sage's lip curled in disdain. "Wolf."

"We have an alliance." She parroted Lucas. "Now, shoo, baby brother."

"Nice try but I know you can't stand this one." He bent to pick up his gear, missing her guilty expression. "Dinner tonight? Bas just got back from New York, and Grey's got the night off."

Mercy nodded, her skin tight with expectation. "Text me the details." But her attention was on the wolf who'd stroked her into wild ecstasy only yesterday. Her lower body clenched and she all but bit through her tongue to force down the rising wave of arousal. She so did not want Sage picking up on that little bit of info.

Her brother said a civilized hello to Riley as they passed. Riley responded with a nod, then jerked his head toward the exit. She went—no way did she want an electronic audience to their conversation.

"Can't stay away from me?" she asked when they were safely on the grass verge outside the building. Set in an industrial/professional area, foot traffic was light, the grass neatly trimmed. It appeared they were alone.

Riley glanced up at the building behind them. "I can feel them watching me."

"Yep. So don't try anything funny." It came out an invitation.

His eyes went dark with a kind of knowledge that made her internal furnace go straight from hot to explosive. "I was passing by, thought you might be interested in some stuff we didn't discuss on the phone earlier."

"Passing by?" She raised an eyebrow.

"I went to visit those kids from the burger place, check they were okay."

Something melted in her heart. "I called them today."

"Yeah, they said." He held the eye contact, all calm and solid and practical . . . except for the blazing heat in that gaze. "Your cat wouldn't leave it alone either, would it?"

"Nope." It was an integral part of them—that need to protect. "They seem to be doing good. That girl Jen, she's a smart cookie."

"She wants to be you when she grows up."

Mercy grinned. "I forgot to tell you something else—we're being stonewalled on what exactly Nash is studying."

"Give the kid a few days," Riley said. "He might change his mind after he thinks it over."

"Especially since we only need enough information to

protect him properly." She made a note on her datapad to have Ashaya follow up with Nash—the lynx might respond better to a fellow scientist. "So, what did you want to discuss?"

Riley's mouth became bracketed by white lines. "Judd got confirmation that someone pushed that shooter to do what he did, some kind of a mental suggestion buried deep in his psyche."

Damn. Her sympathy for the poor man who'd been made a puppet mixed with a slow-burning anger toward those who used people so heartlessly. "Tempting to call it a Psy internal war and ignore it," she said, "but it's affecting everyone." She told him about the professorial suicide. "He could've taken so many kids with him."

"No way to know if he was programmed."

"Funny coincidence, though, isn't it?" She gritted her teeth. "You know, the Human Alliance might consider the Psy their enemy, but they're fucking twins when it comes to harming innocents."

Riley's eyes gleamed amber. "You need to burn it off. Come for a walk."

Anger exploded under a surge of raw desire. "No, thanks." Especially when the urge to nibble at that strong throat, that stubborn jaw, was a drumbeat in her skull. And double especially when she was considering the mechanics of tangling limbs in a car.

The wolf was a shadow in his voice. "Scared to be alone with me?"

"Busy." Despite her racing heartbeat, it happened to be the truth. "I want to finish what I'm doing here since we have some downtime." *And I need to get a handle on this hunger before it creeps into every corner of my life.* Because if she fell too deep and then he found his mate . . . Mercy knew herself, knew the soul-destroying pain that would accompany such rejection—she wasn't good at holding back. If she gave herself to him, it would be with everything in her. "Don't you have work?"

He ran a hand through his hair, mussing himself up so deliciously that she had to fight the leopard's desire to play with the strands. "Yeah, but it's with Hawke and he's in a shit of a mood."

"Sienna?"

"Who else?"

Mercy thought about the girl who seemed to be the—very short—fuse on Hawke's temper. "What's up with those two?"

"He's my alpha," Riley said, eyes full of challenge. "I'm not going to talk about him to a leopard."

"We're not enemies anymore, remember?" she said, tone arch. "We're allies."

"Political allies—our animals still don't trust one another."

"Which is an excellent reason for us to stay away from each other," she said, seeing another glaring truth—her pack was critically important to her life. Being with Riley, that whisper of tenderness growing and twining like a vine around her heart, it held the potential to shake the foundations of her link to DarkRiver.

A sentinel couldn't give her heart to a onetime enemy/new ally and do her job as the first line of defense for her pack. She had to be able to rip out Riley's throat if the unthinkable happened and SnowDancer broke the alliance to turn on Dark-River.

Her stomach roiled with nausea, but her voice, when it came, was calm. "I'm as loyal to my pack as you are to yours." If those bonds were compromised . . . it would break something fundamental in both of them.

Riley went about his remaining business in the city with impeccable competence, following a checklist in his head. It was the only way he'd found to control the wolf when it got this agitated. Mercy would undoubtedly roll her eyes, but then she had her own ways of controlling things, didn't she? He'd felt her hunger, hot and slick in the sunshine, and yet she'd denied them both.

The light changed to red in front of him. His car came to an automatic stop.

He slammed a palm on the dashboard as the wolf snapped

out, frustrated and angry. And needy. That was the kicker. She'd turned him away, and he was drowning for her. "Fuck." Thrusting his hands through his hair, he used every one of the tricks he'd learned over the years to calm himself down.

It wasn't as easy as Mercy might've believed. Riley made it a point to be in command of his instincts because he knew what would happen if he wasn't. His wolf was wild, ferocious, quite capable of killing without a blink if those he loved were threatened. Only with Mercy did he dare let the leash slip a little. And when their bodies joined . . . hell, what leash? But she seemed to like him that way.

"Not enough," he all but snarled as the car started moving again. The worst of it was, he knew she was right. This wasn't about them in isolation any longer, it couldn't be—if it had been just sex . . . but it wasn't. He'd felt it. So had she. So had his wolf. Now it crouched down in feral anger, but it was also thinking, considering . . . wanting.

CHAPTER 20

For the first time in months, the Ghost heard whispers that perhaps Silence wasn't all bad, that perhaps they'd been hasty in beginning to condemn it. He listened, said nothing, but knew something had to be done.

For while the Ghost had nothing against Silence—nor the peace it granted so many—he knew the Protocol was what gave the Psy Council its power. Take away that method of control, and perhaps the Psy race would rediscover other kinds of freedom.

But first, he had to cut this off at the root, discover who was pulling the strings. The M-Psy in charge of the shooter, the Ghost's unwitting source, had known only of the compulsion, not the why or the who. Now he scoured the Net for information, but this person had been very, very careful. He or she had allowed not even the merest sliver of thought to escape into the Net.

A very clever adversary. But the Ghost had assassinated a Councilor. He knew how to wait, how to listen, how to learn. Sooner or later, everybody betrayed themselves. And he was well versed in how to start rumors that spread like wildfire.

At this moment he whispered that the shooter and others had been manipulated, that the Council was trying to cow the populace with terror. He could've said more, but sometimes, it was better to let people fill in the gaps themselves.

CHAPTER 21

Mercy's brothers had picked a little place in Chinatown for dinner. She walked in to find them arguing over the menu. Grinning, she messed up Sage's hair, kissed Grey on the cheek, and let Bastien grab her in a hug that lifted her off her feet. All her brothers were strong men, but Bastien, the closest to her in age, was the biggest.

"Not if you want to live," she said, after he laughingly threatened to throw her into the air. She saw the pretty waitresses give her envious looks—though it was obvious she was related to Bas. He had hair as darkly red as her own, though his eyes were a sharp, incredible green. Her brothers were all gorgeous on their own, but collectively, they made temperatures rise like nobody's business. She'd spent half her teen years scaring off the girls who'd come sniffing after one or the other. Not that the idiots had been grateful.

"You look good, sis." Putting her on her feet after another squeeze, Bas let her get into her seat.

"Yeah, nice dress." Grey actually sounded sincere.

Mercy looked down at the short, royal blue cheongsam she'd bought in this very part of town. With her hair pulled up into a high ponytail and some makeup on her face, she felt good. Even if the knife-edge of need continued to twist relentlessly in her stomach, immune to the practicality with which she'd held Riley at bay this afternoon. "Thanks, Shadow."

"How come he gets a cool nickname?" Sage muttered. "I get Herb."

"Hey, don't knock it," Bas said. "You want to be called Frenchie instead? Sounds like the name of a fucking condom."

They all choked on their oolong tea and one of the waitresses fluttered over, ready to offer all kinds of help. She saw her brothers check out the petite beauty—*men*—but though they gave her charming grins, they didn't extend an invitation. Clearly disappointed, she took the order they finally put together, and headed off.

"What?" Mercy looked around the table. "You guys take up a vow of celibacy?"

"Now that you ask," Grey murmured, brown eyes twinkling.

"Hah." She snorted. Grey might be the quietest, but he was also the most cunningly feline. "I'll believe that the day I"— Normally, she'd have said "sleep with a wolf" but since that option was out, she settled for—"grow wings and fly."

Bas put a hand on her back, as if checking for wings. "This stuff is really soft."

Sage, next to her, fingered the sleeve. "Yeah, it is. How come we rate getting you in a soft, pretty dress?"

"How come I rate the three of you all shiny and spic-and-span?" She raised an eyebrow at their outfits. Jeans, shirts, and T-shirts, nothing out of the ordinary. But all new, or clean and pressed, much nicer than necessary for dinner with their sister.

"We thought we'd go dancing." Grey winked. "You're coming."

"I am?"

"Yes. We need you as bait to draw the other women."

And since Mercy was a sucker for her brothers when the three of them ganged up on her, she went dancing with the demons. The serving staff at the restaurant looked so mournful as they left that she wrapped an arm around Bas's waist and shook her head. "I don't think the three of you should be allowed out in public together."

He swung his own arm over her shoulders. "And I just know I'm going to have to punch someone for trying to paw you in that dress." He sounded very eager.

She didn't remind him that she was fully capable of punching out people on her own. Bas was her brother—he couldn't help protecting her. As Riley couldn't help it. It was like a switch went off in them at times. Mercy could bend when necessary, she wasn't always a hard-ass. Bas had in fact, punched out people for her. She could deal.

The problem with Riley was, he didn't seem to have any give in him. She didn't want her only glimpses into his soul to be after the crushing darkness of nightmare. For her cat to trust him, he needed to trus—

"Hey." Bas squeezed her shoulder. "Where did you go?"

She glanced ahead to where Grey and Sage were strolling, checking out the window displays in the adjacent shops. "I'm dealing with stuff."

A silky pause. "What's his name?"

"As if I'd tell you."

"You chased off my last girlfriend."

"She was a hyena." Not literally, but in heart. "Wanted you for your money." Bas was smart, crazy smart. He made money on the stock market simply by breathing. Which was why he was in charge of DarkRiver's financial assets.

"My ego bleeds." A hand rubbing pitifully over his chest.

"We're going to be wiping up blood for weeks, it's so colossal."

He hugged her closer. "Come on, you can tell me. It'll be our secret."

"And you'll go hunting him the second I'm distracted. I don't think so." But she hugged him back. "So, no new hyena for me to chase off?"

"I'm still healing the scars from the last one." A piercing look. "I know who it is."

"No, you don't."

"Riley."

Her mouth fell open. She looked up. *"What?"*

"Jesus." He stopped walking. "It was a guess, but I'm right. You're . . . they're . . . he's a wolf!"

She snapped around to make sure the other two hadn't heard. "How did you even make that guess?"

He thrust a hand through his hair, almost making a woman on the other side of the street trip, she was looking at him so hard. "Only dominant male I could think of that you'd been reacting to lately. You bitch about him a lot."

She glanced again at her two younger brothers, currently distracted by a display of lanterns. "Don't tell them."

"Why the fuck not?"

"Because you know they'll do something stupid."

"So will I." He jerked his head and they started walking again. "I might not be a sentinel, but I'm your brother. And I know how to kick wolf ass."

"Bas."

"Don't 'Bas' me. You might be able to control Grey and Sage but don't even try it with me."

She glared at him. "This is my business." She trusted Riley not to hurt her brothers, but a lot could go wrong when men got stupid—especially when those men had claws and teeth meant for hunting prey.

"Should've thought of that before you told my *ex*-girlfriend I eat live kittens for breakfast."

A tiny twinge of guilt. Then the cat wondered what Riley would think of her last successful "shoo-away." "Who knew she'd believe me?"

"Oh no? When you 'accidentally' opened the cupboard to expose my 'kitten cage' full of the poor, sad kitties I was going to snack on?" A raised eyebrow. "Wasn't the cage next to my special 'kitten defurring' tools?"

"They were obviously fake."

Bas just stared at her.

Mercy snarled. "Damn it. Let's go dancing."

"Yeah, let's. I need to plan how I'm going to fillet this bastard if he hurts you."

* * *

Riley couldn't do it. He couldn't stay away from Mercy. However, her cabin proved empty. He debated calling her, then realized that would betray far too much of the driving need in him. And he couldn't let her learn that, couldn't give her that much power over him. Shoving the phone into his pocket, he headed back to his vehicle.

That was when he scented *him*. Another male. One of the South Americans. His wolf bared its teeth inside him, but it was possession, not rage. The man had been here but wasn't any longer. He'd probably come looking for Mercy. It was tempting, oh-so-tempting, to track him down and make sure he understood that Mercy was off-limits, but Riley knew his cat. She wasn't the kind of woman to play off one man against another.

And if he went after Eduardo and Joaquin, she'd assume he didn't know that.

"Fuck." Logic was a bitch sometimes. Forcing himself to get in the vehicle, he turned around and went home, parking the four-wheel drive in a designated spot miles from the den and completing the rest of the distance on foot.

The exercise burned off most of his frustration and anger, but he couldn't make himself stay inside the network of beautifully constructed tunnels that had protected SnowDancer from enemy eyes more times than anyone could count. Instead, after showering and pulling on a fresh T-shirt and jeans, he went outside and found a seat on a storm-fallen tree on the edge of the White Zone.

He was sitting there, second-guessing his decision not to track Mercy down, when someone tracked *him* down. Catching the strawberry and candy scent on the breeze, he kept his back to his visitor, allowing her to decide if she wanted to talk to him.

A moment later, a small hand tugged on his sleeve.

Turning, he chucked Sakura under the chin. "Shouldn't you be in bed?"

"It's only nine and I had a nap today." A smile and a hopeful look.

Knowing he was a sucker, but unable to resist, he picked her up—doll and all—and sat her on his lap, where she curled into a contented little ball, her ear over his heart. A wave of tenderness swept over him and he cupped the back of her head in a gentle hold.

"Riley?"

"Hmm?" He stroked his hand over the sleek black fall of hair she'd inherited from her mother.

"Have you seen my daddy?"

Riley went over the roster in his head. "Elias should be coming back within half an hour."

"I'll stay and wait."

"Did you tell your mom?" he asked, thinking that while the hair had come from Yuki, the eyes were indisputably Elias's.

A nod. Tiny fingers braiding her doll's silky hair. "Riley?"

"Sakura."

A giggle. "Did you see my tooth?" She tilted up her head. "See, I lost two."

"Where'd they go?" he teased.

Another giggle, innocent and bright. "Mom said you should come have coffee with her and Dad."

Riley raised an eyebrow. "She did?"

"Uh-huh. And she even made pecan pie."

Riley loved pecan pie, as Yuki well knew. "Your mom's sneaky."

"That's what Dad says." She snuggled closer and he tightened his arms, very aware of her fragility. He couldn't believe one of his tough soldiers had produced this tiny creature, but it was true. Half the time, Elias didn't seem to believe it either. The other half, he strutted around like the proud papa he was.

"How come she's sneaky?"

"She wants to ask me questions, and she's bribing me with pie." He had no doubts that Yuki wanted to grill him about Mercy. Damn nosy packmates.

"Oh." Her attention was on her doll. "Do you think she looks pretty?"

"Very. Just like you."

A sunny smile was his reward. "I like you, Riley."

Riley felt his heart tighten. He liked Sakura, too. Brenna had once asked him if he'd had enough of parenthood what with having to shoulder so much responsibility in raising her and Andrew, but Riley had never seen it that way. To protect and raise a child was a gift. "What's your doll's name?"

"Mimi." Putting the doll on her lap, she patted his chest. "Riley?" A whisper.

He bent his ear to her lips.

"I ate some of your pie when Mom wasn't looking."

Riley burst out laughing, realizing she'd come to hide from the results of her misdemeanor. It amused the wolf in him, too. Because this pup was one of his own, part of a pack both man and wolf had vowed to protect. Now another loyalty was starting to rise, and it confused him on every level, making him question truths so integral to his life that they simply *were*.

Until her.

If this fire between them turned dark and exploded outward, it had the potential to devastate both SnowDancer and DarkRiver.

Still, he wondered how Mercy felt about kids . . . if a child was even possible between two such divergent changeling groups.

CHAPTER 22

Councilor Anthony Kyriakus looked at the husk that had been Samuel Rain and turned to the M-Psy standing next to him. "His chances of recovery?"

Laniea glanced reflexively at the electronic chart she likely knew back to front. "Small but not negligible. We were able to go in and remove the last threads of the compulsion, relieving the pressure on his brain."

"But?"

"But there was a lot of damage. We're not going to know how much until he wakes . . . if he wakes."

Anthony knew Samuel Rain had been a brilliant robotics engineer. What would it do to him if he woke to a reality where he could never again create anything? "The signature on the compulsion was degraded. Did you find anything else during the scan?"

Laniea shook her head. "The compulsion was woven by a highly experienced telepath—the signature was the first part of the programming to go."

"Send me the details. I may have missed something in my initial scan."

The telepathic transfer was concluded in less than a second. Laniea put the chart on the end of the patient's bed and shook her head. "There's one thing I haven't factored into his chances of survival and perhaps I should."

Anthony waited.

"His will." The M-Psy shook her head. "He shouldn't have been able to fight the compulsion, but he did. Maybe he'll fight death with that same strength."

It was a diagnosis that came perilously close to taking emotion into account. But Laniea knew Anthony would never betray her.

"Perhaps," Anthony said, "we lost more than our emotions when we embraced Silence. Perhaps we sacrificed the very thing that made us fight for our right to live."

"If it's waking again," Laniea said, "it's doing so with violence."

"But not in Samuel Rain." Anthony saw in this young man's refusal to surrender, a beacon of hope for his entire race. "In him, it woke to avert violence." Faith, he thought, would be so happy to hear that. His daughter saw too much darkness, her foreseeing gift dragging her deep into the abyss.

And yet despite it all, she kept growing ever stronger. It was dangerous for a Councilor to feel pride, to feel anything, but deep in the recesses of his mind, hidden behind a thousand shields, Anthony was proud of the woman his daughter had become. Now, he nodded to Laniea and left to update Faith on Samuel's condition.

CHAPTER 23

Mercy woke the next day to the clawing viciousness of her cat, a twisting, agonizing need that refused to let her rest. What worried her was that it wasn't only sexual. She *missed* Riley. "Oh, God."

She'd have sublimated her need in work, but she'd been ordered to take time off by Lucas, given the "ridiculous number of extra shifts" she'd pulled over the past few months. Saying he needed all his sentinels fully functional when this calm broke, he'd gone so far as to cancel her rotation on the city surveillance, meaning she was utterly free.

And miserable.

Hoping a cold shower would snap her out of it, she dragged herself to the bathroom. A message was waiting for her on the comm panel when she exited. Noting the familiar number, she called through. "Ashaya, what's up?"

Ashaya's distinctive blue-gray eyes widened in surprise. "That was quick."

"Lucas ordered me to take the day off. The cheek."

Ashaya smiled—that smile was still new, but there was no

doubting it came from the heart. "I was going to ask you for a favor, but you should do something fun on your day off."

"I'm going insane," Mercy muttered, rubbing a hand over her heart. "*Please* give me something to do."

Ashaya's smile faded into concern. "Mercy? What's wrong?"

"My hormones are taking over my brain." God, she was going to bite Riley hard for doing this to her. How had he addicted her to him so quickly?

"Oh," Ashaya nodded. "I've had a few of those moments since my defection." Turning, she laughed at something Dorian had probably said before looking back. "As for the favor—I promised Amara I'd bring up something I've been working on. Do you think you could do it for me?"

Ashaya's twin was seriously nuts, but she was also smart as hell. "Won't she want to see you?"

"No, we've set up a meeting at a later date."

"What am I transporting?"

"One of those chips we found on the humans who attempted to kidnap me," Ashaya said. "I've been taking it apart bit by bit, trying to figure out how it works, what it does. Amara has a copy of her own, but I want her to see something I've found, get a second opinion."

"You get the report with my notes on Bowen's take on the things?" she asked.

"Yes, I'm attempting not to jump to conclusions, however. I also got your message about speaking to Nash."

"Any luck?"

"No," was the disappointing answer, "but I'll try again in a day or so. He may just be overwhelmed right now." She turned again, the electric curls of her hair shifting with abandon. "Wait, Dorian wants to say something."

The screen switched to audio-only and she realized Dorian must've taken the portable handset outside. "Merce, I did that Enforcement check for you. The same knife was used in both kills in Tahoe."

"Damn."

"I've renewed the alert to our people in that area and they'll get the word out to the nonpredatories. Drew's handling the info-spread on the SnowDancer end. Problem is, Enforcement's got nothing else yet, so we can't get specific." His voice dropped and he blew out a breath. "Where the fuck do they keep coming from?"

"I wish I knew, Blondie." She used the childhood nickname on purpose, nudging him away from the edge of darkness. He'd become so much more balanced since mating with Ashaya, but she knew he'd always mourn his murdered sister. So would she—as a child, Kylie had been determined to be included in all of Dorian and Mercy's nefarious schemes, no matter that she was far littler.

After Kylie's death, Mercy had made a determined effort to remember the good times, the mischief, but her heart still hurt at odd moments—like when she saw something she knew Kylie would've loved. She couldn't imagine how much worse it was for Dorian. Swallowing the lump in her throat, she said, "Or should I call you Boy Genius? That one seems to be catching on."

"Watch it, Carrot," he said, then chuckled. "I'm handing things back to Shaya—Keenan says I'm missing the best part of today's episode."

The comm filled with Ashaya's face again, her curls looking wilder than before. "What've you been doing?" Mercy asked with a grin.

Ashaya blushed. "Let's say Blondie is a fast mover."

Any lingering concern Mercy might've had for Dorian disappeared. "I'll be by in, say, two hours? That okay?"

"We'll probably still be curled up in bed, watching cartoons." Her eyes filled with affection. "My mate and son have discovered a mutual love of superheroes and breakfast in bed. They're determined to convert me."

The image Ashaya had sketched—of a lazy family morning—was so appealing that Mercy was almost surprised. Almost. Because she'd realized long ago that family was an integral part of her dream. "Don't get crumbs on the sheets."

As she hung up to the sound of Ashaya's laughter, she realized that Sierra Tech, where Amara worked, was smack bang in the middle of SnowDancer territory.

Riley's territory.

The leopard came to attention. So did the woman. And that fast, all sensible thought was buried under a crashing wave of anticipation.

Riley finished going over his worklist for the day, and handed out the assignments by phone. Unfortunately, the routine task didn't succeed in keeping his mind off Mercy—for the first time in months, he'd dreamed not of Brenna's abduction, but of a redheaded cat who refused to come to him. It had left him sweaty, the sheets tangled around his limbs like so much plastic.

Even in his dreams, she defied him.

However, despite his jaw-clenching frustration, he was almost finished when Hawke came in and grabbed a seat. "What's my assignment?" he asked after Riley hung up.

It was a serious question. Riley's job was to coordinate their resources. Hawke was the best they had. It would've been a waste not to use him—though Riley always had to have a backup in place in case Hawke got pulled away on alpha business. "I've got an assignment you'll love."

Hawke blinked, the slow, lazy blink of a predator very much on alert. "If the name Sienna appears in that assignment, I'm going to shred you open, tie your intestines in a bow, and feed you to the feral wolves."

Riley smiled and kept going as if Hawke hadn't spoken. "You need to take care of a certain juvenile Psy female you gave sanctuary to when her entire family defected from the PsyNet."

"I should've given orders to eat them all."

"Psy taste rubbery," Riley said straight-faced. "I know. I tried to chew off Judd's arm once while we were hunting."

"Stop laughing," Hawke said, though Riley hadn't made a sound. "Just tell me what she's done now."

"Nothing." Riley dropped the bombshell and waited as Hawke's mouth fell open.

His alpha took several seconds to recover. "Nothing?"

"Nothing," Riley repeated. "But you've been slacking off. You need to find her a position in the pack."

"She's—"

"No more excuses, Hawke." Riley folded his arms. "She's been eighteen for almost three months now, and she's been in training with Indigo for what—ten months?" He brought up Sienna's file on his handheld. "No, you stuck her in training over a year ago. She can protect herself well enough to do a number of tasks."

"She's volatile." Hawke's jaw tightened.

"She's a telepath, a strong one." Sienna was a cardinal—her abilities were off the scale.

"She's got abilities aside from telepathy. I've seen her lose control—she can do serious damage." Hawke shoved a hand through his hair.

"So can you," Riley said pointedly. "She's learning. Just because she—"

"Don't go there." A growl.

Riley raised an eyebrow. "I was going to say, just because she's Psy doesn't also mean she's not an eighteen-year-old going stir-crazy."

"Fine." Hawke was gritting his teeth. "I'll handle it."

"Then I'll leave it with you." He'd made his point and Hawke was certainly not stupid. "I'm going to go up, check out the bear population in sector 2. There've been reports they're getting sick." If it was something serious, their vets would need to go up and investigate. Because whatever was affecting the bears could trickle down through the other animal groups in the area, decimating entire herds. And as the pack that claimed territorial rights over this area, SnowDancer was also its caretaker.

More than that, Riley needed a chance to get out of the den before his frustration led him to strike out. The wolf was starting to claw at him, pacing this way and that, wanting blood if it couldn't have sex.

Mercy handed Amara the chip Ashaya had packed in a small, impermeable case.

"Is it all good?" she asked Ashaya's identical twin.

Amara didn't reply until she'd checked it under a microscope. "Yes."

Having a conversation with Amara was hard. She didn't throw out verbal cues like most people— but at least she wasn't homicidal any longer. "Anything you want me to take down to Ashaya?"

Familiar blue-gray eyes looked into hers, but Mercy had a feeling she'd never mistake Amara's gaze for Ashaya's. "Not at this stage."

"Cool." Nodding at the test tubes lined up on the workbench, she asked, "Looks interesting."

"Don't worry," Amara said, "I'm not creating another monster virus."

Since that was exactly what Mercy had been thinking, she grinned. "Never crossed my mind. What is it?"

"A child's game—to make colors." She lifted a stunning blue one. "Copper sulphate."

"You don't strike me as the playing type."

"A perceptive observation." She put the test tube down next to one with a bright yellow compound inside. "But Sascha Duncan says I must try."

With any other person, Mercy would've waited for them to continue. With Amara, she had to be blunt. "Why?"

"She says play appears to help with . . . emotion." Shrugging, she picked up an empty test tube. "I don't pretend to understand the workings of an E-Psy, but if I do this, she leaves me alone for a few days."

Mercy hadn't known Sascha had been spending that much time with Amara—especially given what she knew of Sascha's initial reaction to Amara's absolute coldness. But their alpha's mate was nothing if not determined. Amara needed to be helped in this unfamiliar new world, so Sascha was helping her. It was nothing more—and nothing less—than that. "Play teaches us things," she said to Amara now. "It lets us try out ideas without worrying about whether they'll work. Think of it as a creative form of brainstorming."

Amara stared at her. "That's extremely astute."

"Somehow, I don't think that was a compliment."

Amara said nothing. After a second, Mercy realized it was because she hadn't asked a question. "Was it?"

"Of a sort," Amara said. "I thought changeling soldiers were pure brawn."

"Your sister's mated to Dorian and you think that?" Her fellow sentinel was hella smart.

"I still want to kill him sometimes, so Ashaya doesn't leave us alone much."

Mercy's lips twitched at the straightforward answer. "Don't worry—he gives me homicidal thoughts at times, too." Then she got serious. "Fight it. Fight whatever it is that wants to drag you down. Giving in is for wusses."

Isn't that what you're doing with Riley?

Even as her mind bucked against that unexpected mental whisper, Amara blinked. "It's no wonder my twin says you're her favorite. She never gave up either. Even on me."

Deciding that would do for today, Mercy turned to leave—she couldn't deal with her own rebellious thoughts and Amara at the same time.

"Mercy?"

She turned back at the door. "Yeah?"

"Look." Ashaya held up a new vial. "It's the color of your hair."

Hawke strode toward the Laurens' quarters—Sienna had chosen to remain with her uncle, Walker, his daughter, Marlee, and her own brother, Toby, even after she turned eighteen and was entitled to a separate one-bedroom unit in the den. Whatever else he might say about Sienna, one thing was undeniable—she was a good cousin, a good sister. Marlee and Toby both adored her. So, for that matter, did a lot of the other pups.

Too bad she turned into a demon every time he came within breathing distance. "Riley's right," he muttered under his breath, staring at the closed door of the apartment. Half the reason Sienna was bent on driving him insane was that she had too much spare time on her hands.

She was bright, and her uncles had ensured she was enrolled in a distance-learning degree course run by a major university. But that did nothing to release her physical energy. Indigo, too, had been nudging at Hawke to get Sienna into a position within the pack—because, for better or worse, she was now part of SnowDancer, and not being given a position was an insult.

Hawke felt his jaw set. Insult or not, he had to balance the rights and well-being of every single member of the pack—Sienna had less control over her impulses than almost anyone else in her year group. He couldn't chance her not following orders when it might mean life or death for the rest of her team.

And how do you think she escaped the PsyNet? By being a ninny and disobeying Walker and Judd?

Sometimes he hated that voice in his brain, the one that slapped him upside the head anytime he got too stupid. Funny, it happened a lot with Sienna.

"Whatchya doing?"

He glanced down at the owner of that tiny voice, having scented his miniature shadow several feet down the corridor. "Looking for Judd." The lieutenant hadn't been in his quarters, and Hawke wanted to get his take on Sienna's psychic control.

Ben took a slurp of his orange popsicle. "Not here."

"Yeah?" Crouching down, he made eyes at the popsicle.

Ben immediately turned it in his direction. "Wanna bite?"

"No, I was just kidding." This pup, he thought, would grow up into the kind of man any pack would be proud of. An alpha simply knew with some. "Do you know where Judd is?"

"Outside. With Brenna." Another slurp. "Doing kissy stuff."

Hawke grinned. "And you know this how?" Ben was too

young to be allowed out of the White Zone, and Judd surely wasn't doing "kissy stuff" in the area where the little ones played.

"He told me."

"He *told* you?"

"Yeah. I asked him how come I couldn't come, and he said he was going to kiss Brenna so I'd probably get grossed out." This time he took a bite and chewed. "I decided to come visit Marlee instead."

"She in there?"

"Yeah. With Sinna and Toby."

"Then I guess I'll be speaking directly to Sinna," he said, saying the name as Ben had. "You knock."

Ben tapped with a little fist. "Are you mad?"

"No."

"You're scowly."

And that was when Sienna opened the door.

CHAPTER 24

The Information Merchant had a partial list. He considered how to get that list to those who had hired him. Most people would've used a comm screen, or a secure phone link, but the Information Merchant took being careful to the extreme.

He thought about a face-to-face transfer, but determined that that wasn't necessary at this stage. Instead, he decided to use an old-tech method. Slipping into an office building utilized mostly, though not exclusively, by humans and changelings, he dropped the envelope containing the data into a nearly full out-box while the receptionist's back was turned, and sat down to read a newspaper on his organizer.

The automated mailroom cart came by ten minutes later, impeccably on schedule, and emptied the out-box. It would be in the post within the hour. Satisfied, the Information Merchant got up and walked to the elevators, heading up to a meeting he'd set up earlier that week. He didn't believe in leaving loose ends.

Especially when he was trading the most treasonous of secrets.

CHAPTER 25

Riley was an hour out from the bears' territory when he caught a very familiar scent. Wolf and man both came to a halt, on alert. The wind ruffled the wolf's fur, a cool, gentle stroke. The earth, the wind, the sharp bite of the evergreens, it all served to calm him . . . normally. Today, excitement beat in his blood.

Instead of chasing the scent, he stalked it. Careful, careful, the wolf whispered to the man. Be patient, or she might disappear. And he didn't want her to disappear. He used every trick he knew to hide his scent as he came ever closer. And then there she was, curled up on a warm, exposed rock, her coloring golden, the rosettes on her body dark. She was his natural enemy, but the wolf agreed with the man this one time—this leopard was too magnificent to attack. Perhaps he stood there for a minute, perhaps ten. But when he finally padded out of the shadows, her head didn't jerk up in surprise.

Instead, sleepy eyes opened to half-mast. They were a vivid color close to gold in this form, as if the brown had been heated by internal sunlight. Her eyes seemed to say, "What?" and "Go away, I'm napping," in equal measures.

Holding her gaze, he shifted. The pleasure/pain of it swept through his body. A familiar thing. And yet, new each time. He came to crouching on the forest floor, his eyes still locked with the leopard's. "You're in my range."

A disdainful sweep of her tail. Even in this form, she found ways to sass him.

"Kitties get eaten up here."

A yawn this time, full of teeth. Oh yeah, Mercy knew how to play.

"I'm heading up to check on the bear population," he said, realizing he'd intended to make the offer all along. "Come with me." His entire body tightened as he waited for her answer.

I'm as loyal to my pack as you are to yours.

As a lieutenant, he knew he was playing with fire by continuing to pursue Mercy. He knew that . . . but he was also a man and she was a woman who acted like a drug to his senses. If she denied him again, would he continue to try to change her mind? Yes, he thought, unsurprised. He was stuck on Mercy, and when Riley got stuck, unsticking simply wasn't on the agenda.

But he could be patient, which was good, because the leopard female took her time thinking about it, yawning several more times before reluctantly getting up and padding off the stone. He knew it was all for show—she was as curious as her feline brethren. She stopped face-to-face with him, showing him her teeth.

"I'm scared."

Those teeth threatened to bite his neck. He jumped out of reach and shifted, trusting her to follow the rules of play and not interrupt. She didn't. But the instant he was wolf, she attacked. He rolled in the lush richness of the fallen leaves, knowing the scent would cover him when he returned. He might play a game with the kids, get them to guess where he'd been. It was how they learned.

But for now, he was intent on avoiding Mercy's jaws. Her claws were sheathed this time, and she wasn't really coming at him. Neither was he. He blocked the attack, then rolled her, threatening to grip her neck. Shaking him off, she shot him a haughty look and began to pad away. Time to go.

Coming up beside her, he deliberately pushed at her with his shoulders, so they walked side by side, their flanks rubbing. A little warning light went off in his brain at the act, an act the wolf in him recognized immediately, but he was in too good a mood to listen. The run to the bears' territory passed in easy play. Mercy took off more than once, daring him to catch her. When he did, she sniffed and continued on in a lazy way, as if it mattered nothing.

More games.

More alarm bells.

He ignored them all.

When they reached the bears, he nodded as she went left, while he went right. Mercy might be wildfire to his solid, rooted earth, but when it came to work, they functioned with clockwork synchronicity.

They met an hour later at the starting point. By unspoken agreement, they went back to the stone where he'd first met her before shifting. "The sun's moved," she complained.

"There's another stone as good."

Making a face, she walked over to the second flat slab with silent feline grace. She had no shame in her naked body. Neither did he. But, he noticed her. And that wasn't the changeling way. Not with normal members of the pack—either Snow-Dancer or DarkRiver. Nakedness after shifting simply was. Nothing to be remarked on.

But his brain was remarking plenty on Mercy. Her fire red hair curled just above the curve of her buttocks, drawing his eye to their sweet, toned shape. Mercy was a soldier, her muscles lean and strong. But she was also very much a woman—all smooth, soft skin and luscious, strokable curves.

And her breasts. He swallowed a groan as he caught teasing glimpses of them as she jumped lightly on top of the rock—very much like the cat she was—and lay down on her front, giving a moan of pure, sensual bliss at the heat. "Stop checking me out and come give me a massage."

He walked over, his body heavy with need. But he wasn't

an idiot. He wasn't going to assume she'd accept him into her body again. Making such assumptions with predatory changeling females got men nothing but bruised egos and possibly, missing body parts. He climbed onto the rock with steady steps that were more natural to him than her quicksilver grace. "Damn it, Mercy," he said the instant he saw her back. "You're fucking black-and-blue again. You should've told me I was—"

"It wasn't playtime with you that caused this, Kincaid."

Fury rolled through him. "Who?" He'd rip them to shreds.

"Training, so cut it out." Turning her head, she shoved her hair out of the way and glared. "It doesn't hurt. It's just my skin—and it's not black-and-blue. I saw it in the mirror today; the marks have almost entirely faded."

He scowled, wanting to do damage to whoever had dared harm her.

"My muscles, on the other hand, do ache. So massage me while I tell you what I picked up about the bears."

"You sure you don't hurt?"

"Riley, I'm a natural redhead." A snicker. "In case you didn't notice."

Of course his gaze dipped downward. "Turn over so I can check."

She laughed. "Massage me already."

Still not happy with the marks, he straddled her. She moaned at the first firm touch of his hands on shoulders.

He didn't say anything, choosing to stroke over her back again. "Bears?" he finally asked, though it was the last thing on his mind.

"They're ooo-kay." The last word was a moan as he hit a tight muscle. "I like your hands."

He didn't say anything. Couldn't. Touching her was scrambling his brain cells. And that would surprise almost everyone who knew him. Riley Kincaid didn't get scrambled. He was the one you could count on to be snapping out cool, collected orders while the world turned to custard. Right now, it could've been raining icicles and he wouldn't have cared . . . except to protect Mercy's body.

"The bears are fine," she said, her voice pure indolent cat.

"I scented a couple dead, but no signs of sickness—might be there was a fight. What did you get?"

"Same." His voice sounded like sandpaper to him, but Mercy murmured in agreement and stayed quiescent under his hands.

This, he realized, was another kind of trust. Normally, she'd allow only a packmate to do this. Under his hands, her muscles grew loose, limber. Finishing with her shoulders, he slid down to work on her back. Despite the bruises that continued to anger the wolf, her skin felt soft as satin, warm and tempting. His fingers brushed the sides of her breasts as he did her sides.

"Hey, no copping a feel."

Leaning over, he nipped her ear. "Quiet."

He saw the edge of her smile. "Do the rest."

Her languid laziness was so feline he couldn't do anything else but stroke her. After he finished her back, he swept the heavy weight of her hair to cover her. *Pretty,* his wolf said as he ran the strands through his fingers.

Mercy didn't hurry him up, and he realized she liked having her hair played with. It was a surprising discovery, it was such a feminine thing. But it fit her. Releasing the strands after long, long minutes, he ran his fingers down to trace the delicate lines of the tattoo at the base of her spine. It was a fine blade anchoring and twined by beautiful curling lines.

Feminine and martial.

He liked it. Just as he liked the fact that she had another tattoo on her right arm—slashing lines that echoed the markings on her alpha's face. Loyal. This cat was loyal. And that both drew him and frustrated him. But he wouldn't think about that today.

These minutes, these hours, were for Riley and Mercy. Not a lieutenant and a sentinel. Here, they were two ordinary people who happened to set one another aflame . . . and, perhaps, touch each other far deeper than either of them was willing to admit.

Drifting lower, he ran his knuckles over her buttocks. No protest. So he kneaded her muscles with careful hands, learning her far slower than he had either of the other times they'd been together.

By the time he reached the tops of her thighs, the scent of her arousal had wrapped around him like a thousand soft whispers. But he didn't push. He was enjoying having her under his hands—Mercy rarely stopped being in motion. To have her like this was a rare treat, one to be savored.

The sole of her foot hit his back lightly as she bent it in a lazy movement. He squeezed her thigh. Instead of dropping the foot, she tapped him again. So he stroked his hands back over her body and off her shoulders, bracing them palms-down beside her head as he bent to nip at her ear again. Except this time, it was gentle, a question.

Reaching up to sweep her hair off her back, she bared the line of her neck. He was agonizingly hungry for her, but he didn't immediately move to take. The other two times, he'd been in a fury. Today, he wanted to savor, to taste her in slow sips and little bites. Another nip, the graze of his teeth along her jaw. She made a complaining noise that wasn't really a complaint. "Wolf."

He stroked his hand down her side, over the curve of her breast, her hip, then back up. "Cat."

She arched into the caress, but the move was languid, relaxed. "Pet me some more."

"You always this greedy in bed?" But he was doing what she wanted—petting a warm, compliant, and sexually aroused Mercy was no hardship. Hell, if he was honest, it was an erotic fantasy come to life.

"No." She was purring under his touch. "But I'm not promising anything."

"Of course not." He got off her and the rock.

"Hey!"

"The stone's hard." And there was no way he was chancing adding to her bruises. "Come down here and I'll pet you as much as you want."

"Bribery doesn't work." But she got up with a slow, graceful movement and flowed off the rock. It was the only word he could think of to describe it. She was pure liquid silk. And then she was in front of him, her arms around his neck, her body pressed to his.

As he leaned down to kiss her, he was hit by a fantasy of her hair sliding over his skin, wrapping around his cock. Groaning, he deepened the kiss, stroking his tongue against hers. Her hands tunneled into his hair and she made little noises in the back of her throat that let him know she liked what he was doing.

"I'm ready." It was a whisper against his mouth, her lips sliding along his jaw, soft and lusciously feminine.

"I'm not." Kissing his way down to her throat, he sucked. Just enough to leave a mark.

"I know what you're doing."

He smiled. And bit her. Her body jerked but she kept her claws sheathed. "Behave, Riley." A lazy warning.

"You, telling *me* to behave?" he asked, dipping his head to tug a nipple into his mouth.

Her hands clenched in his hair. "Mmm." That purr was vibrating against him, setting off a thousand small charges in his nervous system. His cock throbbed.

She began to slide one hand down his body. He caught it, brought it back up to his shoulders. Pulling his head up, she pointed to her lips. It wasn't a hard order to follow. And her kiss . . . oh, but her kiss. All heat and lush, seductive pleasure. It was a promise, that kiss, a promise of a slow ride to oblivion.

"So patient," she murmured against his mouth. "Will you be patient for me?"

He blinked. "Er . . ." And then told the blunt truth. "I'm not good at giving up control in bed."

A chuckle, a glimmer of amusement in those golden eyes. They'd turned leopard on him, he realized, but she was a leopard well pleased, willing to let him play. "Where are you good at giving up control?" A flick of her tongue over the pulse in his throat. "Obviously not in the forest. Hmm, how about on the kitchen table—"

As if he needed any more erotic images to torment him at night. "Mercy."

"—in the shower—"

Mercy's skin, all wet and slippery. Her body pinned to the wall by his. His hand clenched in her hair and he took her mouth with raw possession. When they parted, her lids were at half-mast, that teasing smile still curving her lips. "Definitely the shower, then."

Shuddering, he ran his hands over her back to squeeze her buttocks. "You trying to make me crazy?"

"Everyone needs a hobby."

His fingers touched her core. Hot. Slick. So ready. She moved against him, her words breathless when she said, "Now, Riley."

Since he was about to burst out of his skin from the molten buildup of pleasure, he took her down to the grass without argument. Except this time, he made sure he was on the bottom. She braced herself over him, all red hair and sexy, sexy mouth. That mouth curved again as he closed his hands over her hips. "I need a Stetson."

He waited.

"So I can ride you like a cowgirl."

The visual almost made him come. "I'll buy you one for Christmas." He didn't know where he found the willpower to say that, because she'd raised herself up on her knees and was brushing the damp heat of her core over and across him. *"Mercy."* He pulled her down to sheathe him. She could've resisted. She didn't.

Instead, she moved above him in a sinuous curve of fire and gold, her beauty bathed in sunshine. The fire fractured minutes later. And Riley's wolf could do nothing but watch her as pleasure gripped him tight, then broke him wide open.

CHAPTER 26

In an ordinary—if coolly upmarket—section of the city, not far from the Palace of Fine Arts, a brown-eyed, brown-haired man walked into a corner store and paid the extravagant markup on a number of cleaning supplies. "Emergency," he told the old lady who whispered to him that he could get a better deal at the supermarket a few blocks away. "New apartment has slime mold." He made a face. "My girlfriend's threatening to go back to her parents if I don't clean it up *right now*."

The old lady smiled and patted his arm, wishing him the best of luck with his girl. He grinned and tipped his baseball cap at her. There was nothing at all remarkable about him. The corner store manager forgot him as soon as he walked out, and had he, for some reason, needed to check the security footage, he'd have found that the stranger had somehow managed to either have his back to the cameras or his head bent, shadowed by the bill of his cap.

The same scene, or a variation of it, was repeated throughout the city. The customers all bought different things. Innocuous things. So long as you didn't put them together.

CHAPTER 27

Mercy nuzzled her face into Riley's neck and breathed deep. He smelled of earth and forest, heat and man. Beneath her, his body was warm, muscled, the silky-rough hair on his chest teasing the sensitive skin of her breasts.

He lay there and let her kiss his neck, the line of his shoulder, the dip below his throat, his hand lying loosely on her lower back. She wasn't fooled. It was a possessive touch. But she figured she'd let him get away with it this once—he'd earned it. And he'd earned more than a little petting.

When she raised her head and nipped at his jaw, he lifted his lashes a fraction, but didn't say anything, his hand stroking over her bottom.

"So," she said with a slow smile.

He raised an eyebrow, his gaze now holding a distinctly wary look.

"How do I compare with wolf females?"

"You're hoping I'll tie my tongue into knots trying to answer that, aren't you?"

"Damn." She propped her chin on folded hands. "Busted."

He pinched her butt.

"Hey!"

"You deserved that."

Maybe she did. But—"You didn't answer my question."

"I don't kiss and tell."

"Or maybe there's nothing to tell, huh?" She sat up to straddle him, her fingers playing over his chest. "Been a dry spell, Riley?"

His eyes watched her with intense concentration. That was the thing with Riley—he always made her feel as if he was focusing utterly on her. Before, she'd thought it was so he could find ways to tell her she was doing something wrong. But now . . .

"Look who's talking, kitty."

She dug her nails into his chest, but not hard enough to hurt. "Watch it. The endorphins are only going to last so long."

His hands closed over her thighs. "I'll remember that for next time."

"Don't get too cocky, wolfboy. Maybe three times is enough for me."

"Maybe you're a liar."

She narrowed her eyes. "Did you and Indigo ever hit the sheets?" Jealousy was a spike inside her, a dangerous spike born of an even more dangerous emotion.

"Why is that any of your business?"

"Just curious."

"No," he said. "We're colleagues."

Surprised he'd answered, she took a few moments to think about it. "You don't like strong women, do you?"

He stared at her, clearly annoyed. "Indigo's one of my top lieutenants."

"I'm not talking work." She waved it away. "Personally— you *really* do want a domestic-type woman as a mate, don't you? You weren't jerking my chain."

"There's something wrong with that?"

She told herself the twinge in her chest wasn't from the sting of rejection. "No. My mom's a maternal female and I respect her absolutely." For a leopard, the term "maternal" encompassed so much more than motherhood. The soldiers might ensure trouble stayed far from their innocents, but it was the maternal females who were the true glue of the pack, forging the threads that tied them all to each other. "Was your mom like that, too?"

Riley's face closed over. It was like seeing shutters coming down. He'd been tight-lipped with her more than once, but never had he been this remote. "No." The word was flat, eerily toneless. "I'd better be getting back."

Her natural instinct was to probe. It wasn't only the cat's inquisitiveness—the human part of Mercy was also desperate for a glimpse inside this quiet, contained wolf. Because Riley mattered. There, after avoiding it for so long, she'd said it. He mattered. She was incredibly curious about him. But though she'd been intimate with him several times now, had known him for much longer, he'd never really let her in. Not even three nights ago.

Don't ask me any questions tonight, Mercy.

And for all her brashness, that was one line she would not cross—if he wanted to invite her in, he'd have to do so of his own free will. She wasn't so arrogant as to rip the scab off hidden emotional wounds without thought to how it might hurt him.

Riley, she thought with a fierce burst of protectiveness, had been hurt quite enough—first with the loss of his parents, and later, with the horror of Brenna's abduction. She had no intention of adding to his scars. If the memories were shared in trust . . . that would be a different matter.

Trying to make up for raising an obviously painful topic, she dipped her head and kissed him with delicate promise. "I'll run down with you."

The Psy Council met in the closed vault of the Council chambers, deep in the heart of the PsyNet. They were scattered around the world—Tatiana in Australia, Kaleb in Moscow, Shoshanna in London, with Henry on route to that city, Anthony and Nikita in California, and Ming in France—but that mattered little. The PsyNet allowed them to navigate vast distances in split seconds, their minds going where their bodies couldn't.

Now Kaleb watched the vault close and the seven minds within it spark bright. The Psy Council was in session. Nobody was in any doubt as to why they were there.

"The spurts of public violence," Nikita began, "do we have further confirmation that someone is driving it?"

"No, only the shooter from the fast-food restaurant," Anthony said. "The others either died during the acts, or committed suicide afterward."

"But," Ming said, "given the similarity in incidents, especially the compulsion to commit suicide, I'd say we're looking at a planned series of events."

"Agreed." Anthony's distinctive mental voice. "Henry, what's the possibility it could be Pure Psy?"

"I've heard nothing from them on any such plan," the other Councilor replied. "And what would be the point? Their aim is to ensure Silence doesn't fall. These incidents are throwing the Protocol into question."

"On the contrary." Shoshanna entered the conversation. "I'm beginning to hear whispers in the Net that say the incidents are a result of the *breakdown* of Silence."

"Surely that's to our advantage?" Tatiana, the second-youngest member of the Council and the most unknown.

Kaleb had spent considerable time and effort trying to track down Tatiana's history, but the other Councilor was smart. She'd covered her tracks from the beginning. Everyone knew she'd killed the Councilor whose place she'd taken, but she'd done it with such calculated coldness that no one would ever be able to prove anything. Kaleb didn't care about proving the charge. What mattered was knowing her weaknesses. Currently, she had none.

"No," he said now. "It may seem that way, but this individual is acting outside Council authority. He's challenging our control of the Net."

"Kaleb is right," Nikita said, backing him as per their agreement. That agreement was fluid, but for the time being, their aims coincided.

"We can, however," Tatiana pointed out, "take the idea and utilize it on a much larger scale."

"That's an option," Ming said, "but I'd vote against it."

"Your reasoning?" Shoshanna.

"Such open degradation may cause the populace to cling to Silence, but it will also have a flow-on effect. The more violence, the more ripples in the Net."

"A continuous feedback loop," Kaleb said, seeing the truth of it. The PsyNet was a closed system—what went in didn't dissipate except into the Net itself. The more violence done by Psy, the more the Net would echo with violence. "Using such methods to maintain Silence will, in the end, fragment the pillars of it even further. It's already happening—we've had a fifteen percent rise in acts of interpersonal violence in the last week alone."

"Correct." Ming said nothing further.

Tatiana was the next to speak. "I see your point, Ming. But it seems to me that we've lost considerable control over the past five years. Perhaps we should reconsider Henry's suggestion of mass rehabilitations."

"We've been over this," Nikita said. "We come down too hard, and the rebels might succeed in turning the populace."

"Working in the shadows is our specialty," Tatiana responded. "Surely we can eliminate the troublemakers faster than we've been doing to date."

"There is an alternative." Nikita.

Everyone waited.

"We open the Center for voluntary reconditioning." She paused, as if to ensure they were paying attention. "Silence suppresses all emotion, but everyone in this vault knows that some primal instincts are difficult to completely eliminate. Such as the instinct to survive."

No one argued with her.

"Right now, there are millions in the Net who're starting to feel the pressure of recent events. These individuals will cling to Silence, to that which is known, if given the choice. We offer them that choice."

"And plant compulsions when they come in?" Henry asked.

"Not necessary." Ming evidently saw where Nikita was going. "The more people who get themselves reconditioned, the calmer the Net. And the calmer the Net, the less the rebels have to work with."

"We won't get that many," Shoshanna said. "People try to avoid the Center."

"You'd be surprised." Tatiana's voice. "Deep down, past Silence, past every line of conditioning, every barrier, our race fears the monsters within. They'll come."

And Kaleb knew she was right.

Mercy had surprised him, Riley thought as he exited his room the next morning. He'd expected an inquisition, and gotten a caress. "Cat," he whispered under his breath.

"Riley!" It was Indigo's voice.

He turned to wait for her, Mercy's words whispering through his mind. He hadn't lied. He respected Indigo a hell of a lot. She was one of the top-ranking people in SnowDancer—there wasn't anything he wouldn't trust her to handle. It irritated him that Mercy had questioned that trust. What irritated him more was that she'd made him question his personal preferences—was it so wrong to wish for a mate who'd stay at home rather than be out there facing God-knows-what?

Safe, he thought, a maternal female would be *safe*, protected within the domestic sphere that was her domain.

Unlike Brenna. Unlike his mother.

"What is it?" he asked, shutting the lid on those memories.

Indigo put her hands on her hips, namesake eyes bright with intelligence, black hair pulled back in a high ponytail. It reminded him of how Mercy did her hair. Both women were no fuss, no mess. But only one drew him with an intensity that was a claw in his gut, a fist around his throat.

Mercy would never play it safe, never allow him to shield her.

"Where were you yesterday?" Indigo asked, nostrils flaring as she tried to guess.

He wasn't worried. Because Mercy wasn't bound to him in any way, her scent wasn't embedded in his skin. As his wasn't on hers. Which meant no one knew of his claim—including the two South American sentinels who continued to sniff around her. His hand fisted.

"Checking on the bears," he answered, forcing himself to release that fist. "Were you trying to reach me?"

"Yeah—Rats say Alliance mercenaries are moving in the city. No specifics yet."

"Then the surveillance isn't having an effect."

"Wouldn't say that—they're having to dodge us to do anything. That's got to be hurting."

"Let's hope it hurts enough that they pack up and get out." He glimpsed a small, cardinal-eyed boy walking up the corridor. "Hello, Toby."

Judd Lauren's nephew gave him a sweet, shy smile, one that made him want to smile in return. The kid had that effect on people. "Hi, Riley. Hi, Indigo."

"Hi, kiddo." Indigo ruffled his hair.

Toby bore the indignity in silence. "I'm going to wait for Sascha."

"Sascha's coming up?" Indigo asked, one hand on the boy's shoulder.

Toby nodded. "She's gonna help me with some stuff." He tapped the side of his head to indicate that "stuff" was mental, probably an aspect of his psychic abilities.

"Go on," Riley said. "You don't want to be late."

Toby smiled again. "Okay." But before he left, he reached into his pocket and pulled out something wrapped in brown paper. "This is for you." He put it in Riley's surprised hand and ran off before Riley could ask him what it was.

"Hey," Indigo said, voice amused, "I don't rate a present."

"I'm his uncle." The relationship was through Brenna's mate, Judd, but Riley didn't stand on such restrictions much. "I wonder what it is."

"Open it." Indigo made no move to leave.

"Ever heard of privacy?"

"No."

A smile tugged at his lips. "You've been hanging out with Mercy."

"We talk some," she admitted. "It's . . . not hard, but different, being a powerful female among this many men."

He looked up in surprise. "But you're not alone. We've got Jem—"

"Yeah, she's a lieutenant but posted out way over in the L.A. region," Indigo said. "Mercy's the only one nearby who understands these things."

"What things?"

"Well, if you could understand them," she said with exaggerated patience, "I wouldn't be talking to a cat, would I?"

He didn't back down. They didn't call him the Wall for nothing. "Do you think the pack's leadership structure is unbalanced?" Changelings weren't human or Psy. Female dominants were an expected part of the pack. But now that Indigo had pointed it out, he realized that of the ten SnowDancer lieutenants, only two were female.

"Nah." She waved her hand. "It just turned out that way this generation. Remember—when your mom was lieutenant, it was six-four in favor of the females."

It was the second time in less than twenty-four hours that someone had mentioned his mother. If he'd been the superstitious type, it might've concerned him. But he wasn't. And it didn't. "True," he said, and unwrapped the package.

"Oooh." Indigo picked up the tiny, interlocking wooden puzzle and ran her fingers over it. "This work is too smooth for a child."

"Walker probably helped him." Judd's brother was very good with his hands, something that seemed to surprise him as much as anyone. "It's a wolf."

Indigo gave it back to him. "Yeah, stylized but discernible."

Riley played with the pieces, thinking Mercy would probably enjoy this. He'd jumble it up and give it to her, just to see the look of feline concentration on her face.

A hand waved in front of his eyes. "Earth to Riley."

"What?"

"I asked how come you got a present." She looked suspicious of his lapse in focus.

He thought about it. "I've been spending a bit of time with him, teaching him tracking, things like that."

"You're good at that."

"What?"

"Being a big brother." A smile. "And uncle now. Brenna and Drew are lucky to have you."

As she walked away, he wondered if his siblings thought that. Raising them, with the pack's help of course, wasn't anything he'd ever resented—he was who he was. Solid. Rooted in earth. But now he wondered—was he too solid, too practical, to continue to captivate a woman as wild and as bright as Mercy?

And why, if he was set on finding a maternal female for a mate, did it matter that he be fascinating enough to enchant a sentinel?

CHAPTER 28

Entering the White Zone, Sascha waved off her escort—Dezi and Vaughn—and walked over to take a seat on the ground in front of Toby. He'd chosen a peaceful spot where the little ones wouldn't disturb them but which kept him from breaking the rules about venturing too far. "Hello, sweetheart."

"Hi." A bright smile that showcased a truly gentle soul.

It was a miracle, that smile. Toby had been a shocked, too-quiet child when she'd first met him. Now he could've been any child in either pack, with as much mischief in his heart as laughter. But, she thought, he was a little more sensitive than even the healers. "How about we start with you telling me how things have been going?"

"Well, the rainbows are stronger."

The "rainbows" were pieces of color that floated in the dark spaces within a neural network. The PsyNet had no such rainbows. The Web of Stars had had it from Sascha's first glimpse—because those rainbows were the psychic emanations of an E-Psy, an empath. Sascha didn't consciously create those emanations—they were simply part of who she was. But in the PsyNet, that truth had been buried under a thousand shields.

As had Toby's.

The boy wasn't an E-Psy. His main ability was a variant form of telepathy, but he had enough E in him to affect the LaurenNet. "Do you think it'll get any stronger?" She had a theory—that if the LaurenNet had had a powerful E-Psy in its midst, Toby's latent ability would have remained that way. But because the LaurenNet was without its own empath, need had compelled the strengthening of muscles that might otherwise have lain dormant.

The boy frowned in thought, easy in showing emotion. His face was a masculine version of his sister, Sienna's, intense and compelling. "I'm not sure," he said at last, "but I don't think so. It feels . . . finished now."

"That's what I think, too." She touched his hand, and their fingers intertwined. "Have you been feeling people's emotions?"

A nod. "It's not all the time now—the shields you showed me work good."

"Excellent." She'd had to learn her skills rough. There were no other E-Psy—no *free* E-Psy—around to teach her. With the recent discovery of the Forgotten, the descendants of the large rebel contingent that had dropped from the Psy-Net a hundred years ago, she'd hoped for more knowledge, but the Forgotten had evolved in different ways, their bloodlines enriched with human and changeling blood. They'd been able to give her some help, but not much.

It had been disappointing, but not catastrophic—she'd been well on her feet by then. Her shielding skills had always been excellent, even in the PsyNet, so she'd had a good base to work from. One thing she'd learned since mating with Lucas was that she didn't always have to leave herself open to the emotions of others—it was draining, and more than that, it invaded their privacy. But there were some things an E-Psy couldn't control. "Are you still picking up on people's emotional resonance?"

"Like sort of knowing what they're feeling without trying?"

"Yes." It was second nature to her, as effortless and as unstoppable as breathing.

Toby nodded. "But it doesn't hurt or anything. It's normal."

"That's exactly it—being aware of others' emotional states is normal for us." No one, she thought fiercely, remembering her own childhood, would tell this bright, beautiful boy that he was *flawed*. No one would crush his smile. Sascha would make sure of it. "It's like the wolves can scent where people have been, or who they've touched."

"I saw Riley before I met you," Toby volunteered.

"You did?"

"He was sad." Quiet words. "Not crying-sad, but deep-inside-sad. Old-sad."

Sascha understood in a way most people wouldn't have. "Like the sadness is buried so deep, he might not even know it's there?"

"Yeah." A pause. "Was that . . . unethical?" He said the last word with frowning concentration. "That I knew that about him?"

"Well," Sascha said, "it depends on how you found out. Did you use your abilities consciously, or did you just know?"

"I just knew." A definitive nod. "Like I know when Sienna's grumpy, and Marlee's happy."

"Then I see no reason for worry." Smiling, she brushed his hair off his forehead, the gesture more of affection than necessity. "Now, shall we practice your shielding?"

Riley was heading into his office to clear the decks when he heard the strangest thing. Sienna was speaking to Hawke in his office, and since the door was open, he could hear everything. That wasn't the strange part. The strange part was that Sienna was being *polite* to their alpha.

"I appreciate you giving me a position in the hierarchy," she said, sounding more mature than he'd ever heard her.

Silence. Then, "You earned it." Short, clipped. Hawke probably wasn't sure what the hell she was up to now.

"I won't let the pack down," Sienna added. "Indigo says I

pretty much have the physical aspect of soldier training down—it's a case of becoming familiar with the other parts."

Riley wasn't surprised at the rank Hawke had decided to assign her. Sienna was a dominant. She'd be far happier doing jobs associated with protecting the pack than otherwise.

"See that you do. Or Indigo will flay you alive."

"I will."

Okay, this was getting beyond strange. Sienna wasn't built for such unresisting compliance. She was like Mercy. A little wild, full of passion, incredibly vivid. Instinct told him that whatever was happening in Hawke's office was important.

"Is that all?" A harsh question from Hawke.

"Yes. Bye." And then Sienna walked out. She saw Riley and gave a little wave but didn't come over to say hi. Riley narrowed his eyes, almost able to feel the vicious strength of the control she was keeping over herself. One hard push and that girl would shatter. "What the fuck is going on?" he asked, stepping into Hawke's office and shutting the door.

"You're asking me?" His alpha's jaw was clenched so tight, Riley could almost hear bones grinding.

"She's closed up tighter than a fucking drum." And Riley knew that was wrong with every fiber of his being. "If she was wolf, I'd say she was trying to choke her animal."

"Fuck it, Riley." Hawke pushed back from his desk and paced across the office. "I don't know what's up. I went to talk to her, gave her the option of becoming a trainee soldier."

"And?"

"And nothing." Hawke kicked the stone wall violently enough that it had to have hurt, then turned and walked in the other direction. "She said 'thank you' and 'I'm happy to accept.'"

"That's not Sienna."

Hawke's pale eyes were wolf furious. "Apparently it is now. Good thing for the den, too." Except he didn't sound convinced.

Mercy opened her front door to a gorgeous male. Unfortunately, it was the wrong one. "Joaquin. What a lovely surprise." Her tone said otherwise.

He reached up to push a hand through that sleek black hair of his, dark eyes watchful. Unlike Eduardo, he didn't flirt. But that only meant he did his hunting in a stealthy fashion. "I thought we might have breakfast together."

"I don't recall inviting you."

"I'm here at your grandmother's behest." A gleam of feline cunning in his eyes. "She said you'd treat me as an honored guest."

"She probably told you I'd kick your ass to Mexico." Mercy snorted and folded her arms. "But what the heck. I have to eat."

Joaquin didn't move from the doorway. "Won't you invite me in?"

"You just want to come in so your scent will be inside." And if Riley walked in and smelled it, she wouldn't be able to stop the resulting bloodshed. Part of her was irritated that she was allowing a male's possessiveness to dictate her actions, but the other part of her was thinking like a sentinel. And buried below that was a raw protectiveness that broadsided her with its strength. "I'm not having you create an interpack incident. We'll go to a pancake place."

To her surprise, Joaquin turned out to be an interesting breakfast companion. He also clearly adored her grandmother. "Isabella is an alpha we'd follow to our graves, no questions asked."

"Isn't that the definition of a sentinel?" she said, taking a bite of her maple-syrup lashed stack. "I'd do the same for Lucas."

"We're both lucky. I've heard of packs with a weak alpha, one who doesn't command such respect. It ends up killing the whole pack."

Mercy nodded. "So is that why you're here? She asked?"

"It would've been a good enough reason, but she showed us videos of you." A smile in his eyes. "I was away when you visited us. If I hadn't been . . . well, perhaps you'd be roaming the Amazon now."

"In your dreams." Laughing, she finished off her coffee and stood. "I have to get to work, but Joaquin, you have to know—the field is not open. Go home."

Implacable dark eyes. "You still don't wear his scent."

Rolling her eyes, she left him to the temporary duties Cian had assigned as part of the agreement to allow two out-Pack sentinels into their territory. But the way he'd said those last words, the confidence in them, niggled at her. Scent layers only became ingrained in long-term lovers or mates.

She'd only been intimate with Riley a handful of times, but they spent a lot of time together. And still no scent? It was her, she thought, taking an unflinching look at the almost mutinously independent nature of her leopard. That leopard was suspicious of even the ties between lovers. What if the suspicion never ended?

That thought worried away at the edges of her mind even as she got to work in a CTX station in Oakland. It was a relief to get a call from Ria, Lucas's administrative assistant—she was sick of going round and round in circles inside her own head.

"Sentinel meeting tonight," Ria told her. "At Lucas's place."

"Time?" She circled a possible security hole in the blue-print in front of her, her mind flicking to the last time she'd been in an underground garage. Damn but she missed the wolf already. And, scent layer or not, that spelled trouble.

"Seven. Sascha's doing dinner."

"God save us all." Sascha had decided she liked cooking. Unfortunately, cooking didn't like her back.

Ria chuckled. "She's improving. She made me a cake the other day, and it was only a little salty."

"That makes me feel a whole lot better."

"Don't worry—tonight it's tacos. She told me there's not much she can do to destroy that particular meal."

"We'll see," Mercy joked. "Any other news?"

"Zara's designing for us again as of today."

Mercy liked the changeling wildcat who'd been on con-tract to DarkRiver's construction arm before heading back to her own pack. "Say hi to her for me. Tell her Sage still has a crush on her."

"Aw, cute. How come your brothers are single?"

"They say I scare the women off."

"More likely they're spoiled—they're not going to settle for any woman who doesn't match the standard you've set."

Buoyed by the compliment, Mercy shook off her odd mood and focused on the work. The rest of her day, including a security shift in the city, passed with surprisingly little drama—the Alliance had gone cold again, and Bowen and his crew were still behaving. Even Eduardo and Joaquin were nowhere to be seen, for which boon, she could only thank the heavens.

And if she continued to find herself thinking about a certain wolf much too often, she was sentinel enough to keep her emotions from interfering with the job. But those feelings were fresh in her mind when she got a call as she was about to leave to change for the meeting.

"Come up and meet me tonight." That deep, now familiar voice soaked through her skin, rich, dark, and tempting.

Her hand clenched on the receiver. "Can't. Got something else."

"When's it finish? I'll meet you."

"No."

"That's it—no?" The edge of a growl in his voice. "I thought we'd settled this."

The sheer arrogance of his *commands*—not requests, commands—made the cat snarl. "Doesn't mean you have an entry into my pants anytime you please."

"Jesus, Mercy, I just wanted to talk to you."

She felt a little twinge. Of guilt. Of hunger. "Talk now."

"Fine." He told her about the conversation he'd witnessed between Hawke and Sienna.

Mercy's antennae twanged. "Something's seriously wrong."

"Yeah, that's what I thought. I want you to tell Sascha. She's the one Psy we know who might have a shot at getting to the bottom of this. Judd says Sienna's stonewalling him."

"Why didn't you call her yourself?"

Not even a pause. "Because it's you I want to talk to." No lies. No subterfuge. No hiding his intent.

"Damn it, Riley. This'll leave us both broken in the end." The naked emotional response pushed out past any logical rebuttal. She was starting to think of him as *hers*, but he wasn't, might never be. Not when her leopard wouldn't even accept the bonds of scent.

"And is fighting it any less painful?"

No. No, it hurts just as bad.

CHAPTER 29

He was only twenty-two, a telekinetic with a Gradient rating of 7. Powerful, he was truly powerful. And he'd lost control.

Trembling, he levitated the fallen bureau off his roommate's body. The Tp-Psy lay crushed, his organs static, his brain destroyed. *Dead.* The Tk-Psy swallowed the word past the jagged glass of a parched throat. He'd never seen a dead person before. That wasn't part of the Psy curriculum.

But now his roommate was dead, and he was a murderer.

He didn't even try to hide it. Didn't want to. He wanted to find an answer, something that would stop him from doing the same thing ever again. Enforcement processed him quickly, since there was no question of culpability.

When a representative from the Center came to offer him mild rehabilitation in lieu of a sentence, the Tk-Psy didn't hesitate. Even if they'd said he had to do the sentence, he still wouldn't have balked. Because he never again wanted to feel his powers sliding out of his grip, never again wanted to see blood seep into the carpet.

For the first time, he truly understood the salvation that was Silence.

CHAPTER 30

Mercy sat in her car, staring out at the light show of a cloudy dusk. Her hands tightened on the steering wheel until she felt like she could break the damn thing. When the first flick of rain hit the windshield, she finally turned on the engine and headed to her cabin, wanting out of her work clothes before going over to Lucas and Sascha's aerie.

Turned out she was the first to arrive. Sascha was in the kitchen, looking mournful. "Lucas went to grab some take-out."

"You found a way to destroy tacos?" Mercy raised her eyebrows. "This, I have to see."

Sascha threw a tomato at her. "I dropped the box of taco shells and managed to break every single one into a million pieces."

Looking into the box, Mercy whistled and put down the abused tomato. "Wow, sure you didn't throw this at his highness's head?"

A guilty look. Mercy burst out laughing. "That does my heart good."

"What?"

"To know you two still fight."

Sascha's lips tugged up at the corners. "It's fun."

"Yeah, it is." Grinning, she used one of the broken pieces to scoop up the salsa Sascha had already made. "I got some info for you on Sienna." She filled Sascha in.

"Hmm, I'll have to go up and see what's happening. I've been working with Toby, but I don't think I've talked to Sienna in several weeks." She leaned against the wall and looked at Mercy with those penetrating cardinal eyes. "You're wound up tighter than tight."

Mercy decided to take up the implied offer. "Riley's pushing."

"That's what predatory changeling men do." A meaningful glance at the broken taco shells.

"Not that kind of pushing—though he does that, too. He's pushing for more than sex." She paused, then admitted the truth. "It already is more than sex." The strength of these new emotions threatened to crush her heart, steal her breath.

"Ah." Sascha took a few moments. "Is there a possibility he could be your mate?"

"I'm not what he's looking for in a mate, trust me." A stab deep in her soul, a twisting pain that seemed to get stronger with every day that passed.

"That hurts you."

She went to deny it, then decided it was unmitigated stupidity to lie to an empath on the subject of emotions. "Yeah, it does. But I'm glad he was honest—that's more important than anything. As long as he doesn't try to mold me into what he wants, I can deal." Because she wanted him, too, the idiot.

And maybe, since he wasn't asking for a lifetime, her leopard wouldn't resent being tied down, perhaps even find some peace in it. Except . . . "The way he draws me, the sheer strength of it . . . I don't know what to do."

Sascha gave her a surprisingly mischievous smile. "Doesn't mean you can't enjoy him while you figure it out."

And the tension broke, just like that. Mercy threw part of a taco shell at Sascha. "Some help you are."

They were still laughing when Dorian arrived, followed

by Clay. The four of them managed to demolish the salsa by the time Lucas returned, with Nate and Vaughn on his heels. None of the sentinels' mates had come today, which was surprising. Mercy said as much.

"Kids are at Tammy's—Tally's gone to dinner with Ria," Clay told her. "They're calling it a strategy meeting—how human females deal with changeling males."

Everyone but Dorian laughed. His next words told them why. "Shaya's with Amara."

"She'll be fine," Lucas said. "Your mate's tough."

"Yeah." A proud smile. "I can't help but worry, though. Keenan's at Tammy's."

"Faith, too," Vaughn added. "And Brenna was there when I left."

No one found that strange. Brenna and Faith had quietly become very good friends over the past months. "Did Judd come down?" Mercy asked.

"Probably." Dorian passed her a box of take-out fried rice. "He has trouble letting Brenna out of his sight."

"Oh, please," Mercy muttered, "you're all so overprotective you'd be delighted if you could pack your mates in cotton wool and put them inside glass bubbles."

Sascha started laughing so hard, she almost dropped her egg roll. "I think that's Lucas's secret fantasy."

Her mate growled at her. "All I said was that you looked a little tired. You didn't have to blow a gasket."

"You told me to go lie down." Sascha poked her chopsticks in his direction. "Do I look like an invalid to you?"

Of course, that was just an invitation for the men to throw in their support behind Lucas, while Mercy had to back Sascha on principle. Come to think of it, the cardinal did look different. Not tired exactly. A little more fragile. Softer. More breakable.

"Enough." Sascha cut off the discussion with a hand. "We have actual work to do."

"Right," Lucas said. "Clay, you had some intel."

"Rats." Clay named his source. "They're catching hints that a group of people are gathering chemicals that could be used to make bombs. Low-tech bombs, but they'll do the job same as high-tech."

Everyone went quiet.

"Alliance?" Dorian finally asked.

"Unconfirmed but from the surveillance footage we were able to get, one of the buyers looks very similar to a face we flagged as a possible Alliance mercenary from the flights that came in around the time of Nash's abduction," Clay said. "Teijan has his people on it twenty-four/seven, but whoever they are, they're being very careful. No clue as to where they've set up base yet."

"We'll find them," Lucas said, eyes grim. "No one makes trouble in our city."

The night after his frustrating call with Mercy, Riley was antsy. It was tempting to blame it on his day—DarkRiver and SnowDancer had both upped their already visible presence in the city in silent warning to the Alliance, but they weren't any closer to running down the operatives. Since he'd just come off a full day shift in the city, it would've been easy to lie to himself.

But that wasn't who he was. "What would you say if I asked you a hypothetical question?" he asked after giving Hawke his report.

Hawke's eyes gleamed. "That there are no such things as hypothetical questions."

"That's what I thought." He lapsed back into thought.

Hawke stared at him. "I can answer your hypothetical question, though."

"You don't know what it is."

"I know you're jumpy as hell for Mercy. Go find her. Get naked. The end."

Riley looked at his alpha. "That's your pitch to women? Let's get naked?" He snorted. "No wonder your balls are blue."

Hawke gave him a one-finger salute. "Go take care of your own balls."

"Maybe I will." He got up. "I have an answer for you, too."

"I don't want to hear it."

"Too bad. Lieutenant privileges." He put his hand on the door to the office. "I know why your balls are blue."

Silence.

"Whatever the hell is happening between you two, make a note that several different men, me included, will kill you if you touch her. She's not ready."

"I don't know who you're talking about." Hawke's voice remained unconcerned, but his hand was squeezing his pen so tight, he'd probably shattered it.

"But none of us will kill you for spending time with her." He pulled open the door. "Track her down, taunt her into a sparring session. It'll get you skin-to-skin contact."

Hawke's eyes were pure wolf when they met Riley's. "I don't think so."

Riley looked at his alpha and gave a slight nod. "Yeah, I see your point." A little contact would only enflame the wolf. "You need to draw some blood?" It was an honest offer, wolf to wolf, frustrated male to frustrated male.

"Not yet." Putting down his mangled pen, Hawke shoved both hands into his hair, leaving a streak of bright blue ink on the pale strands. "You'll find me when I do." He sounded disgusted.

Riley shrugged. "It's my job." Being the senior lieutenant was about more than responsibility to the pack. It was about responsibility for the alpha as well. With Hawke unmated—and likely to remain so—Riley had to make sure the other man never went too close to the edge. Hawke, in turn, kept a watchful eye on him, too.

Now the alpha raised his head. "You're so fucking calm you fool everyone else, but don't fool yourself, Riley. You're in no better condition than I am."

Leaving Hawke to his own demons, Riley got changed into workout gear, found an empty training room, and began to go through his usual sparring routine, but without a partner—he was in no mood to hold his punches. Hawke could've taken him, but his alpha already saw too much. He didn't want to betray anything else.

"Riley?"

"Go away." He'd heard Brenna enter, had decided to ignore her.

But Brenna had never been easily dissuaded. "Drew said you're not sleeping well—that you were up most of last night."

He went through a vicious series of moves and ended a foot from her, breath calm, eyes furious. "Drew has a big fucking mouth."

"Yeah, tell me something I don't know." She grinned, but there was worry in those magnificent eyes she'd turned from a scar to a badge of courage. "Riley, is this . . . I . . ."

Scowling, he closed the distance between them to cup her cheek. "It's not about you." Her hurt haunted him, but he wasn't going to put that weight on her back. That was his cross to bear. "I'm not sleeping because I want sex."

Her mouth dropped open. Then she went bright red. "Too. Much. Information!"

Satisfied at having distracted her from the past, he raised an eyebrow. "You did ask."

"Argh." She rubbed at her temples. "Am trying to erase image from mind."

His temper lessened at her theatrics. "What, you think I'm a monk?"

"Might as well have been," she said with a shrug. "You haven't been with anyone for months."

"And that's not too much information?"

"That's looking after my brother." She poked him in the chest. "And if you're—you know—why don't you go and do something about it?"

He stroked a hand down her hair, reassuring himself for the millionth time that she was still alive, still breathing. God, he felt for Dorian. The other man's sister hadn't come back. That heartbreaking truth was why Riley had allowed Dorian to strike the killing blow when they'd hunted down the monster who'd stolen so much innocence. "You think it's that easy?"

"You've got confidence leaking out your pores."

"The bigger the ego," he muttered, repeating something Mercy had said to him, "the louder they pop."

Brenna laughed. "You never had an ego problem, Riley. You had a responsibility problem. You didn't even go away to roam—you were always there for me and Drew."

"You were more important. And Pack centers me."

"Maybe now's your time to roam?" She grinned at him. "With a certain redhead."

"Out," he said, pushing her to the door. "There are some things little sisters don't need to know."

He shut the door on her grinning face, but as he went back to his routine, his mind circled back to the problem that had driven him here in the first place—the gulf that would always separate him from Mercy. His wolf was blood-loyal to the pack, to his people. Her leopard felt the same about Dark-River.

He knew all that.

And still he wanted her with a fury that made him snarl at the idea of any other male laying a hand on her.

CHAPTER 31

The men and women tapped for the second San Francisco operation were loyal, had reasons to be loyal.

"A Psy killed my family," one man said to his workmate, "but the Council covered it up, said there was no violence among their race. They made it seem like my father killed my mother."

"Fucking bullshit," his teammate muttered. "They've got those Jax junkies, strung out on the streets. That's violence—they're killing themselves every time they mainline that stuff."

"I never thought about it that way," the first man said, "but you're right." A pause. "Why did you sign up?"

"I'm sick to death of being at the bottom of the food chain." A shrug. "Maybe we succeed, maybe we fail, but no one will ever dismiss us again."

"DarkRiver and SnowDancer know we're here," his partner replied. "I almost got caught today."

"We lost a bunch of supplies, too—no one can get near the pickup point." A word that turned the air blue. "People are making mistakes. We do that, we might as well give it up."

"You really think we can pull this off in wolf and leopard territory?"

"Sure." He shrugged. "They're searching for a needle in a haystack."

"Where do I put the wire?"

"Here." The explosives expert completed the low-tech but stable bomb and handed it off to the third man. "You know what to do?"

The man nodded. "I'll make sure no one sees me."

"Hey," the first man said. "Why are you here?"

For a minute, the other man was silent. Then he said, "One of them wanted something I knew. I wouldn't give it to him. So he tore into my mind and took it."

The word wasn't used, but they all knew it—rape. The Psy had been getting away with it for far too long. Now they would pay. And if this attempt failed, the Alliance would rise again. And again. And again.

Because the Psy wouldn't stop until they were forced to.

CHAPTER 32

Mercy was not amused to come home after a night shift in the city to find breakfast waiting for her. "Out," she said to both the males on her porch. "And I'm not messing today."

Eduardo raised his hands in surrender. "I'm heading home. This is good-bye."

"Thank God for small mercies," she said. "And you?"

Joaquin gave her an enigmatic smile. "Still no scent."

"Suit yourself." Grabbing a muffin, she walked into the cabin and shut the door. She heard Eduardo laugh and Joaquin curse, but she really wasn't in the mood. Eating quickly, she showered and got ready to catch some shut-eye. When she looked out the window, it was to find the men gone, though they'd left the food behind in a thermal container. Reluctantly impressed by their refusal to give in, she stored the food in her kitchen, then crashed, planning to be up by one in the afternoon.

If she'd known what was going on in the woods not far from her house, her sleep might not have been as smooth.

* * *

Riley had come down to talk to Mercy and found Eduardo and Joaquin. This time, he wasn't in a walking-away frame of mind. Stepping out behind the men as they left Mercy's cabin, he waited for them to turn.

They did, faces predator-sharp. These two were sentinels, strong and well trained. But they didn't have violent possessiveness running through their veins. "I thought she told you to get lost."

It was Eduardo who answered: "Leopard females that dominant don't take well to males who do exactly what they say. But you wouldn't know that, *wolf*."

"I know her far better than either of you ever will." He watched their eyes, waiting for an aggressive move.

"She doesn't carry your mark in her skin," Joaquin said, and it was obvious from his tone that he wasn't ready to leave the field.

"And I bet she hasn't let you lay a hand on her." Her knew Mercy. She was easy with skin privileges in the pack, but she zealously guarded her privacy outside it.

Joaquin smiled. "Her skin is soft, creamy."

It was a taunt meant to make Riley's wolf see red and it succeeded, but he was also a lieutenant honed in fire. He narrowed his eyes. "Me and you. Eduardo stays out of it."

"Done." Joaquin's claws slid out. "I win, you walk away."

"Never going to happen." He released his own claws, slicing them through skin with the thoughtless ease of someone who'd grown up semishifting.

"Hold it," Eduardo said, scowling. "What the fuck are you doing, Joaquin? We didn't come here to mess up DarkRiver's pact with the wolves."

Riley waved him off. "I give you my word this won't impact things politically."

Eduardo raised an eyebrow. "Yeah? Then go for it. I can't wait to see how you explain this to Mercy."

Riley was no longer thinking. Joaquin had moved a bare

fraction of an inch, but Riley knew it was in preparation for a strike. He was proven right an instant later as the South American sentinel came at him in a rage of claws and speed. Joaquin was good, Riley thought, moving out of the way even as he used his own claws to shred the other man's sides.

There was no blood, though Joaquin's shirt was in tatters. The sentinel had twisted away in a fluid move no wolf would ever make. But a wolf could utilize that fluidity against his prey. He went as if to strike, Joaquin shifted left . . . and Riley struck up with his free hand.

"Fuck." Joaquin hissed out a breath as his blood scented the air. "Lucky hit."

Riley didn't speak, watching. But he wasn't quite fast enough to evade the kick that almost dislocated his shoulder. Moving with the kick, he grabbed Joaquin's foot and twisted. Bones would've snapped in a human. But they weren't human. The other man landed on his feet, but his balance was slightly off. Riley had damaged something.

Not allowing his opponent to regain control, he attacked, his driving possessiveness giving him an edge even Joaquin's feline grace couldn't counteract. Slamming his claws to within a breath of the leopard's throat, he gritted out the words, "Be on the next plane out of here or I won't stop next time."

Joaquin's aggression was a golden glow in his eyes. "You're faster than you look."

Taking that as acceptance, Riley drew back.

Joaquin straightened, wiping blood off his lips. "Good luck." He held out a hand.

Unsurprised, Riley shook it. Changelings stuck to their word—it was part of the code of honor that kept peace among their kind. "Make sure your alpha doesn't send replacements."

Joaquin rubbed his jaw. "That, I can't promise. Isabella is a law unto herself."

"Then tell her that anyone else she sends up," Riley said quietly, "I'll be sending back minus body parts."

Eduardo grinned. "That, she'll understand. You sure you want to mess with Isabella?"

"If she's Mercy's grandmother, I'll have to deal with her

eventually." He nodded once as the two men headed off. Part of him wanted to follow to make sure they truly were leaving, but the other part wanted desperately to see Mercy, to drive his scent into her skin so no other male would dare what Joaquin had. The field *was not* clear.

Trusting the honor of the two sentinels, he walked left, to Mercy. He was on her doorstep when he realized he was bruised and bloody. One look and she'd know exactly what he'd been doing. He didn't care. Raising a fist, he knocked.

The door was pulled open a few moments later by a sleepy-eyed cat dressed in an old T-shirt. Those eyes widened when she saw him, but he kissed her before she could say a word, clasping the back of her head to keep her in place as he fed his need for her. He was expecting to feel her claws any instant, but it was her hands he felt, under the torn fabric of his T-shirt. Shuddering when she flattened her hands on his back, he deepened the kiss until it was a melding of mouths, raw and hot and honest.

That was when her claws pricked him, hard enough that he knew he'd have bruises. Breaking the kiss, he looked down into eyes gone leopard in anger, though her lips were soft, full, so tempting.

"Riley Kincaid, you have Joaquin's blood on you." Her nostrils flared. "Dead or alive?"

"Alive." He winced as her claws dug deeper.

"I told you to stay away from them."

"I'm not a pet dog," he growled, closing his hand around her throat. "Don't try and leash me, kitty cat."

Those golden cat eyes shimmered with the sharp bite of feminine anger. "Get your hand off my neck."

Leaning in close, he breathed his next words against her lips. "Make me."

A taut moment, as they stared at each other, both furious, both unable to walk away. He waited to feel real pain—predatory changeling females could do serious damage when riled, and he'd made her plenty angry—but he didn't care. Right now, this moment, it was pure ambrosia.

Mercy's lashes lowered, and when they came back up, he

saw the cat prowling behind the irises. "You're insane, Kincaid." She bit his lower lip hard enough to make her point. Then, withdrawing her claws, she raised a hand to her throat and pulled at his pinkie. "I'll break this if you don't get your hand off me."

He knew instinctively that he'd pushed her far enough.

"Good choice," she said as he released her. "Now come in and maybe I'll patch you up."

Realizing he'd somehow skirted the icy blade of her anger, he walked in. She padded away into the bathroom and he followed, pulling off his T-shirt as he entered. She stared at the claw marks on his chest, the cuts on his side, his face. "You don't need stitches." Putting her hands on his arm, she tugged. "Turn."

He decided to obey because it felt so good to have her touch him.

"Hmm. No stitches necessary here, either, though you'll have some enormous bruises. Most of it will heal within the next couple of days."

"Do you have anything for the bruises?" Stiff muscles could be dangerous, slowing reaction time when it mattered most.

Coming to face him again, she said, "Maybe. Shower off the blood and find me. I might be in a good mood. I might not."

He blocked her exit from the bathroom, very aware of the sleek nakedness of her body beneath that old T-shirt. "Stay." God, he was starved for her touch. Just that, just touch.

She looked at him out of eyes that continued to hold a golden edge. "Shower and I'll let you sleep with me. I did a night shift."

He moved immediately out of the way. "Why didn't you say so? I wouldn't have kept you from bed." He scowled, the protectiveness he felt toward her trumping everything else. "I'll be out in five."

He was as good as his word, rubbing his hair dry as he walked naked into Mercy's bedroom. She was curled up, half-asleep below the sheets, but waved him over. "Bruise cream."

"I'll put it on."

"Shuddup and lie still."

Throwing aside the towel, he lay down on top of the sheet. Her fingers felt like perfection on his flesh, feminine and strong and uniquely Mercy. When she'd put the cream over all the bruises, she yawned and got up to wash her hands before crawling back into bed. He was waiting for her beneath the sheets, and to his surprise, she didn't say a word as he spooned his body around hers, their lower limbs tangling, his hand flat on the warm skin of her abdomen.

"Take off the T-shirt," he murmured against her ear.

"Pushy." But she gave him what he wanted, surprising him once again.

Mercy, he thought, was an intrinsically generous woman. He'd known that, but today, he saw another facet to that part of her nature. She was angry with him for fighting with Joaquin, but even so, she was giving him what he needed. She could've made him beg—he was so starved for her, he might just have done it. Instead, she'd allowed him into her bed, allowed him the most intimate of skin privileges.

That truth made something in his heart unsnap, unlock, and he wasn't quite sure what it was.

A feminine hand curled over the arm he had around her waist. "Sleep."

Holding her tight, awash in the warmth of her, he did as ordered. And unlike the night he'd spent awake and walking the halls of the den, this sleep was utterly peaceful.

Mercy was smiling that afternoon as she sat in DarkRiver's business HQ. Sleeping with Riley again had been nice. Really nice. They'd woken together, made love with a lazy slowness that had turned her blood to treacle. It had been tempting to stay in bed, but Riley had an afternoon shift on the patrols they were running in the city, and she had to complete several of her security reports.

She'd just finished a call with a firm specializing in high-tech intrusion detection systems when the phone rang. The ID was exquisitely familiar. She answered by switching the clear screen of her computer to comm mode. "Riley?"

His response was audio only, with a little icon that told her he was on a cell phone. "Mercy, you still in the city?"

The sound of his voice crawled inside, touched the cat . . . and wasn't immediately clawed away. "Yeah, what's up?"

"We got a tip that something odd was going on in one of the new warehouses they're building along the Embarcadero," he said, referring to the long stretch of road that ran around the eastern edge of the bay. "Near the Bay Bridge."

Excitement sparked. "I'll be there—"

"No rush. I went in with a small team, checked things out. They—"

Mercy tried to counsel patience and failed. "You what? This is *our* op, Riley. Not yours. You knew I was in the city, that I could've been there in minutes, but you still didn't call until after you'd gone in?"

He didn't bother to lie to her, to make up something about using their resources wisely or some other crap like that. He just said, "I made the decision. Deal with it."

Deal with it? Fine. "What did you find?" she asked, hand curled into a fist so tight, she could see tendons push up white under skin.

"This particular warehouse is almost complete and the foreman says no workers have been inside for two weeks. But someone was here and very recently," he said, sounding a little guarded at her apparent calm.

Good, she thought. "Alliance?"

"From the human scents and the fact that we found some bomb-making apparatus, I'm saying it's a good bet."

"Damn." She tapped her fingers on the desk. "They're actually going to do this, blow something up in our territory."

"I fucking hope not. If they do, it's war."

Mercy took a moment to think. "Maybe the target has nothing to do with us—could be they're here to eliminate Bowen's group."

"With a bomb?" Riley's disbelief was obvious. "It'd be easier to shoot them in some dark alley. They blow something up, it's about getting everyone's attention. Right this second," he continued, "their motivation matters less than finding them. From all the evidence, they're staying on the move, but we've got a scent now."

"I'll get some leopards on it, too." She was already making a mental list of those in the city or close by with the necessary tracking skills. "I'm on my way."

She kept her anger contained on the drive over, and said nothing when she first saw Riley in the warehouse. Instead, she confirmed his findings, then set Aaron, Jamie, Barker, and Kit to tracking. "Kit, I want you paired with Barker."

Kit opened his mouth to complain but she shut him up with a look. "I know you're a good tracker, but you're still in training. Seriously, boy, do not give me any shit today."

Kit blinked. He carried the scent of a future alpha, and one day soon, he'd be able to overpower her in a fight—but she'd be his senior until he became alpha. And not only did Kit know that, he knew how to deal with dominant females, having grown up with Rina for a sister. "Someone made you mad today," he murmured, hands up. "Glad it wasn't me. Is Barker here already?"

"Should be outside. Check in with me by phone every fifteen minutes."

"Will do." Nodding, the young soldier headed out.

The warehouse was clear of everyone but Mercy, Riley, and the scene processing people ten minutes later. Leaving the scientific types, Mercy headed out to her car, Riley by her side. "I've got one question for you," she said as they walked, "what was the tip?"

"That there was a lot of late-night traffic in and out of a warehouse that was meant to be off-limits to anyone but the construction crew."

"That's it?"

"One of the soldiers patrolling this area thought she smelled something dangerous—probably caught a whiff of the chemicals. Rats came through with the same info two minutes later."

Mercy knew he'd received that data directly because he

was in charge of city security at the relevant time. "So you knew you were going into danger." She put her thumb to the car door to unlock it.

"It was a possibility." His eyes were calm when he looked at her, but the hand he closed over her door when she slid it open and back, was white-knuckled.

"And is that when you made the decision not to call me?" she asked, holding his gaze without flinching. "When you realized it might be life-threatening?"

"We had no idea what we might be walking into," he said. "The place could've been rigged to blow."

"Answer the question." She didn't break eye contact.

"Yes. I didn't want you exposed to that unstable a situation."

She was so angry she was trembling inside. "That's what I thought—and it wasn't your call to make, Riley."

"What the fuck use would it have been to put us both in the line of fire?"

"Again, not your call." She tried to breathe, but her throat was knotted up with too much fury and air barely seemed to get in. "We're allies. If you start holding back information, that alliance falls."

His jaw tightened. "You know damn well this had nothing to do with the alliance."

"Yes," she said, "it did. Everything we do impacts our packs."

He didn't answer, but she could feel the pulse of his anger.

"Don't you dare treat me like *your woman* ever again," she said, teeth gritted. "Not when it concerns the safety of my pack. Which is all our 'relationship' is going to concern as of this moment."

"No," he said, grabbing her elbow. "You don't get to end us. Not over this."

The cat growled and she let the sound travel up through her vocal cords. "I get to do whatever I want." She wrenched her arm from his. "I invited you into my home," she said, nose to nose with him. "I *trusted* you. You just shit on that trust." Sliding into the seat, she pulled the door shut.

He refused to let it close, leaning down to look at her. "I did not break your trust."

"Tell yourself that if it makes you feel better." This time, she pulled hard enough to make her muscles scream, kicking out at his shins at the same time. His grip loosened in surprise, and she got the door moving, sliding her leg back inside in the nick of time. Then she got the hell away from Riley before he did something else that made her heart hurt.

Her eyes burned and that only made her angrier. "God damn you, Riley!" She slammed her palm on the steering wheel hard enough to leave bruises.

CHAPTER 33

Sascha split off from Lucas as they entered the Snow-Dancer den. "What did Mercy say?"

"They found what looks like the Alliance's bolt-hole, but the mercenaries are long gone." He thrust a hand through his hair. "We can deal with this before we go down. Mercy's got things under control."

She nodded. "I need to speak to Toby for a few minutes. You go talk to Hawke."

A quiet nod. "I'll back you, whatever you decide. But, kitten, this could be serious."

"I know." She wouldn't make the decision lightly. "Go on."

As he followed the soldier who'd met them at the door, another led her to the schoolroom where Toby was doing math. "I'll be fine now."

Sing-Liu gave a nod. "See you around."

Watching the other woman leave, Sascha was struck by the changes wrought over the last year and a half. The first time she'd come here, Hawke would have never allowed her to wander freely. Even now, she knew there were certain sections where she'd be denied access, but all in all, it was a definite improvement.

Toby's teacher glanced her way right then and, a short conversation later, the boy walked out to meet her in the corridor. "What's the matter?" he asked at once, his E senses telling him she wasn't as calm as she appeared.

"Come with me." She walked him to an empty classroom and, closing the door, took a seat opposite him. "Toby, I need to talk to you about Sienna."

"Oh." She could almost see the struggle in him. "Loyalty's important."

"I know, kiddo." She took his hands. "I don't want you to betray her. I just need the answer to one question." A question Toby could answer better than even the adults in his family.

"Just one?"

"Just one."

"Okay."

She held his gaze. "Does Sienna need help?"

Toby bit his lip and nodded, the movement jerky with emotion. "She's so afraid, Sascha. It's breaking her in here." He fisted a hand and circled it over his chest.

"Oh, baby." Getting up, she knelt down to hug him, stroking her hand over his back. "Have you been trying to help?"

A nod against her, boyish arms holding on tight. "Before, she was afraid but it was okay. I could help her. But now she's all shut up. I can't get the rainbows inside."

"You did good, Toby." He'd no doubt helped Sienna far more than he realized. If the girl was splintering on the psychic plane, having a brother with empathic abilities would've leached off some of the pressure. But now Sienna wasn't allowing even her adored baby brother inside. That meant serious trouble. "Okay, sweetheart, I want you to go back to class and try not to worry."

"Will you help her?" Cardinal eyes looking solemnly into hers.

"I'll try my hardest." She wouldn't lie to him. "But Sienna's stubborn. She'll fight me."

That actually made Toby relax. "Yeah. She's fighty."

Sascha laughed. "That she is."

Dropping Toby back in class, she made her way through the SnowDancer tunnels to Hawke's office. She needed to speak to Sienna, and for that, she'd need Hawke's permission. Which was going to be a hurdle in itself.

Frowning, she stopped, realizing she'd gone completely out of her way. Strange. She knew how to get to Hawke's office, but instead she was heading toward the paintings that lined the entranceway. It would've been logical to turn and put herself back on the right path, but she was no longer in the Net. Logic didn't rule supreme.

Trusting instinct and her growing abilities, she continued on toward the hallway lined with an amazing array of images of wolves at play, at rest, even in combat. She wasn't as surprised as she should've been to see Sienna Lauren at the farthest end of the tunnel—the part closest the door. The teenager's face was stark white, her free hand clenched rigidly enough to hurt. She was running the fingers of the other over what looked like some kind of a fracture in the wall.

"Sienna." Sascha kept her tone soft, able to sense the distress coming off the girl in waves. It was the first time she'd seen her this close to breaking. Sienna had turned eighteen that summer, but except for her run-ins with Hawke, she acted with a maturity beyond her years—unsurprising, given what Sascha suspected of Sienna's abilities. The girl's training had to have been brutal. "Sienna," she said again, putting a hand on the girl's shoulder.

Sienna jerked away from the wall. "I didn't mean to." On the surface, it was an angry declaration. "I didn't, Sascha."

Sascha wasn't close to Sienna, but she was coming to realize that as an empath, she had a shortcut to people's trust. It was a responsibility she intended to honor . . . no matter what. "It's okay," she began, trying to soothe.

"No," Sienna interrupted. "Hawke will go crazy." There was no fear in her, just a staggering sense of having done something bad. Something very bad.

Hawke? Sascha frowned, then looked at the wall. The fracture, the crumbled paint. "You did this?" she asked with utmost gentleness, taking the girl's hands in her own and turning them over—powdered stone clung to her skin.

"I didn't mean to," she said again. "I only wanted to look at them—they're important to Hawke. I—" Her voice hitched, her breath broke. "My emotions are going haywire, Sascha. And without control, I can't—" She cried out, wrenched her hands away. A second later, *power* filled the air. It was so strong, it raised the hairs on the back of Sascha's neck.

Fear threatened to take over but she stood her ground. Panicking would just make it worse. Everything about Sienna pointed to a combat ability—which one, Sascha wasn't sure, but one thing was certain—such Psy were very, very, *very* unstable until trained. Before Silence, many on the extreme end of the scale had died when their powers turned on them. "Sienna," she said, drawing the girl's attention. "Look at me." She infused her voice with command, made the girl meet her eyes. "Focus."

Sienna blinked eyes that had gone inky black, drowning the white stars, and nodded in an uncoordinated jolting motion. A minute later, her hands uncurled and the sense of power disappeared. Both of them breathed a sigh of relief. A single, clear tear escaped Sienna's phenomenal control. Her heart twisting up, Sascha gathered the teenager close. "Shh, we'll figure this out."

"I'm the horror in the closet, Sascha, the nightmare even Psy hide from." She held on tight, her face pressed to Sascha's shoulder.

"Don't be melodramatic." Sascha couldn't believe the pain contained in the fragile body she held. Sienna's emotions were so tormented the girl was close to shattering. It made no sense, not when she had to have been fully conditioned before she left the PsyNet. "You have combat-grade abilities. It's not limited to mental combat, is it?"

A shake of the head. "No."

Sascha had the sense that Sienna was hiding the whole truth, but now wasn't the time to push. "Your uncle has ex-tremely powerful abilities—he's learned to control them. So will you." Judd's stated ability was telepathy, but Sascha had a feeling that that was a front for other, deadlier gifts. The man had been an Arrow, an assassin no one ever saw until it was too late.

"I'm not like Uncle Judd." A flat statement. "I'm worse." No more tears, no weakness in that voice, only a truth so painful no one should have to endure it. "You know it and so do I. One slip and boom, I take out the entire den."

Sascha knew that wasn't teenage grandeur at work. "Your cardinal status isn't telepathy, is it?" As with Judd, that was the skill everyone knew her to have.

A pause. The answer was less than a whisper. "No."

My God. Sascha held the girl closer, disbelieving. Cardinal Psy with furious combat abilities were beyond deadly. Sienna *could* possibly take out the SnowDancer den if she lost her grip on her powers. "You've been trying to manage it?"

"I shut up everything inside. Everything." Words ground out through clenched teeth. "I thought if I could hold it, just hold it, it would be fine. But it's not."

"Why?" she asked. "Why are you losing control this badly?"

The answer, when it came, broke Sascha's heart.

"Hawke." It was an almost soundless whisper.

"Oh, Sienna." She stroked her hand over the girl's hair, even as her mind worked at piercing speed. "Has it been cumulative?"

Sienna nodded. "The second I met him, everything crumbled, my shields, my conditioning, everything! And Sascha, I *need* that conditioning. Judd showed me how to short-circuit the pain controls but I haven't— I'm not like him, I don't think I can stop without the pain."

Sascha squeezed her eyes shut, sending Sienna soothing waves of reassurance. But she didn't brush aside the girl's words. Silence had been undertaken for a reason. It had become perverted over time, but at the start, the Protocol had been their salvation—it had saved people like Sienna, Psy who couldn't think for the virulent strength of their gifts. It was possible the girl simply couldn't exist without Silence.

And if that was so, it would send shock waves through both the Lauren family and the SnowDancers.

"The LaurenNet," she said, referring to the small psychic network that linked Sienna's entire family, "is it strong enough to survive your not being in the den?"

Sienna nodded immediately. "Marlee and Toby are settled. They won't attempt to rejoin the PsyNet. And with Brenna in our net as well, it's gained in strength. But I can't leave for long—maybe a week or two. Toby's my responsibility."

"Of course," Sascha said. "But you need a break, you know that. And we're close enough that someone can drive you up here when necessary."

"I can drive. Uncle Walker taught me." A pause, then a slight shake of her head. "But these eyes, Sascha. We can't hide them."

Sascha smiled. "Sometimes, I don't want to stick out either, so I've been working with our techs to develop a new type of contact lens. It's not perfect yet, but it's good enough—you can wear it up to a month before it needs replacing."

Hope lit Sienna's face. "I could be free. I mean, not leave or anything, but I could go out into the city, move about."

"Yes." Sascha touched her hands again. "But not until you can control yourself."

A shaky nod. "I don't know who can help me—Judd's done a lot, but there's no one else like me."

Sascha felt a flash of worry. What if . . . ? No. Cardinal X-Psy were a myth. Even midrange Xs were rare, their gift turning on them during childhood. None but the very weak survived to adulthood. "Sienna, what's your combat ability?"

"I can't tell you." Sienna's jaw set in a way most would've read as stubbornness. They would've been wrong. It was desperation. "I *can't*. No one can ever know."

Sascha stroked her hand over the teenager's hair again. "Don't worry—I'm not going to withdraw my offer. But I need to know this—will you be safe around my pack?"

Sienna took long moments to think about it, strengthening Sascha's faith in the girl. "I was *cold* in the Net, Sascha," she said at last. "Really cold—maybe even colder than Judd. It's being here, in this den, that breaks me. If you get me out of here, my conditioning should spring back."

Sascha knew precisely what Hawke would think of that, but if Silence would keep Sienna functional, then she'd fight tooth and nail for the girl. "Did the Council know about your abilities?"

"Yes." She swallowed. "Ming wanted me to join his Arrows, become his protégée. Then he found out I was stronger than him. And that's when my family got the order for rehabilitation."

"It's not on you," Sascha said firmly. "It's on the Council—they made the decision to destroy their own people."

"Sascha . . . I might have to go back."

Both of them knew exactly what Sienna was talking about—the dark skies of the PsyNet, Silent and cold, might be the girl's only hope.

CHAPTER 34

Riley knew he'd fucked up. Even his wolf knew he'd fucked up. What he didn't know was how to fix things. That was what he did—he fixed things. For his family, for his pack, for everyone who mattered to him. But he had no idea in hell how to fix something so crucially important to him. Mercy had been so *angry*.

"Riley?"

He looked up to find Elias running toward him, sweat rolling down his temples. "How'd it go?" Eli was one of their best trackers, his nose fine-tuned in either human or wolf form.

But this time the SnowDancer soldier shook his head. "They're smart—went straight from here to Pier 39, far as I can tell."

"Shit." Pier 39 was always jam-packed with people, and with the blue skies they'd had today, it was doubtless worse than usual. "The trail dead-ended?"

Eli nodded. "I didn't say anything to the others, didn't want to influence them in case they caught something I missed." Said with a soldier's calm acceptance that he was part of a team. "That cat—Kit—he's really good. He might be able to pick up the trail again."

But half an hour later, when Mercy called him, it was to say that Kit had only been able to get two piers farther down. "He thinks they might've had water transport. But we've got their scent now," she said, her voice terse, businesslike. "I'm sending everyone who knows that scent to do sweeps of the city."

"I'm doing the same."

"Teijan's coming over to take a sniff. Don't shoot him."

Teijan, Riley knew, was the Rat alpha. "Fine."

He wanted to say something else, anything else, but she'd already hung up. Gritting his teeth, he put the phone in his pocket and—after Teijan had come and gone—decided to join in the sweeps. If the bomb makers had acted smart and gone to ground, then they wouldn't find a fresh trail, but that didn't mean they had to be careless.

Sascha waited until she and Lucas were almost ready to leave to pull the lid on a powderkeg of trouble. She'd already broken the rules and spoken to Sienna's uncles—Walker and Judd had both agreed that something needed to be done. Their worry for the daughter of their lost sister was an ache beneath their skin, though neither man showed much on the surface.

"Sienna needs a break from the den," she said point-blank to Hawke. "I've offered her a room at the aerie." It was as well that Lucas had added an extra room once Julian and Roman started sleeping over on a regular basis. "I need you to release her from her duties here."

"Hell, no!" Hawke slammed a hand on his desk. "She's a liability. The Council gets any idea she's alive, they'll begin hunting the whole family."

"It'll only be for a week or two," Sascha said, "and we can disguise her. She's agreed to cut her hair, get contacts. She doesn't even walk like a Psy anymore after almost two years in the den. She'll fit right in."

"Cut her hair?" Hawke repeated.

She could understand his shock. Sienna's hair was incredibly beautiful, a rich, unique shade that burned with inner fire. It had darkened over the past year until it wasn't truly red. Closer to port, or the dark heart of a ruby. The color was so distinctive that they'd have to bleach it before dyeing it and the process would be easier with short hair. However, Sascha intended to talk the teenager into keeping the length—it would be a psychological anchor, very necessary when everything else was falling apart around her. "You have to let her go," she told the alpha. "She needs time to rebuild her shields."

Hawke's pale eyes glittered. "And why will a change in location help?"

Lucas stirred beside her, but didn't step in between. "Because," she said, "you won't be there."

Everyone went quiet. Then Hawke swore. "Damn it, Sascha. I haven't touched her. She's a kid."

"I don't think Sienna has been a child for a very long time." She looked into his eyes. "And she's growing up faster every day."

Another pause fraught with anger. Hawke finally thrust a hand through his hair, blowing out a breath between pursed teeth. His eyes were bleak when he met hers again. "You're right. Take her and help her. Maybe she'll get over her crush."

Sascha didn't know why she said what she did next. "If she doesn't?"

White lines bracketed Hawke's mouth. "Then tell her I can't give her what she wants." Unspoken were the words: *Because I've already given it to someone else.* Sascha felt a deep sense of loss, of pain, and knew that Hawke had lost his mate.

Lucas touched her lower back. "We'll protect the girl," he told the other alpha, one male to another.

Hawke nodded. "Take good care of her. And bring her back in a week or I'll do the job myself."

* * *

Riley made his way back to the den a little after six. The sweeps had netted nothing, but had served to make the populace aware of a threat in their midst. It would make them more vigilant, watchful. He'd discussed a public broadcast with Mercy—though "discuss" was probably the wrong word for the clipped words they'd exchanged—but they'd decided that with this little information, they risked starting a panic.

Instead, they'd told their people to quietly get the word out to those they trusted. The Alliance had to be finding it increasingly difficult to procure a hiding place—the stress might lead to mistakes. And when it did, the changelings would be waiting. This shift, that responsibility was in Indigo and Nate's hands.

Deciding he didn't particularly want to talk to anyone, he parked his vehicle on the very edge of den territory, shifted into wolf form, and loped off into the trees. He caught the scents of several other packmates along the way—Eli's whole family, including little Sakura; D'Arn with his mate, Sing-Liu; Tai and Judd.

That latter pairing would've normally made him grin. Tai thought Judd walked on water. The boy turned up at every training session and followed Judd's merciless discipline without a single word of complaint. Riley and the other lieutenants, including Judd, all knew Tai had both the mental and physical strength to make lieutenant after he grew up a bit more. Right now, he still had the edges of boyhood on him.

He spied the faint hint of Hawke's trail and veered off in the opposite direction. The last person he wanted to see right now was one of the very few men who could beat him into submission and make him talk. He didn't want to talk, didn't want to consider why he was so angry and frustrated . . . and lost.

But Hawke had other ideas. The alpha wolf moved out in front of him, having muddied his trail through experience and trickery. Riley wasn't pleased to see him. Baring his teeth, he warned Hawke to get the hell out of his way. Right now, all he wanted to do was brood. Or failing that, draw blood.

Hawke apparently realized that. But instead of leaving, he attacked. And he was *fast*.

Riley didn't have Hawke's speed. But he had something his alpha didn't. A body that could take just about any damage and keep going. Hawke had called him a fucking stone wall on more than one occasion, the reason behind his nickname.

Now he braced for impact and took it hard. Then rolled and rose to his feet, uninjured. Hawke was already coming for a second strike, and since Riley's aggression had been building ever since that fight with Mercy, he met his alpha in midair. The contact was raw, bloody, no-holds-barred.

Riley was one of the extremely small number of people in the den with whom Hawke didn't bother to hold back. He was alpha—stronger, faster—but Riley was dogged. He simply wouldn't go down. That leveled the playing field in a way that left them very well matched. And today, even their anger was well matched—they weren't fighting with logic. They were fighting like the wolves they were, driven by instinct, by emotion, by the need to savage their opponent.

There was no mercy in either of them.

Ten minutes later, they were both still standing . . . and bleeding, their sides heaving. They stared at each other, Riley looking into pale, pale eyes that never changed, no matter what form Hawke took. Staying in position, he watched as a mirage of color appeared around the wolf, and split seconds later, a man crouched in its place.

Riley shifted an instant later, touching his hand to his side. He was cut, but even with having fought Joaquin earlier, the injuries would heal fairly fast. "I'm bleeding. So are you. But you have a bruise the size of a cantaloupe on your ribs. That means I win."

Hawke snarled. "Shut up." But he winced as he sat down. "Damn wall. I think I broke a hand." He flexed his fingers.

Riley sat a little ways to the left, where he could keep an eye on Hawke's face . . . and use the night shadows to disguise his own. "What's got you so angry?" Easier to be the lieutenant, to make sure his alpha was fully functional, than think about the mess he'd created for himself.

"Sienna's gone to stay with Lucas and Sascha for a while."

"Good." Sascha might be able to help the girl as she'd helped Brenna after his sister had been violated, her mind close to broken. Riley would take a bullet for the empath without blinking—some debts could never be repaid. "But why does it matter to your wolf?"

"She's a juvenile," Hawke said. "My instincts tell me to protect her, that's all."

"Okay."

That only seemed to irritate Hawke. "You piss me off, Riley."

"Yeah?"

"All grounded and practical and shit."

"That's what she says."

"Ah." Hawke's face relaxed a fraction. "So Ms. Mercy's the reason you were out here sulking."

"I brood. You sulk."

Hawke bared his teeth. "I'm your alpha. Show some respect."

Riley snorted, though he was anything but relaxed. "I saw you puke your guts out after you stuffed yourself on chocolate cake. Respect's not coming easy."

"I was seven. And I seem to recall you threw up first."

"You have a faulty memory."

Hawke's eyes were wintry pale when he glanced over. "Enough dancing, Riley. You think I trailed you and got myself beaten up because I want to shoot the breeze over old times?"

Riley shrugged.

"You and the cat—something happened." It wasn't a question.

Riley blew out a breath. "She won't let me look after her." And after his devastating failure in protecting his sister, he desperately needed to take care of the woman who'd become so much more than just his lover.

"Mercy's not the kind of woman who needs looking after."

"Thanks."

"Sarcasm doesn't suit you, Mr. Stick-in-the-Mud."

Riley turned to stare at a grinning Hawke. "How the fuck do you know about that?"

"I have big ears." He flicked an ear currently hidden behind messy strands of thick silver-gold hair.

"Then stop fucking listening." He stared out at the cool black of night in the Sierra, the early stars diamond pinpricks in the sky, the firs pointed silhouettes against a backdrop of mountain and rock. "I don't know if I can accept that."

"Then you'll lose her." Serious words. "She won't accept restrictions."

"Brenna did."

"Brenna humored you for a while because you're her big brother and she adores you. Mercy's probably not in the adoring stage, and even if she was, I can't exactly see her being happy to give up her duties as a sentinel to darn your socks."

"Darn my socks?" Riley shook his head. "Where do you get this stuff?" In spite of the light words, he couldn't stop thinking about the painful intensity of his emotions for Mercy. At first, it had been lust. Bright, sharp, changeling in its wildness. There was nothing wrong with lust—especially when she'd been in lust, too.

But now, other things had invaded, taking a clawhold on his soul—including this gut-wrenching need to protect. Then there was the simple but visceral need to see her, hold her, have her accept him into her world. "I don't want to cage her," he said. "I just can't stand the thought of anything happening to her." It was a deep-rooted fear, one that twisted around his gut like razor wire.

"Then walk away." Quiet words. "Walk away while you can still do it as friends."

"Too late," he muttered. "She's barely talking to me." He told Hawke what he'd done.

Hawke stared at him. "I thought you were smart, Riley."

"Obviously not."

"She's right," Hawke said. "You two don't have the luxury of acting as if your actions matter only to you. You're critical parts of your packs—what you did today came very close to breaching our agreement to share intel."

"Lucas isn't going to get into a pissing contest with you over that."

"No, he'll leave it to Mercy to sort out. Like I'll leave it to you."

"I can't just treat her as a sentinel now." It was impossible. He saw her as a woman first—an intelligent, beautiful, strong woman.

Hawke thrust a hand through his hair. "Then I need to assign someone else as liaison."

"Do it and I'll rip your throat out."

"Think for a second," Hawke said, tone granite-hard. "I chose you as liaison because I knew you weren't hotheaded. I need someone who isn't going to jeopardize this alliance."

If there was one thing Riley had never been accused of being, it was hotheaded. "I'll work it out with Mercy."

"She really gets to you." Hawke's voice was contemplative. "As the SnowDancer alpha, I want to tell you to back off before things get even more messed up."

Riley waited.

"But as your friend, I say go for it . . . Women who get to you that deep don't come along more than once in a lifetime."

Riley caught something in that statement, was ready to follow it, but the truth when it came to him wasn't soft, wasn't gradual. It was a head-ringing mental slap that left him stunned. "I'm so blind."

"Talking to yourself?" Hawke rubbed at his jaw. "Want me to leave you alone?"

Riley barely heard him, and when, ten minutes later, Hawke followed through on his offer, he hardly noticed. Because—"I never figured it'd be her." And he'd known her for a long time. Had respected her strength even as she drove him insane. Hell, he'd admired the lithe sexiness of her body more than once—he *was* male, after all. But why had he never known it was her?

It didn't matter. Because now he did . . . and there was no way he was ever letting her go.

CHAPTER 35

Councilor Nikita Duncan stared at the book sitting in the center of her desk, bound in leather that was stained and marked with coffee rings, the edges curling, and asked herself why she'd tracked down a copy of this very rare, very out-of-print volume. It had cost her a considerable amount of cash to acquire.

She could, of course, have infected the bookseller's mind with a mental virus and simply taken it, but she'd wanted to do this without attracting any attention whatsoever. So she'd created a false identity, that of an eccentric human collector. Because the bookseller would never *ever* have knowingly let this volume fall into Psy hands.

She'd patiently ensured his security checks came back to the same rich human identity. And then she'd paid the exorbitant price for this stained, browned book. The pages were moth-eaten at the edges, but the words . . . the words were visible. That was why it had been so expensive. Nothing was missing, nothing had been torn out.

Nikita knew she should destroy it and reclaim the cost from the Council coffers. None of her fellow Councilors would blink an eyelash—this was a legitimate expense. But she hadn't bought it to destroy it, though if anyone did ever track the sale back to her, that was what she'd tell them.

She picked up the book, redid the packaging, and put it in a simple brown waterproof envelope. Then she wrote the name of the recipient on the top: *Sascha Duncan*.

Again, she asked herself why she was doing this. "Power," she told herself. That was why she did anything.

CHAPTER 36

Mercy had just walked into her cabin after working late when the comm panel flashed an incoming call. She answered audio-only. "Hi, Gran."

"Don't 'hi, Gran' me," Isabella snapped back. "What's this I hear about you and a wolf?"

"I'm going to kill Eduardo and Joaquin." They had to have caught an airjet to get home so fast.

"Those two didn't say a word except to tell me anyone else I send up had better be prepared to come back sans body parts."

"Then how do you know anything about my life?"

"I have ears. I use them." An impatient sound. "Put me on the viewscreen so I can see your face."

Blowing out a breath, Mercy did as ordered. An instant later, her maternal grandmother's face appeared on-screen, beautiful, determined, and dangerously intelligent. Isabella was on oddity in her part of the world, with pale cream skin and hair that had been a rich dark gold before it turned a stunning white, traits she'd bequeathed her daughter, Lia—Mercy's mom. Family legend said some *bandido* way back when had stolen away with the daughter of a French admiral, and now, every so often, the genetics kicked up an unexpected blonde. Mercy didn't know if that was true, but Isabella was certainly regal. She'd undoubtedly look as haughty at a hundred and thirty.

"A wolf?" Isabella repeated.

"No."

Isabella narrowed her dark brown eyes. "Lying to your grandmother is a mortal sin."

"It's not a lie. He's an ass."

"I could've told you that." A sniff. "I know wolves can be attractive, but seriou—"

"Back up." Mercy held up a hand. "How do you know?"

"None of your business."

Mercy grinned. "Played with a wolf, did you?"

"If I did, I came to my senses in time." But her lips were twitching. "Be careful, Mercy girl. They're different from us."

"Gran."

"No, you have to know—they are different. They tend to be more brutal in their pack structure, for one."

Mercy thought of Hawke's rule, compared it with Lucas's. Yeah, there were differences, but both men would kill for those under their care. "We're the same as far as the things that matter."

"If you mate with him—"

Mercy all but screamed. "Who said anything about mating? I just had my own bit of fun. End of story."

Isabella raised an eyebrow. "Never seen a man rile you up like this before."

"I'll get over it." She had to. Because what he'd done . . . "He fucking hurt me, Gran."

Sascha lay curled up in bed beside Lucas, playing her fingers over his chest. "Do you think Sienna's alright?" They'd decided to stick with the girl's real name. With her eyes covered up and her hair dyed a temporary brunette, she looked nothing like her old self.

"Kit knows who she is—he'll make sure she's not overwhelmed."

"At least it's an outdoor dance, easier for her to acclimate—she can walk off if things get too much." The older juveniles and young adults had thrown together the dance/dinner/excuse for flirting after Sienna had "come to visit from Talin's hometown."

The fact that she was actually sleeping at Lucas and Sascha's fazed no one—packmates were used to accommodating others and Tally's house was full. So the logistics had been neatly skirted, but still . . . "She's been so sheltered, first in the Net, then in the SnowDancer den."

"She'll be fine. I made sure everyone knows she's under my protection." He squeezed her. "Not that it's necessary—Kit won't leave her side."

"I'm worried it's too soon."

"The whole point of this week is to give her some time out." He spread his fingers over her lower back. "If she can get things under better control—"

"She's already more stable," Sascha said, having felt the girl settle as soon as they left the den.

"Good. That'll give her more time."

But Sascha knew what he wasn't saying—sooner or later, Sienna was going to need more training than anyone in either pack could provide. No one knew, however, just who might be able to train a cardinal with her destructive abilities. "She's safe around the pack," Sascha said. "Judd and Walker have an eye on her through the LaurenNet, and she knows to contact me for telepathic assistance the instant something happens."

"Can you calm her down?"

"Yes, for a while. We decided that if she gets really bad, Judd will hit her with a telepathic blow that'll cause unconsciousness. Not what I would've chosen, but it gives her the confidence to move about without worry."

"Which means we have the aerie to ourselves." He grinned. "Kit said she could crash at his and Rina's tonight since it's closer, but I want you to check she's comfortable doing that, with it being her first night."

"Hold on." Her telepathy was enough for a quick conversation with Sienna, given the girl's much longer reach. Sienna could "hear" the barest whisper.

First, a polite mental knock. When Sienna responded, she asked, *Are you still fine with staying over at Rina and Kit's?*

Yes. Kit said I can have his room and he'll take the couch.

Be careful. His room's probably a pit.

No, Rina told me he's soldier-neat. A pause. *I'm okay, Sascha. I'll 'path you if anything happens?*

Catching the rising intonation, Sascha said, *Of course. Now go enjoy yourself.*

Dropping from the link, she pressed a kiss to Lucas's shoulder. "She's coping. But I can already feel her itching to return to the den."

"I don't think that's anything either of us can change." Worry laced his tone. "Hawke called to check that she was settling in—I talked him into letting her stay with us indefinitely, with regular visits up to see Toby and the others."

It was more than Sascha had ever expected. "How?"

"I told him the truth—she's better down here." He blew out a breath. "Keep an eye on her, kitten. That kid's got a hard road ahead of her."

Sascha nodded. "Do you think . . . maybe?"

"Even the panther doesn't know the answer to that." Turning, he looked down at her, bright green eyes gone night-glow. "But it knows it wants to pet its mate."

"Well, it just so happens that I need some petting," Sascha murmured and was about to kiss him when he went hunting-quiet, then relaxed.

"Dorian's here—let me see what it's about."

"I hope nothing's wrong." She sat up, sheets clutched to her breasts.

Kissing her on the lips, Lucas got out and pulled on a pair of jeans, which, Sascha thought, was a shame. As if he'd heard the thought—and he might have, through the mating bond—he turned to throw her a grin. "You can bite my ass in a minute."

She threw a pillow at him but she was laughing. Falling

back onto the bed, she realized she really did want him—quite desperately. The need between her and Lucas was a wild, growing thing, but she'd been extra aroused this past week. She'd never had a problem with letting Lucas know she wanted him—it was easy when the man could tell by her scent. But she'd all but ripped off his shirt an hour ago.

He'd loved it. She thought she was turning into a sex maniac.

"Sascha." The tone of his voice had her sitting up.

She glanced over his shoulder. "Where's Dorian?"

"Gone." Walking over, he sat beside her, a package in his hand. "He took Ashaya and Keenan out to dinner, popped into HQ to pick up something, and was there when this was delivered. There's no return address, but . . ."

"But what?" She swallowed, scooting closer to his warmth. "Lucas?"

"It has Nikita's scent on it."

Whatever she'd expected, that wasn't it. "It's not—"

"Not dangerous," he reassured her. "You know Dorian—he ran every diagnostic test he could on it. It's inert. A book, from the weight and size."

"Why would my mother send me a book?"

He handed it to her. "Let's find out."

"I—" Her fingers were trembling too much to undo the packaging.

Lucas's hands closed over them. "She can't hurt you here." Panther-green eyes looking into hers. "You're stronger, far stronger, than she'll ever be."

He knew that for the truth with everything in him. Sascha was a healer of minds, of souls. She walked undaunted into darkness, into nightmare, for no reason than to help others. It took a courage Councilor Nikita Duncan would never possess.

Now he saw her straighten her shoulders, tuck the edges of the sheets firmly under her arms—the burst of familiar modesty delighted and amused him in equal measures—and take a deep breath. "If you would, Mr. Alpha," she requested.

"As you please, Mrs. Alpha." Sliding out one lethally sharp claw, he tucked it under the flap and slit it open.

"You're awfully convenient to have around," she said in her best prissy Psy voice, and he knew his Sascha, with her quiet strength and warm heart, was back.

Wrapping an arm around her, he said, "I live to please," and watched as she slid out a book that had been meticulously wrapped.

"So much packaging," she said as she peeled off layer by layer. "Must be something important."

Or Nikita could be playing with her mind. He didn't want to say it, knew that Sascha was still vulnerable where her mother was concerned—and how could he not understand that? "Kitten," he began.

"I know, darling." A shaky smile. "I know. I lived with Nikita's politics and ethics for most of my life." Reaching out as she found herself at the last layer of fine tissue, she gripped his thigh and peeled the edges of the paper apart with one hand to uncover the title. "*The Mysterious E Designation,*" she read out loud. "*Empathic Gifts & Shadows.* By Alice Eldridge."

Mercy kicked out a leg and spun, hitting her target—her favorite tree. She called it Riley, having been driven to kick it after their first real meeting. Now she "ran" up the tree and did a backflip, coming down on her feet, no wobbles. Though it was closing on eleven o'clock, she was too wired to sleep. Even talking to her gran hadn't helped with the angry pain that continued to rip through her veins.

Another kick. "Stupid." Slap. "Male." Slap. "Wolf."

Fury expressed—at least for now—she took a deep breath, centered herself, and began going through the martial arts routine her original trainer had helped her devise. She'd embellished and changed it over the years to take her increasing strength and flexibility into account, and Dorian had taught her several new moves, but as a training routine, it still worked perfectly. It kept her toned and supple, something that was often more of an advantage than brute strength.

As she moved, she felt joy. This was who she was. And it

felt good. A dance of the soul. One no one had the right to steal from her. Not even the man who made every female instinct in her sit up and pay attention. Her anger threatened to derail her rhythm, but she gritted her teeth and kept going.

Once, a long time ago, she'd worried about her tendencies—she'd been a young teen and, like her peers, had just wanted to fit in. The phase hadn't lasted long. How could it? Her mentor, Juanita, had been a soldier, her grandmother an alpha, and even her nondominant mother had a spine of pure steel. They'd all taught her that being a strong female was a good thing, a thing to be cherished.

Too bad Mercy had had to go and find herself attracted to a throwback like Riley who wanted little wifey at home with an apron and a dress and a "Oh, honey, I missed you—I can't do anything without you" smile on her face.

"Ha!" She speeded up the routine, hoping it would stop her brain cells from firing.

No such luck. Instead, she began to scent Riley on the air currents. At this rate, she'd be seeing him—"Fuck!" She continued with the workout, knowing he was watching her. She hid nothing of her speed or strength, doing her best to intimidate him.

To show him the truth of who she was.

He leaned against the tree and watched her with the intense focus of a soldier who'd trained more than a few young ones. He was watching for mistakes, errors, not because he'd get pleasure in pointing them out, but because it was habit—it was better to warn a fighter in training, than have them fail when it meant life or death. Mercy knew—she did the same thing herself.

Finally, a good twenty minutes later, she lowered her speed and began to go through a cool-down routine.

Riley didn't speak until she'd finished and was wiping the sweat off her face using the towel she'd hung on a tree branch.

"You move like liquid lightning," he said quietly. "I've never seen anything that beautiful."

Her mouth dried out. Damn it. She'd been good and mad at

him. And now . . . "You're a lieutenant. You'll have seen lots of people train."

"No one like you." He shook his head. "It's like you're dancing. I almost wanted to put two swords in your hands."

"I can do that, too," she told him, grinning at the unhidden spike of interest in his eyes. "Someday, when I'm in a good mood, ask me and maybe I'll play with knives for you."

"Why do I get the feeling that if any blood was spilled, it would be mine?" Dark eyes, steadfast gaze.

She shrugged, very aware of the sweat molding her black sports bra to her body, the airy thinness of the loose white *gi*-style pants she preferred over tights. "No pain for Riley, no fun for Mercy." She was still so mad at him, but now that he was here, the anger was dulled, covered by . . . hope. Because he'd come. The arrogant bastard had come to her.

"Merciless," he said. "Is that why they call you Mercy? To be ironic?"

"No."

"No?" Open interest in his expression.

"It's because my mother would always say 'Have mercy on my nerves, baby!' after I pulled one stunt or another," she said, not sure why she'd shared that childhood memory. "It stuck."

"Your poor mother." He stepped out of the shadows. "What stunts did you pull?"

"Why don't you tell me what stunts *you* pulled."

He gave her a pensive look. "Sorry. I was a pretty good kid."

She knew he'd helped raise Brenna and Andrew, but his parents had been alive till he was ten. "What, you behaved even when you were seven or eight?"

"Yes." He watched her, so intent it was almost a physical touch. "My mother used to say I'd been born old."

"Do you agree?"

"I am who I am."

It was such a Riley answer that she smiled. "What you are is a pain in the ass when you want to be." Especially to her.

"Never said I didn't pull stunts as an adult."

Clever, clever. Her cat liked clever. "What're you doing here, Kincaid?"

"Looking for a cat to play with."

"Hmm." She put a hand on her hip. "I think I saw a nice tame tabby over thataway." She pointed over his shoulder, in the opposite direction from her home.

"Still mad, huh?"

"You could say that."

He reached up to rub the back of his neck, and it was a nervous gesture . . . from a man who didn't seem to know the meaning of the word. "You confuse me, Mercy." Not said as an excuse, but as a frank truth. "I don't know what I'm doing around you half the time."

"New experience?" she asked, leaning against a tree opposite him.

"A little." Dropping the hand from his neck, he shoved both hands into his pockets. "Actually, a lot."

"Big brother and lieutenant," she said. "Both positions that require you to lead."

"It comes naturally."

But it had been honed by his position in his family, in the pack. "Ever tried letting go of the reins?"

"No."

There it was again, that blunt honesty that hit her in the gut every time. "Never?"

"Not that I can remember." A drawing in of breath that sounded painful. "Hawke's sometimes been able to push me back—like when I wanted to rip Judd to pieces after he and Brenna first got involved, but I've never submitted in my life." A pause. "Is that what you want?"

CHAPTER 37

"What?" She blinked. "Submission? From you?" The idea was so extraordinary her mouth fell open. "What do you think?"

"That's just it—I don't know." It sounded like he was having teeth pulled.

"Knock it off, Riley." His discomfort was cute, but that's not what she wanted from him. "You know the answer."

That made the wolf bare its teeth. Mercy could feel the aggression in the air, though Riley was doing an impressive—and irritating—job of keeping it locked behind bars of steel.

"I think you'd chew up," he said, "and spit out a submissive. And I think you're smart enough to know that that wouldn't make you happy."

"That makes me smarter than you." It was the cat clawing at him, still pissed at the way he'd attempted to turn her into something she wasn't. She waited for him to come back with a justification that she had every intention of shredding into a million pieces.

"Yes," he said, poking a big fat hole in her balloon of indignation. "But no one ever called me stupid—just thickheaded."

She raised an eyebrow, as if he hadn't punched the air right out of her.

"Maybe," he said, dropping his hands to his sides and moving closer, "I realized my mistake."

"Did you, now?" She shook her head. "Stop right there, wolfie."

He actually obeyed. Hmm, the leopard thought, perhaps they might forgive him after all. But it wasn't yet a fait accompli. "And what," she asked, "did you realize?"

He folded his arms.

"Body language," she pointed out with a—just slightly—gleeful smile.

"You're not making this easier." He kept the arms folded.

Stubborn wolf. "If I did, I wouldn't be me."

"Yeah." A slight smile curved his lips as he dropped those arms.

And for now, for the cat in her, it was enough. She had no desire to humble him—this, what he'd said, what he'd done, it was a big step. "So, you leaving now that you've done a half-assed job of an apology?" It was very deliberate provocation.

"Invite me in and I'll give you a massage." It was a playful offer from a man who, she was learning, rarely played. "I'll attempt to turn half-assed into full."

"I got that last time." She put the towel around her neck and swung around to walk to the cabin. "What else you got?"

He prowled behind her. "The ability to give you mind-blowing orgasms."

"Let me think about it." She was playing, too—he had to have scented her readiness by now. It was getting to the point that simply being around him aroused her, and wasn't that a kicker since she'd first bitten into him to assuage her hunger? "Amuse yourself while I shower."

"Okay."

She was a little suspicious of his ready agreement—Riley was practical, focused, honest, but he was no pushover. It made complete sense to her that they called him the Wall—this man wouldn't budge once he decided on something. He'd fight for it to the death. That's why, despite everything, she liked him.

And right now, it was obvious he wanted her. He'd come down here with the intention of smoothing matters over between them—and she knew full well that if she'd made things easier, he'd have taken it. Hell, he was a man, a proud, dominant man. But he'd been ready and willing to have her carve out a pound of flesh, which was why she hadn't clawed him as much as she'd thought she would.

But she wasn't in any way mistaken about the fact that Riley was who he'd always been. Smart, rooted in earth, and very, very determined.

So when he got all meek and compliant, the hairs on her arms rose in suspicion. Still, he seemed to be genuinely relaxed as he grabbed a beer out of her eco-cooler and sprawled on the sofa. Deciding that maybe he was trying to charm his way into her good graces—not that it would work if she didn't want it to work—she walked into her bathroom, stripped, and entered the shower.

The door opened a minute later to expose Riley standing there, beer in hand.

Scraping damp strands of red off her face, she glared at him. "I don't remember giving you an invitation."

"You said to amuse myself while you shower." A slow, slow, deliciously slow smile.

It said *gotcha*.

And Mercy realized that when a man who rarely played, played with a woman, hell, it was better than any kind of sophisticated charm on earth. Sniffing as if she wasn't completely delighted, she turned her back to him and lathered up her hair. She could all but feel his gaze sliding over her body.

Rinsing out her hair, she felt it slick down her back, pasting itself to her skin. Riley's arousal wrapped around her, vivid, strong . . . familiar. Her body responded, echoing and strengthening the erotic fusion of scents. It was another level of pleasure, a soft, invisible sea that caressed and tempted.

"Turn around." It was a husky request.

She glanced over her shoulder to meet his eyes. "Alright."

He didn't bother to hide either his surprise or his appreciation when she gave him the view he wanted. Those dark chocolate eyes had gone wolf on her—a stunning amber full of heat. "Pretty," she whispered, fascinated all over again.

He didn't seem to hear her, his eyes following the lazy movements of her hands as she used the fluffy loofah to lather herself up with peach-scented soap. Just because she was a sentinel didn't mean she wasn't also very much a woman. His eyes followed her every movement as she stroked the loofah down her neck, over her breasts, and across her nipples.

The beer bottle hung forgotten from his hand, his erection pushing so hard against his jeans it made her want to lick her lips. But she kept up the slow, seductive show. Because—and quite aside from the fact that he'd acted like an ass, but then turned up to take the heat—it was Riley's turn. He was an incredibly generous lover. She knew if she walked out to him and whispered an erotic request in his ear, he'd give her exactly what she wanted. Of course, his generosity also allowed him to retain control.

Mercy wasn't planning on letting that happen tonight. Because if they were doing this—and it appeared they were—then they were doing it together.

Stroking the loofah over her stomach, she spread her legs just a fraction . . . and dipped between.

He breathed out something that turned the air blue and placed the bottle on the ground before putting his hands on the bottom of his T-shirt.

Her eyes narrowed as he ripped it off to expose that mouthwatering chest. "You've got new bruises."

"They'll heal. And I wanted a fight." His hands went to the top of his jeans.

"I didn't say you could touch," she murmured, watching him toe off his boots.

"Yeah, you did." He unsnapped his jeans. "I scented it bright and clear."

She stroked herself between her legs, aware his eyes hadn't moved off her hand. "Ah, the good behavior's over?"

"Something like that." The jeans and underwear were kicked aside and he was walking over, stark male demand in every step.

He took the loofah from her hand. "Put your hands above your head."

The command in his voice curled around her, making her center throb. She'd always known she'd need a strong man so that didn't worry her. As long as what went on in bed, stayed in bed. Or in the shower. "Are you going to break my trust again, Riley?" There could be no mistakes, no blurred lines here.

He met her eyes full on. "Not on purpose. Never on purpose." He took a deep breath. "But I'm likely to fuck up when the wolf's riding me."

It was her turn to be surprised. "I should kick you out of this shower right now."

"Probably." Then he kissed her. "But you don't seem like the kind of woman who'd let fuckups ride."

She smiled. "No." Raising her hands, she crossed them above her head. "But, Riley, I'll only bend so far. You can't meet me halfway, this will end." It wasn't a threat. No, it was something far more important.

And he understood. "I'll try, Mercy. I'll give it everything I have." It was a raw promise, from the heart of the wolf, from the soul of the man.

It would do, she thought, her own heart clenching. It would do. Because Riley would honor that promise with everything in him. And if it didn't work, if they were both too strong-willed, too stubborn, to meet in the middle, it wouldn't be because they hadn't tried. And it would hurt like hell. She knew that. Accepted that. And decided to give it a shot. "Tell me, Riley," she said, teasing, "what would you do to me if there were no boundaries?"

He dropped the loofah and replaced it with his fingers. "Tying you up sounds like a good idea."

"So, staid Riley Kincaid has a kinky secret." She moved on his fingers, relishing the building tightness in her body, the sheer pleasure on his face. "Do you have a whip?"

"With you, it might come in handy." His fingers slid inside her.

And she came.

Just like that.

A wild burst of ecstasy that swept over her in short, jagged waves and left her breathless. Chest rising and falling in a ragged rhythm, she looked up through lids gone half-mast. "You didn't even kiss me properly. What kind of a woman do you think I am?"

"The kind that means trouble." But he bent his head and gave her a kiss straight out of her hottest dreams, all tongue and demand and sex. When they parted, he put his hands on her hips, as if to lift her up.

"Wait." Pushing him back until his body blocked the water, she shook off his hands and sank down to her knees.

His hand fisted in her hair, and when she looked up, it was the wolf's eyes that she met. She knew hers had gone cat at orgasm, and she let them remain that way. Gaze locked with his, she put her hands on his thighs . . . and used her mouth on him.

His grip on her hair tightened almost enough to hurt before he let go, slamming both hands palms-down on the tile in front of him. "Mercy!"

Smiling, she flicked her tongue along the underside of his erection, and purred. Debauching Riley was the most exquisite task she'd ever had. Now she let the cat out to play, stroking him with quick, feline flicks of her tongue before sucking deep and hard.

His hips jerked. Once. Twice. And then he froze. *"Mercy."*

She didn't release him, didn't submit to the command in that tone. Instead, she ran her nails deliberately down the backs of his thighs. He swore a blue streak, but managed to hold on. She refused to let him—no way was Riley getting out of this without surrendering to her, at least this little bit. It mattered. Wasn't just sex. They were changeling—if he trusted her physically, he'd eventually trust her with his thoughts and secrets, too.

But first, she wanted his beautiful body to come apart for

her. Taking her mouth off him, she looked up, met his gaze . . . and licked her lips. He shuddered. And this time, had no hope in hell of holding back.

It was well after midnight when they fell into bed. She was almost asleep when Riley said, "I dream only good dreams when I sleep with you."

Breath catching in her throat, she pressed her lips to his heart to tell him she was there, that she was listening. He didn't say anything for several minutes, but when he spoke, the undisguised emotion in him tore her to pieces.

"Brenna was so small when our parents died. She couldn't even walk properly, just do that grab-anything-and-hope-I-don't-fall wobble."

Mercy smiled at the image. "A baby."

"Yeah." His voice dropped, grew husky. "And she was my baby. You wouldn't believe how possessive I was over her and Drew."

She rubbed her nose against his chest. "That's the one thing I have no difficulty believing."

"Cat." A squeeze. "We were adopted into another family, but the whole pack looked after us. We were almost spoiled with all the attention we got. But even then, I always knew Drew and Bren were *mine* to take care of."

Conscious of what was coming, she stroked her hands over his chest, pressing another kiss to his heart. Skin privileges of the most tender kind. Her cat wanted desperately to protect this wolf, but knew this poison had to come out, had to be purged.

"But," he said at last, "when it mattered, I wasn't there. The things that bastard did to her—" A sound that held indescribable pain mixed with absolute rage. "It destroys me that the girl I cradled as a baby had to suffer that. She must've cried for me, but I wasn't there. *I wasn't there.*"

"You *were*," Mercy said fiercely.

"The rescue was—"

"I'm not talking about that." She pulled herself up on the

bed until they lay face to face, side by side. "Sascha said that Brenna's will was a steel flame, so strong, so beautiful."

Violent pride in Riley's eyes. "I know."

"But, Riley"—she cupped his face in her hands—"where do you think she learned that strength, that will? Who do you think taught her that she *was* that tough, that she could beat anything?"

Flickers of understanding in his gaze, but he shook his head. "I always protected her."

"But you didn't cage her," Mercy said, knowing he'd only tried to do that after the rescue. "You brought her up to be a proud, strong wolf. *You* gave her that foundation, Riley."

A long pause and the wolf glimmered in his eyes. "I need to think about this."

She smiled. "You do that, wolf." Part of him would always worry after Brenna. That was normal. But perhaps, in time, he'd stop being haunted by a monster's crime. "And remember, Brenna made it." A brush of fingertips against his lips. "She'd probably like her big brother back."

He dropped his forehead against hers in unspoken affection. Stroking her hand through his hair, she decided that was enough for one night. But she didn't want him to fall asleep with such solemn thoughts on his mind—she wanted to give him a smile, guarantee his dreams *would* be pleasant. "Still want to know about the Bikini Babe contest?"

Chocolate brown eyes that were suddenly alert. "Hell, yes."

She came so close their breaths mingled as they spoke. "Needless to say, you repeat this, I'll sharpen my claws on your ribs."

A slow blink. "It won't leave the room."

"Okay," she said, taking a deep breath. "When I was fifteen and *very* stupid, I had a crush on this other cat."

"Who?"

"Not important. And I mean that," she added to make sure he'd drop it. "I was already stronger and faster than most boys my age. I thought this boy could handle that—he certainly seemed confident. Turned out he was a snotty-nosed twerp."

"You going to tell me what he did?"

"If you stop growling."

A startled pause. "Sorry."

"It wasn't that big a deal," she said with the maturity of age, though it had devastated her at the time. "I gave him a Valentine's Day card—he opened it in front of his friends, and made sure my friends and I were nearby, too. He laughed after he read it out, said he'd never go out with another *boy*." The insult had spread through the school like wildfire, savaging Mercy's fledgling feminine confidence.

"I'll kill him."

She nipped at the wolf growling in her bed. "No need. I took care of it."

A gleam of interest.

"At first I was humiliated." She'd cried on her mom's shoulder until Bas and Dorian had both been ready to do murder. "Then I got mad. I decided to show him *exactly* what he'd missed out on."

Amusement had his mouth curving. "I'm liking this story."

"Knew you would." It released the tension in her soul to see laughter in him again. "You can guess this part—there was a Bikini Babe contest that summer to publicize this new line of swimwear for teens. You had to be sixteen to enter and then only if you had parental permission—I was a few weeks too young, but Dorian hacked into the computers to get me entry."

She couldn't help the truly gleeful smile that spread across her face. "After I won, I printed up this poster of me wearing the winner's sash—and a truly tiny bikini—and pasted it on the twerp's locker, with the words 'Dickless wonders need not apply' at the bottom."

Riley burst out laughing. "You're fucking amazing."

"Thank you. I was also grounded for months, along with Dorian. And I got detention for the poster prank, too." She grinned. "I didn't care. I was the hottest property on campus. You've never seen a more miserable face than the twerp's— he looked like he was about to cry every time he saw me at the beach that summer. And I made sure to be at the beach a lot."

Riley's smile hadn't faded. "Why don't you like people knowing about this? He messed with your cat, you took care of business. Where's the shame in that?"

"I was an idiot, Riley—I let that moron influence how I saw myself. I lost interest in tormenting him pretty fast once I saw how weak he was. Then I was mad at myself." A pause, and without warning, the wickedness in her took over. "You know, I can still fit into the winning bikini . . . though it's gone from tiny to microscopic."

"You're tormenting *me* now."

Chuckling, she kissed him. "Sweet dreams, wolf."

CHAPTER 38

The Information Merchant walked to his meeting in a deserted boathouse off a private marina with steady steps. Perhaps other men might have had concerns about coming to such an isolated area to meet individuals who'd already proved willing and able to kill, but he was a high-level telepath. He could and had crushed human minds with a single focused thought.

And, he was an information seller. That was his trade, and people paid him well for it. Clients seldom wanted to kill the golden goose. If they did, they'd discover their mistake. Reminded, he pressed a preprogrammed code on his organizer, utilizing the wireless link to his home computers, then slid it into his pocket.

Taking a last look around the dark, fog-shrouded street, he opened the small side door and walked in.

The bullet hit him hard, shoving him against the wall.

Staring down in disbelief at the . . . *dart* lodged in his chest, he attempted to gather his psychic resources for a deadly blast.

Only to find his mind mired in ice.

"Consider the experiment successful, gentlemen." A voice from the shadows. "We're all still alive."

The Information Merchant gripped the dart and tugged it out. "Why?" The agony of the loss speared down his spinal column, spread through his nervous system.

"You know the answer—information. Unfortunately, you know too much."

Steps coming in his direction.

Then a burst of pain inside his heart and everything stopped.

CHAPTER 39

Just after nine the next morning found a sleep-deprived but otherwise happy Mercy sitting across from Hamilton, the SilverBlade sentinel she'd had some fun with many, many moons ago. Staring at him, she suddenly realized he was a very good-looking man. Okay, she'd known that already, but only as an adjunct to his strength and speed. But today, she really saw his face—the chiseled planes, the luscious sun-kissed skin that had come by way of a Mediterranean ancestor, the vivid topaz eyes and jet-black hair.

"Why are you looking at me like I'm a bug?" he asked, passing her the files he could've as easily e-mailed.

It was a big, giant hint. But he hadn't acted on it, which made Mercy suspicious. "I just realized how beautiful you are."

He went red. Bright red. "God damn it, Mercy!"

"Sorry." She grinned.

"No, you're not." Rolling his eyes, he leaned back in his chair. "I don't suppose your pack has anyone else like you?"

"No, I'm one of a kind." She stared at him. "Are you trolling for women?"

"Would you shut up?" But he was laughing. "No, but I'm keeping my eyes open—I'm getting antsy to settle down."

"That's an oxymoron." Flippant words but her mind was connecting the dots. "You came back to see if I was your mate?"

He shrugged. "We had good chemistry and we're friends. I figured it couldn't hurt to come have another sniff—you know what I mean so stop gagging—and make sure. I can see I'm too late."

Mercy got a very bad feeling in the pit of her stomach. "And you know this, how?"

"The scent layer's new, but it's unquestionably there. You're marked, babe." He grinned. "Does the poor man know what's in store for him?"

Mercy's intestines tied themselves into a giant knot. It wasn't surprising that Hamilton had picked up the scent layer faster than those in her pack. They knew how much time she and Riley had to spend together, probably figured it was a surface layer of contact. But she'd showered this morning after Riley left, then slicked pretty-smelling body cream over herself. And if Hamilton could still sense Riley . . .

No need to panic, she told herself. Lovers often wore layers of scent that made it clear who belonged to who—females and males both. "What's the scent layer like?"

Hamilton gave her a keen glance, then whistled. "You didn't know."

"Answer the question."

"I picked it up the instant I walked in the door—I'm getting a very definite 'hands-off' vibe."

Mercy swore under her breath. Then again. "It's the start of the mating dance."

"Which is why I'm sitting wayyy over on this side of the desk and making no physical contact," Hamilton said, raising his hands in the air. "I have no desire whatsoever to be hunted by some rabid male who's decided I touched his woman."

"I'm no one's woman."

"Not yet anyway. Am I the first to sense it?"

She nodded, trying to find her footing when the world had just shifted sideways.

"Since no one in your pack's exactly a slouch," he commented, "it means the change is recent. I probably picked it up because I haven't seen you for so long."

"And you're single," she said between gritted teeth, realizing the dance had to have kicked in the night before. By accepting his word that he'd try to never again hurt her as he'd done yesterday, she'd trusted Riley on a level she'd never before trusted a lover. More than that . . . he'd trusted her. "Every male I've seen this morning has been mated. The scent wouldn't register as strongly to them."

"So, who's the lucky guy?"

"I'm going to kill him," she muttered. "He knew and didn't tell me." Changeling males *always* knew when the dance began.

"Ah, Mercy . . . I wouldn't tell you, either."

She felt her eyes go leopard. "Men!"

"Please," he drawled out. "Look how you're reacting. Dominant females don't like the idea of being tied down. So if it was me, and you somehow didn't notice the scent, I'd make sure we were well and truly entangled before I said anything. Less chance of you deciding not to accept the mating." Getting up, he gave her a mock salute. "Are you sure you don't know any more like you?"

She thought about it. "Indigo."

"The wolf lieutenant?" He whistled. "She's all kinds of *fillne*. Would she date a cat?"

"Ask her."

"Damn if I won't." He held out his hand for Indigo's number.

Mercy gave it to him in thanks for the fact that he'd spilled the beans about the mating dance. She also threw in a bonus warning. "Don't try any dominant shit on her—she'll eat you for breakfast then suck the marrow from your bones for dessert."

It was a measure of Hamilton's confidence that he grinned

as if he'd just been told he'd won a million bucks. Hah, she thought as he walked out. He was all fun and games now, but if it got serious, he'd probably turn as crazy as Riley and try to keep Indigo from harm. Now that, Mercy thought, would be a fireworks show she'd pay to witness.

Of course, Riley *had* seen the error of his ways. More, he'd offered her a glimpse of his heart, something she'd never expected. It had undone her.

Ten minutes later, he surprised her again. "We need to go look at a corpse."

Mercy blinked. "Wow, so romantic."

"Intel came to me since I'm in charge of city security this morning. But I thought you'd want in on it. I'm on my way to pick you up."

"I'll grab a kit with gloves and things."

It didn't take them long to get to the body—found by a couple of the Rats in one of the less accessible corners of the bay, the information had traveled to cat and wolf ears rather than Enforcement, which meant they had free rein at least for a short time frame.

The body was wedged between several rocks, having apparently been washed up at high tide. Parking the car in the shadow of a large tree, the two of them headed down the tiny dirt access road to check it out. Though the sea had done a credible job of smothering the man's natural scent, they both caught the faint metallic tang.

"Psy," Mercy said, crouching beside the body. "Those squads that Sascha and Judd told us about must be combing the city, searching for him." All Psy who disappeared from the PsyNet without explanation were tracked to verify the reason for their sudden disengagement.

Riley nodded. "The instant word of his body gets to Enforcement, we lose all hope of figuring out how he ended up here."

"I've got enough training to process this," she said. "We bring in our techs and we give away the game." There was nothing much out here—two people might skate under the radar, but a team would be highly visible.

"That's what I thought."

"Anyway, it could be simple drowning or suicide." Putting on thin protective gloves, she checked the corpse for evidence of how the male might've died, while Riley took photographs with a small but high-resolution camera. "Fish have nibbled a bit and he's been banged around, but I'm not seeing anything that screams murder. Of course, I'm no expert."

He tapped a finger on his knee. "Can you take samples without it being obvious you took them?"

"No problem—I'll go through one of the bite sites." She was drawing blood as she spoke. "Haven't done anything like this for a while."

"Remind you of med school?"

A pointed glance. "That background check sure was thorough."

"Of course." He kept an eye out around them as he spoke, making certain to look skyward, too. "Falcons are coming today. They want us to grant them permission to fly over pack land."

She took a number of swabs, making quick notes on where they'd been taken from. "Been in the works for a while." The WindHaven clan occupied territory—a large slice of Arizona— that bordered SnowDancer land. Their request wasn't unprecedented. The bird changelings, especially the species that were meant to fly far and wide, often negotiated such treaties—the right to flight along strictly drawn paths.

If WindHaven wanted even limited landing privileges, they'd have to agree on some kind of an alliance, but first SnowDancer—and DarkRiver, as the wolves' main ally—had to find them worthy of an alliance. A weak partner could cause incredible damage. However—"They seem pretty solid."

"Guess we'll find out when we meet." He looked at her as she removed her gloves and put them in the biohazard bag before closing the lid on the whole kit. "Done?"

"Yeah. At least we got this much." She made a face. "Probably won't be enough for any real answers."

"Maybe we'll get lucky with the blood work." He held out his hand for the kit. When she raised an eyebrow, he didn't so much as blink. "I'm stronger. Suck it up."

Her mouth fell open as he turned something she'd said to him more than once, right back on her. Taking the chance to grab the kit, he loped over the rocks and up to the car ahead of her.

Since his back was turned to the cat prowling up behind him, he missed the smile tugging at the curve of her lips.

Mercy checked her phone when they got back to the car. "Falcons postponed," she told Riley. "Meet's set for day after tomorrow instead."

"Must've been something big," Riley murmured. "They've been working for months to reach this point."

Agreeing, Mercy cleared the message. "I'm thinking we get a Rat to call in an anonymous tip on the body. No use leaving him out there to rot. Who knows what's in his system."

"I have to meet more of these Rats. Teijan wasn't what I was expecting."

Mercy made the call before answering him. "They don't like you wolves as much as us leopards," she said, closing her phone. "Apparently, you've been known to threaten to skin any Rat you see sniffing around."

Riley gave a grim smile. "That was when they were spies with no allegiance to anyone. Now they're valued associates."

Mercy snorted, but the cat was intrigued by his logic. As agile as it was, it needed a mate who could match it mentally as well as physically. "Getting back to the body—I can't quite figure out how this guy fits into the recent slew of Psy going nuts. You heard of anything going down where the perpetrator wasn't found?"

"No."

"Me, either. But it's not like Enforcement sends us memos."

"What about that cop?"

"Who? Max?" Mercy frowned. "He went back up to New York."

"He might have contacts."

Mercy nodded. "I'll ask Clay to tap him. But if the Psy decide to hush it up, no one will know anything." She blew out a frustrated breath.

"Mercy." A tone so restrained, it spoke of the greatest emotion.

"What is it?"

"Am I out of the hole I dug myself with the last op?"

"Maybe." But she couldn't help it—he was so serious. Reaching across, she brushed her fingertips over his jaw, tenderness tugging at her very soul. It would, she thought, be so very easy to hurt this man and never know she'd done it, he held everything so close. "You're out of *that* hole."

He winced. "You found out."

"How long did you think the mating dance was going to escape my notice?" She folded her arms, though she wanted only to stroke him.

"Can we talk about this later?"

"Hmm." She glanced at the kit he'd put on the backseat. "After we drop off the samples."

"I'll get one of my men to take it up to Sierra Tech. Work for you?"

Mercy nodded. Most of the respected R & D company was commercial, but a small area had been set aside to research things the packs needed to know. Since DarkRiver and Snow-Dancer paid for that section out of their own funds, the minority shareholders weren't bothered. And both packs had a place where they could get work done in efficient privacy. "Let me call Ashaya and tell her about the samples. She'll probably want to head up."

As she was finishing the conversation with the M-Psy, she remembered something else. "Did you manage to talk to Nash again?"

"Yes, but he wouldn't share any details of his research over the comm link," Ashaya replied. "I'm sorry—I know you need more to evaluate his protection needs."

"Not your fault." She leaned back against the seat. "Let me see if I can set up a face-to-face. Might get something that way."

"Good luck."

The NetMind came calling while Faith was sitting in the office Vaughn had rigged for her—an office she absolutely adored, because it was as wild as the man who was her mate, being situated in a hollow cavern off the spectacular main cave that Vaughn had made into a home. The walls in this cavern glittered with embedded minerals, setting off the glow in the thin tubes threaded through the walls of the entire "house." Those tubes provided both heat and light in an eco-friendly way, leaving her cocooned in warmth.

It was, she thought, just one element in the whole that added up to a feeling of total safety. No one would dare touch her now that she belonged to Vaughn, but it was nice to be able to work without any worry whatsoever—the route to her and Vaughn's home was booby-trapped in every way you could imagine, and some most people never would.

Lying back in her favorite easy chair, she began to go through the list of forecasts she'd been requested to make. She never made any business predictions alone, of course. There was always the potential for a Cassandra Spiral, the major mental cascade that could destroy her—the mating bond limited the danger, but neither she nor Vaughn wanted to take chances. Not when she was already so vulnerable to the dark visions, the ones that entered her mind without warning.

But even there, she thought with pride, she'd learned to use the mating bond to anchor herself so the nightmare didn't take her over. In comparison, this—playing with the list, "priming" her brain—was utterly safe.

It was as she was going through the list for the third time that the NetMind "knocked." She couldn't really see it—had never been able to. She simply knew it was there, a vast, endless presence that was at once ageless and childish. Today she caught the tumble of roses it threw into her mind in its version of hello, and laughed.

Talking to the NetMind was difficult—it seemed to understand images better than words, and yet it was the librarian of the PsyNet, holding on to and organizing the billions of words that passed through the Net. And it was a sentience, one that changed with the Net. Now its roses were followed by torrent of images Faith could barely process.

Violence. Blood. Suicide. Over and over.

She showed the NetMind a hand, palm-out, their by-now familiar signal for "slow down." It obeyed, though its version of slow was still almost too fast for her brain to process. But it was better than before. Catching the avalanche of images, she put them aside for later review, sensing the NetMind's distress. Worried, she sent it an image of a woman colored in darkness.

The DarkMind.

It was the twin of the NetMind, created out of all the horror, the hurt, the badness that the Psy had Silenced. Faith knew from painful experience that the DarkMind was mute—but it had found a way to scream, to vent its rage through acts of violence committed by those fragile minds already predisposed toward darkness.

Now she asked the NetMind if its twin was behind the wave of violence.

The answer came within a split second, less.

The image she'd sent was returned to her, but with the DarkMind scrubbed out. So this wasn't the DarkMind trying to speak in whatever limited, tortured way it could. But then the NetMind sent her another image—of the PsyNet, with tendrils of darkness creeping through it. Except this darkness wasn't normal, wasn't healthy. It was putrid in a way Faith couldn't explain—she just *felt* it deep in her soul.

An image of a thousand tears overlaid the snapshot of the PsyNet.

The PsyNet was dying, Faith thought, and the NetMind *was* the PsyNet in many ways. Her heart stuttered. But this sending also had another message—the DarkMind might not be driving these acts, but its influence had subtly corrupted another, or others. However, though it was tempting to think of the DarkMind as evil, Faith knew that was wrong. It was also a sentience, and the blame for its insanity lay in Silence.

She sent the NetMind an image of arms outstretched, an offer of help.

The response was of a globe, but a globe colored in the shades of the Net—white stars against a background of black velvet. Around that globe was a shimmering shield that repelled her hands.

The Net wasn't ready for help.

But there were cracks in the shield. She touched a finger to one crack, and knew that was Judd. The one next to it, Walker. And not far from them, Sascha. So many fine, fine cracks. The most isolated one, the newest . . . no, this was the very first, but it was hidden, hidden deep. And it was male, powerful, so *very* powerful. When this ghost . . . "Oh," she whispered, realizing who it was she touched. "The Ghost." When the most notorious rebel in the Net broke his Silence, the shield would well and truly shatter.

What the NetMind couldn't tell her, and her foreseeing gift refused to see, was if the PsyNet would survive . . . or drown.

CHAPTER 40

"It's later."

Riley looked around Mercy's office, curious. It was neat, but with an indefinable flair that was indisputably her. "Where'd you get this?" He gestured at the striking wall hanging behind her desk.

To his surprise, she didn't push him. "Peru. I went roaming down south after I decided medicine wasn't for me." Coming to stand beside him, she smiled. "That was a hell of a lot of fun. I hung out with my grandmother's pack for a while— even went to *Carnaval* in my leopard form."

He could see her in the wild color of Rio de Janeiro. "With Eduardo and Joaquin?"

She laughed at his tone. "No, they were doing some roaming of their own."

"Why did you choose to study medicine?"

"You know how we double up—I talked to Tammy and we decided it'd be nice to have someone else medically trained. But it didn't fit." She shrugged. "So I took some time off, went back and majored in communications instead. Much better fit."

Riley nodded. "I didn't study beyond high school."

Mercy was surprised to hear the hint of hesitation. "Riley, you've been working in the pack since forever. You did an apprenticeship—I bet you're the go-to guy for everything and then some."

He gave her a slow smile that rocked her heart. Ah, damn. Pretty soon this wolf was going to become indispensable to her happiness. And the leopard both craved and feared that.

"I think," he said, "I'd like you to take me to *Carnaval* one year."

It was the last thing she'd expected him to say, but it succeeded in making her heart melt. For her, *with* her, Riley was willing to play. "You didn't roam, did you?"

A shrug. "I chose that—the pack wouldn't have minded if I'd taken off for a while. But I couldn't."

Because that wasn't who he was, Mercy thought. The predator's need to protect had overcome its need to roam free. "I'll take you to *Carnaval*," she said, stepping up to stand in front of him, hands braced against her desk, "if you stop avoiding the reason we're in here."

He thrust a hand through his hair, and when he looked at her again, any hint of vulnerability was gone, replaced by steely determination. "I'm keeping you."

Mercy blinked, so startled the leopard wasn't sure whether to snarl or stare. "Isn't that up to me to decide?" Females always had the last say in the mating bond.

He stepped closer, every inch the SnowDancer lieutenant. "You're my mate. End of story."

She raised an eyebrow. "You can't dictate that."

"Mercy, we're in the mating dance—just being around you turns my wolf crazy." Making a sound of sheer frustration, he did something she'd never have expected from staid Riley Kincaid before he showed her his wild creative streak. He reached forward, curled one hand around her neck, put the thumb of his free hand on her chin, and had her mouth open before she realized what he was about.

The kiss was long, deep, breathtakingly sensual.

And his hold, it was proprietary in the extreme.

It was, she had to admit, some kind of wonderful to be kissed so deliciously by the only man who'd dared play with her cat with the intention of winning.

He bit her lower lip.

Her eyes snapped open. "Kiss it better."

"No." He nipped her again. Sharp. Sexy. "You make me so fucking insane, I want to mark you all over. So everyone knows you're mine."

The leopard growled in her throat. "Not yours." She was her own person, a predator same as him.

"We'll see about that." This time, he dipped his head . . . and bit her neck in a suckling kiss that made her moan and thrust her hand into his hair, tugging him back.

"Stop that."

Instead of obeying, he reached up to squeeze her breast through her T-shirt, as if he had every right to be fondling her in her own office. And maybe glancing down to see that big, tanned hand on her body was mind-blowingly erotic, but . . . "*Oh.*" He'd stopped nibbling at her neck and now nipped at her ear.

Mercy was astounded at the discovery that her earlobes were exquisitely sensitive. "Again," she ordered, one hand in his hair, the other on his shoulder.

"No." He raised his head, eyes glittering. "You can't have everything you want unless you give me what I want."

She narrowed her eyes. "Don't play games with a cat."

"Who else am I going to play them with?" A squeeze of her breast, a kiss pressed to her parted lips. "Play with me."

It was the one invitation he could've made that soothed the cat, made her want to relax, maybe tease him a little. But first—"You said you were going to try last night. Are you going to take this, take us, for granted because of the mating dance?"

"No." His hand was still around her throat, his fingers stroking in a possessive caress. "It's not just about having a mate."

"Then what is it about?" She pushed off the hand on her breast and stood upright. That free hand immediately settled on her butt. Pushy. But she liked him that way.

Leaning down, he locked eyes with her. "It's about having a mate who adores you."

She didn't know which one of them he was talking about, whether it was a promise or a declaration, but she did know that no woman could've resisted him at that moment. "Then we dance, wolf." A slow, teasing smile as she raised her arms to wrap around his neck, even as something deep in her screamed in warning—there was a danger she wasn't seeing, a shock she'd never be able to bear. But Mercy was too caught up in the lush hunger of the mating dance to listen. "Let's see if you can catch me."

He skated his hand from her neck and down her body to close over her hip. "I already did, remember?"

"New game." She pressed a kiss to the base of his neck, a spot she was becoming very fond of. Especially since he always blew out a breath when she licked her tongue over it. Like now. "New rules."

"Tell me the rules." He didn't seem to realize he was holding her head against him.

Hmm, she thought, Riley *really* liked having his neck kissed. She was so going to take him necking out in the woods. Smiling, she began to nibble on that strong column, feeling her cat purr as he shuddered and angled his head to give her better access. "The rules," she whispered, drawing the warm, masculine scent of him into her lungs, "are that there aren't any rules."

He froze for an instant, then groaned. "You're going to drive me to the asylum."

She smiled. "That's the point." Riley liked rules. She didn't. Let's see if her wolf could drop his guard enough to tantalize a cat.

Sascha sat in her home "office"—the balcony outside the aerie—and stared at the book her mother had sent her. She kept hoping for a distraction so she wouldn't have to open the pages, wouldn't have to consider why Nikita had done this, whether it was a trap or a peace offering.

As if on cue, the comm panel chimed. Relief washing through her like a rainstorm, she answered using the handset she'd placed on the balcony table. "Sascha speaking."

"Sascha, it's Nicki."

"Hiya, kitten." Looking away from the book, she stared out at the trees. "What's up?" Nicki was only eighteen, but had recently become apprenticed to the pack's historian, Keely, after it became obvious she'd been born for the role.

"Keely asked me to do some research—she said you were interested in Alice Eldridge?"

The feeling of buoyancy deflated. "You found something already?"

"I got super lucky with the first person I spoke to—one of Keely's contacts." The sound of rustling, as if she was settling papers. "Sorry," Nicki said. "I never expected to be given something this cool so soon—it's exciting."

Sascha made a murmur of agreement and waited.

"Okay, so the deal is, Alice Eldridge was a Ph.D. student who was doing this big study on different kinds of Psy around 1968."

Nineteen sixty-eight—the year before the concept of Silence was first floated. "She got permission?"

"Yeah, looks like it from the info I was able to hunt up. All the stuff about her is buried deep—I got most of my intel from a rare books dealer slash conspiracy theorist after I turned up in person this morning and convinced him I wasn't Psy. I actually had to show him my claws, if you can believe it."

"He was that hesitant?"

"Oh yeah, and once he told me the history behind Eldridge, I understood why." A long inhale. "Okay, so it seems that midway through her study, Alice Eldridge decided to focus only on E-Psy, and her results were considered groundbreaking, the best work on E-Psy ever done."

"Her work was well-known?"

"In academic circles, yes. The original 1972 print run—done through a university press—was small, around two thousand, but there were rumors she'd been approached by a bigger publisher. Her style was apparently one that would've translated well to the popular market." Nicki paused to take a breath. "Unfortunately, Alice Eldridge died in a mountain-climbing accident in 1975, and that deal never eventuated."

A chill rippled down Sascha's spine. So close to the implementation of total Silence, had it truly been an accident? "Why isn't there any mention of her online?"

"That's the thing—the rare books guy told me that her work was destroyed in a massive purge around a hundred years ago."

Sascha's hand fisted. Silence had been fully implemented in 1979, a hundred and one years ago. And that was when E-Psy had become a liability . . . so they'd been buried, broken, erased. Somehow, she found the voice to say, "That's great work, Nicki."

"Thanks." The girl sounded so pleased that the chill melted a little. "I found a few bits and pieces on her other book—do you want that information, too?"

"Sure." Anything to delay the return to her "gift."

"Actually," Nicki corrected herself, "it wasn't a book but a manuscript. It seems Eldridge had begun to research another group of Psy after she finished her thesis."

Sascha frowned. "If it was a manuscript, how did you find out about it?"

"Well, it's sort of the Holy Grail to Eldridge scholars," the girl said. "The woman I spoke to—after the rare books dealer introduced us—told me that Eldridge was openly working on a new project before she died. Helene—my source—said there's a reference to it in the book on E-Psy."

Sascha made a mental note to keep an eye out. "Go on."

"The thing is, after her death, no one could find any hint of that work in her office or home. It was like she'd been doing nothing for several years." Nicki hummed a spooky tune. "Weird, huh?"

"Very," Sascha said, but she saw another angle. "The conspiracy theorists think someone got rid of her work."

"Bingo. Even though they don't know what that work was." A pause. "I mean, they *think* they do—according to Helene,

the information was passed down through the family of a col-
league of Eldridge's—but they have no clue what it means."

"Did they give you any hint of what they think she was
working on?"

"Yes. Helene said Eldridge was doing a long-term project on X-Psy." Nicki paused again. "Do you know what the X
stands for?"

Sascha swallowed and sidestepped the question. "You did
a fantastic job, Nicki. I'll be sure to tell Keely."

Nicki made a little noise of delight. Laughing, Sascha was
about to say good-bye when Nicki said, "Oh, wait, Sascha, I
almost forgot—a copy of Eldridge's book goes for over five
hundred thousand dollars, it's so rare. Any that are left are
mostly in very private collections."

"Thanks, Nicki." Breath lost, she hung up and just sat
there for several minutes. *Five hundred thousand dollars?*
Dear God. Not that Nikita couldn't afford it—that amount
was nothing to her—but still . . .

She stared at the book once again, knowing it might provide the very answers she'd been seeking. Freed from the
bondage of Silence, her empathic powers were changing, de-
veloping, *growing*. What she didn't know was what they were
growing into.

Her hand reached out. Withdrew. "Am I being a coward?"
she asked out loud, then shook her head. "No, I'm being cautious." Picking it up, she took it back inside the house—storing
it in the safe hidden under the eco-cooker.

Despite her questions, her curiosity, she wasn't yet ready
to face her mother's gift. Nikita had cut her off without a
blink. It would take time to see anything but rejection when
she looked at Eldridge's book.

Riley headed out from Mercy's office with a deep sense of
rightness in his gut. She'd accepted the mating dance. He had
no intention of letting her escape the mating itself, no matter
what he had to do.

Walking into the underground garage, he raised an eyebrow

when he saw the tall, red-headed male leaning against his four-wheel drive. "Bastien."

"Riley."

"Where are your brothers?"

Bastien smiled and it was nothing friendly. "They'll be along soon. So, what makes you think you have any right to lay a hand on my sister?"

"She gave me that right." He met those bright green eyes without flinching. In a physical fight, he knew he'd win. But this wasn't about the physical. It was about something far more important—Mercy loved her family. He was not going to fuck up their relationship by beating on her brother. "Seems to me she's a woman who knows what she wants."

"She's also my sister." Bastien straightened. "And you're a wolf."

The hairs on Riley's nape rose as another man entered the garage. He was older, his hair lightly threaded with gray. "I didn't expect your father."

"When you're touching his baby girl?" Bastien snorted. "Hi, Dad. Shall we kill him here or take him out to the forest?"

Michael Smith folded his arms and fixed Riley with a gimlet eye. "You going to hurt my girl?"

"No, sir."

"According to her grandmother, you already broke my Mercy's heart."

Riley's stomach pitched, not at the words, but at the memory of how he'd hurt her. "She's not that fragile." He felt a sudden kinship with Judd. Riley and Drew had made his life hell after he first started seeing Brenna.

"No, she's fucking not." Bastien grinned as Sage and Grey entered the suspiciously otherwise-empty garage. Riley was now surrounded by Smith men. He didn't make any aggressive moves toward the two youngest, though they were pushing into his space. Pups, they were just pups. Bastien could be dangerous, but in this, Michael Smith was the one who truly mattered.

Now the older man stepped closer. "She ever beaten you in a fight?"

"Almost." And he knew full well that if she ever came after him with lethal intent, he might not end up the victor—predatory changeling females were inexorable hunters once they decided on blood.

"How'd that go down?"

Riley understood that was the most crucial question of all. He could've lied. He didn't. "Like sandpaper."

Michael blinked, as if surprised. "Then why are you with her?"

He held the other man's gaze, let his own fill with the raw fury of the wolf. "You know why. And you know I won't walk away."

CHAPTER 41

Two hours after Riley left, Mercy tracked down and talked to Teijan. The Rat alpha was visibly frustrated, his normally *GQ*-tidy hair wind-tousled, his black shirt wrinkled. "I know something's happening, but damn if they aren't good at hiding their tracks."

Mercy thought about that. "Humans have learned to be invisible. These guys take it to the extreme." And if the Human Alliance wanted to show muscle, display what it was capable of, it would send its best. Her cat suddenly sat up, seeing an answer to a riddle.

Leaving Teijan to reorganize and disperse his troops, she found a private spot and made a call to Lucas. "Have you considered the fact that maybe we should be using Bowen and his team?" They'd know all the tricks their ex-compatriots might use.

Lucas blew out a breath. "Yeah."

"Just 'yeah'?"

"I'm your alpha, Mercy," Lucas said, voice quiet. "I picked up the mating dance this morning."

She sucked in a breath. "You telling me you're already using Bowen and his team, but don't want Riley to know?"

"He's not rational on this. Neither, for that matter, is Dorian."

"But it's Riley you're worried about with me." Turning, she fought the urge to kick at a nearby wall. "I'm a *sentinel*, Lucas. My loyalty is to DarkRiver." Again, an alarm flared in her head. Again she didn't listen, too angry to understand what it was attempting to tell her.

"I'm not questioning that." Lucas's tone changed, became openly alpha. "But the mating dance screws with your emotions—I didn't want to put you in a tough spot."

"I don't spill things during pillow talk," she said, frustrated and hurt that he'd think so little of her. "I can keep Pack secrets."

"I know you can." This time, the panther was in his voice. "Shit. I'm sorry, Merce. It was never meant as a comment on your loyalty to Pack."

The cat was still bewildered by the blow that had come from nowhere, but she couldn't doubt her alpha. Lucas didn't lie to his sentinels, no matter if the truth was a bitter pill to swallow. "So?" she asked, releasing her fisted hand.

"We checked out Bowen and his team—everything we found backs their story. Right now, I've got them working on tracking down the new Alliance squad, but their major strength is in information. If we manage to unearth the name of the target . . ."

Mercy nodded. "Much easier to work backward. Who's running Bowen and his people?"

"I am. I'll let you know the instant they come up with anything—that was never a question."

Feelings soothed, if not totally mended, she nodded. "Alright. I'd better get back to work."

But she didn't immediately return to her patrol area after hanging up, feeling a strong urge to speak to her mother. Comfort, she thought. She was like a cub seeking comfort. She didn't care. Coding in the number for her childhood home, she waited until Lia answered. "Hey, Mom."

"What's the matter, darling?"

Her throat closed up at the unconditional love in that single sentence. "Things are a little mixed up." She bent to pick up a marble that had seen better days and threw it lightly into the air, catching it on the way down. "I guess I just needed to hear your voice."

"Come to dinner, baby."

"I don't know if I can tonight, Mom." She'd be lousy company in her current frame of mind. "But I'll be by this week."

"Mercy, sweetheart, does some of this 'mixed up' stuff have to do with a certain wolf?"

Mercy winced. "Who told you?"

"Well, I kept expecting you to do so . . ."

"I planned to," she said, rolling the marble between thumb and forefinger and wondering why she'd ever thought anything could remain a secret from her mom.

"It doesn't matter, baby. I took matters into my own hands." A familiar hint of steel.

Mercy's leopard sat up. "Oh?"

"I called Riley a few minutes ago. He's coming to dinner tomorrow at seven. Don't be late, sweetheart."

Mercy hung up after a few more words, knowing a summons when she heard one. If she didn't turn up, well, Mount Vesuvius had nothing on her mom.

It seemed to be her day for calls because no sooner had she gone to shove the phone into a pocket than Ashaya rang through. "We did a very, very quick run-through with the samples you brought up from the body," the scientist told her, her voice excited. *Too* excited. Mercy went to ask what was wrong, but Ashaya was already continuing to speak. "He had traces of the same drug in him that we found on the men who tried to kidnap me."

"Damn." Mercy closed her fist around the marble. "You figured out what's so special about it yet?"

"Possibly." Ashaya paused. "I'm supposed to make sure I deliver reports to DarkRiver and SnowDancer simultaneously on this issue."

It was normal procedure, but after the call with Lucas, she

found herself irritated. Fighting the irrational emotion, she said, "Riley's in the city. I'll get him to meet me at HQ."

Hanging up, she called Riley with the message before making her way back to the medium-sized office building DarkRiver owned near Chinatown. She should've felt more comfortable in her own office, but her cat refused to settle, its hackles rose—as if it could sense a danger the human side of her was too dense to see. Frustrated, she pushed the amorphous knowing to the back of her mind. Nothing, she thought, could be worse than having her loyalty questioned—if only by implication.

"You called?" Riley pushed through the office door, locking it behind him.

The leopard didn't like that, seeing in it a possession that threatened an integral part of her life. "Ashaya's got something to tell us." Switching the clear screen of her computer to the comm function, she coded in the call.

Riley walked around to stand beside her chair, one arm along the back, fingers grazing the top of her head. She flicked him off, to his surprised expression. When he frowned, she concentrated on the screen, knowing that to him, her behavior had to be inexplicable. "Ashaya, we're ready."

The scientist came on-screen, blue-gray eyes vivid against smooth mocha-dark skin. "Alright," she said, and recapped what she'd already told Mercy. "I've been working with Amara on this in order to speed things up, and we believe we've discovered the purpose of the drug."

"Go on," Mercy said, at the same time that Riley said, "What is it?"

Folding her arms, Mercy leaned back in her chair.

Ashaya looked from one to the other, but didn't ask questions. "We can thank Amara for this. My twin decided that since it appears the targets of this substance are Psy, she'd inject herself." Her hand was shaking when she lifted it to push back her hair—which was secured in two tight braids.

Mercy jerked upright. "Is she okay?"

"Yes, yes. She's fine. Now." Ashaya dropped her hand. "She took a very small amount."

"And?" Riley prompted.

"And she found she couldn't use any of her psychic abilities for five minutes."

Annoyance forgotten, Mercy caught Riley's eye. She saw the same tight excitement in him that she felt in her own gut. Glancing back to Ashaya, she said, "Can we replicate it?"

Ashaya didn't look happy. "It's like a drug that would stop you shifting, Mercy. How can I possibly justify reverse engineering something that painful? Amara would've had a breakdown if I hadn't been linked with her through the entire process."

"Shit, I didn't think of it that way." Mercy rubbed her face. "The thing is, if we had that drug, then we wouldn't have to kill Psy on sight." Right now, there was no talking, no negotiation. If a Psy came after a changeling, the changeling aimed to kill.

"It'd be a deterrent," Riley added.

Ashaya shook her head. "Amara's heart stopped."

Mercy froze. All at once, she remembered the sudden, odd panic she'd felt on patrol a couple of hours earlier. She'd put the fleeting emotion down to her hyperawareness of her surroundings, but what if it had been something else, Ashaya's scream for help? After all, as Dorian's mate, Ashaya was in the Web of Stars, the blood-bonded network that connected Dark-River sentinels to Lucas. "I thought you said she was okay."

"I managed to get it restarted." Trembling fingers pressed to her lips. "Amara couldn't use her abilities for five minutes, but she crashed at the thirty-minute mark. Depending on the dosage, the drug could stop a Psy heart in any time range."

Mercy brushed aside the information for the moment. "I'm going to call Dorian for you."

"He's almost here." Ashaya lifted her hand in silent thanks, even as anger filled her expression. "They likely developed this drug to block Psy powers, but now they're using it to weaken and kill."

"Do you think they know?" Riley asked.

"It has to have been tested. They must've decided the risk was worth it."

"Why?" Riley persisted. "What's the point if the target dies?"

"Given the dosage we found in the darts, if they'd shot me during the kidnapping attempt, they would've had at least a ten-minute window either to give me some kind of an antidote—one that would've neutralized the fatal element—or be ready with equipment to restart the heart." She took a deep breath. "They're being extremely confident about its use, which makes me believe there is an antidote. There was medical equipment in one of the vehicles they drove to the ambush site."

"But no possible trace of an antidote." Mercy shook her head. "I'm more inclined to think they're playing Russian roulette. Hearts don't always restart."

Ashaya nodded. "Either way, the Human Alliance is a real threat." With that, she clicked off.

Riley rose to his full height. "If this drug didn't have lethal side effects, would the ethics worry you?"

She took time to think about it. "It would devastate me if I couldn't shift, but if the hit was temporary, I'd live. Right now, we don't allow any Psy aggressors to live." Because Psy could kill with a single violent mental blow.

"Still, to have a limb or a sense cut off, that's brutal stuff." His words were solemn, his presence intrinsically dominant.

"This is war." A quiet one. A stealthy one—until the Human Alliance had started to take it public. But a war nonetheless. "And a drug like this *could* act as a very strong deterrent, keep the Psy from picking fights." Looking at him, she suddenly knew why she'd reacted so strongly to Lucas's admission, and then to Riley himself. It was a vicious kick to the gut. *Oh, Jesus.* "I have to get back to work. Bye."

"Mercy."

"Go away, wolf." She stood, and strode over to unlock and pull open the door. "Don't push me." An angry truth churned in her, violent and distrustful. Had he known? But she wouldn't ask him that right this moment, when the leopard was riding her with brutal ferocity.

He came to stand toe to toe with her. When he angled his

head for a kiss, she showed him teeth. So he nipped her on the neck instead. Angered at the wildfire that streaked through her at the fleeting caress, she shoved at his chest and sent him out the door. "And don't come back tonight, either. I've got better things to do—"

A hand flat against her door, holding it open. "You're not the kind to blow hot and cold. So what the fuck is this?"

She was so emotionally ravaged by the realization she'd just had that she clawed at him, the words coming out in an unthinking rush. "This is me being real. I'm busy—I don't want to play tonsil hockey. Look, you're okay in the sack, and we work well together, but I need my space. I don't particularly want a man full-time in my life."

His hand fell away. "I guess that's going to make this mating hell for both of us."

CHAPTER 42

The Ghost watched as word spread of the offer of voluntary mild rehabilitation—a process that would strengthen the basis of the conditioning that was Silence. For the first time, going to the Center didn't mean death, but life . . . and people were beginning to seriously consider it. Predictably, the idea appealed most strongly to those with the most dangerous abilities.

The Ghost understood. His own ability could be incredibly destructive. But never would he submit to the M-Psy at the Center. Perhaps Silence was a cage that kept the monsters inside, but it was a cage nonetheless. He knew what it was to grow up inside a cage—a cage so tight, so restrictive that he'd almost forgotten how to breathe.

To willingly embrace the silver bars of another prison was not something he'd ever countenance. But he found himself hesitant to step in the path of those who were making the opposite choice. Did he have the right to turn them away from that which might save them? So many were cracking, breaking, shattering. Murders had increased in the past few months, a slow creep that tainted the Net with darkness. Even at that very moment, violence flickered on the edges of his vision.

That violence had always been a part of the Net, but now it was starting to rise to the surface, to grab control. But there was no symmetry to it, no sense of the scales being balanced. These bursts were like mini eruptions, destroying all in their path. Could he blame those who chose the cage of Silence if chaos was the only alternative?

He realized he didn't have the tools to answer that question.

For the first time, the Ghost, a being of Silence, found he needed answers from someone who understood emotion.

CHAPTER 43

Mercy didn't like feeling like a bitch. And she didn't think of herself as one. But she'd been a bitch to Riley today. Pushing him away like that. Telling him the one thing she'd known would make him back off. Predatory male changelings were *proud.*

And it wasn't as if he'd done anything to provoke her. He'd been acting exactly who he was, and she'd savaged him for it. "Damn it!" She clenched her hands on the steering wheel, feeling worse with every passing second.

Of course he hadn't known and hidden the truth from her. Riley wasn't a liar. He'd never have held back something this important, not when he'd given her his word that he'd try. For her. For a cat who had hurt him so much today.

I guess that's going to make this mating hell for both of us.

Her leopard didn't want that. But neither did it want to face the inevitable repercussion of mating with him. However, one thing was certain—Riley would come after her again. He wouldn't be able to help himself. She was his mate, and given the fever of the mating dance, the depth of his hunger had to be driving him half-insane. So he'd bury his pride and he'd return—probably to shake some sense into her.

Her lips quirked, but she removed her hands from the steering wheel and got out of the car. The SnowDancer den was an easy fifteen-minute run from this point. It was tempting to call and ask him to meet her outside, but that would be cowardly. And Mercy was no coward. Taking a deep breath, and paying no overt attention to the scents that told her she was being watched by an invisible screen of guards, she headed in.

Andrew was waiting for her by the open door. His eyes were twinkling. "Hello, future sister-in-law."

"Out of my way, shrimp."

"My heart bleeds." He put a hand to said heart, melodramatic in the way only younger brothers could be. "Are you the reason Riley almost ripped off my head a few minutes ago?"

"None of your business." She pushed past him. "Show me the way to his quarters."

"Shouldn't you talk to Hawke, make sure it's alright for you to be up here?"

"Drew, today is really not a good day to mess with me."

Andrew walked beside her, pointing left when they reached a fork in the tunnels that made up the den. "In that case, rest assured I'll take care of the formalities."

"Thanks." She shot him a suspicious look. "Why are you being so helpful?"

He shrugged. "I like my brother. And I especially like watching him off balance." An evil grin. "You and he are the best entertainment I've had in years."

"Why hasn't Riley killed you yet?"

"I keep bouncing back." A shrug, wide-eyed innocence.

Charmed despite herself, she came to a stop in front of the door he'd led her to. "Now, listen carefully," she said, leaning close, "if you dare come back here tonight, be prepared to sing soprano the rest of your life. *Capisce?*"

Andrew's eyes widened. "Man, you're scary. Lucky Riley." And she could tell he meant it, too. "I'm outa here." But he paused. "Be gentle with him, Mercy. He's got a heart as big as Texas—he'll die for you without blinking. But he doesn't expect anyone to do the same for him."

Knot in her throat at the unexpected burst of seriousness, she nodded and watched him walk away. Then, straightening her shoulders—and ignoring the large number of wolves who seemed to have something to do in this corridor all of a sudden—she knocked. Riley had to have scented her by now, so the fact that the door had remained closed didn't bode well.

Several seconds passed.

Frowning because such pettiness wasn't like him, she went to knock again when the door was wrenched open and she was pulled inside. Against a warm, wet, very naked male chest. "Oh," she whispered, leaning back against the door he'd shoved shut, "you were in the shower."

Pushing damp hair out of his eyes, he put his hands on either side of her shoulders and said, "What are you doing here?"

She was too interested in the view to reply. He'd hitched a towel around his waist, but it looked precarious. She bit her lip in an effort to fight the urge to accidentally-on-purpose nudge it out of the way. 'Cause Riley all wet and smoldering got her motor running in a serious way. His body was pure muscle, muscle she'd touched more than once, and yet she found her mouth watering as if she'd never seen him before. *Mine,* part of her purred, even as another part threw the solemn ramifications of that thought into her face.

Right then, she didn't care. Because this was her mate. How could she not touch him when he was in front of her? How could she not give him what she knew he needed, the simple skin-to-skin contact they both craved?

"Mercy." The snarl in his voice said the wolf was very much in control.

She went to speak, then decided to hell with it. Framing his face in her hands, she took his mouth in a slow, possessive kiss that made her toes curl. He kissed her back, but his arms remained planted on either side of her body. Still mad. That was okay, she thought, nibbling at his lower lip. Coaxing Riley sounded like a fun night to her. Especially if it involved getting that towel off his body.

His eyes were wolf-amber when she drew back, his cheekbones drawn sharply against his skin. "Come by for an 'okay' time in the sack?"

Not mad. Seriously angry. "Maybe I came to apologize," she said, linking her arms around his neck. "And maybe you'll hear it if you stop snarling at me."

"What, you're going to tell me I'm a better than okay lay?"

Oh, man, but he was pissed. In his defense, she thought, men had a way of becoming that way if you insulted their sexual prowess. And coming from the woman meant to be his mate . . . damn, how was she going to fix this? "Of all the things I've said to you, that's the one you decided to take to heart?"

An unwavering amber stare.

"Damn it, Riley, you know you make me crazy in bed," she said, consigning any attempt at subtlety to Hades.

"Do I?"

"I'm ready for you right now and you know it. My panties are so damp it's embarrassing."

"Oh?" And then he was unsnapping her jeans and one big hand was sliding into said panties, parting her liquid-soft flesh with a single smooth move.

She yelped. *"Riley."*

"Just checking the evidence." His face was implacable, but his skin, his skin burned so hot, she could feel the heat brush against her in lapping waves. "Maybe I want to see it, too."

Her eyes were all but rolling into the back of her head from the exquisite pleasure of his stroking fingers. He knew just how to caress her . . . including how very much it frustrated her to have her clitoris circled but never touched. "Kincaid, you have a mean streak."

"Only around you." He slipped a single finger inside her, teasing her body into moving on him. "You make me act like a damn juvenile."

"Good." Curling her fingers in the damp hair at his nape, she leaned in for another long, wickedly sensual kiss. "Now, stop teasing."

He withdrew his hand.

She moaned. "I didn't mean that! Come back."

"You ready for a full-time man?" Hard words. "Because I don't do part-time."

"Neither do I." Her words had been said in anger, thoughtless, unmeant.

"I haven't heard an apology yet."

"Oh, God, Riley." She ran her hands over his chest. "You're an incredible lover. Now, can I play with your beautiful cock?"

He blinked and the wolf retreated to show the man. "Christ, Mercy."

But she was already pushing that damn towel to the floor to expose him. Her breath came out in a shuddering sigh as she closed her hand around the rigid length of him. "Oh, I have plans for this gorgeous thing."

Riley jerked in her hand, his next words a growl. "Give me your mouth." The kiss was wild, untamed, real. They were both breathing in jagged gasps by the time it ended, and she was sliding her hand up and down his length in desperate need. It didn't surprise her when her clothes ended up shredded on the floor and Riley lifted her up against the door.

"My boots," she muttered.

"Hot," Riley muttered, tugging away her hand so he could grip her hips and ease her onto him slow and easy.

Trembling, she held on to his shoulders and decided she'd died and gone to heaven. The man was simply magnificent—possessiveness, dominance, and all. He was also hers. If only she could figure a way out of the minefield between them.

Riley stroked his hand through the silky red hair spread across his chest. It was a kick to the gut to see Mercy here, in his domain. The wolf wanted to bite her again, not to hurt, never to hurt. Just to make sure she really was here.

Then she stirred, scratching her claws lightly over his skin in lazy affection. "I still have my boots on."

He grinned. "A naked redhead with her boots on. Nirvana."

"Smart-ass." A kiss pressed over his heartbeat, a hand stroking across his chest, playing with his chest hairs in a way that was very feline. Petting him, he thought. She was petting him. He wasn't a man anyone petted. But coming from his mate . . . he relaxed into it, content.

"Riley, about this afternoon."

"We're square, kitty cat." More than square. Never in a million years had he thought that wild, untamable Mercy would come to him.

But she gave a frustrated sigh and sat up, pushing her hair off her face. When he couldn't help but stare at her beautiful breasts, she growled in her throat and flipped the long strands back over them.

He looked up, scowling. "Now what?"

"Have you thought through the consequences of our mating, Riley? Have you?" She poked a finger into his chest. "One of us is going to have to break from our pack. One of us is going to have to cut out our heart." *Her.* She was the one who'd have to break. She knew that beyond any shadow of a doubt . . . because Riley *was* just a fraction older, just a fraction more dominant. Not enough to change the dynamic of their relationship, but more than enough to rip her from Dark-River.

"We'll still be close physically—"

"That's bullshit. You know it and I know it." Fisting her hands, she thumped them on her thighs. "DarkRiver is as much a part of my soul as SnowDancer is yours. Sentinels don't leave their packs, not unless they choose to follow a new alpha. Neither do lieutenants."

"We have an alliance," Riley said, feeling a chill creep up his back. "There's no reason for either of us to break from our packs."

"But we will! Soon as we mate, for one of us, the connection to our alpha, to our pack, the blood bond, will break. We'll feel it right here." Mercy slammed a fist into her heart. Because he understood her—damn it—he didn't say it, but she knew he was as aware as she was that it would be her.

"You're not going to give up your mate to stay in your pack." Ground out through clenched teeth.

She couldn't argue with him. "No." Having a mate was a gift, a brilliance of being. "But it'll destroy a part of me. I won't be the same woman. I'll be less." That was what had so terrified her this afternoon, the recognition that to be with this man, with her mate, she'd have to give up not only her pack . . . but part of herself. "I don't know if my leopard can accept that."

Riley swore, then reached out to close a hand over hers. The leopard snarled, making her jerk back in reflex. His mouth tightened. "You're not just a leopard, Mercy, you're human, too. You won't be less—you'll adapt."

"I might be human," she said, aching to touch him, yet angry with him at the same time, "but I'm also a pack animal. I'm not a loner, Riley. I never have been. I can't be whole without my pack." She sucked in a breath. "If it had been another leopard pack, it would've hurt like hell but I think my cat would've learned to adapt. But to come into a pack of wolves—"

"If that happens, if yours is the bond that breaks," Riley said, sitting up to face her, "SnowDancer will treat you as its own, you know that. You *know*."

"The woman understands," she said softly, breaking his heart with her sorrow, "but the leopard doesn't. All it knows is that if I take my wolf, I might lose everything else that ever mattered."

CHAPTER 44

The next morning, by mutual agreement, Mercy and Riley drove to meet Nash down the road from Nate and Tamsyn's house. The entire Baker family was staying there while their home was being fitted up with all sorts of high-tech security.

The drive was quiet. Neither of them mentioned the painful truth they'd talked about in the den, but the fact that they hadn't been apart since the night before . . . well, it spoke for itself.

"Thanks for meeting me out here," Nash said, taking a seat at a picnic table in the backyard of Zach and Annie's house—the couple had already left for the day, but Zach had called Mercy with the location of the hidden key. Using that key, she'd put on the coffee while Riley escorted Nash over. She'd figured the boy would do better with a male.

Now she put three empty mugs on the table as Riley headed in to bring out the insulated pitcher. "You didn't want to worry your parents, right?"

A nod from the young man across from her. Brown eyed,

with hair a few shades lighter, he was good-looking in a gentle kind of way. But there was an underlying toughness to him, the lynx within.

"Coffee." Riley poured and grabbed a seat. "I'm going to cut to the chase, Nash. It's been a week and we're still not clear on why the Alliance targeted you rather than any number of more experienced researchers. MIT's playing the commercial sensitivity card and you haven't exactly been cooperative, either."

"Secrecy's vital to our funding." Nash met Mercy's eyes. "We all had to sign complex nondisclosure agreements."

Given the alacrity with which the lynx had agreed to this meet, Mercy had a feeling he simply hadn't wanted to say anything in a medium that could be recorded or traced back to him. "Okay, I get that," Mercy said. "But we need to calculate the odds of another attempt—whether by humans, changelings, or Psy. It'll affect not only the security arrangements we make for you, but your family's as well."

Nash didn't even take a moment to think about it. "Odds are very high. Any of the three, but changelings probably not so much."

"Damn, that's what I was afraid of." Mercy chewed on her lower lip. "This company that's sponsoring you, will they pay for bodyguards?"

"I think so."

Riley nodded, as if following Mercy's line of thought. "We'll provide the bodyguards."

"You would anyway," Nash said. Then smiled. "But the sponsor doesn't have to know that. The pack might as well get paid for protecting my ass."

Mercy grinned. He was okay, was Nash. "They're also the most likely source of the leak."

"Yeah. I had a call from the managing director to say they're going through all personnel who might have links to the Human Alliance."

"Good." Riley tapped a finger against his coffee mug. "This company—your gut reaction?"

Nash's face turned serious. "They're out to make money, but they're willing to put in the hard time funding research that might never go anywhere. I figure that's fair."

Mercy agreed. "Their ethics?"

"They've agreed that if I'm successful, they'll allow medical use at cost or less if possible. Everyone else will pay a premium." Nash met Mercy's eyes. "The owner's daughter has a condition that might be helped by my work. Believe me, he won't withhold it from other kids. He's one of the good guys."

That convinced Mercy as nothing else could've done. Heart, love, it had a way of fighting off darkness. "I have to admit I'm curious as anything about what you're doing, but I understand commercial sensitivity. We can work with what we've got."

Nash thrust a hand through his hair. "When I started, I didn't realize all the implications. I was thinking of purely medical use, but, well . . . everyone wants to be stronger."

Mercy went motionless at the oblique hint. "No wonder the Alliance wants you." She despised their tactics, but could see what drove them. Humans were the weakest of the three races—Psy were weaker physically, but had psychic abilities to compensate. If humans could at least level the playing field so they had changeling strength . . . yeah, she could see the temptation.

"It's a very long-term project," Nash told her. "I think the Alliance thinks we have functioning prototypes. We're nowhere near close."

"But you're on the right track," Riley said. "Enough to make you a serious target."

Another shy grin. "Good thing I have leopards and wolves on my side, then."

In a van parked on a street packed with tourists out to sample the area's world-famous crabs, several screens came to life. "We have eyes on Nikita Duncan," said the operator.

His partner watched the Councilor enter the office building and—frustratingly—take the stairs to the mezzanine floor, where she apparently had a meeting, judging from the focus with which she walked toward the first door on the left. "Damn."

"Don't worry. She'll move."

"It wasn't supposed to be like this—we were meant to act when we *knew* what her exact movements would be."

"We're still on schedule."

"But we lost hours trying to keep ahead of the wolves and cats. Our reconnaissance wasn't anywhere near as good as it should've been." A pause. "Maybe we shouldn't have killed the information broker."

"It's done now."

"Yeah."

"Anyway, the chairman seems to have some kind of a top source of his own—he's been giving us good tips."

"Hmm." A pause. "What a waste."

"Huh?"

The man shrugged and brought up a screenshot of Nikita Duncan's form. "Look at that face, those cheekbones, those legs." The Councilor had an exotic mix of Irish, Japanese, and Russian blood and had inherited the best from all sides. Tall and lithe, she had the almond eyes of a goddess, and the kind of silky hair men liked to see on their pillow. "Too bad she's a heartless bitch."

"She'll be a dead bitch soon enough."

Mercy was meant to be doing a shift on the continuing security patrols in the city, but after she and Riley went their separate ways, she asked Clay to cover for her so she could drive to Tammy's. She'd deliberately picked the one sentinel who wouldn't ask questions, but to her surprise, he gave her a narrow-eyed glance and stroked the back of one hand over her cheek. "You okay?"

Surprised by the affection from a leopard who'd been all but stone a few months ago, she felt every one of her emotions threaten to come to the surface. Damming the storm back with effort, she touched his hand in thanks. "I will be."

He let her go without further comment, but she knew he'd be keeping an eye on her. It made her cat settle—today, she needed the comfort of Pack, of knowing she was part of a cohesive and vital unit. How could she possibly exist without the blood bond that tied her to DarkRiver so fundamentally?

When she arrived at Tammy's, the healer took one look at her and dragged her into the kitchen. "What's the matter?"

"The Bakers?"

"Gone exploring in the woods. They've got an escort. My babies are at playgroup. Now talk."

She just blurted it out. "If I mate with Riley, will we be able to have kids?" It was another part of the dream, something she'd always imagined. If she couldn't . . . it would hurt, no doubt about it.

"Of course you will," Tammy said at once. "I've been researching that ever since you two showed an interest in each other. Inter-changeling unions between predatory species aren't that common, so the info is scattered and incomplete."

Relieved, Mercy rocked back on her heels. "It's because the animal prefers its own kind."

"Yeah." Tammy leaned over and took Mercy's hand, eyes shining. "But sometimes, the human heart loves so deeply that it overcomes the objections of the animal."

Mercy felt a knot form in her throat.

"I'm so glad you have that," Tammy continued. "Of all the sentinels, it's you I worried most about."

Startled, she stared. "Me? Why?" When Clay had almost gone rogue and Dorian had come close to self-destructing? "I'm probably more stable than anyone but Lucas."

"Exactly," the healer said. "People tend to ignore the ones who seem okay. And we shouldn't. You're an integral part of the pack, and I worried that we'd left you too much on your own."

Mercy rolled her eyes. "You worry way too much. Shall I tell you how alone I've been lately?" She didn't wait for an answer, pulling out a chair and turning it around to sit with her arms on the back while Tammy perched on a stool at the counter. "Ever since word got out about me and Riley, I've had an uncountable number of teenage girls sidle up to me and ask if wolves are good lovers."

Tammy choked. "No!"

"Oh, yes. Their eyes, they are wandering."

"Oh, dear God." Tammy looked torn between horror and laughter. "If the teenagers start dating, Hawke and Lucas will both have aneurysms."

"Oh, you haven't heard the best part." She paused. "An entire pack of male juveniles cornered me the other day to ask if I didn't think leopards were good enough for me."

Tammy rubbed her forehead. "I think I have a headache."

"You don't get to have a headache. Only I get to have a headache." She tried to keep a straight face. "When I pointed out that I could gut them all with a butter knife but that I might have difficulty doing the same to Riley, they turned green. You might have to pet a few later on—I think I scared them off sex with leopard females."

Tammy was looking a bit green herself. "Do I want to know more?"

"Probably not." She ran a hand over her face. "Enough stalling, Tammy. Will my babies shift?"

"Yes, absolutely." Hopping off the stool, she went around the counter to pour some coffee. "I didn't realize you were concerned about that."

"I heard that when two different changelings mate, the animals cancel each other out and the child can't shift."

"Old wives' tale." Tammy made a face as she brought the cups to the table. "Makes no sense genetically. Genes don't cancel each other out."

"But some are recessive and others aren't," Mercy said. "How's that work with changelings?"

"We screw up those neat genome charts the biologists like to keep," Tamsyn said.

"So we don't know what'll happen?"

"No. We do. All healers keep extensive records, and I've been on the phone and on e-mail with hundreds of healers across the world over the past few days." She took a sip of coffee. "We're pretty sure what goes on, even though scientifically, we have no proof."

"I'll take healers over science any day." Especially when it came to changeling genetics. They confused normal scientists. Having been best friends with Dorian since childhood, she knew that better than most—the other sentinel had been born latent, unable to shift into the animal form that was his other half. His parents had taken him to the best M-Psy out there. None had been able to help. It had needed a woman locked into his very soul to do that.

"Okay." Tammy put down her coffee and took a deep breath. "You know how you and Riley are always fighting over dominance?"

Mercy nodded.

"Yeah, well, your babies are going to have the final word on the subject."

Mercy stared at Tammy. "How final?"

"Very. When two changelings of different species mate, it's the more dominant one in the pair whose genes are expressed as far as shifting goes." Tammy's eyes gleamed with hidden laughter. "Of course, no one knows when things get set in stone—it might depend on who's feeling more feral the day you conceive."

Mercy's hand fisted even as wonder bloomed inside of her at the thought of carrying a child. "We're not bonded yet." There would be no babies until her leopard accepted Riley without boundaries, without conditions, with absolute trust.

"I guessed . . . do you want to talk about why?"

"No. We're dealing with it. I'm just glad to know if we do make it through, our babies will be able to shift."

"You don't mind that your kids might not shift into cats?"

"They'll shift. That's what matters." She squeezed Tammy's hand, knowing the healer understood. "Dorian never talked about it—he's so fucking male—but I know how much it hurt him not to be able to go leopard. I've been way more worried about whether or not my kids *would* shift, than what they'd shift into."

* * *

On the other side of the world, Councilor Kaleb Krychek drove home through the pitch black of night on the outskirts of Moscow. Putting his vehicle on automatic navigation half an hour from his destination, he used his organizer to connect to the house's security node—he always checked his defenses before he ever entered the zone he considered safe. He had no personnel at his home, no one who could betray him. But the entire area around his property was alarmed and protected. He knew if a butterfly landed on his balcony.

He also knew when people had been creeping around where they shouldn't be.

Tapping into the full security logs, he saw the presence of a number of bodies a hundred feet beyond his outer perimeter. Of course, that wasn't his actual perimeter. He'd set alarm lines well into the fields that surrounded his isolated home, all the way to, and *across*, the properties of his neighbors.

Kaleb liked his privacy.

He double-checked the data. No way to tell if the people lying in wait were human, Psy, or changeling. Their estimated body weight tilted them toward non-Psy, as Psy of the same size and height had a slightly lower bone density. He rechecked the data for the third time, putting it through the filters of his own mind.

He knew the BlackEdge pack—the wolves that controlled the greater Moscow area as far as changelings were concerned. Selenka Durev, their alpha, didn't like him, but she was willing to work with him to keep the city peaceful, so long as he kept his nose out of her business. The agreement worked because Kaleb had no interest in changeling affairs—though he kept a very close eye on Selenka and her pack. Wolves were smart, dangerous, and could be lethal adversaries, as Nikita Duncan had discovered in her own region.

His agreement with BlackEdge had put him in close contact with several changelings. He was a Tk, used to manipulating kinetic energy. He'd watched their movements, noted the way their muscles and bones shifted without even realizing he'd taken in the data. Now he compared those movements against the intruders.

Not wolves. And not bears, either, the other major group in the area. At present, the StoneWater clan had a wary truce with BlackEdge. The bear changelings moved less gracefully, but with a distinctive style that was as good as a brand. Neither matched. And since both BlackEdge and StoneWater would kill any other changelings who came into their territory without permission, that meant this was most likely a human assault force.

He looked up through the windshield, the entire security check having taken him only three minutes. The next question was—what did they want? Surveillance had to be the answer, as there was no way they could get past his security. He glanced at his organizer and pulled up the data again.

And saw what he'd missed in the first sweep.

Humans had learned to compensate for their lack of psychic or shifting abilities. Especially in the area of weapons. The portable guided missile launchers almost hidden in the mass of body heat were likely primed and ready to level his house the instant he stepped inside. A fast, quick kill. The only way to take a cardinal Tk by surprise. Too bad he knew they were there.

CHAPTER 45

Several hours after the wrench of leaving him, Mercy tracked Riley to the former Alliance hideout on the Embarcadero. His wolf flashed into his eyes when he saw her, and it was all she could do not to press close, and simply savor the warm masculine scent of him.

It wasn't professionalism that held her back. It was the knowledge that to do what she craved would be to torment them both. "What're you doing here?" she asked.

"I always do a pass through here in case one of them doesn't realize it's been made. Might get a new trail." His gaze never moved off her, his jaw a brutally hard line.

Such control had to hurt.

She couldn't let him hurt. Closing the distance between them, she stood so they brushed shoulder to thigh. He sucked in a breath, his hand shifting to lie on her lower back. "I can't be near you and not touch."

She nodded. "Who were we kidding?" The humor was fragile, the truth inescapable. "But that's not why I came."

Riley watched as his cat took out a small datapad and pulled up a map of the city proper. "Something bugs me about the tips we've had about possible Alliance movements." She overlaid the map with the location of those tips. "If we remove the clear outliers, and focus *only* on the tips that really had some substance behind them, we end up with this."

He leaned in, until the wildfire vitality of her filled his every breath. "A very rough circle." He studied the diagram. "It's still a massive area. Includes the warehouse Bowen and his group are using."

"I know, but all this"—she waved a hand—"the bomb making, the cloak-and-dagger stuff—seems too coordinated for a small hit like that." She pulled out a laser pen and began making *X*s. "If it's revenge they're after, for the squad we took out, they could hit our pack HQ, the central CTX station, a couple of other places, but most of our stuff is spread farther out—toward Yosemite."

"You think it has to do with the Psy. That corpse?"

"Yes, and because then, the centralization makes sense. Plenty of Psy targets in the city." She annotated major Psy institutions, including banks and, nauseatingly, schools.

He knew why—the Alliance had given them no reason to believe it had a conscience.

"But why San Francisco?" he asked, playing devil's advocate. "It's not a logical choice—we know to be on the lookout for them. We've already disrupted their operations to a degree."

Mercy pursed her lips in a way the wolf found fascinating. He'd never seen that expression before, never seen that facet of her. "A particular target?" She shook her head almost at once. "There's nothing unique about these places. They're important and it'll cause chaos on a major scale if they go down, but the Alliance could find the same caliber of target in New York, Los Angeles, a dozen other cities."

The wolf came to attention. "But we do have one thing no other city does." Taking the pen, he put an *X* on one of San Francisco's most well-known buildings.

"Nikita?" Mercy's mouth dropped open. "No."

"What better way to leave a mark?"

"Flaming idiots!" she yelled, igniting without warning.

"Whoever the fuck is driving this operation needs to have their head examined, preferably after it's been ripped off! No way would anyone be this much of an imbecile!"

To Mercy's surprise, Riley chuckled and leaned down to press a kiss against her parted lips. "God, my mom would've loved you."

Her heart almost stopped. "Riley?"

"She was a lieutenant," he told her, his voice husky. "So was my dad. They died defending the pack."

She turned to wrap her arms around him. "They were protectors."

"Yeah." He nuzzled into her neck, as if soaking in her scent. "My dad, he was the strongest man I ever knew, but he used to turn to putty in Mom's hands."

"That sounds like the perfect mating."

He chuckled. "You'd like that, wouldn't you?"

"Damn straight." Kissing his neck, and smiling at his responsive shiver, she hugged him extra tight. "I think your mom and dad would've been so proud of the man you've become. If I ever have a son," she whispered, "I want him to be like you."

He shuddered. "We'll figure it out, kitty cat. Somehow."

She was about to respond when her cell phone rang.

A tenseness filled his body. It was gone an instant later. "Answer it," he said. "You're a sentinel."

The leopard batted at him with playful humor. "Damn, but you're trying to be good, Kincaid."

"Glad you noticed."

His hands settled around her hips as she dug out her phone. "Hello?"

"This is Bo. Lucas told me to call you directly if I found anything."

It was a vote of confidence from her alpha and she appreciated it. "What have you got?" She slapped a hand on Riley's chest when he started to growl, having heard Bowen because of the way they were pasted together.

"I think I know why they're building bombs."

She dug her claws into Riley this time, shooting him a

"hush" look. He winced and toned it down; however, she could all but feel his need to tear Bowen's throat out with his bare hands. "How good is your intel?"

"Good but not foolproof. The chairman's been known to shut others out of the loop."

"Who's the target?"

"Not target. Target*s*." And then he told her the names.

Mercy closed the phone and stared at Riley. "Someone *is* that much of an imbecile. I don't believe it."

"If he's right and they succeed, it'll plunge the world into wholesale war." Riley was already pulling out his cell. "I'll call Faith."

Mercy nodded and pressed the quickcode for Sascha. "Pick up, Sascha. Pick up."

Sascha closed the cell phone and swallowed. It rang in her hand moments later. "Lucas?"

"Sascha, I can feel you hurting. What is it?"

And that quickly, her terror was buried under a flood of love. "I need to get hold of Nikita." She relayed what Mercy had told her.

"Damn." A pause. "You want me to call?"

"No, I'll do it. I'll call you after." Hanging up, she coded in a number she'd never expected to use again.

Nikita answered on the first ring. "You got my package."

"It's not about that." She kept her tone even with effort—Nikita didn't understand her daughter's emotional nature. She probably never would. But she was still Sascha's mother. "We've had a tip that Councilors have all been targeted for assassination. Check the building for explosives."

It was a reflection of the world she lived in that Nikita didn't argue, just hung up after telling Sascha she'd get back to her. Shaking from the impact of that short conversation, the first nonbusiness one she'd had with Nikita since her mother disowned her, Sascha slid down the aerie wall and to the floor. Tremors shifted over her body from head to foot.

She wanted Lucas. *I need you.* A thought sent through the

mating bond, needy and vulnerable. It was as if she'd lost all her strength, become the fractured creature she'd been after she first learned what had been done to her, how her gift had been stifled, her mind almost destroyed. *Lucas.*

Her mate's love moved to surround her, comfort her, hold her. She closed her eyes and wrapped that feeling around her very senses, cocooning herself in the savage wildness of him. But a footstep sounded on the balcony what felt like an instant later, breaking her concentration. She looked up to see a striking blond male with the mark of a sentinel tattooed onto his arm. And she knew Lucas had sent him.

Dorian sat down beside her. "Hey." When he put his arm around her shoulders, she resisted. "Come on, Sascha darling." A gentle tease. "You've helped me more times than I can count. Just think of me as Luc's stand-in."

Softening, she let him hug her. "What about Ashaya?" The other woman was both Psy and newly mated. She might not understand that at this moment, Dorian was simply giving a packmate what she needed to hold herself together until her mate got to her.

"She's seen inside me, seen how you helped me stay sane—"

"You did that yourself." He'd always been impossibly strong.

He squeezed her. "I'm saying she understands. She's the one who sent me to you."

"I thought Lucas?"

"I got his call after Shaya's. She felt something from you in the Net." He rubbed his cheek over her hair. "We get to look after you sometimes."

Giving in, she turned into his hold, but other than asking him to call Vaughn to make sure Faith had gotten a message to her father, she said nothing . . . not until Lucas appeared in the doorway. She was barely aware of Dorian leaving, her eyes focused on Lucas. He was sweating, his T-shirt soaked. Tearing it off, he threw it to the side and scooped her up into his lap as he sat down on one of the huge cushions that served as their sofas.

Once, she would've considered her need for him a flaw, a weakness. Today, she all but crawled into him, the scent of him as familiar to her as the sound of her own heartbeat.

"I'm all sweaty," he murmured some time later.

She pressed a kiss to the side of his neck. "You look good sweaty." Laying her head on his shoulder, she sighed. "You must've broken a few speed records getting here." He'd been in the city office, which meant he'd driven as far into the forest as he could, then run the rest of the way on foot.

"We'll be paying fines till the next century." A stroke down her back. "You okay?"

"It hit me hard. Hearing her voice." She swallowed. "I've been avoiding any business meetings with her lately and you've been letting me."

"We all get a few free passes." Another stroke. "She say anything to hurt you?"

"No. She's checking for explosives." A tear streaked down her cheek even as she finished that sentence. "What's *wrong* with me?" Frustrated, she dashed away the streak of wet. "I'm not this weak! I'm an alpha's mate!"

"Hey." Lucas grabbed her fisted hand. "You had a shock, the adrenaline's probably still screaming through your system."

"No." She shook her head, scowling even as another tear escaped her control. "This is too much. I'm not this fragile, not anymore." And it was true. She should've been able to handle Nikita without falling apart. "My emotions have been seesawing all over the place the past few days."

Lucas went very quiet against her. Then he buried his face in the curve of her neck and breathed deep. The joy that shot through her an instant later was so pure, so beautiful, and so utterly protective that she turned in his arms, eyes wide. "How can you know?"

His smile was fierce. "I know." His arm tightened as one hand spread over her abdomen. *"I know."*

Putting down the briefcase he'd carried in, Kaleb took off his suit jacket and removed his tie before opening the first few buttons on his shirt and rolling up his sleeves. He never ever did the latter while outside his home.

No one could be allowed to see the mark on his forearm. Most would have no idea what it meant. Perhaps no one would know. But the PsyNet was the biggest data archive in the world—he couldn't take the chance that someone, somewhere, knew the story behind the mark. The room had been processed by Enforcement, after all. There had to be pictures, though they wouldn't have found DNA. Santano Enrique had been too careful for that. And he'd taught Kaleb everything he knew.

Now, having neutralized the threat from the humans, Kaleb considered his next move. The men had been from the Human Alliance, but unfortunately, he hadn't been able to tear their secrets from their minds. First, they'd had some kind of a block, and second, the instant he eliminated the first, the others had all been killed by remote.

He looked at the chip in his hand. Each intruder had had one in the back of his neck. Clearly, it was equipped with some kind of a suicide strategy—or perhaps murder was more apt. But why would the Alliance target Kaleb? Not that their reasoning mattered. The assassins had signed their death warrants the instant they set out to destroy the house.

Because this wasn't truly Kaleb's house. He was only a caretaker. And he took his responsibility very, very seriously.

Mercy got off the phone with Vaughn and blew out a breath. "Faith's father is safe," she told Riley as they stood in the driveway to her parents' home. Dinner had come up on them so fast, they'd hardly had time to shower—luckily, Riley had begun to carry an overnight bag in his vehicle. Mercy's cat was a little leery of that hint of permanency, but not enough to take a step back. Not now. Not when the vines around her heart had grown so fiercely strong. "They found explosives at a building where Anthony was supposed to have a meeting at tonight."

Riley glanced at her, eyes contemplative. "How about Nikita?"

"A charge hidden in the elevator shaft—the working theory is that someone hacked into the surveillance system, intending to detonate the charge once Nikita was inside. Since she lives on the penthouse floor, it was a smart plan."

Riley shook his head. "How is she still alive?"

"Blind luck. She made an unplanned trip to New York last night, and went straight from the airport into negotiations on the mezzanine floor when she got back today. The other party kept her longer than estimated. Almost certainly saved her life."

"Judd hasn't been able to get in touch with his contact, but we should get more information when he does."

"Never thought we'd be helping Councilors stay alive." Mercy reached over to brush away a lock of hair that had fallen across his face in a gesture that seemed exquisitely familiar, exquisitely theirs. Heat arced through her fingertips, and it took her a second to realize she'd closed the distance between them until their bodies met.

"You're connected to Nikita and Anthony through Sascha and Faith," Riley said, his hands closing over her hips. "You couldn't let a packmate lose a parent."

"No," she agreed, wondering what he'd say if he knew Anthony's true loyalties, wishing she could tell him. "But I think I'd have done the same even if we didn't have Faith and Sascha in the pack—after Marshall Hyde's recent assassination, I don't think the world could survive the shock of losing a second Councilor."

He stood there and let her run her fingers through his hair, over his jaw, along his lips. "You're right," he said, eyes going wolf on her. "Much as I hate the Council's guts, the Psy are still the most influential race on the planet—if they crash and burn, we'll all pay the price."

"And the Net's not ready," Mercy said. "That's what Sascha, Faith, and Ashaya all say. Too much too soon and millions of innocents could die."

"It's like the Alliance *wants* to destabilize the world."

Putting both arms around him, she drew in the scent of him until it was in her very veins, twined with her own. "My theory—someone smart but morally corrupt has a thirst for power."

"Much easier to become king if the world's in chaos," Riley said, his lips brushing her own as his hands pressed her flush against his muscular frame.

"Hmm." She was rapidly losing interest in the conversation, far more—

"Get a room!"

CHAPTER 46

Mercy released Riley to turn and face her middle brother as he lounged in the doorway. "You have something to say, Herb?"

"I can't believe you're smooshing faces with a wolf," came the acerbic comment. "You really that hard up?"

Growling low in her throat, she ran toward him, aware of Riley's bitten-off curse as he followed. Sage, the idiot, had taken off through the house to come to a standstill behind their mother's petite figure. Mercy skidded to a stop on the kitchen tiles and pointed a finger. "Wuss."

Sage stuck out his tongue from behind their mother, wrapping his arms around her waist as she stood shredding lettuce into a salad bowl. "That was so easy, Mercy. You must be seriously hormonal—ouch!" He raised a hand to rub at his left temple—where their mother had reached up to pull his hair. "What was that for?"

"For being a brat," Lia Smith said without stopping in her task. "Sometimes, I think you're all still in short pants."

"Only when we come here," Bas drawled from the back

doorway. "It's like I enter this house, and boom, I lose twenty years."

Mercy, adrenaline lowering now that Sage had gotten his comeuppance, found that she'd somehow ended up leaning against Riley as he stood with his back to a wall, his hand a rough warmth along her arm. He was petting her, calming her. Doing what a mate did.

Awash in bittersweet joy, she looked at Bas. "Where's Grey?"

"Right here." Her youngest brother came in through the kitchen doorway with her father. "Hi, Riley."

"Hi."

Her eyes narrowed when no one bothered to introduce themselves. Even her father just gave a curt nod and kissed Mercy on the cheek before going to his mate. She looked at Bas. "Did you four gang up on Riley?"

Absolute silence in the kitchen except for her mother's exasperated breath. "Michael T. Smith, I told you to leave the boy alone."

The "boy" held her tighter against him, obviously not the least bit worried. "I'm fine, Mrs. Smith. And I have a sister, too."

Lia turned her gaze on Riley. "Good God, Mercy. You brought another one into the family?"

And Mercy knew it would be a good night, no matter the worry that continued to pierce her heart.

Sascha stared at Tamsyn in the rosy evening glow. "You're sure?"

"Sascha, darling," Tamsyn said with teasing patience, "it's a pregnancy test, not rocket science. Even if it wasn't positive, the fact that Lucas says you are is gold—you're probably around two weeks along. That's when males tend to pick it up."

"He told me my scent's changed, that my body's already shaping itself to accommodate the new life in my womb." His eyes had glittered with protective emotion, his soul there for her to see.

"A mate always knows," Tammy said with a gentle smile. "The rest of the pack will begin to pick it up now that he has."

"How?"

"Something happens when the male member of a pair knows—it's like his protectiveness coats you, and your own scent changes with it, to something unique, something that speaks of life newly begun."

Life. Sascha laid a fluttering hand over her abdomen. "I still can't quite believe it." A soft warmth lay curled in her belly, a presence that she sensed with every empathic sense in her. It was a spark now. No, a tiny fraction of a spark. So tiny that she had to focus all of her power to feel it. "I never expected to be a mother." Perhaps that's why she hadn't understood what her body had been trying to tell her.

Tamsyn looked surprised. "Really? But you love children."

"Yes." She reached out for Tammy's hand, wanting to share the depth of her joy. "But when I was in the Net, when I thought I was flawed, I swore I'd never submit a child of mine to that kind of an existence."

Tammy leaned forward to kiss her lightly on the cheek. A gift. A comfort. "You're not in the Net any longer."

"And," a deep male voice said from the doorway, "you were never flawed."

She raised her head to look into the face of the panther who was her heartbeat, and now, the father of their unborn child. "You were supposed to stay downstairs."

"Yeah," Tammy said, even as she released Sascha's hands and walked to the doorway, "this was a girls-only session."

A slow smile crossed Lucas's face. "I wonder if it'll be a girl."

Tammy passed him, brushing her fingers over his arm in an affectionate gesture. "Way too early to tell."

Lucas stayed in position after Tammy left, his green eyes stroking a caress over her. "Scared?"

"Yes." She didn't know how to be a mother. "Nikita was hardly a good role model."

"I'm scared, too."

"You're the alpha of the pack," she said, finding they'd somehow moved toward each other without realizing it. "You're only saying that to make me feel better."

He took her hand, placed it over his heart. "Listen."

It was jagged, touched with a tinge of sheer terror. "Why?" she whispered.

"My parents were wonderful," he told her, continuing to hold her hand. "But they couldn't protect me. It terrifies me that I won't be able to protect our child."

She shook her head, pressed her hand more firmly against him. "They died fighting for you. If that's the legacy we leave our child, that child will grow up knowing he or she was loved, loved so completely."

"Such faith in me, kitten." He cupped her cheek with his free hand, his touch warm, wonderfully familiar. "Have the same in yourself."

Leaning into him, she drank in the beat of his heart. "Give me a few months. I have to study the mother thing."

"Ah, Sascha." He laughed, and the sound of it wrapped around her like a sensual blanket. "I'm sure you'll have a graduate degree in it by the time the kid decides to pop out."

She fisted her hand and thumped him on the chest, fighting the smile that threatened to edge her lips. "Don't tease."

He kissed her, a quick, wild burst of easy male affection that echoed down the mating bond. "I'll take you to the book-store."

"Will you read the books?"

"I won't have to—you'll read them to me." He smiled and it was a slow, feline curve of his lips. "I do love the things you say in bed."

She burst out laughing, the emotional chaos of the day buried under the incandescence of their mingled joy.

Everyone was early to the Council meeting. "Are we all secure?" Nikita asked.

There was a round of confirmations.

Kaleb asked the next question. "We need to have an idea of what they're capable of. I'm willing to share what I found—I'm assuming I was the hardest to get to?"

"Correct," Ming responded. "Your teleportation abilities made you the most difficult target. However, Tatiana is also close to impossible to get to without warning."

Kaleb had heard rumors the other Psy could strip shields, enter any mind she chose. She hadn't yet broken his shields, and he made sure never to be anything but absolutely guarded against her. "Tatiana?"

"I see no harm in sharing the information," the other Councilor said. "Downloading the details now."

Streams of silvery data began to flow against the pure blackness that was the psychic vault of the Council chambers. Kaleb caught the vital facts on the first pass. "They planned to poison you."

"It appears that way," Tatiana said. "It's difficult to fully guard against insects in my part of Australia. The perpetrators released a number of toxic funnel-web spiders around my property."

"That strategy has a high chance of failure," Shoshanna pointed out.

"Yes," Tatiana agreed. "From what I discovered afterward, I think it was an opportunistic ploy after their first one failed. I was meant to be on a private jet to Papua New Guinea today—that jet, I'm now told, developed mysterious engine failure and crashed into the ocean, killing all on board."

"How did they get to the jet?" Kaleb asked. "I assume it was yours?"

"That's a critical security breach—I know it wasn't any of my people." Her tone of voice made it clear how she knew. "We're still working on it."

Kaleb decided to speak next. "They attempted to blow up my house from a distance." He gave them the necessary facts without betraying his own security protocols.

One by one, the others laid out their data. Surprisingly, it was Ming who'd come the closest to being killed. The assassins had made no attempts at stealth for the most militarily inclined Councilor. Instead, they'd fired at his armored vehicle using high-explosive antitank rounds. The car was so much twisted metal. The sole reason Ming was alive was because one of his Arrows, a true teleporter, had been with him at the time. Vasic had blinked everyone out of the vehicle in the minuscule fragment of time after the rounds hit.

"We have a leak," Kaleb said after scanning the data. "Someone in the upper tiers."

"The body of a man who was known to sell sensitive information washed up yesterday," Nikita told them. "I had it sent to the lab for processing."

"I agree with Kaleb," Ming said. "Even a top-level information thief couldn't have discovered *all* our locations on a particular day and time without massive effort—even if he was the conduit, he needed to have sources."

"The other option," Nikita pointed out, "is that this was a long-term plan. They watched and waited for the perfect opportunity."

"Possible," Henry agreed, speaking for the first time. "With the recent defections, they consider us weak."

"That's their mistake." Kaleb would allow no one to shatter that which he considered his. And for now, the PsyNet needed his fellow Councilors. When it no longer did . . .

"Perhaps, instead of speculating, we should reconvene once we have further details of the attacks." Shoshanna.

"We do have another issue to discuss," Kaleb pointed out. "The programmed violence. It's stopped."

A pause of several seconds as the other Councilors brought up their files. Tatiana was the first to speak. "Councilor Krychek is correct. All the most recent interpersonal violence has been one on one, or in families. No cases with the potential for mass fatalities."

"The timing is certainly fortuitous." Nikita.

Kaleb waited for Henry to speak. He did. And confirmed all of Kaleb's suspicions about the identity of the shadowy puppet master.

"It may be," the other Councilor said, "that the aim of the events has been realized. We are now, after all, offering voluntary reconditioning. It's a step in the right direction—toward perfect Silence."

The dinner passed without bloodshed. Mercy wasn't quite sure how, but she had a feeling her mother had a great deal to do with it. Which was why she left Lia to ride herd on Riley, Bas, Grey, and Sage while she went into the kitchen to help her father put on the tea and coffee.

"Sit," she was told the instant she entered.

Having guessed this was coming, she pulled herself up onto the counter and watched him move about. Michael Smith was a big, strong man. A man a woman could rely on.

"So," he said, "that's the best you could do for a mate?"

Mercy snarled before she could stop herself. And an instant later, knew she'd been had. "Dad!"

"Aw, don't be like that, baby girl." Ruffling her hair, he tapped her cheek, a smile curving over his lips. "I suppose I should've known you'd never do anything the easy way."

She made a face at him and opened the cookie jar to take out one of the biscotti her mom always kept in there. Bas loved the things. The rest of them had picked up his addiction. Nibbling on the treat, she said, "So?"

"So what?" He raised one dark red eyebrow.

"Do you like him?" It mattered, his opinion, her mother's. Not that it would make her give up Riley, but she *was* a pack animal, and inside the walls of this house, within this family, Michael and Lia were the alpha couple. They always would be, even if Lucas and Sascha came over for dinner.

Michael glanced at her with quiet eyes. "He looks at you right."

"Right?"

"Hmm." A teasing smile. It was obvious where Grey had inherited his wicked sense of humor. "Eat your biscotti."

Knowing she'd get nothing more out of him, but her heart lighter at the confirmation that Riley would be welcomed into the family, she did as ordered.

* * *

Riley stared across at Mercy's brothers, very aware that only the small-boned woman on his left was keeping them from trying to play tic-tac-toe with his bloody bones.

"Grey," Lia said, putting more dessert onto Riley's plate, "why don't you play the sax for us?"

Grey looked like he'd been asked to strip naked and do a lap dance. "Only if you make Riley sing."

A snicker went around the table. Lia scowled and it immediately quieted. All at once, Riley could see Mercy doing the same at their own dinner table. Their children would likely be hellions, but his mate would keep them in line, no question about it. *His mate.* His heart clenched.

I won't be the same. I'll be less.

How could he do that to her? And yet, how could he possibly let her go?

"Riley." Fingertips on his arm. "I suppose you can't sing a note?"

He smiled. "Actually, I can."

Grey looked crushed. But it was Bastien who spoke next. "But can you take care of my sister?"

"Your sister can take care of herself." No matter how much he wanted to do the job for her. The wolf was alternately proud of her strength and frustrated by it. Perhaps it would be that way their entire life. Or, perhaps, they'd find a middle ground. "But I'd walk through fire for her."

Lia squeezed his forearm, and when he looked down, he saw a blazing inner strength that told him where Mercy had gotten her grit. Reaching up, she pecked him on the cheek. "You'll do, Riley."

CHAPTER 47

Things were in an uproar in Venice. The chairman made sure to tell the other members of the board to get the hell out of Dodge and keep their heads down. He liked control, but he was no traitor. As he made his own escape, ready to go under the knife and assume an identity he'd set up years ago, he considered the events of the past twenty-four hours.

Some would consider the entire thing a failure. He considered it a first strike. The Psy would never again underestimate the Human Alliance. As a bonus, if the Council stuck to its normal mode of operations, Alliance people would soon begin to die. And the chairman's point would be made without him having to say a word—in the end, the Psy were killers, monsters, and they would crush anyone who dared rise against them.

As for the changelings, the chairman truly had no disagreement with them, but they couldn't be allowed to keep getting in the Alliance's way. Tonight they'd pay the price for their interference—let's see how they liked being helpless for a change.

Raising his hand almost compulsively, he touched the chip

at the top of his spine, currently covered by the stiff collar of his suit jacket. It was a modified version of the chips worn by the soldiers. Too bad Bowen and his team had had the beta versions—unlike the men who'd gone after Councilor Krychek. The chairman felt sadness, but he was resolved. This was a war. And those men had died in battle. They were heroes.

CHAPTER 48

Riley knew Mercy was up to something, but couldn't figure out what. As he drove her home, he tried to think like a cat. *His* cat. It was close to impossible. She never did anything predictable.

"Do you have to return to the den tonight?"

He shook his head, his blood heating. "No. I planned to talk my way into your bed."

"Talk?"

"Maybe push."

Laughing, she fell silent again. He decided to let her be, and by the time he brought the car to a stop near her place, he thought she might be close to asleep. "Kitty cat?" He brushed his fingers down her cheek, needing to touch her, to reassure the wolf she was still there, that she hadn't chosen the ties of Pack over those of mating.

"Come on, wolf," she said, sounding not the least bit drowsy, "I've got something to show you."

Curious, he got out of the car and walked alongside her as she took him deep into the night-dark of the forest she called home. It was peaceful, and perhaps, if his senses had been human, quiet. But he could hear the scurrying of forest creatures as they went about their business, the whistle of the wind through the treetops, the sound of his mate's unbound hair sliding against her back.

Reaching out, he ran a hand over that shimmering fire, enthralled all over again. "Where are you taking me?" Not that it mattered. His need to simply be with her was so strong, he'd walk through the forest forever if that was what she wanted.

"You'll see." Smiling, she picked up the pace.

Fifteen minutes later, they emerged into a glade screened by the mist of a waterfall he knew would shimmer with rainbows in sunlight. But the moon ruled the night, and its rays reflected off the water to cast a silvery glow over the lush vegetation. Things glittered to his night vision, fascinating and wild, even as ultrafine droplets whispered over his skin.

Mercy walked behind him as he stood soaking in the beauty. Not saying a word, she wrapped her arms around his waist, her cheek pressed to him. He realized then that she'd shown him a secret place, given him a present wrapped in the intrinsically generous nature of her spirit. His heart tightened to the point of pain, and then the pain spread out in a wave of indescribable warmth.

Closing his hand over hers, he said, "Thank you."

She nipped at him, but it was playful. Her purr was something else altogether. Fingers dancing up his shirt, she tugged at the buttons. "Off."

He was more than happy to oblige. She peeled it off from behind and dropped it to the ground, then said, "Everything else."

Smiling at the command, he decided he had nothing to lose by obeying. And everything to gain. She didn't change position even when he was naked, his skin gleaming in the moonlight.

Fingers running down his spine, skating lower, then back up. This time, she spread her hands and stroked, petted, caressed until he felt a light sweat break out over his body. As he waited, held in place by her pleasure, she pressed a kiss to the part of his back closest to her. "I like the way you're built, Riley. All hard and solid and bitable."

Every dominant instinct he had urged him to take control. But something else, another set of instincts, pulled him back. If his mate wanted to tease him to insanity, that was her right. And, difficult as it was to restrain his wolf, he liked this, liked knowing his mate found him attractive.

Teeth grazing over his back. "Beautiful."

"Come here." A husky request.

"Not yet." But she stroked her hands up his body and pressed herself to him. She was still completely dressed.

"I want skin."

Hands gliding over his arms, testing his muscles. "And I want to pet you."

The wolf was a master negotiator. "You can do it as much as you want if you take off your clothes."

Soft feminine laughter. "It'll torture you."

"I like being tortured by you." Damn if it wasn't the truth. "Mercy, kitty cat."

Claws digging into his skin. "I'm still not sure I like that nickname."

"Tough." When dancing with a leopard female, the trick, he'd realized, was to give a little, but never too much. "You'll get used to it."

Those claws didn't release. "Or maybe I'll peel the skin from your bones."

Playing, he thought in wonder, his mate was playing with him. "I didn't realize you liked to talk dirty in bed."

She laughed then and the claws were retracted, his unbroken flesh kissed over by soft feminine lips, flicked by a tongue he wanted to feel on every part of his body. God, when she'd gone down on him . . . his head had about exploded. Now his cock twitched, eager. Shuddering, he felt her draw back, heard the soft susurration of her shedding her clothes . . . but not her boots.

His entire body turned into one big flame.

He expected her to press herself up against him again, but

she came around to face him instead. Groaning, he raised a hand to cup the lush heaviness of her breast. "You're the one who's beauti—" The word ended in a growl as she closed her fingers around his erection and pumped once. "Mercy!" His hands were in her hair, and his mouth on hers before the shout ended.

She tasted like fire and earth, true and real, strong and unique. On his cock, her hand was a brand, and he realized in the dim depths of his mind that he was being taken in a very feminine way. So when she tore away her lips to run them down his neck—oh, God, the pleasure of it—he didn't force her back. Instead, he angled his neck so she could close her lips more easily over him . . . so she could close her teeth more easily over him.

The bite shook him to his toes. Not with pain—he had so many endorphins in his system by now, he doubted he'd feel anything less than a deathblow—but with the heartbreaking pleasure of it. She'd marked him, in a place no one could miss. It was a claiming and it soothed his predator's soul as nothing else could've done.

Perhaps there would be no easy answer to their mating, no solution that wouldn't tear their hearts to shreds, but they belonged to each other. Nothing could change that.

"You taste good, Riley." A soft purr of sound against his pulse as she laved her tongue over the mark she'd made.

Shuddering, he decided he'd been good quite long enough. "Mercy." He tried to pull her hand off his cock.

She tightened it. "You said I could pet you as long as I liked."

"Didn't say I wouldn't try to fuck you in the middle of the petting."

Her eyes snapped up to meet his. "That's feline logic. You're a wolf."

"I'm learning from the best." He couldn't get her to let go of him, and to be honest, he wasn't trying very hard. She was a hot glove over his aroused flesh. "I want wetness," he whispered in her ear, nibbling on the lobe.

She squeezed his cock in reaction and he almost came. Barely able to stand upright, he swore. "Are you trying to make me a eunuch?"

A laugh, a flush of air against his skin. Strokes along his cock, slow, sure, possessive. "That's one thing I'd never do—it'd be a crime against Mercy." Finally, after one more tortuous caress, she released him, only to start sliding down his body.

"No." He halted her, using his superior strength. "It's my turn." His turn to lick and suck and taste and adore. Nipping at her mouth when she growled softly, he cajoled her into a prone position on the ground—though of course, he made sure he was on the bottom, with her lying on top of him.

She kept kissing the mark she'd made, and every time she did, he felt a wave of raw emotion pass through him, a violent mix of tenderness, possession, hunger, and devotion. Desperate to shower that devotion on his mate, he urged her up his body. "Higher," he said when she straddled his chest.

Her eyes, night-glow in the darkness, shimmered bright gold. "Are you sure?" And then she stroked her fingers down, through her own curls, and let out a gasp.

Having lost the power of speech, he just watched as his cat rose up on her knees and showed him slick, feminine fingers sliding through folds his mouth watered to taste. But he couldn't stop this. It was the most erotic sight he'd ever seen. It was also, he realized in a primitive corner of his brain, an act of trust. Mercy was making no effort to keep an eye out for danger, leaving the task up to him.

She was, he understood with a twisting in his heart, letting him take care of her in her own way.

They were learning each other. Finding a middle ground. God, he adored her.

And then he stopped thinking. A subconscious part of his mind, a part that never really turned off in dominant changeling males, stayed watchful, alert for anything that might harm his mate, while the rest of him simply gloried in the beauty and sensual delight of her. The glide of her fingers through flesh damp with heat, with need, it pushed him one step closer to insanity.

"Mercy," he said when he couldn't take it any longer, not knowing if he was saying her name or asking for leniency. Gripping her waist tight, he pulled her up and took over the task of pleasuring her with his mouth. There was little patience in him tonight, but she seemed perfectly happy with his rough strokes, the grazes of his teeth, the relentless demand of his kiss.

She came on his tongue the first time, hot and wild. And when he shifted her limp form back down his body, coaxing her into sitting up enough to take him inside, she was a scalding silken glove, one made for him alone. He didn't last long.

The last thing he remembered was his cat licking over the mark she'd made.

CHAPTER 49

The Ghost preferred to meet his fellow rebels in person so he could gauge their voices, their body language. He trusted no one. But Judd Lauren and Xavier Perez had been with him long enough that he didn't expect them to betray him. That in itself was a concession he'd never thought he'd make.

Looking down at the untraceable cell phone in his hand, he considered which one of them to call. Xavier was human, Judd a Psy defector. Xavier had lived with emotion his whole life. Judd had only just begun.

Perhaps this time, the man who'd known Silence, and now knew something else, would be the better choice. Coding in the number as he stood in a desolate location no one would ever trace to his real identity, he called Judd.

The other man picked up after five rings. He had to have been asleep but his voice was clear when he said, "Didn't expect to hear from you today. Guessing the Net's in an uproar."

The Ghost thought about his next words. "To what are you referring?"

"Still don't trust me?" There was no rancor in the comment. "Councilors are being targeted for assassination."

"It wasn't limited to Councilors," he told the other man. "Several high-ranking people in the substructure are dead."

"But," Judd said in a way that reminded the Ghost he'd once been an Arrow, an assassin, "it's not the catastrophe it could've been. So, what do you need?"

"The answer to a question." He laid out the facts dealing with the offer of voluntary rehabilitation. "Do I have any right to stand in the way of those who want to strengthen their conditioning? I've never been concerned with destroying Silence itself." His goals were deeper, older. He wanted to cut out the rot, excise the sickness that threatened to destroy his people all over again . . . while their Council watched, complicit in their deaths. "But the Protocol is a weapon the Council uses to keep the populace in line."

Judd took a long time to answer. "There's a difference between making a free choice, and making a choice because you're afraid of change. No one knows what the Net will be like with emotion—"

"We know," the Ghost said. "Before Silence, our race was on the verge of extinction." Violence and insanity had run rampant, savaging the PsyNet from within.

"Yes, exactly—before Silence. The Protocol's changed us, changed the Net. I'm alive today because of what I learned from the conditioning process. We won't go back to what we were."

The Ghost considered this new avenue of thought, realized Judd was right. There could be no comparison between past and present—the future was a true unknown. "The weak ones won't survive without Silence." They'd break under the weight of their gifts.

"No," Judd agreed. "Let them go. We can't make the choice for them—we can only show them that maybe, they can find another way. Emotion is a powerful tool."

Long after the conversation was over, the Ghost stood in the desolation of his lonely location and considered Judd's words. Emotion . . . No, he thought. That was a path he couldn't take. Not yet. Perhaps not ever.

Because if the Ghost lost control, the Net would truly shatter.

CHAPTER 50

Mercy had intended to spend the morning discussing their untenable situation with Riley in the hopes of finding some kind of an "out," but he got roused from bed three hours before dawn. "What?" she said, barely lifting her lids as he answered his cell phone.

His claws shot out. Realizing something was very wrong, she sat up and put a hand on his lower back as he finished the call.

His eyes were wolf when he glanced at her. "Three young men from the pack didn't come home last night."

Fully aware how wild the young ones could be, Mercy knew there had to be something more. "No question it's foul play?"

A nod as he got up and began to dress. "Hawke called all three on their cells—those boys are over twenty and in training. No matter what they were up to, they'd answer."

Mercy pulled on her own clothes. "We'll mobilize our resources, help you look for them. Last known location?"

"A club in the city. It's—" His head jerked to Mercy's phone as it trilled an emergency code.

Grabbing it, Mercy answered. "Vaughn, what is it?"

"Get to the city. We're missing Nicki, Cory, Mia, and I'm sorry, Merce, but Grey's missing, too. They went out to dinner, never came home."

Grey. If someone had hurt her sneaky, funny, youngest brother . . . Stomach tight with a raw mix of fear and rage, she had to struggle to find the breath to tell Vaughn about the SnowDancer kids. He swore. "Start driving. Indigo was already down here for a night shift—I'll coordinate with her so everyone goes out in teams of one leopard, one wolf."

Hanging up, Mercy told Riley what had happened. Her voice broke when she got to Grey's name.

Riley gave her a crushingly tight hug. "We'll find them. Your brother struck me as someone who knows how to take care of himself and those around him."

She nodded. "He's tough. He fools everyone with that musical genius facade, but he can put Sage and Bas in the dirt when he's in the mood." Finding comfort in that, she drew away. "Let's go."

Riley looked at her. "How're your hands?"

Startled, she held them out. "Rock steady. Why?"

"Because I think this situation calls for your style of driving."

Mercy put her foot on the accelerator and made it to the city in half the usual time. They'd got a message to converge at Union Square, where search grids were being assigned, so she double-parked and they ran to the spot.

"Anyone think to check on Bowen's group?" she asked Vaughn. Her leopard hadn't sensed deceit in Bowen. Power, yes. A determination that could make a man do many things, yes. But not deceit. However, the leopard wasn't infallible.

Her fellow sentinel nodded. "They're clean—they're helping us look for the missing in their section of the city. Stupid not to use a crack team when we've got them sitting there."

Mercy glanced at Riley to see how he was taking this. He raised an eyebrow. "I guess the enemy of my enemy is my friend." Quiet tone, but the wolf was in his eyes—she knew the anger was directed at the bastards who'd dared harm those under their care.

Feeling that same sense of violation, she slid her hand into his before returning her attention to Vaughn. "Are you sure the missing are still in the city?"

"No," the jaguar said, making her stomach sink. "Dorian's working airport and highway surveillance; SnowDancer's checking satellite footage; Faith's running telepathic scans. We'll leave no stone unturned, Mercy."

She swallowed, nodded. "What do you need from us?"

"We want you two visiting all known Alliance sites. I've already sent people through but you know their movements better than anyone else."

"What makes you think this is connected to the Alliance?" Riley asked.

Vaughn shoved a hand through his unbound hair. "One of the Rats was partying Above and he's almost certain he saw Grey get into a van with a human. But the Rat was more than a little tipsy, so I'm covering all our other bases, too—Sascha even woke up Nikita to ask if this was a Psy op. Nikita says no."

"She's not exactly trustworthy," Mercy muttered, "but this has the smell of the Alliance. Psy teams don't like to attract attention."

Riley nodded in agreement as they headed off, deciding to take the car since they had a lot of ground to cover and others were already working the streets. They came up blank at the Embarcadero warehouse, and in the Tenderloin, though they got out and traversed the entire suspect section on foot. All other known sites yielded the same result.

Panic threatened to twist Mercy's heart into a knot. It was all she could do to keep it together. "Where else?! God damn it!"

Sweating despite the cold air as they stood beside the car, Riley tried to think. That was his strength when it came to chaotic situations. Right now, the mating dance was playing havoc with his mind, but with Mercy beside him—even a distraught Mercy—he found a measure of control. "Let's go back to the basic facts," he said. "Our grid covers the Alliance. So we work on the assumption that the Alliance did this. No ifs, no buts."

She nodded, eyes full of fire.

"Then, the next question becomes—why would the Alliance take them in the first place?" he said. "It's very deliberate—three SnowDancers and four leopards."

"Either a declaration of war," Mercy muttered, kicking at a tire, "or a big fat 'fuck-you.'"

He considered that.

"Riley, the killings—there have been two confirmed cases in Tahoe. What if—?"

"Damn." He reached out to brush sweat-damp strands of red off her face. "I forgot to tell you in the mess yesterday—one of the comm techs forwarded me a bulletin. Seems the two victims were lovers. Enforcement's charged the husband."

The sheer banality of the crimes seemed to shock Mercy out of her burgeoning panic. "Oh." A quick nod, a jerky breath. "Okay, okay." She shoved her hands through her hair and he could almost see her pulling her sentinel skin around herself.

"If we can't answer the why, let's try the how." She placed a hand against the hood. "I can see how your three boys might've been taken—pretty girl distracts them, another spikes their drinks, then the girls 'helpfully' lead them out. Everyone thinks they're drunk boyfriends, nothing sinister. But our kids were out having dinner, not in a club."

Riley nodded. "If it was me, and I had to get four sober people to do what I wanted, I'd grab one while he or she was separated from the group, then force the others to follow by threatening the one I had."

"The thing is, you know about how loyal we are—would the Alliance?"

"They've proven to be smart. They study the enemy before striking."

"So your scenario is a possibility." Mercy's claws were out, though she didn't seem to realize it. "But unless there were a lot of attackers, it'd be hard to control that many changelings, especially once you had them in a van or truck."

"Unless you use the threat of death against one to force the others to behave"—his brain made a cognitive leap—"or to dose themselves with a tranquilizer." Every single captured changeling would've tried to find an escape hatch, but if someone was holding a gun to the head of a friend, they wouldn't have dared risk an action that didn't promise a hundred percent chance of success. Packmates did not sacrifice one to save many. The Psy called that a weakness. Riley thought it their greatest strength. "But even if they're all knocked out, what then?"

"Exactly." Mercy began to pace up and down the street, both of them deliberately ignoring the fact that the tranq doses in their scenario could've been fatal. "If it's a message, we need to receive it. Otherwise, we don't know who did it, and they don't get credit. And the Alliance likes to make a splash."

"We need to factor in another thing—the kidnappers need time to get away after delivering the message." The wolf in him saw a hint of possibility. "We need to be searching isolated places where the missing wouldn't immediately be found, but where they wouldn't *not* be found in a reasonable amount of time."

Mercy apparently located a hair tie in her pocket because she began to pull the flowing strands of her hair into a messy ponytail. "They're not totally familiar with this city, so they won't go far from their 'circle' of movement."

"We need to dumb the search down." Riley straightened, seeing the truth. "We've been searching in places they probably have no clue how to even find."

Mercy's eyes turned night-glow. "There were reports of possible Alliance movements in the streets leading up to the Palace of Fine Arts. It fits. It's not so isolated that the missing wouldn't be found, but it's isolated enough that likely no one will pass through it at this time of the morning." The clock had just ticked over five thirty.

They were already moving as she finished speaking. Adopting Mercy's hell-on-wheels driving technique, Riley had them on the Palace grounds five minutes later.

Magnificent in daylight, the huge pillars that curved out from the rotunda were ominous in darkness. Mercy deliberately avoided looking at the glassy surface of the lake to her right. No going there until necessary.

Using her night vision to negotiate around the pillars, she kept her body low to the ground, trying to pick up a scent. What she found instead was a jagged claw mark in the grass. "Riley." This had been made by a wolf.

He was beside her in a second. "Scent's dissipated, but it's fresh."

They all but crawled on the ground, alert to any other hint that the mark might've been made by one of their lost packmates. Riley found the next bread crumb—an earring with dangling glass beads.

Mercy's heart jumped into her throat. "Mia. She's learning to work with glass—she's so crazy-proud of those earrings, she'd never have dropped one accidentally. Not if she was conscious."

A few feet later, she saw a worn, handmade button. "Grey." He loved that blue shirt despite the fact it was all but threadbare. Sage had made the buttons in one of his fits of creativity, and their mother had cut out and sewn the shirt itself. "They left us a trail. Maybe they weren't knocked out."

"Or the drug began to wear off."

It was tempting to speed things up now that they knew the missing had come through here, but they stuck to the trail. This was a large area—better to be a little slow than miss them altogether. It was as well that they fought the instinct to chase blindly . . . because four minutes later, they found both the cats and the wolves. All were propped around a pillar shaded by overgrown greenery, and so deep in shadow Mercy and Riley could've easily passed them by. All seven had also been doused in a light perfume that would've played havoc with changeling noses.

They appeared dead.

"No." Dropping to her knees, Mercy began to check pulses. Her relief when she felt the first sluggish beat threatened to

stop her own heart. "Alive, all of them." Her hand lingered on her brother's face. "God, I love you, brat."

Riley relayed their find by phone and both Tamsyn and Lara, the SnowDancer healer, arrived what felt like seconds later. All seven young men and women were on the way to the hospital within a span of minutes. Lucas rode with the healers, while Hawke remained behind to see if they could get anything more from the scene.

Mercy had been planning to go with Grey but decided to stay at the Palace when her parents called to say they were almost at the hospital. She wanted to find the bastards who'd dared this. Returning to Riley's side after the others had left, she found him talking to Hawke.

"The messages pinned to their chests were all the same," Riley was saying. " 'Stay out of Alliance business, or next time, they won't be breathing.' "

"Nice of them to leave a calling card," Hawke said, clearly furious. "We sure it was the Alliance?"

"Techs are still working on it, but initial word is the prints on the notes match those we found at the warehouse."

Hawke shook his head. "Everything points to a power play, but the timing makes me think something big's happening soon and they want us distracted."

"Could be both," Riley murmured, his beautiful hair turning bronze in the quiet dawn light. "A very deliberate demonstration of power, and a smoke screen."

"They failed with the assassination attempts on the Councilors," Mercy said. "Which leaves Bowen and his group as the most likely targets."

Riley was thinking along the same lines. "We need to warn them."

"And get the bomb squad out there." Mercy pulled out her cell phone.

"After you do that," Hawke said, "I need both of you to head up to the Glade."

Riley felt Mercy bristle. "You're not my alpha."

"Technicality," Hawke said with his customary arrogance. "It's for the meeting with WindHaven."

Riley decided he'd have to punch Hawke—several times—when Mercy turned to him after the other man left to talk to someone else, and bit out, "I don't care what we have to do, I'm not leaving my pack even if we mate."

"Even if?" He grabbed her arm, pulled her toward him. "You are not doing this to me. We're as good as mated." If she took back everything that had happened between them, if she said it hadn't mattered, it would fucking break him.

"I'm still not a wolf." A baring of teeth. Then, to his surprise, she kissed him with all the firestorm intensity of her nature. "And I'll never call that asshole my alpha."

Riley didn't even consider defending Hawke. "There has to be some way to leave you connected to DarkRiver."

"I can't think how." She sounded frustrated, angry, at the end of her rope. "If I lose that . . . if the blood bond snaps . . . God, Riley, what will I do?"

He closed his arms around her, understanding exactly how she felt. Being a lieutenant wasn't a position, it was part of who he was. "Mercy, I—" What the hell could he say? There was no way to fix this. One of them would have their blood bond to their alpha broken. And if it was tied to dominance, as it most likely was, then there was a high chance it would be Mercy. "I wish I could fix it so I'd be the one who'd have to leave my pack."

Her body tensed. "You'd hate giving up your blood link to SnowDancer."

"Not as much as I hate being helpless while you're hurting." He held her tight. He was her mate, her protector. And yet he knew that if they became one, he'd hurt her as no one had ever before hurt her. That was unacceptable.

"Maybe we can manipulate the dominance somehow," he said, seeing possibilities, "fix it so it's me who shifts packs." It would rip out a massive chunk of his heart, but if it was the only way to protect his mate, he'd do it a hundred times over. "Dominance is fluid, capable of change. All we have to do is find the right trigger."

"Riley—"

"Shh. Just let me hold you. Just for a second."

She softened in his arms, showing a courage he wasn't sure even he possessed. "Kitty cat, we'll figure out a way." Because he never wanted Mercy to feel less, feel broken. He'd savage himself before he'd allow that.

CHAPTER 51

The Information Merchant was dead. But his computers weren't. They ran with quicksilver efficiency. And when the final check-in deadline passed with no contact from their master, the computers shifted operations.

The Information Merchant had been an honest man as far as spies went. He'd found information and he'd handed it over for the agreed price. He'd never held anyone to ransom, never used what he'd discovered for blackmail. It was bad for business.

However, he knew that not everyone was like him. So he'd made contingency plans—he saw no reason to maintain the faith with anyone who would kill him. Five seconds after the final deadline, his computers sent comprehensive details of his last employer—the Human Alliance—the information he'd found, *and* the plans of his associates to the Council.

But the computers didn't stop there. The Merchant had decided to leave a mark on the world. A second set of data, this one limited to the details of the *other* plans he'd managed to unearth, was sent to media stations in the affected areas, the information routed through servers around the world to confuse the trail.

Only after those tasks were complete did the computers begin the total erasure of their files. Ten minutes later, the Information Merchant truly was dead.

CHAPTER 52

Mercy was in the car on the way to the isolated warehouse that Bowen and his people were currently evacuating, when her phone rang. "Sage? What is it? Is Grey—"

"It's not Sage," said an unfamiliar female voice. "It's Clara, from CTX. I'm using Sage's office line. I knew he'd have your number as a quickcode—"

"Slow down, kitten," Mercy said over the girl's rapid speed. Clara, she recalled, was a human intern. A very young one. "What do you need me for?"

"An e-fax came through a minute ago and I can't find anyone—" A pause, the sound of air being gulped. "Sorry. I'm just freaked. There are probably people here but I thought you should know—the fax says there's going to be a bomb going off in the city in half an hour. Exactly 7:32 a.m."

Mercy sat up. "Details?"

When Clara read them off, Mercy blew out a breath. "Anything else?"

"It says the Human Alliance is behind this and other fatal attacks around the world, and asks for a boycott of their businesses in protest. Shall I send the fax to your phone?"

"Yes." She shot it to both Hawke and Lucas as soon as it landed in her in-box. "And, Clara—good call."

Hanging up on the relieved girl, she turned to Riley. "Floor it. We have a deadline."

Riley did as asked, and they made it to Bowen's group in plenty of time. Warned by Mercy, the team had cleared out with military precision. Though Bowen was pissed.

"How the fuck did they get a bomb inside?" Near-black eyes narrowed. "It had to be one of us, someone they turned."

The tiny Eurasian woman beside him frowned. "We can't know that."

"Where the hell is Claude then? I haven't seen him for twenty-four hours."

Mercy left them arguing in low voices and headed over to rejoin Riley. "Chance of collateral damage?" she asked, looking around in the unexpectedly cloudy morning light. At least the fog was manageable, barely licking at their ankles.

Riley shook his head. "None. Other warehouses are empty. Bowen and his team swept them for vagrants on their way out, and I did a second sweep."

"Good." She rubbed her forehead. "Bomb squad's setting up now—they might be able to find and disarm the device using one of their bots."

Glancing around to ensure that everyone was out of the danger zone, he nudged her to follow. "We need to clear the perimeter."

As they walked, Mercy could sense his wolf clawing at the surface of his skin. Her leopard wasn't much better. But she knew it was worse for him. It was just the way nature worked—the mating dance could push a predatory changeling male close to insanity. Riley was holding it together. For her.

And for a wolf changeling of his possessive, intensely protective nature to fight the instincts of his beast . . . it had to be a trip through hell itself.

I wish I could fix it so I'd be the one who'd have to leave my pack.

It had been no false promise. She knew he'd do it if it was

in any way possible. Riley would give up everything to keep her from being hurt.

He's got a heart as big as Texas—he'll die for you without blinking. But he doesn't expect anyone to do the same for him.

Maybe, she thought, her own heart expanding past all fear, all worry, it was time Riley learned what it was to be mated to a leopard. That leopard was finally ready to take a leap in the dark, trusting he'd catch her on the other side. And for her, it was very much a conscious decision—she was too strong, too independent, to fall into this by chance.

She slid her hand into his, twining their fingers together. Leopard and woman were both in agreement—this man, this wolf, he was strong, he was smart, and he was willing to fight for his mate, no matter the cost to himself. The leopard could do no less.

Riley shot her a smile that was the merest curve of his lips. "There goes my macho image." But his hand tightened around hers. Masculine heat, callused palm, the touch of a man who'd never let go.

Her soul grew painful with need, with an emotion unlike anything she'd ever before felt. "I have something for you."

He tugged her over the perimeter line—given the size of the explosives mentioned in the e-fax, as well as those found in Nikita's building, the blast wouldn't make it even halfway to this distance. But no use in being stupid—they intended to wait behind a deflective wall set up by the bomb squad. And Riley didn't stop until they were on the other side of that wall. "Yeah? What? Is it shiny?"

Her cat wanted to tease him back, but someone interrupted before she could say anything. It was Indigo. "I've got everyone else moving," the lieutenant told them. "You two going to stay here?"

At their nods, she continued. "Fire crews are waiting one street over like we agreed. Soon as anything goes, they'll haul ass."

"Good." Mercy glanced at her watch, holding on to her

impatience with her teeth. "The tip said it was set to blow in about ten minutes."

They both waited until Indigo had jogged away before resuming their conversation. "So," Riley asked, "what have you got for me?"

Taking his hand, she placed it palm-down over her heart. It would hurt like a bitch, she thought, but he was hers to protect as much as she was his. "Me." And she opened up her soul, laid herself bare.

The mating bond shoved through her body like white lightning, hot and wild and right. Incredibly, wonderfully right. His energy was different from hers—wolf, not leopard—but it laced itself with her own until their combined strength was far greater than either would've ever been alone. "Wow."

He blinked, swaying on his feet. "Damn."

She gripped his chest to keep him upright, a difficult feat since she was feeling intoxicated herself. They both almost fell over, laughed, and then they were kissing. The physical connection between them had never been in any doubt, but the mating bond added a new resonance to it, until she could feel his touch in every cell of her body. "Mmm, I like."

Riley heard Mercy's words but couldn't respond, his wolf still stunned from the impact of a bond he'd always known about, but never truly understood. This wasn't anything like he'd imagined—it was more, it was better, it was . . . damn fucking amazing. Sweeping his tongue into Mercy's mouth, he groaned.

Some time later, he raised his head. "That building's supposed to explode soon."

"Hmm." Dreamy eyes looking into his. "Who cares."

Riley felt like agreeing. "We're drunk." He didn't dare approach the subject of her sentinel bond. He could feel his own blood bond to Hawke strong and sure, which meant his precious Mercy had lost a chunk of her heart. He'd make it up to her, he vowed, love her so deep and true that it would bury the pain of that devastating loss.

However, right then, she looked so content, he didn't want to break the moment, didn't want to destroy their mingled joy. His mate, *his mate* had given herself to him. It was more than he'd ever expected from this wild, independent leopard he adored. Stroking a hand over her hair, he held the beauty of the moment tight to his heart, a secret treasure no one could ever take from him. Mercy's gift. "I think," he said through the thickness of emotion, "this is better than being drunk."

"Yep." She dropped her head to his chest and rubbed her face against him. He knew what she was doing—rolling in his scent. He wanted to do the same. Preferably with her all long, lean, and naked below him.

They stood there for several minutes, getting themselves under some sort of control. At long last, Mercy glanced at her watch. "One minute to time of detonation if the tip was legit."

"I hope it wasn't." Because if it was, then things were going to get ugly.

"Yeah."

"I don't know about internal Alliance politics," Riley said, "but I don't like the way they use up their people like they're nothing."

Mercy nodded. "And if they kill— Oh, my God!"

Riley followed her gaze skyward to see something plummeting in what looked like an uncontrolled dive. It was too big to be a normal bird. "Hell." He looked around for something to cushion the blow, but the entire area was old-fashioned concrete and wood. "Flare your wings," he said to the falling bird between gritted teeth. "Slow it."

"Come on, come on." Mercy rose on tiptoe, as if she could reach up and catch the other changeling.

Three seconds before impact, it was as if the falling one heard them. His wings spread, though one looked strange . . . broken, Riley realized. It slowed his descent from killing to crippling. The changeling also managed to shift his trajectory so he slammed into a pile of old wood instead of the concrete, but he came down hard, a falcon in full animal form.

They were both running before he hit, heading back toward the building. Riley hated that his mate was going into danger, but his wolf respected her strength. This was who she was, and she was perfect. The falcon lay as if dead, but when Mercy put her hand on its body, she nodded. "Alive."

Riley gauged the bird's weight. "Big son of a bitch." Carrying him in animal form would be awkward, but if he was this big as a bird, he was likely bigger as a human. Bird changelings did seriously weird things with their weight when they shifted, but in general, their animal form was smaller. In the end, it took both of them.

He slid his hands under the falcon's back half, while Mercy took the front. "Ready?"

"Go." They headed away from the scene, knowing they only had seconds.

But they didn't even have that. They smelled the ignition at the same moment. Riley looked at Mercy. *"Shift!"* Their animal bodies were lower to the ground, would take the impact better.

Laying down their burden even as they shifted, they covered the injured changeling with their animal forms as the world turned to fire around them.

The wolf's howl lifted above the city, mournful, sad, so desperately sad that everyone who heard it felt their heart tremble in echoed grief. Running from the Palace of Fine Arts at a speed that made the humans in his way gasp and wonder if they'd really seen what they thought they had, Hawke followed the sound to a patch of concrete not far from a collapsed building. Dust and smoke clogged the air, but he didn't need to see to find them.

A large gray wolf stood in front of an unconscious leopard. The wolf was licking at her muzzle, patting her face with his paw, trying to nudge her to wakefulness. But the leopard lay still, so still that it was almost as if she wasn't breathing.

A falcon lay a little to the left. It was alive. Good enough. Hawke turned back to those who were his own and knelt down beside them. The wolf didn't turn to look at him, all its attention focused on the fallen leopard. When Hawke went to check the leopard for injuries, he moved slowly, ensuring the wolf knew he didn't intend to do harm. Even so, the wolf stood ready to strike, those amber eyes watching Hawke's every move.

That was when Hawke noticed the wolf's left back leg was broken. He didn't tell the male to sit. Instead, he focused on finding the leopard's injuries. The most dangerous one was obvious the instant he looked at the downed feline's side. A massive gash split the black and gold of her soot-covered fur, probably caused by flying debris.

Hawke swore and pulled off his T-shirt to stop the blood flow. He could've helped the wolf, but sharing strength with a leopard was beyond his abilities. It agitated the alpha wolf inside him—this leopard, this woman, was Pack. He had to help her. "Hold on, Mercy," he murmured, shoving a hand into his pocket to close around his cell phone.

It proved unnecessary.

Lucas ran out of the smoky haze that very instant, followed by Tamsyn. Behind Tammy and Luc, he saw two other falcons land and shift. In normal circumstances, they'd be dead for having invaded another predator's territory, but Hawke knew they'd likely been coming in early for the meeting at the Glade.

"Lara had to stay at the hospital," Tammy said in a quick-fire report. "One of your young men is having a bad reaction to the tranquilizer they used." A glance at the wolf who stood in silent watch. "Can you take care of Riley?"

"He won't let me," Hawke informed her. "Not until Mercy's okay."

"Men," Tamsyn muttered but she was already removing his wadded-up T-shirt and checking the wound. "It's bad, but she's a fighter. Come on, Merce." Putting her hands over the wound, she closed her eyes.

Hawke could feel the healing energy emanating from her, though her energy was unfamiliar—feline. Healers calmed everyone when they began working; however, the injured wolf stood guard, ears raised, but mouth closed. Watching. Waiting. If anyone made a wrong move, that unfortunate individual would find their jugular sliced clean through.

Riley was in no way rational right now.

Placing one hand on Mercy's head beside Hawke's, and the other on Tammy's shoulder, Lucas frowned. "Sascha's got her, I think."

Hawke knew Luc and Sascha had a strong connection, but he hadn't realized it was telepathic to a degree. A twinge of envy uncurled in his gut. Like the leopards, changeling wolves mated for life. He'd never had that chance—the girl who would've grown into a woman he adored had died decades ago. And now his wolf walked alone.

It was as well, he thought, that Riley had mated. They needed a strong male-female bond at the top of the leadership structure. It would center the pack, anchor it. Now he felt the strength of that mating bond flow into Tammy, and through her, back into Mercy. Changeling healers fixed things with touch, but the energy had to come from somewhere. Riley nudged at Mercy's nose with his own, touching her with one careful paw.

That was when Hawke felt something tug at him. Similar to when Lara drew power during a complicated healing. He glanced at Tamsyn. "You feel that?"

A distracted nod. "It's from Riley."

No, Hawke thought, it wasn't. It was coming from him, too. And that meant Riley and Mercy had completed the mating. His gaze met Lucas's.

"You can't have her," the leopard alpha said, as if he'd read Hawke's mind.

Their eyes clashed, alpha to alpha, wolf to leopard. The air stilled.

"Fight over her later," Tammy hissed, her voice a lacerating whip. "Come on, Mercy, wake the hell up."

But she didn't. No matter how many times the wolf tried to nuzzle her back to consciousness.

CHAPTER 53

The Councilors didn't bother to have a full meeting to deal with the Alliance issue. They simply agreed on a course of action and dispatched squads to take care of it. If the Alliance wanted a war, they'd get a war.

But the chairman had miscalculated on one crucial point. The Council chose stealth, not public violence. With the recent surge of hostile behavior by Psy, overt bloodshed would've run counter to their attempts to calm the populace. Instead, things were taken care of with such subtlety, it was impossible to prove Psy involvement.

And the Psy didn't kill everyone. Instead, minds were scanned and dossiers built. The one called "the chairman" had escaped the net, but three of those at the top of the food chain had been tracked and eliminated. The others would be found sooner or later. The worker bees had been left alone . . . with their memories of what had happened intact. Their leadership had abandoned them to take the heat, knowing the assassins would come.

The Psy had had a century to learn the cold logic of demoralizing the enemy.

Now, the paramilitary arm of the Alliance was crumbling from within.

CHAPTER 54

Lucas and Hawke stood looking down at the badly injured male prone on the hospital bed. "What the fuck happened, Adam?"

"I got shot out of the sky. Like a damn plane." Ignoring the myriad other wounds that marked his body, the tall, heavily muscled man stared at his shattered wing, having remained in half-shift form to allow the wing to set properly. "Fuck, that's going to take weeks to heal."

"Only reason you're not dead," Hawke pointed out, "is because you're alpha in waiting."

"Wing leader," Adam corrected, an odd catch in his voice. "It's you four-legged beasts who have alphas."

"Insulting us?" Hawke drawled, though his mood was anything but buoyant.

Lucas looked over, his own face drawn. "I don't think he realizes he's in our territory and we can bury his body where no one can find it."

"Ha-ha." Adam's sarcasm was rendered less effective by the fact that his normally copper-colored skin was dull with injury—where it wasn't black-and-blue. "Is Naia here? Our healer?"

"Yeah, she was on your tail. With one of your wing-seconds." Hawke raised an eyebrow.

"Shut it," Adam snapped. "She's one of the highest-ranking members of the wing. She needed to be at the meeting." A wince. "Jesus, my head hurts."

"Naia had to shave off your hair to check for injuries," Lucas said. "Turns out you're too hardheaded to hurt."

Hawke folded his arms, forcing himself to focus on this problem and not the one he could do nothing to solve. "But you're not as pretty anymore without those long, silky— what's the word—yeah, tresses."

Adam was giving Hawke the finger when a softly curvy woman with the mystery of the Greek Islands stamped onto her features walked into the room. "Out," she said. "Both of you. He needs to heal."

"We'll go, Naia," Lucas said, his voice quiet. "But we need to know what Adam brought into our territory."

"Nothing," Adam said.

"I might believe it if I heard it from Aria." Hawke scowled.

"There's been a change in the structure of our wing."

"What change?" Lucas asked when the other man fell silent.

"Aria's dead."

Hawke sucked in a breath. "Hell. I liked her."

"She had a good life," Naia said, eyes drowning in sorrow. "She was a good wing leader." A short glance at Adam, and Hawke understood without words why Naia, and Jacques— now the second-highest-ranking member of WindHaven, had come with Adam. Aria hadn't only been their wing leader, she'd been Adam's grandmother. They'd probably been worried he'd blow the negotiation by picking a fight with either Lucas or Hawke just to let off steam. Both men would've understood, but it would've delayed things.

"She was," Lucas agreed. "So we have to deal with your feathered ass now."

"You've been dealing with me for years," Adam reminded them. "Now there's no filter so we have to become friends." The sarcasm fairly dripped. "Did you get the bullets?"

"No. One went through your body, the other shredded your wing and disappeared." Hawke didn't like it. His men would shoot down an enemy, but only after checking with him. Lucas had already told him it hadn't been one of his people. "We'll find out who it was."

"Jacques knows the location," Adam murmured, the words hazy. "He was . . ."

Naia waved them out as Adam lost consciousness, exiting herself a few minutes later.

"How did Aria die?" Lucas asked.

"Old age." Naia's face was sad, and yet there was peace in it. "We knew it was coming. She somehow survived her mate's death, perhaps because she was wing leader, but the life went out of her—she only lasted six months after he took his last breath. There was no foul play."

Which made it less likely that someone had targeted Adam. Since neither Lucas nor Hawke liked unknown threats in their territory, they went out with Jacques. What they found was unexpected—spent shells and eight dead men with chips in the backs of their necks.

Mia and Kenyon, one of the SnowDancer boys who'd been among the missing, identified three of the eight as having been involved in their kidnapping.

"I'm going to call Bowen," Lucas said, "see if he can shed any light on this."

The Alliance man arrived twenty minutes later, took one look at the dead men, and nodded. "Two of them worked directly for the chairman, probably saw his face." He bent down by one particular body, sorrow in every line of him. "Damn it, Claude. Why?"

"Your chips seem to have a kill switch," Lucas said, feeling a stab of pity despite himself. "Their brains are literally leaking out their ears."

Sorrow morphed into cold rage. "No one told us."

But the evidence was plain to see. Whether these men had attacked Adam in retaliation for DarkRiver and SnowDancer's interference in their plans, or whether they'd been given orders to simply cause chaos, it didn't matter.

Because it seemed the chairman was cleaning house.

Riley hated seeing Mercy so still, so quiet. He could feel her in his soul, a vibrant presence, but in front of him, she was pale, unmoving. Tamsyn was worried about a hidden infection—Mercy should've woken by now. Riley's wolf grew frantic with every passing second. God, he'd just found her. He couldn't lose her. Who'd jerk his chain when he needed it most? Who'd make him laugh at himself?

He closed his hand around her fingers and squeezed. "Wake up, kitty," he said, trying to reach the wildness in her. "I need you." He hadn't said that to anyone since the day his parents died.

Deep in his soul, he thought he felt a pulse of love, of warmth, but the mating bond was new. He didn't know if it had been real or if he'd imagined it because he needed it so much. In his hand, her fingers lay quiescent, so unlike the woman he adored with every part of him.

All those years they'd danced around each other, all those insults they'd hurled at each other, all those times they'd stood nose to nose, toe to toe, it had been preparation, he thought. They hadn't been ready for each other then. But now they were and damn if he was going to let fate steal the future from them.

Getting into bed beside her with effort, he held her to his heart. And then he dropped every remaining shield, every barrier, and *willed* her to heal.

Bowen and his team left San Francisco two days later, heading for Venice. Bowen had been recalled by the remaining members of the security team. "I can't believe you're taking over the chairman's job," one of his men said, shaking his head in disbelief.

"I'll be making it my own," Bowen said, his mind full of

the images of death. So many of his friends gone, all so the chairman and his cronies could rule supreme. "I will not send my people out like cannon fodder, and I'm through with picking fights just to prove I can beat the big boys. From now on, we do it like the changelings—become so strong within ourselves that no one dares pick fights with *us*."

"The temptation, though, Bo," Lily said. "It's gonna be a kicker. And you're not a politician."

"Yeah?" He grinned. "Then how come I have the beginnings of a business agreement—maybe more—with the two strongest changeling packs in the United States?"

Lily's mouth dropped open. "How? I thought you were persona non grata."

"I fucked up," Bo said, still angry at himself for his part in terrorizing a child. "But I owned up to it, too. Honesty matters with changelings. When I got recalled, I set up a meet with the alphas and said maybe we could turn a bad start into something good."

"And they listened?"

"It's a work in progress. They've agreed not to boycott Alliance businesses—it's a temporary deal, but it's a deal." DarkRiver and SnowDancer hadn't reached where they were without being highly intelligent operators. They were fully capable of slicing away all contact with the Human Alliance— as you would a diseased limb—if Bowen didn't manage to clean up an organization that had gone from hope to violence on the back of one man.

The chairman had fouled something humans had created after the Territorial Wars as a way to rebuild their lives. Now that powerful business/education network was under fire around the world, with innocent men and women being accused of masterminding violence. Bowen had to prove the Alliance was more than that—first to their members, then to the world. "We've broken, Lily," he said, thinking of Claude. "I want to bring the pieces back together."

"Do you think you can?"

"Yes." It wasn't too late. The chairman's evil hadn't yet taken root. "The 'leadership' might've tried to find glory

through war, but we can give our people something concrete—
used correctly, the chips *could* level the playing field once and
for all."

Her nod was slow, her glossy hair reflecting the light. "No
one would be able to strip our shields, steal our secrets." There
was old pain in those words, memories of terror.

"Yes." Bowen squeezed her hand. "I want humans to become integral to the fabric of the world. To do that, we have to
be willing to step out of the shadows and take our place on
the negotiating table. No more blood."

His adoptive sister looked at him, a strange clarity in her
large gray eyes. "You're not going to stay security chief for
long. You'll lead."

On the other side of the world, Tatiana Rika-Smythe rose
from a chair and drank two glasses of a protein mix. Her body
was close to skeletal. She'd paid a high price for this gamble,
but if it had all gone according to plan, she'd now be the sole
surviving member of the Council, and no one would've considered her a factor in the deaths of her peers. As there were
no aspirants strong enough to become Council, she would've
effectively owned the Net.

At the time, the cost-benefit ratio had seemed satisfactory.
That was no longer the case.

I believe you have served your purpose.

She waited as the chairman paused and considered if his
chip was faulty.

*Your chip is defective. I made sure of it the night I found
you—your mental shield makes you careless about more
physical means of attack. Such a human failing.*

Trembling, the man slid a hand under his hair.

*Mind control takes large amounts of energy, and I really
can't spare any more.*

The chairman drew himself a bath with no prescience of
danger. He was dead five minutes later.

Tatiana sighed in exhaustion as she retook her seat. She
would've preferred not to lose him—as a tool, he'd been perfect.

When she'd found him three weeks ago, his mind had already been full of both hatred toward the Psy, and a willingness to use violence to achieve his aims. All she'd had to do was nudge him until he'd set out to destroy the Council itself.

Every other action, from pushing the kill switch on his men, to going after the changelings, he'd taken on his own. Tatiana had no interest in anything unconnected to the murders of her fellow Councilors. But that very independence of thought had made the chairman too dangerous to leave alive.

It would, of course, have been better if she'd been able to control the Alliance as a whole, but even one mind-control link was draining. She'd been forced to watch the continued development of the chip and the drug, but that, she decided, was a minor issue, one she could deal with when she was stronger.

Right now, she had to recover . . . and reassess the other Councilors' weaknesses. Perhaps, she thought as she walked haltingly to her bed, she might eventually program the next leader of the Alliance. Humans made such perfect stalking horses.

CHAPTER 55

Mercy woke in a spacious but unfamiliar room. *No.* She remembered seeing it before, but the images were hazy. Most likely, she'd woken earlier, then slipped back into sleep. Her side ached, and when she reached down to investigate, she found bandages wrapped around her middle. Still, she thought, it didn't feel too bad—not like when that piece of tin had sliced into her.

Yawning, she snuggled deeper against the familiar male body beside her. "Riley?"

Silence.

Surprised, she raised herself up on her elbow and looked down. His face was drawn, lined with fatigue. Stupid man, she thought, he'd been staying up to watch over her. She'd *felt* him as she slept, knew he hadn't left her side. Even though the plascast on his leg and thigh told her he'd suffered an injury himself. The break had to be a bad one if Lara had cast him so solidly. He should've stayed in animal form for the healing, but it didn't surprise her that he hadn't. She wouldn't have, either, had their roles been reversed.

Kissing him on the jaw and petting his chest until his face

relaxed, she groaned and got out of bed on wobbly feet. Riley's fingers immediately clenched on the sheet where she'd been. "Sleep," she said, holding on to the headboard as her muscles got used to being upright again. "I'm right here."

After a few more soothing words, he slipped back into a deeper rest.

It was, Mercy thought, standing there looking at him, inexpressibly wonderful to have a mate she loved with every breath in her. With no one around, she could be as sappy as she wanted. But of course, there *were* people around. However, they were giving her and Riley privacy and that's all that mattered.

Dragging herself to the bathroom, she did what needed to be done, then showered. From the putrid color of her bruises, she figured she'd been out for days. Her body was clean, which meant either one of the healers or Riley had taken care of it. She didn't feel any embarrassment at the thought—he was hers. Of course he'd care for her. As she'd do for him. In a heartbeat.

Feeling refreshed, she went back out to the bedroom encased in a fluffy white robe. Her bandages had some kind of plas coating so they'd survived unscathed. After grabbing a hairbrush, she sat down beside Riley and began to smooth the tangles. He instantly turned to wrap his arms around her waist, his face at her hip.

She smiled when one hand dropped down to nudge aside the robe until he found skin. Strong fingers closed over her thigh. He was still asleep. But even there, he was pushy. Exactly as she liked him.

Putting the hairbrush on the bedside table, she stroked his hair and shoulder for a long time. Perhaps an hour. It didn't matter. She was simply happy to be here, with him. Made lazy by the petting, she slipped out of the robe and into bed beside him. Half an hour after that, his hand moved on her thigh, his thumb making lazy arcs. Yawning into his chest though she wasn't sleepy, she pushed him down when he began to roll over on top of her.

"Watch your leg," she ordered, the leopard in her tone.

He tugged at her curls in revenge. And not the ones on her head.

"Riley Aedan Kincaid," she said. "I know you're awake."

He cupped her, bold and possessive.

She shuddered. "On your back, wolf."

He obeyed, removing his hand from between her legs. She'd have been disappointed if she hadn't had something so much better to look forward to. Sitting up in a careful motion, she looked down at his naked body, checking to make sure he hadn't been harmed anywhere else. Only when she was satisfied did she give in to the need to be one with her mate, to anchor the bond with touch. "Yum, yum, all mine."

"You don't have the energy to do this. Do you know how many days you were out?"

"I *need* this," Mercy said, and it was the truth. "I need you."

Dark eyes didn't smile. His hands brushed over her bandages, and the darkness intensified. She couldn't allow that. If Riley put up his walls again, it would break her heart. "Grumpy." She nipped at his jaw. "If you brood, I won't go down on you."

He blinked. Then a tiny smile edged those full male lips.

"That's better." She pressed a kiss to each side of his lips, her heart so full, she didn't know how she bore it. "I know I was hurt, but so were you. It's life. It's who we are."

"You almost died."

"But you brought me back." She cupped his face in her hands. "I always knew you were there. Death didn't have a chance against the Wall."

A long silence.

"I reserve the right to go a little crazy," he said at last.

She spread herself over him, skin to skin across their top halves. "Ditto." Another kiss, his hands sliding across her, gentle over her bandages and bruises. She accepted his tenderness, his care, giving him back the same. "This feels so right," she whispered against his lips.

Wolf-amber eyes looked back at her. "Good."

"Arrogant." But she was smiling, because her Riley was back.

* * *

They emerged an hour later to find the cabin deserted. Mercy grinned. "We scared them off."

Riley's smile was pure wolf as he balanced himself on crutches. "Made them jealous, too."

Chuckling, she walked out to the porch . . . and felt her heart sigh in utter delight. "This is stunning." They weren't in the high Sierra, but neither were they down in DarkRiver territory. The firs were green, the air crisp but not cold, and the house—"Wow. Swiss chalet fused with mountain cabin." She'd glimpsed a stone fireplace inside, and now saw the outside was made out of logs that blended the home seamlessly into the forest. "Whose place is this?"

"Ours."

She stared at him. "What? Since when do you own this?"

"Five years ago." He shrugged. "I had it built for my mate."

"The cute little housewife?"

"I'm an idiot," he said, "but obviously, I'm an idiot who even then knew he was an idiot."

She folded her arms, staring daggers at him.

"Mercy, look around you. It's rugged as hell. Can you see some submissive little creature surviving out here?"

Blinking, she did take a good look around. "She'd pee her pants at the first strange noise." Arms lowered, she walked over and poked him in the chest. "Have you had other women here?"

"No one's been here. I've never even spent a night inside." Dropping one of the crutches, he reached up to cup her cheek. "I built it for two, not one."

Well, she had to kiss him for that, didn't she?

"Kitty cat," he said, face solemn. "I'm sorry."

She frowned. "For what? You had nothing to do with the explosion."

"No . . . about your sentinel bond."

Her heart clenched and then released as she realized . . . "I don't feel any different."

"You should." Riley looked half worried, half relieved. "I

definitely felt it when I got bonded, and there's a connection to Hawke, to the other lieutenants. It's hard to explain."

"I know what you mean—it's like being near a fire and feeling the warmth." She shook her head. "And I tell you, I can still feel that warmth."

"Well . . ." He ran his hand over her hair. "That's good. But if you want to be physically closer to your pack, we can move."

Ah, damn but the man had a way of saying the most tender things in that deep, solid voice of his. "I'm good." And it was the truth. Being with her mate was . . . joy. Such joy that it filled every cell, made her blood golden with the beauty of it.

His head lowered even as she rose on tiptoe.

"Ahem." A pointed cough. "Didn't you two already get that out of your system?"

"Go away, Hawke," Riley said without looking.

The wolf alpha came up the stairs and tugged on Mercy's hair. "Red. Pretty."

Mercy smiled . . . and flashed up her claws. But Hawke was already on the other side of the porch, a smirk on his face.

"Now, now," he said, "I'm your alpha—"

"Bullshit." Mercy sheathed her claws and turned so her back was cradled against Riley's chest as he leaned on the railing. "I'm a DarkRiver sentinel."

The wolf alpha's eyes gleamed. "You sure about that?"

Catching a couple of familiar scents on the breeze, she waited. Lucas and Sascha stepped out of the forest a few minutes later. Mercy took one look at them and bit back a grin, but Hawke didn't bother to resist the urge to make a comment.

"You have a leaf stuck in your hair, cat."

Nonchalant, Lucas reached up to pull it off. "Jealous, wolf?"

"Boys," Sascha said. "We're here to discuss something important." Walking up the steps, she hugged Mercy. "I'm so glad you two are alright." There was a change in her eyes—an impossible new depth of soul, of empathy. And her scent . . .

Mercy's leopard all but pounced on Sascha in excitement. "Holy crap! Congratulations!"

Sascha smiled, and glanced at Lucas. "I don't think I can quantify our excitement." Then she turned back. "But that's not why I'm here. It's about the Web of Stars and the equivalent thing with the wolves."

"You should sit," Lucas said, and he wasn't talking to Mercy.

Sascha stared at him. "I didn't realize pregnancy of four weeks' duration made me incapable of standing upright."

"It makes me incapable of reason," Lucas said, charm in every inch of him. "Humor me."

Rolling her eyes, Sascha turned back to Mercy. "We should go in and grab seats—Tamsyn was here when you woke this morning and she said you're going to be fine, but you need more bed rest. Lara gave the same orders to you." She pointed an admonishing finger at Riley.

"Sascha darling, I don't know what you and the cat get up to in bed, but those two aren't resting." Hawke padded over, and Mercy noticed that though he was wearing jeans and a white tee, he was barefoot. Crazy wolf.

Lucas cut Hawke off, opening the door to usher his mate inside. Mercy went in with Sascha and Riley followed. They heard a thump an instant later, and then some swearing, but when the two alphas walked in, there wasn't a bruise on either of them. Sascha gave them both a narrow-eyed glance, got choirboy smiles in response.

"I'm assuming," Mercy said, trying to control her laughter, "that something weird's happened with the Web?"

Sascha nodded. "When you and Riley first mated, it was as if the Web and the SnowDancer network didn't know what to do. In most cases, I think one of you would've been pulled out of your network—a connection *across* networks is theoretically impossible."

Riley's fingers played over her hip. Worried. Possessive. She leaned into him. "So what happened?"

"The impossible." Sascha's eyes sparkled. "The mating

bond snapped into place between you two, without removing either of you from your respective webs."

Riley stirred. "Are you saying you can see both the Snow-Dancer and DarkRiver networks now?"

"Not exactly." Sascha blew on the surface of the glass coffee table to steam it up, then used her finger to draw the connections as she explained. "Lucas and Hawke have a blood bond because of the alliance, so the packs are already bonded on some level."

Hawke shifted and Mercy's cat picked up an edge in his movements. Not directed at anyone in the room but there. "Why didn't our networks merge?" he asked.

Sascha looked from wolf alpha to leopard alpha. One was by the fireplace. One behind his mate. Opposite sides of the room. "Because neither of you will submit to the other."

"Hell, no!" From two different throats.

"See." Sascha threw up her hands. "I think a changeling network has to have an alpha at the core—and you can't have two alphas. But the alpha-to-alpha blood bond has obviously had some psychic effect. I can't see the wolf web," she explained, "but I can sense that it's now side by side with Dark-River's web on the psychic plane. The mating bond goes from Mercy and disappears, and since you two are mated . . ."

"It means it reappears on the other side." Mercy thought about it. "If the blood bond hadn't been there between Dark-River and SnowDancer?"

"Honestly," Sascha said, "I don't know. Could be we'd have ended up with the same result. You're both so dedicated to your packs—with changelings, such things seem to matter a great deal when it comes to the psychic plane."

Riley straightened his unbroken leg. "You want us to choose." A glance at Hawke, then back at Lucas.

"It's necessary," Hawke said, pale eyes intent.

Lucas nodded. "Your animals won't like not having a concrete answer. Plus, we need it for the stability of the pack structure."

Mercy turned to Riley and raised an eyebrow. "Okay?"

Nodding, he looked to Hawke. "I'll stay SnowDancer, she'll stay DarkRiver."

"There won't be a loyalty issue," Mercy said. "My loyalty is to my mate first, then my pack." It was how it had always been. Pack was built on the ties of family. And family began with mating. "Don't ask us to keep secrets from each other."

Lucas made a mock obeisance at her pointed reference. "As if we'd even try," he said, rising to his full height. "Mates come first."

Riley brushed his lips over Mercy's hair in a caress so tender, her toes curled. "It would also," he said, "make our domestic life easier if you two didn't declare war against each other anytime soon."

"Why would we do that when we now have the liaison team of our dreams?" Lucas was all but rubbing his hands. So, for that matter, was Hawke.

"I hate you both," Mercy said without heat.

Riley put his arm around her. "Me, too."

EPILOGUE

There was a celebration in the Pack Circle a week later, after Tamsyn and Lara had cleared both Mercy and Riley. It was a joint celebration—of the new life coming into the pack, and of Riley and Mercy's mating.

Bas thumped Riley on the back. "Look after her or I'll scalp you in your sleep." A smile so feral that if Mercy hadn't known better, she'd have thought her brother didn't even know what a suit was, much less a financial market.

"Judd said one day it would come back to bite me," Riley muttered, leaning on his crutches.

"He won't hurt you," Mercy teased. "If he does, I'll use his kitten defurring tools on him."

Bas showed her teeth. "I'm bigger than you. And I intend to cheat."

Laughing, she pulled him down for a kiss on the cheek, then pushed him into the dancers. "Go make some woman's night." And there were a lot of them giving Bas the eye.

Grinning, he blew her a kiss and merged into the dancers. Grey, she saw with a surge of warmth in her heart, was flirting outrageously with Mia, both of them none the worse for their short kidnapping. Sage was operating a camera somewhere, recording this for Keely's archival files.

"This is nice," she said, leaning into Riley's side as they stood with their backs against a large tree trunk. "Both our packs here."

"And everyone behaving." He nodded at the two groups of juveniles, one on either side of the Pack Circle. That the event was being held here was another step into trust. Changelings guarded their Pack Circles zealously. During Dorian's mating ceremony, certain wolves had been invited down, but it had been a limited number.

But with Riley and Mercy's mating, Lucas had decided it was time to extend the hand of friendship. Hawke had snarled, but he'd taken it. There was going to be another joint party up in the SnowDancer circle a month from now. However, the SnowDancer alpha had only made a fleeting appearance at this party—Mercy had a good inkling why.

"Hey, as long as they don't claw into each other," she said, putting the issue from her mind, "I don't care how much they glare."

"Poor Sascha," Riley said, a laugh in his voice. "She can't find a minute to herself."

Mercy glanced over to see Sascha being offered food, drink, a blanket, suggestions for baby names, and God knows what else. Changelings adored children, but their fertility rate wasn't as high as that of humans or Psy. As a result, any birth was cherished. And any pregnant woman was cosseted, petted, and generally driven out of her mind by the others in the pack—male *and* female.

As Mercy stood there, amused by the knowledge that Lucas would most certainly be getting a strip torn off his hide later tonight, she glimpsed Kit slipping off into the forest. That wasn't unusual. He was a twenty-year-old male, after all—a gorgeous one. What was unusual was the girl holding his hand. Sienna Lauren.

Oh, shit.

Mercy was about to go after the two—if only to stop an interpack incident, when Riley said, "Look at her."

She followed his gaze to find Brenna laughing up at Judd, her golden presence a stark contrast to her mate's quiet intensity—but no matter what he looked like, there was no doubting the bond between the two. "They're good together."

Riley hugged her to his side. "Yeah, they are." And for the first time, there were no shadows in his eyes when he looked at his sister. It was, Mercy thought, an excellent start. "God," he continued, "I can't believe I used to play horsie for her when she was a little bit." He shook his head. "What games did you play with your brothers?"

"I considered Bas my own personal doll. I used to dress him up in sentinel gear and take him on raids."

Riley laughed and it was such a rich, open sound that her leopard was enchanted. "Dance?" she asked.

He looked down at his cast. "If you don't mind staying in one place."

"If that's pasted up next to you, sounds about perfect to me."

Riley proved adept at balance. And fully capable and willing to hold on to his mate when the going got shaky.

Later that same night, tired but unable to sleep, Sascha went to the safe and took out the Eldridge book.

"Sascha?" Lucas called out. "Come pet me."

"Only if you pet me, too."

The response was quick-fast. "Deal."

Smiling through her trepidation, she walked into the bedroom and lay back against her mate's seated form. "Before we do that, I think it's time we read this." Because this wasn't about her anymore. It was about her baby, too, a child who might be born with his or her mother's gifts.

Lucas ran a hand through her hair and nodded. "Let's do it."

Taking a deep breath, she flipped to the first page of text.

Introduction

The E-Psy, or empaths, as they are called in the vernacular, are something of a peculiarity. The powerful among them can heal the most devastating of emotional wounds. Folklore says they can cure insanity. That has never been proven. What has been proven is that they can certainly help people through difficult emotional times, absorbing negative emotion in a way that defies even psychic explanation.

During the course of my research for this thesis, I was privileged to interview one hundred E-Psy in the greater New York region, of which three were cardinals, twenty were high-range (Gradients 6.5–9.9), thirty-seven were midrange (Gradients 4.0–6.4), and forty were low-range (Gradients 0.1–3.9).

"Lucas, that's a lot of E-Psy in one location. If she got that many for a thesis project . . ."

"Means there were a lot more around in the Net."

Sascha nodded. "Backs up what Faith told us—the Net-Mind is hiding so many others." Snuggling against him, she continued reading . . . and found Alice Eldridge's thoughts mirroring her own.

E-Psy have never been rare, but not much is known about them, perhaps because we study that which we are afraid of. And no one is afraid of the empaths. After having near-constant contact with them for close to twelve months, I feel it is safe to draw the following conclusion: E-Psy are some of the warmest, most welcoming people on the planet. They are quite delightful companions and are rarely seen alone.

However, it is this very warmth and generosity of spirit that makes the other aspect, or in some cases, expression, of their ability troubling to many. It is the ethical dilemma which disquiets them the most and one I will be focusing on in the second half of this book.

Sascha broke off to look at Lucas. "That doesn't sound good."

"Wasn't it you who told me nothing can ever be black or white?"

She thought about it. "Shades of gray." She nodded. "If I was utterly good, I'd never understand badness."

"On to the next page?"

"Oh, yes."

Riley didn't say a word for several minutes when Mercy mentioned the Kit-Sienna thing sometime in the wee hours of the morning. "That," he murmured at last, "could be a problem."

"That's what I thought."

"We can't do anything about it—they're adults." He ran his hand down her back. "But we can keep an eye on *all* the players."

"Agreed." A laugh bubbled out of her. "Look at us, in bed and talking Pack business."

A pause. Then, "You make my heart beat, Mercy."

Her heart jumped into his hands all over again. He was so damn calm and he made those statements as if they were facts of life. *"Riley."*

Kisses on her cheek, along her jaw. "So, how many bratlets do you want?"

"As many as it takes to drive you insane." Her throat was husky with emotion.

"Then one redheaded little girl should do it."

"I love you." Beyond the mating bond, beyond the sensual draw, she quite simply loved Riley. "More every single day." And she didn't care how sappy that sounded.

A slow, perfect Riley smile. Just for her.

Turn the page for a preview of
Nalini Singh's next
Psy-Changeling romance

Blaze of Memory

Available November 2009 from
Berkley Sensation!

DEATH

Death followed the Forgotten like a scourge. Relentless. Without pity.

They'd sought to find hope when they dropped from the PsyNet, wanting only to build a new life away from the cold choices of their brethren. But the Psy in the Net, their hearts iced over with the emotionless chill of Silence, refused to let the dissidents go in peace—for the Forgotten, with their hopes and dreams of a better life, were a roadblock to the Psy goal of absolute power.

Among their numbers the defectors counted a large contingent of telepaths and telekinetics, medical specialists, men and women gifted in psychometry, and so much more. These powerful individuals, these *rebels*, stood as the only real psychic threat to the increasingly omnipotent Psy Council.

So the Council cut them down.

One by one.

Family by family.

Father. Mother. Child.

Again and again, and *again*.

Until the Forgotten had to run, to hide.

In time, memories were lost, truths were concealed, and the Forgotten almost ceased to exist.

But old secrets cannot be kept forever. Now, in the final months of the year 2080, the dust is rising, light is shining through, and the Forgotten stand at a crossroads. To fight is to face death once more, perhaps the total annihilation of their kind. But to run . . . is that not also a kind of annihilation?

CHAPTER 1

She opened her eyes, and for a second, it felt as if the world shifted. Those eyes, the ones looking back at her, they were brown, but it was a brown unlike any she'd ever seen. There was gold in there. Flecks of amber. And bronze. So many colors.

"She's awake."

That voice, she remembered that voice.

"Shh. I've got you."

She swallowed, tried to find her own voice.

A raw hiss of air. Soundless. Without form.

The man with the brown eyes slipped a hand under her head and tilted it up as he put something to her lips.

Cold.

Ice.

She parted her lips, working desperately to melt the ice chips in her mouth. Her throat grew wet but it wasn't enough. She needed water. Again, she attempted to speak. She couldn't even hear herself, but he did.

"Sit up."

It was like trying to swim through the most viscous of fluids—her bones were jelly, her muscles useless.

"Hold on." He all but lifted her into a sitting position on the bed. Her heart thudded in her chest, a fluttering trapped bird.

Beat-beat.

Beat-beat.

Beat-beat.

Warm hands on her face, turning her head. His face shimmered into view, then twisted impossibly sideways.

"I don't think the drugs are fully out of her system." His voice was deep, reached deep, right into her beating fluttering heart. "Have you got— Thanks." He raised something.

A cup.

Water.

She gripped his wrist, her fingers almost sliding off the vivid masculine heat of his skin.

He continued to hold the cup out of reach. "Slow. Understood?" It was less a question than an order—in a voice that said he was used to being obeyed.

She nodded and let him bring something to her lips. A straw.

Her hand tightened on him, she was so thirsty.

"Slow," he repeated.

She sipped. Rich. Orange. Sweet. Despite the ruthless edge in her rescuer's voice, she might've disobeyed and gulped, but her mouth wasn't working right. She could barely draw up the thinnest of streams. But it was enough to soothe the raw flesh of her throat, fill the empty ache in her stomach.

She'd been so hungry for so long.

A flash of something in the corner of her mind, too fast for her to grasp. And then she was staring into those strangely compelling eyes. But he wasn't just eyes. He was clean, almost harsh lines and golden-brown skin. Exotic eyes. Exotic skin.

His mouth moved.

Her eyes lingered on his lips. The lower one was a little fuller than seemed right on that uncompromisingly masculine face. But not soft. Never soft. This man, he was all hardness and command.

Another touch, fingers on her cheek. She blinked, focused on his lips again. Tried to hear.

". . . name?"

She pushed away the juice and swallowed, dropping her hands to the sheets. He wanted to know her name. It was a reasonable question. She wanted to know his name, too. People always exchanged names when they met. It was normal.

Her fingers clenched on the soft cotton sheets.

Beat beat.

Beat-beat.

Beat-beat.

That fluttering bird was back, trapped in her chest. How cruel.

Not normal.

"What's your name?" His eyes were piercing in their directness, refusing to let her look away.

And she had to answer. "I don't know."

Dev looked into that cloudy hazel gaze and saw only a confused kind of fear. The need to protect ignited in his gut, but it was a need he couldn't afford to indulge. "Glen?"

Dr. Glen Herriford frowned from the other side of the bed. "Could be a side-effect of the drugs. She was pretty doped up when she came in. Give it a few more hours."

Nodding, Dev put the juice on the table and returned his attention to the woman. Her lashes were already dropping. Not saying anything, he helped her down into a position flat on her back. She was asleep moments later.

Jerking his head to the door, he walked out with Glen following. "What did you find in her system?"

"That's the funny thing." Glen tapped the electronic chart in his hand. "The chemicals all add up to plain old sleeping pills—not even an overdose."

"That's not what it looks like." She was too disoriented, her pupils hugely dilated.

"Unless . . ." Glen raised an eyebrow.

Dev's mouth tightened. "Chances she did it to herself?"

"There's always a chance—but someone dumped her in front of your apartment."

"I went inside at ten p.m., came back out at ten fifteen." He'd left his phone in the car, had been irritated at having to stop work to return to the garage. "She was unconscious when I found her."

Glen shook his head. "No way she had the coordination to get through security then—she'd have lost her fine motor skills well beforehand."

Fighting the rush of anger provoked by the thought of how helpless she must've felt, he glanced back into the room. The bright white overhead light glinted off the woman's matted blonde hair, highlighting the scratches on her face, the sharp bones slicing her skin. "She looks half-starved."

Glen's usually smiling face was a grim mask. "We haven't had the opportunity to do a full checkup but there are bruises on her arms, her legs."

"You telling me she was beaten?" Raw fury pulsed through his body, hot and violent.

"Tortured would be the word I'd use."

Dev swore under his breath. "How long before she's functional?"

"It'll probably take forty-eight hours to flush the drugs out completely. I think it was a one-time hit. If she'd been on them longer, she'd have been even more messed up."

"Keep me updated."

"Are you going to call Enforcement?"

"No." Dev had no intention of letting her out of his sight. "She was dumped in front of my door for a reason. She stays with us until we figure out what the hell is going on."

"Dev . . ." Glen blew out a breath. "Her reaction to the drugs say she has to be Psy."

"I know." His own psychic senses had picked up an "echo" from the woman. Muted but there. "She's not a threat right now. We'll reassess the situation after she's up and around."

Something beeped inside the room, making the doc glance at his chart. "It's nothing. Don't you have a meeting today with Talin?"

Taking the hint, Dev drove home to shower and change. It was just after six thirty when he walked back into the building that housed the headquarters of the Shine Foundation. Though the top three floors were broken up into a number of guest apartments, the middle ten were taken up with various administration offices, while the floors below the basement housed the testing and medical facilities. And today—a Psy. A woman who might yet be the latest move in the Council's attempts to destroy the Forgotten.

But, he reminded himself, right now, she was asleep and he had work to do. "Activate. Voice code—Devraj Santos." The clear screen of his computer slid up and out of his desk, showing a number of unread messages. His secretary, Maggie, was good at weeding out the "can waits" from the "must-responds" and all ten onscreen fell into the latter category—and today hadn't even begun. Leaning back in his chair, he glanced at his watch.

Too early to return calls—even in New York, most people weren't at their desks by six forty-five a.m.

Then again, most people didn't run the Shine Foundation, much less act as the head of a "family" of thousands scattered across the country, and in many cases, the world.

It was inevitable that he'd think of Marty at that moment.

"This job," his predecessor had said the night Dev accepted the directorship, "will eat up your life, suck the marrow from your bones for good measure, and spit you out on the other end, a dry husk."

"You stuck to it." Marty'd run Shine for over forty years.

"I was lucky," the older man had said in that blunt, no-nonsense way of his. "I was married when I took on the job and to my eternal gratitude, my wife stayed with me through all the shit. You go in alone, you'll end up staying that way."

Dev could still remember how he'd laughed. "What, you have a very low opinion of my charm?"

"Charm all you like," Marty had said with a snort, "but women have a way of wanting time. The director of the Shine Foundation doesn't have time. All he has is the weight of thousands of dreams and hopes and fears resting on his shoulders."

A glance filled with shadows. "It'll change you, Dev, turn you hard if you're not careful."

"We're a stable unit now," Dev had argued. "The past is past."

"Dear boy, the past will never be past. We're in a war, and as director, you're the general."

It had taken three years into the job before Dev had truly understood Marty's warning. When his ancestors had defected from the PsyNet, they'd hoped to make a life outside the cold rigidity of Silence. They'd chosen chaos over control, the dangers of emotion over the certain sanity of a life lived without hope, without love, without joy. But with those choices had come consequences.

The Psy Council had never stopped hunting the Forgotten.

To fight back, to keep his people safe, Dev had been forced to make some brutal choices of his own.

His fingers curled around the pen in his grip, threatening to crush the metal. "Enough," he muttered, glancing at his watch again. Still too early to call.

Pushing back his chair, he got up, intending to grab some coffee. Instead, he found himself taking the elevator down to the subbasement level. The corridors were quiet, but he knew the labs would already be humming with activity—the workload was simply too big to allow for much downtime.

Because while the Forgotten had once been as Psy as those who looked to the Council for leadership, time and intermarriage with the other races had changed things in their genetic structure. Strange new abilities had begun to appear . . . but so had strange new diseases.

However, that wasn't the threat he had to assess today.

If they were right, the unknown woman in the hospital bed in front of him was linked to the PsyNet itself. That made her beyond dangerous—a Trojan horse, her mind used as a conduit through which to siphon data, and implement deadly strategies.

Dev would allow *no one* to harm that which was his.

The last spy he'd found had discovered very well that

Devraj Santos had never left his military background behind. Now, as he looked down into the woman's bruised, scratched, and emaciated face, he considered whether he'd be able to snap her neck with cold-blooded precision should the time come.

His fingers dug into his palms, instinct coming up hard against the icy practicality that drove the director of the Shine Foundation. It was as well that the decision didn't have to be made right then. Turning away from that still yet oddly compelling face, he was about to leave the room when he noticed her eyes moving rapidly under her lids. "Psy," he murmured, "aren't supposed to dream."

"Tell me."

She swallowed the blood on her tongue. "I've told you everything. You've taken everything."

Eyes as black as night with a bare few flecks of white stared down at her as mental fingers spread in her mind, thrusting, clawing, destroying. She swallowed a scream, bit another line in her tongue.

"Yes," her torturer said. "It does seem as if I've stripped you of all your secrets."

She didn't respond, didn't relax. He'd done this before. So many times. But the next minute, the questions would begin again. She didn't know what he wanted, didn't know what he searched for. All she knew was that she'd broken. There was nothing left in her now. She was cracked, shattered, gone.

"Now," he said, in that same always-patient voice. "Tell me about the experiments."

She opened her mouth and repeated what she'd already confessed over and over again. "We doctored the results." He'd known that from the start, that was no betrayal. "We never gave you the actual data."

"Tell me the truth. Tell me what you found."

Those fingers gouged mercilessly at her brain, shooting red fire that threatened to obliterate her very self. She couldn't hold on, couldn't protect them, couldn't even protect herself— because through it all he sat, a large black spider within her mind, watching, learning, knowing. In the end, he took her secrets, her honor, her loyalty, and when he was done, the only thing she remembered was the rich copper scent of blood.

She came awake with a jagged scream stuck in her throat. "He knows."

Brown eyes looking down into hers again. "Who knows?"

The name formed on her tongue and then was lost in the miasma of her ravaged mind. "He knows," she repeated, desperate that someone understand what she'd done. "He *knows*." Her fingers gripped his.

"What does he know?" Electricity arced like an inferno beneath his skin.

"About the children," she whispered, as her head grew heavy again, as her eyes grew dark again. "About the boy."

Gold turned to bronze and she wanted to watch, but it was too late.

The Psy-Changeling series from
New York Times bestselling author

Nalini Singh

SLAVE TO SENSATION
VISIONS OF HEAT
CARESSED BY ICE
MINE TO POSSESS
HOSTAGE TO PLEASURE
BRANDED BY FIRE

"Nalini Singh is a major new talent."

—#1 *New York Times* bestselling author
Christine Feehan

"I wished I lived in the world
Singh has created."

—*New York Times* bestselling author
Gena Showalter

penguin.com

First in the Guild Hunters series from
New York Times bestselling author

Nalini Singh

ANGELS' BLOOD

Vampire hunter Elena Deveraux
is hired by the dangerously beautiful
archangel Raphael. But this time, it's
not a wayward vamp she has to track.
It's an archangel gone bad.

**"NALINI SINGH IS A
MAJOR NEW TALENT."**
—Christine Feehan

penguin.com

M415T0209